# PLAYS BY THE BOOK

## CAROLYN MILLER

Visit Carolyn Miller at www.carolynmillerauthor.com

Edited by Roslyn Howe.

Cover Art by KT Designs.

# CHAPTER 1

*Saint Paul, Minnesota*
*August*

As far as ordinary went, Britta Jane Johnson thought there was nobody more ordinary than herself. Below average height, above average weight, brown eyes, hair neither blonde nor brown, all her life she'd heard words like "plain" thrown at her. But even though some might think being considered ordinary was boring, being average had its upsides too. Nobody ever expected much from her, so she had no pedestal to fall from, and any day she felt like she looked good wasn't the norm but a win. Being ordinary meant she had no expectations to live up to, which some might think was a disadvantage, but it meant she could be herself. And as she'd had nearly three decades of figuring that out, and had grown more comfortable in her skin this past decade, it also meant that on days like today she could pull out a move that would surprise—or shock, as the case may be.

She studied herself in the mirror, and smoothed down the bright yellow fabric. Too much? Well, too bad. A swivel of shoulders showed the wings were still attached. Let's see if they lasted until she arrived.

Thirty minutes later she pulled into her parking space, and readjusted her wings, touched up her lipstick, and exited her car. Then bit back her smile as she caught the dropped jaws and wide eyes from several pedestrians passing by.

Yep, this wasn't the usual attire for downtown Saint Paul, Minnesota, even in the heights of hockey mania which saw all manner of wacky costumes along this stretch of road leading to the arena just down the street. But then, she wasn't shooting for average today.

"Looking good, Britta!" Derek called as she neared the library's front door.

"Thanks Derek." She smiled as he lounged against the stone balustrade. In winter, numbers of the city's homeless gathered near the front doors, taking shelter from the bitterness that plunged temperatures to minuses deeper than nearly everywhere except for North Dakota or Wyoming. Thanks, Benny Latimer, for asking her to help with that school homework report that had lodged that piece of trivia inside her brain.

"Did you sleep well?" She paused as she scanned him. Derek seemed well, even though there was a chill in the air.

"Can't complain."

She smiled. "You can, you know. I'd be happy to talk to Pastor Norberg and—"

"You don't want to waste your time doing that."

"Come on, Derek. Don't tell me you're not worth it. I happen to know someone thinks you're pretty important."

"Who? You?"

She nodded, and pointed upward.

He scoffed and shook his head. "Don't go giving me that."

"Doesn't change the fact that God loves you."

He folded his arms and glanced away, his usual sign for this conversation being over.

*One day, Derek, God is going to zap your tough heart, in Jesus's name.* "Have a good day," she called, and offered a wave.

Her bosses didn't like the fact she spoke to the homeless, but she figured her ultimate Boss probably approved. One could take the evangelist out of the church setting but could never take the fire out of her soul.

She moved to the side and accessed the staff entrance, then took her dressed-up self to her desk, stifling a chuckle as she passed those dressed far more staid and sedate, whose ideas of heroes seemed to be research scientists or librarians. And fair call, both were true heroes and made a nice change from the caped crusaders that Hero Day usually inspired. Many of the librarians she worked with were heroes to the kids and parents who were so appreciative for the extra support the kids' librarians offered during school time.

"Britta." Margaret Rankin blinked as Britta drew near. "Um, wow."

"I know, right?" Britta swished her ruffled yellow skirt.

"I gather from the antennae and the black and yellow stripes you're meant to be a bee."

*Meant to be?* She clicked her fingers and pointed at the head of the children's department. "Meant to *be*. I see what you did there."

Margaret blinked behind her horn-rimmed glasses. "I, er..."

Britta swallowed a smile. Margaret had a very different sense of humor. Some of the people she worked with, like Kayla, described Margaret as a "boomer".

Her colleague snickered softly, and Britta eyed Kayla's Regency gown and raised her eyebrows.

"Don't start. Jane is a literary goddess."

"And you've dressed as her for the past five years. Wasn't this year supposed to be your chance to break out of your rut and try new things?"

"I know, I know. It's just that John wanted to take me out last night and I ran out of time and... yeah."

Ran out of time when today's event had been on the calendar all year? Okay. She swallowed a sigh. "Well, it looks like it's going to be up to me to celebrate all things sweet and powerful today."

"You look good," Kayla said.

"Thanks." She suppressed the desire to suck in her stomach, courtesy of her overindulgence at the recent State Fair. What was a girl to do—pretend that the Fair's deep-fried ranch dressing triangles or dill pickle tots or a chile mango whip weren't supposed to be tried, at least? Besides, bees were meant to be round after all. And if she sucked in too far then the corset might have issues elsewhere.

"Love the corset." Kayla waggled her eyebrows.

"It's not too much, is it?" Everything was covered, and with the long sleeved black and yellow tee nothing could be seen.

"It's just enough." Kayla winked, which wasn't exactly reassuring. "But I'm not sure if many people are going to understand just why bees are heroes."

"Well, they will after I explain it fifty million times today."

Yes, she knew her outfit was going to prove a stretch to most people's ideas of heroism, but there was a limit to how many times a girl could dress as Jane Austen or Anne of Green Gables. And while she might have Pippi Longstocking-esque height, her body shape had been all woman since tenth grade so that wasn't really gonna fly.

Margaret cleared her throat, ensuring the small team gave her their full attention. "Now, I just wanted to run through the order of events today. We have a busy schedule so we need to stay on the ball."

"I just love when she uses sports metaphors," Kayla

murmured.

Britta grinned. Margaret was the most non-sporty person on their team, the one who always complained whenever the Wild played next door and the sheer volume of fans meant there were always a few wanting to know where the nearest bathroom facilities were.

"We are not a public convenience," Margaret would say with a sigh.

Except their jobs, employed by the city of Saint Paul, kind of suggested they were. Hence the need to practice patience with those who paid their taxes—or even with those like Derek, who probably didn't—to ensure this public facility could remain open to serve the needs of those in the Saint Paul area.

"...and at four, we're expecting a visit from some of the members of the Wild hockey team." Margaret's nose wrinkled in distaste.

"Woohoo!" Kayla called.

Margaret eyed her over her glasses. "You have been assigned to do shelving at that time."

"What? I mean, pardon?" Kayla glanced at Britta who shrugged. Yep, this was a surprise to her as well. "I thought Britta and I were doing the hockey session. You know we *love* hockey."

"Your enthusiasm for the sport has not passed unnoticed," Margaret said. "Which is why I did not feel it appropriate for you to run a session on heroes when you were meeting yours."

"But... but—"

"Mrs. Rankin," Britta interposed. Margaret always preferred the title; no over-familiarity for her. "You can trust us to be completely professional in that situation."

Margaret eyed her. "I'm sorry, but it's rather hard to equate the word 'professional' with you dressed in that attire today."

She refused to take offense. "We all need bees. They're the bee's knees of agriculture, so to speak."

Kayla smothered a snicker, as Margaret frowned. "I'm not sure—"

"I'm not sure that anyone else would know the players well enough to introduce them to the kids," Britta continued. Not that they'd need introducing. The kids who would come today knew every detail about these men they regarded as real-life heroes. Minnesota wasn't known as the "state of hockey" for nothing.

"One doesn't need to know a guest speaker to be able to introduce them." Margaret glanced at her redheaded second-in-command. "I thought I'd ask Carol to do the honors."

"Oh!" Carol blinked behind her glasses, glanced at Britta then at Margaret, and grimaced. "I'm sorry. I just remembered I have an appointment then."

Judging from the resignation spreading across Margaret's face, it didn't look like Carol should expect a promotion any time soon.

"Very well," Margaret said.

Kayla fist-pumped as Britta internally cheered.

"I suppose I shall have to do it."

"What? I mean, pardon?" Kayla said.

"Oh, Margaret, let the girls do it," Carol protested softly. "You don't need to spoil their fun."

*Amen, sister.* Britta smiled at her.

"I don't want to discuss this further," Margaret said. "We have a busy day, so let's get on with it."

"I bet she doesn't want to discuss this further," Kayla grumbled as Margaret moved to the front desk. "She's a dictator, that woman. You know the only reason she doesn't want us to do it is because you did such a great job organizing it last year."

The highlight of her year. "Don't let her pique spoil your day," Britta said softly. "I'm sure we'll still get a way to see them."

"It's not like I'm going to go all crazy fangirl on them," Kayla complained.

Britta eyed her.

"Well, not now I have John anyway. But you still could."

"That would be unprofessional," she said, as primly as she could.

Kayla rolled her eyes. "But they're hot."

"I'm not interested."

"Come on, we both know that's a lie."

"Fine. I would be interested, but they're all taken or not Christians so that's that. Okay?"

Kayla sighed. "I don't know why no guy has asked you out."

One of life's great mysteries, and a question she'd asked God many times before. She might be plain, but she didn't think she was conventionally ugly. Nobody had said that to her, anyway. And her personality mightn't be to everyone's taste, but it wasn't like she had none. An ordinary plain girl had to cultivate a sense of humor, even if just to shield herself from the slights, slings, and arrows of the beautiful and entitled. But dwelling on such things too long was a recipe for discontentment, and not something that helped her remember she was a child of God. "I guess nobody has recognized my inner awesomeness yet."

Kayla smiled. "Or your outer awesomeness. I gotta say this is your best look yet."

Britta smiled. "I tried."

"You slayed." Kayla motioned to her corset. "I know it might not be Red Jellybean approved, but you should keep that on rotation."

Britta laughed, thinking about how well this would go down at her youth group. Yeah, that was something else not worth investigating.

"Girls?" Margaret called. "Get to your stations, please."

Britta joined the others in moving to their appointed places. The front doors would open soon, and it would only be a matter of seconds before the children's area would be crawling with eager kids, ready for children's author talks and book readings and activities. And while missing the hockey talk was disappointing, there would be plenty of other fun activities to stay engaged in.

She pushed back her shoulders and smiled. Today was going to be a great day.

~

TODAY WAS GOING to be awful.

Mitchell Reilly stared at the phone where his latest message to his girlfriend lay unanswered. Unread, even, according to the phone's handy-dandy little messaging thing that announced when his texts had been delivered or read. Why wasn't Georgia picking up?

He flicked back to where the message from the club's PR and community liaison officer lay. He had twenty minutes to get to the venue of the presentation he was supposed to show up for. And read a book. A book! He hadn't read a book in years. Well, apart from the Bible, and even that he tended to read on his phone. There was less chance others might ask him about it if it was on his phone, and he could pretend he was just like the others and how he'd always been. Tough, uncompromising Mitch Reilly, known for his killer checks and his hard-core defense, always ready with a smart-mouthed comeback. Even if some of that wasn't quite what he thought Jesus would do.

He gritted his teeth and took the elevator to his car. Okay, so the fact he was a Christian would come as a surprise to many, as it had to his family. Even if faith had been part of his growing up. But then, that was what the love for a good woman could do to a man. And since Georgia had entered his life, well, he was trying to change and prove he was the man she expected him to be.

And despite his on-ice toughness, he did find it reassuring to know that there was Someone bigger than himself, who could be trusted with his future. Even if he sometimes couldn't remember things like he used to, and what was happening with Georgia wasn't tracking the way he wanted at all.

He steered into his usual spot, where he parked on game days, then jogged to the library entrance, where he recognized a teammate wearing a jersey with the Wild colors of green, Iron Range red, and yellow.

"Hey, Enzo."

Jack Enzo turned and grinned. "Reilly." Backslaps. "How was your summer?"

He shrugged. "Good. Saw the fam in Trinity Lakes."

"Where's that again?"

"Southeast Washington. My sister got married a few months ago."

"Ellie, right?"

"Good memory."

"She's kinda hard to forget."

A firecracker, his sister. Youngest in a clan of boys. She'd looked amazing, totally unlike the tomboy he'd always known, dressed up to the nines at her wedding. Her wedding. His stomach tensed. Was Georgia *still* unhappy about that kiss?

He shook off the concern and refocused on his friend. "How about you? What have you been up to?"

He'd seen a few of the guys in recent months, joining with various ones for training purposes or skills clinics. Living four states away, and spending a lot of time in Seattle trying to get Georgia to pay attention to him, meant he hadn't had as much time as he should've had prepping for this season.

As Jack continued sharing about his family, regret knuckled within that he'd left serious relationships a little late. He didn't like regrets. They felt too much like mistakes, and he didn't want to second-guess his life choices. Yeah, he could've done a few things better—okay, a lot of things—but he was on the right track now. Even if Georgia didn't seem so onboard.

He became aware that Jack had stopped talking, that he was supposed to say something, like he was interested and hadn't been in his own head. "Yeah, well that sounds great," he mumbled.

He wasn't sure if he'd sold his interest, as Jack eyed him then shrugged. "So, you ready?"

"Born ready." He frowned. "What are we doing today?"

Jack shook his head. "It's the kids' Hero Day. Remember?"

He clicked his fingers. How could he have forgotten? "Of course." He smirked. "Not surprising they asked us."

Ahead, someone opened the door, and he glanced at the homeless man lying nearby.

"Wassup?" the dude said.

Mitch nodded, but ignored him and hurried inside. A couple of other Wild players drew his attention and he did the reunion thing again. He really needed to get his head into gear and off the question marks around Georgia and Seattle 1600 miles away.

A middle-aged woman wearing glasses directed him up the stairs to a glass-fronted space behind which little bodies moved, many of them dressed up. In fact, a number of the adults around here had dressed up too, which suggested they took Hero Day pretty seriously. Wait—was that woman dressed as a bee? "What the actual—?"

Matt Barlow sniggered. "Did you see Bee Chick too?"

"Since when is a bee a hero?" He glanced back, saw her with her hands on her yellow and black hips, her antennae bobbing around as she tilted her head and joined the kids in watching their progression down the hall.

They passed that room, and yeah, he might've waved to a few of the kids, who instantly turned to follow them. And maybe that was bad of him, because it quickly became obvious that they had a little entourage following them.

Mitch wasn't unused to fans—his family liked to tease him

about his groupies—but little kids were the best. To have the chance to inspire them just like he'd been inspired all those years ago was awesome.

He joined the other players and they were met by a severe-looking lady in glasses and a cardigan, who looked like she read the encyclopedia for breakfast. Unlike Ms. Bee, who looked like fun.

He frowned at himself, and maybe scared a kid who backed away, so he found a smile, pushing thoughts of Georgia and women in bee costumes far from his mind. Right now was about the kids, not anything else.

"And it's wonderful that you can join us," Cardigan Lady said. She glanced at her notes, adjusted her glasses. "Now, which one of you is Mitchell Reilly?"

He lifted a hand. "I am, ma'am."

She peered over her glasses at him, and he suppressed a shiver as unfortunate memories of a high school English teacher flooded through him. It had been rumored that Miss Wicklow boiled alive students who didn't do their homework, and he'd had her a few too many times to ever truly be comfortable with a woman who wore glasses.

She frowned, peering up at him. "You're very big, aren't you?"

Either that, or she was very small. Probably best not to say that. He opted for a nod instead.

The room had filled with little kids, and some not-so-small ones too. It looked like any press day, but it was apparent the lady wasn't used to the kind of energy young hockey fans brought. The longer she took, introducing his teammates, peering at her sheet of paper, then across at them, the more obvious it was the kids were getting restless. Still, patience was a virtue, according to some. So he dug a little deeper, folding his arms, and glancing across the room, to see another dressed-up woman had entered the space. He huffed to himself—why was this chick dressed like an extra from *Bridgerton?*—then glanced back to see Cardigan Lady was now giving instructions, but he had to fight to hear what she was saying.

He nudged Matt. "What's she saying?"

"Apparently you're going to read a book."

"I'm *what?*"

The room froze, and all eyes swung to him. By now Bee Chick had joined the room too. Cardigan Lady coughed gently, but he couldn't look away from the black and yellow creature. She was short and, to be honest, kinda plain, especially with those glasses, and those horizontal stripes were doing nothing for her. But that corset sure was.

He blinked, glanced down, as heat streamed up his neck. *Sorry, God.* Oh, and, uh, *Sorry, Georgia.*

Man. Was it any wonder Georgia wanted nothing to do with him? He was such a bad boyfriend.

"Hey, lady, when are we gonna hear from them?" A rude kid pointed to Mitch and his teammates.

Mitch threw the kid his best scowl. But he couldn't really blame him. The lady was as boring as bat—

"Oh, Britta, do you mind?" Cardigan Lady looked flustered. "I just remembered I have something to do."

"Sure." The woman dressed as a bee moved forward, and everyone in the room seemed to straighten as if to attention. And to be honest, how could they not, with the small Bee Woman clapping her hands and demanding "Eyes this way, please."

"You got it," Matt muttered.

"Dude, you got a girlfriend, remember?"

"Can't stop a man from looking," Matt said.

Mitch was about to protest when conviction clanged within. Something he'd read recently about a speck in another's eye while he wore a log in his own...

"It's wonderful to see so many fellow hockey fans are here

today."

Fellow hockey fan, huh? He might've known.

"Can we give the wonderful players who have come along today another round of applause?"

He didn't think they'd received an earlier round of applause, but that didn't matter. This woman might be little but she had single-handedly won back the room.

Then in clear ringing tones she outlined what was going to happen, and Mitch found himself beckoned forward—and gently shoved by Matt too—to the seat beside her. She smiled up at him, but he didn't dare look at her for too long, in case people misunderstood where he was looking, given their height difference and all.

"Okay, and Mr. Reilly is going to read to us." She passed him a book, already opened to a page, then encouraged him to sit.

He peered at the front cover of the book, then murmured, "Uh... why am I reading this one?"

"Because it's the one you nominated to read," she murmured back.

Had he? When? Why couldn't he remember? "But—"

"You know how to read, don't you?"

He shot her a look.

"Then sit down and read. Hey guys," she said in a louder voice, "Mr. Reilly needs you all to sit down, then he can start. Okay?"

Mr. Reilly. He might have trouble with remembering some things, but he'd always hated that name.

A kid's hand shot up. "Hey Miss, why are you dressed as a bee?"

She glanced at Mitchell, who instantly looked down at the page. Then she cleared her throat. "Because bees are my heroes. One of my heroes, anyway."

"Why?" the kid asked.

"Do you like to eat?"

13

"Yeah."

"Well, bees are super important because they pollinate most of the food crops and other flowering plants. And in lots of parts of the world they're in strife, so I think it's important to shine a little light on that."

"They're in trouble?" Mitch asked.

She nodded. "In some parts of the world, yes. Some diseases have affected their numbers, which has a knock-on effect on other things."

A ripple of restlessness heaved through the gathering.

"But that's not why we're here," she said in a louder voice. "Who's ready to hear from Mr. Reilly?"

"Me!" a score of voices shouted.

"Then please, let's show Mr. Reilly our best manners and pay attention as he reads from one of his favorite books."

He caught a snicker from one of his teammates, and he felt heat flush his collar. He glanced up from the book, saw the questioning looks of various kids and adults, and knew what hypocrisy tasted like. What on earth was he doing sharing this when he hadn't read a book in years?

He glanced up at Bee Woman, whose smile softened a little, like she recognized that he was struggling, then she nodded. "Just read the first paragraph, that'll be fine."

"Uh, do I have to hold it a special way?" he murmured.

"No. Just read. Loud enough so the kids in the back can hear you."

Man. How could his memory be so bad that he'd forgotten so quickly what he was supposed to do? Why hadn't he spent more time thinking about this instead of thinking about Georgia?

She moved closer, and he could smell a sweetness that he really didn't want tickling his nose.

He coughed, and she backed away. Good. Then he started to read.

# CHAPTER 2

S omeone somewhere had a lot of explaining to do. What on earth were they doing getting an obvious non-reader in to read to the kids? Poor guy.

She scanned the room, saw some of the kids scratching their heads, and some of his teammates squinting like they couldn't believe it was Mitch Reilly there. And truth be told, neither could she. She'd thought his natural arrogance that he used on the ice to such good effect and that he'd displayed before when he'd walked past and interrupted her session would extend to reading aloud, but perhaps this was not his forte.

"And... and then h-he..."

His cheeks seemed flushed, and he was stammering over his words, so she touched his shoulder. "Just finish that sentence," she murmured.

He glanced at her, then his cheeks seemed to go redder still. If she'd been put in charge of this segment, she would've made sure the poor man knew what he was doing, rather than throw him in the deep end like this.

"...and then he went home."

He lowered the book, and she knew she had mere seconds to save him.

"Wow, thank you so much Mr. Reilly. Can we give him a big round of applause?" She led the way, and when some of his teammates seemed to be clapping half-heartedly, she narrowed her gaze at them, which seemed to do the trick as they upped their pace. "Thanks again for doing that, Mr. Reilly. Now, I'm sure many of you who have come today have some questions you'd like to ask your hockey heroes, so I'd like to invite the rest of the Wild team members to come out the front, and we'll have a quick question and answer session. Remember, our theme today is heroes, so it'd be great if you can make sure your questions are focused on that."

One of Mitchell's teammates nudged him and laughed, and the man's cheeks deepened to magenta. Well, they would if she could see past the rusty-colored beard.

"Dude, that was embarrass—"

"Okay!" She grinned to hide the yell in her voice. "Who's ready to ask the first question?" She pointed to a little boy wearing glasses. Yes, she played favorites and always picked those who wore glasses to answer first. So sue her. "Who do you have a question for?"

"I want Mitch."

"Okay, Mr. Reilly—"

"Can you please stop calling me that?" he mumbled.

"Oh! Certainly. Is Mitch okay?"

"Yeah."

He didn't look at her. Weird. But then, he probably wanted to get out of here as quickly as he could, and for that she couldn't blame him.

"Okay, so what's your question?" she asked the boy in glasses.

The next ten minutes passed far more peacefully, and the tension within dropped. Maybe everyone would focus on this side of today's event, when things were going well, rather than remember the embarrassment of before.

"Oh my gosh," Kayla said, sidling up. "Can you believe how bad he was?"

"Stop it," she whispered, her smiling attention on the front. "He was mortified."

"Didn't he know what he was supposed to do?"

Apparently not. But she wouldn't say that aloud and expose Margaret's shortcomings. It was one thing to organize an event, but quite another to ensure all the pieces would flow together. And seeing Margaret had been adamant about doing the kids' Hero Day program herself this year, Britta had thought she'd known what it all involved. Which she obviously hadn't. Which had now embarrassed a poor hockey guy in front of his team-mates and his fans. Regret knotted within. She should've stepped in and risked Margaret's displeasure by checking every-thing was organized properly.

The sea of waving hands soon petered out to the last one, and she invited the girl to ask her question.

"Uh. This one is for Mitch too. I want to know how many goals you think you'll score this year?"

"Great question. Let's say I'll be shooting for my season top score, so maybe forty?"

Britta laughed. "See what he did there? Shooting for... when we're talking about scoring goals?" Okay, judging from the blank faces, maybe they didn't appreciate her penchant for corny jokes like Kayla did. "Right, well, let's thank the team for answering so many questions by giving them a round of applause."

Applause always bought a few moments to breathe, to refocus and get people settled.

Once that was done she steamrollered on. "Now we have one more component this afternoon. Kayla, give everyone a wave." Kayla waved. "Now, if you follow her, she has a number of player cards that the players here are happy to sign, but you'll need to collect a card from Kayla first then hop in line. Okay?"

"Okay," the kids chorused.

"Ah." She held up a hand. "Before you skedaddle, we here at the library want you to know that we've loved having you visit us today, and you should know you're always welcome to visit the library. Books are our friends, after all."

Hmm, the kids looked itchy to leave. Very well, then.

"Okay, once again, thank you to the Wild guys for coming today, let's give them one last round of applause!"

Once that was done she continued. "And thank you for demonstrating that reading is something tough people do too" —although some of them probably could afford to do it more often—"and we hope you've had fun. Now, I'm going to ask the team to take their places and the rest of you can line up and get your card from Kayla at the door."

"Why do you want them at the door?" Matt Barlow, one of the newer Wild team members, asked as the kids scurried to line up.

"Because otherwise it'll be a crush. It's all about the safe movement of people here." She grinned. "And we want everyone to leave with a card with the library's details on it, which is what you'll be signing, so they won't throw it away."

"Good plan," Jack Enzo said.

She smiled modestly. That's what she'd thought when she'd suggested it. "Now, Mr. Enzo, can I ask you to please sit at this table here, and you, Mr. Reilly—"

"Mitch," he insisted.

"Mitch, my apologies, could you sit at this table here near Mr. Barlow. That allows for people to have enough room to take photos and do the things they need to do."

"Uh, sure."

When she'd organized this event last year, they'd found that moving some of the crowd toward the exit had helpfully encouraged some of those people to leave, which meant only the most hard-core fans remained, and that had made things easier. Clearly Margaret hadn't thought through all the logistics of what this event involved.

Twenty minutes later, the last of the stragglers were leaving, which meant only Kayla, Britta and the last two hockey players remained. Time to encourage them to leave also, so they could clean and tidy this space.

"Well, thank you very much for coming. I hope you know that the library truly appreciates your time."

"Sure." Mitch's features settled back into the hard mien he was known for.

"You're welcome," Jack said, far more graciously. He glanced at his friend. "I didn't realize just how bad Reilly was at reading though."

"Well, we'll have to make sure you read next time." She smiled sweetly.

His brow wrinkled, like he wasn't sure if she was being sarcastic or not. And to be honest, she wasn't exactly sure if she was being sarcastic or not either. All she knew was that she felt a strange sense of defensiveness for the man who might exude confidence, but had displayed little in that moment when asked to read a book.

She glanced at Mitch, but he wore a frown too. Whoa. Had he thought she was insulting him? Not that there was any easy way to get out of that. "Um, I should probably let you both go. Again, thank you for your service to the community of Saint Paul."

She held out a hand. They grasped it—nope, no tingles or foot pops, just like there shouldn't be as both men were *taken*—and she waved as they left the room.

"Whoa." Kayla joined her in watching them descend the stairs. "I know you didn't mean it to sound this way, but it did sound a little bit like you thought Mitchell Reilly was dumb."

She winced. "I really didn't mean that to come across like that."

Kayla shrugged as they returned to the room. "Well, not everyone is cut out to read books to kids."

"Apparently." She straightened some chairs.

"Although why he couldn't read a paragraph of his favorite book, I don't know."

"Maybe he was just having a bad day." She picked up the jacket slung on the back of a seat. Whose—?

A cleared throat spun her around. To see Mitch Reilly standing there. His cheeks were pink again. "I, uh, left my jacket."

She lifted it and, at his nod, hurried to hand it to him. "I hope you have a good rest of your day."

"It could hardly get worse now, could it?"

She stepped back, the animosity rippling from him like radiant beams. And not good radiant beams, like in "Silent Night". "I'm sorry if you heard any of that."

"About how bad I am at reading?"

She winced. But she wouldn't admit it was Kayla who had said that. "It wasn't that bad."

He grimaced. "I didn't think bees lied."

"Excuse me?"

He gestured to her outfit.

"Oh. Look, I'm sorry you weren't better prepared."

His eyebrows rose like he was offended. "I don't like to read."

"And that was our fault," she rushed to say. "We should have made sure you knew what to do, so I'm very sorry about that."

"Hey, that wasn't your fault, Britta," Kayla murmured.

"Still, as a representative of the library I feel like I should apologize. So I'm very sorry that today's experience was not what we quite imagined."

He dipped his chin, shrugged into his jacket, then pivoted

away. So much for all her training in people skills. She was a zero for two at the moment with this man.

"I get the impression that he's not very happy with you," Kayla murmured.

"I can't blame him. I feel like he got thrown under a bus." She sighed. "We really should have organized today better."

She didn't want to blame-shift, yet she knew whose shoulders bore that responsibility. And it wasn't theirs.

But once the room was straightened and they returned to their desks it was to see that Margaret had already left for the day. Instructions on the whiteboard listed what was happening tomorrow.

"Well, that's great," Kayla mumbled. "From the looks of that she's probably not planning to come in."

"If she doesn't, then we'll cope."

"Because you do her work for her. When are you going to step up and go for a promotion?"

"I'm happy doing what I'm doing. Besides, if I took on more responsibility, then I'd have less time for my kids."

"Your kids." Kayla rolled her eyes. "You do too much for them anyway."

But for some of them, "I can't do too much."

Kayla sighed. "Well, I'll let you polish your halo. I've got a date with John tonight."

While she had a date with... Hmm. The usual. "Have fun."

"You too." Kayla pistol-pointed a finger at her. "Don't do anything I would do."

"I'm not sure that's how... okay." She watched as Kayla exited the room.

Well, seeing she had no date, and no boyfriend, she was unlikely to do anything Kayla would do. Dinner with her folks for one, and no man in her bed, for two. Kayla might be her friend, but they didn't share the same views about that. Which made life tricky sometimes, walking as a Christian without wanting to come across as judgmental.

She powered down her computer and grabbed her coat, then departed the upper floor, waving goodbye to the janitor as she exited the front doors. Only realized she still wore her bee outfit when a few wolf whistles came her way from those gathered outside.

There were more people with Derek now, but he still called a "Bye Britta" to her.

She waved to him, and hurried through the park to where she'd parked her car. There was still plenty of daylight, but it never hurt to be careful.

Then she paused. What would Jesus do? She veered to a nearby bakery and picked up a couple of croissants, then turned back to where Derek sat and handed the paper bag to him. "Sorry, Derek. They were out of the chocolate ones."

"You didn't have to," he said.

"I kind of felt like He wanted me to." She pointed to the sky.

He shook his head.

She smiled, dimming it a little for the others around, then shrugged into her coat.

"Hey, honeybee, you got some honey for me?" one of the men called.

"Leave my girl Britta alone." Derek lurched like he was trying to stand.

"Don't get up. I'll be fine," she murmured. "See you tomorrow."

She hurried across the road and through the park. A peek across her shoulder saw one of the men was following behind her. She didn't recognize him, he wasn't one of the regulars, and her pulse picked up. But she was safe. This was a fairly popular part of downtown with plenty of restaurants and people milling about. Even if she couldn't see anyone right now.

One of Saint Paul's copious wild turkeys—thanks to a very

successful reintroduction program in the 1970s—scuttled across in front of her, heading to the road, where no doubt it would cause traffic delays as often happened. She peeked behind her—her peripheral vision showed the man was still there—so she drew her bag across her and pulled out her phone. Even if just to pretend she was on the phone would be better than acting like an easy oblivious target. "Hi, Josh." Her mythical husband's name. "Yep, I'll be there in one minute," she said, loud enough so anyone behind her could hear. "Yep, I can see the place now."

Footsteps hastened behind her, and she picked up her pace. The lights from a nearby hotel's restaurant glowed, drawing her in. She'd be there in ten seconds, eight, five—

Then a hand grasped her upper arm and she spun around, kneed the man and screamed.

MITCH WHEEZED, clutching himself as he bent over, as the sound of footsteps faded away. This was the last time he was going to pretend to be a knight to rescue a damsel in distress.

He heard a gasp, then an "Oh my gosh! I'm so sorry!"

"So am I," he rasped, finally finding enough air so he could straighten, and pretend he was all right.

"Oh my goodness." Her fingers clasped his arm. "I didn't realize it was you."

He coughed, then shook off her hand.

"I didn't mean to touch you either."

"I suppose it's good you know about self-defense," he gritted out.

"I teach my girls that."

"Your girls?" That's right. She'd been on the phone talking to a man who must be her husband. But she didn't look old enough to have girls who needed to be taught self-defense.

She shook her head impatiently. "What were you doing?"

Yeah, what had he been doing? "There was this guy following you, and I thought he looked a little weird, and, yeah."

From the way she was looking at him and backing away, he was fairly certain she thought the creepy guy following her was him. Then her face softened. "You were trying to protect me?"

"My mistake. Won't happen again. Clearly you know how to protect yourself."

She took a step forward, and the stupid antennae bobbed, drawing his reluctant smile.

Maybe she misunderstood for her face softened a little more and she smiled too. "Well, thank you."

He nodded. "You're welcome?"

She winced. "I'm so sorry. This afternoon really hasn't gone the way you wanted it to, right?"

"Not your fault." Some of it, anyway.

"Um, just out of curiosity, you were expecting to read today, weren't you? I really feel bad, and that we should've better prepared you."

He couldn't let her take responsibility for his own lack of prep. "Yeah, that was my fault. I agreed to do this weeks ago, but kind of forgot, and yeah, sorry."

*Sorry?* Now that was a word he didn't often say. What was wrong with him?

She studied him, still keeping her distance. Then she nodded, sending those dumb antennae bobbing. He fought another smile.

"What is it?" she asked.

"I like your antennae."

"My what?"

He touched his head, and she touched her hair.

"Oh! I forgot I still had them on." She grimaced. "No wonder people thought I looked weird at the bakery."

"The bakery?"

"Yes, I was just getting some food for Derek and all these people looked at me strangely."

"Who's Derek? I thought you mentioned Josh before." He mentally shrugged. So he'd been accused of being blunt a time or two.

"Oh, Derek is one of the guys over there." She pointed to the steps of the library.

"One of the *homeless* guys?"

"Yep." She eyed him.

"What does Josh think about that?"

"Who?"

"The guy you were talking to on the phone."

"You were listening?"

"You weren't exactly keeping quiet, lady."

"Britta, not lady."

He blinked. "Um, Mitch."

"Not Mr. Reilly, I remember." Her smile sparked. "Why is that?"

No way was he about to spill his loathing for his dad to this yellow and black creature.

Her smile faded, and she backed away. Maybe he was wearing resting scowl face again.

"Okay, sorry for asking," she said. "And look, I'm sorry for things being awkward before. And just for the record, I hope this hasn't put you off partnering with the library in future events."

"Sure," he lied. No way, Jose would he *ever* grace this place with his useless presence again.

"Really?"

Her face lit, like she thought he'd said yes. Which to be fair, he supposed he had. Uh-oh...

"Oh, that'd be awesome! Do you mind if I reach out to the team PR people?"

What, not his phone number, like most groupies would

have? Not that she was his groupie, even if she'd admitted to being a hockey fan. She definitely wasn't his type, especially compared to Georgia, who definitely was.

His heart tensed—he really needed to talk to her—and maybe some of that fell onto his face as she backed away again.

"It's okay. I'm sorry for being pushy."

Huh? She wasn't being pushy at all. She was a weird mix of confidence and grace and quirkiness as shown by her bee costume. "Why bees?"

"Excuse me?"

He pointed a finger at her outfit. "You said something about bees being your hero. Which is weird, by the way."

"Come on. You like to eat, right? Don't you remember what I said before? Bees are the number one pollinators, and essential for food production, so I would've thought a hockey player would appreciate those creatures who are responsible for their food."

Okay.

"Besides, I said bees are *one* of my heroes." She smiled again. "I have a few."

"Yeah? Like who?"

He stilled, as awareness fell on him. This wasn't flirting, was it? It kind of felt that way, though, even though he was only meaning to ask as a way to exchange information. He didn't mean anything more. He couldn't mean anything more. Not with Georgia.

Maybe she felt it too, for she backed away, her face dimming. "We should probably go." She gestured to a couple of kids who were standing nearby holding up their phones. "I know you have a girlfriend, and I don't want to get you into trouble by having any pictures taken that get misconstrued by others."

"Yeah. Okay."

She jerked a nod, stepped back another pace. "Look, don't

worry about coming back to the library. Unless you want to, and your girlfriend knows, and it's okay with her."

Why was she being so pedantic? Georgia wouldn't care. He blinked at that shocking thought.

"And um, thank you for coming to my rescue."

"Even though you're obviously a ninja and you didn't need it."

Her lips perked as she shrugged. "And thank you again for coming today. It's great for kids to associate tough guys with reading."

"Uh, sure."

She studied him a moment longer, then nodded, pivoted, and strode away.

And he glanced across at the teenagers, who scurried away. Then wondered if the Bee Woman—what was her name?—would be safe reaching her car, especially dressed like that, and whether he should follow, just to make sure.

Then realized that would only further muddy the waters, and that she seemed plenty tough enough to protect herself. And that he really needed to call Georgia, and finally figure out why she was avoiding him. Once and for all.

# CHAPTER 3

"So, how did the Hero Day talk go?" her mom asked that night at dinner.

"It was okay."

"Just okay?" Dad asked. "I thought you were really looking forward to it."

"I was. But…" She shrugged.

"It's not the same as when you organized it," her mom guessed.

"I don't have control issues—"

Her sister, Astrid, huffed.

"—but Margaret was pretty adamant she wanted to do things her way. Until she basically dumped me in the middle of things." She winced. "It's such a bad look for the library."

"What do you mean she dumped you?" Mom asked.

Britta explained, and was soon comforted by their understanding.

Some might call it lame that she still lived with her parents at the ripe old age of twenty-eight; she called it being prudent, especially with the cost of living these days. Besides, she'd tried the share apartment thing; it wasn't for her. It was too tricky trying to negotiate apartment rules when those she was living with did not hold similar personal boundaries, such as who was allowed to sleep over. And after days like today, it was good to relax with those who understood, even if she and her younger sisters had occasional moments that added to, not eased, the strain.

Astrid and Milla had inherited the blonde, blue-eyed Norwegian genes from their equally beautiful mother, while Britta had always felt she looked like the first pancake that didn't quite turn out right. But that was okay. And as the eldest she was proud that her sisters were strong in their own ways. Looks didn't have to define a person, anyway.

"You should go for Margaret's job," Astrid said.

"She's been there for years, so it's not like I can move her out and take it on."

"We'll have to pray the right door opens then," her mom said. "Amen."

"Well, I better go to bed. Goodnight, all." Her mom had an early shift as a memory care nurse at a nearby aged care facility.

Britta kissed her mom's cheek and she finished her meatballs —hey, a girl with curves like hers had to maintain them, right?— and took her turn loading the dishwasher, allowing time to think on what she had to do for Friday night at youth group. But stubborn thoughts kept persisting, and she winced. Had she been a little forward today? She hadn't wanted to suggest Mitch Reilly return, even though she'd pretty much said that. Well, she'd like him to return for his sake, for a redemption round, so to speak, but hadn't wanted to imply at all that she wanted him to return for her sake.

*Lord, did I do that?*

She searched her heart, but no. No attraction lay there, so maybe she was safe. Sympathy for a person didn't mean attraction. It just meant they were a fellow human, and as she believed in compassion for fellow humans, she was allowed to feel sorry for a man who'd stumbled and embarrassed himself in front of others. And if she had accidentally smiled a bit much, then that was only because she was trying to make up for kneeing him, and to prove she was a nice person, after all. And she had emphasized she knew he had a girlfriend a number of times, so hopefully he knew she wasn't trying to hit on him, even if she had hit him, so to speak...

"Hey Britta, what's this?" Astrid drew close and showed a picture on her phone.

"Let me dry my hands. No, don't move it higher, I can't see it when you do that."

She wiped her hands on a kitchen towel, then held her sister's phone.

And saw a photo of herself, dressed in her bumblebee outfit, standing very close to Mitchell Reilly. "Oh dear." It must've been taken and uploaded by one of those teens near the park when she'd accidentally touched him. She checked the Facebook site. Saint Paul's Insiders, a local gossip site. Great.

"Um, the man has a girlfriend, right? Georgia, or something."

She handed the phone back. *Lord, let this not make trouble for them.* "Yep."

"Then what on earth—?"

"We were just talking, that's all."

"It doesn't look like that was all."

"Well, it's true." She held her sister's gaze.

Astrid nodded, then returned to the screen. "You should see the comments. Or maybe you shouldn't."

Why, when people said things like that, did it instantly make her want to read them? Even though she knew it was a bad idea? *Lord, don't let this snag my heart.* "I'd appreciate your prayers so that this doesn't blow up."

Astrid sighed. "You are always so good, aren't you?"

Ah, this old chestnut. Which sounded awfully like Astrid wanted her to be bad, and if so, how bad did her sister want her to be? Best to change the topic of conversation. "So, tell me about your work today."

Astrid shared a little about her job at a local elementary school, and she made it through the next ten minutes keeping the conversation firmly focused on Astrid. As the middle sister, Astrid had often complained about feeling overlooked at times, and not getting the attention she thought she deserved, which everyone in the household knew was a lie. Now she was older, Astrid's need for validation was demonstrated via strongly expressed opinions, which honestly got a little exhausting at times.

Thank goodness for Milla who, as the baby of the family, was a lot more chill.

Her dad worked as a factory foreman, and he'd never had time for female histrionics, so he usually put Astrid in her place when she got too critical and self-pitying. But his shifts at work meant he wasn't always here, and Britta had learned the hard way that her well-intentioned eldest sister advice wasn't always appreciated.

She showered, hopped into her PJs and into bed, but not to sleep, instead wrestling with the talk she was due to give at the Red Jellybeans tomorrow night. She was one of the leaders at her church's junior high youth group, and loved her kids, and they loved her. She hoped today's outfit hadn't scandalized any of the kids. Or their parents.

After picking up her phone she flicked back to the photo that Kayla had uploaded to the library site, with all of them dressed in their outfits. She still couldn't quite tell who Margaret and Carol were supposed to be, but there was no mistaking who Kayla was, while Britta's black and yellow outfit stood out.

She zoomed in on the photo. Nope. Everything was covered, so that was the main thing. And yes, the corset had given her more of a waist than she normally had, but she'd never be

Marilyn Monroe va-va-voom voluptuous. She just held her weight, like her body was conditioned for Minnesota's icy winters, and was always prepared with an extra layer of padding in case she got lost in the snow.

The black leggings had slimmed her legs, and the black boots had probably made her look more powerful than she planned. But how anyone could call her sexy while she wore a yellow headband with bobbing antennae needed their eyes checked. Even if Mitch had said he liked it.

Ugh. She was *not* thinking on that man. "Lord, bless him and his girlfriend. Lead them into the future You have for them. But I don't want to think about him anymore."

So to make sure she did not, she pulled out her latest read—Georgette Heyer's *The Nonesuch*—and soon lost herself in the antics of faraway England, and the comfort of a hero who was nothing like those of today. Even if they might both be known for their sporting prowess.

Mitch tapped out a message. *Georgia, we need to talk.*

It was the sixth time he'd tried to reach out to her. Heck, this was dumb. He was going to have to call her.

He tapped her number, unsurprised when she didn't pick up. So he did the next best thing and called his sister instead.

"Mitch? What are you doing calling me?"

Yep, this was a conversation that would go well, he could already tell. His day, which had not been great, was about to get a whole lot worse. "Um, how is married life?"

"Great, thanks for asking. But that's not why you called, is it? Come on, out with it."

Ellie was always a straight shooter. Here went nothing, then. "So, I was wondering, have you heard from Georgia at all?"

He closed his eyes at the silence filling the phone. Silence that said his sister knew something but didn't want to share.

"You have, haven't you?" he said flatly.

"Mitch, I don't know what to say."

He clenched his hand. "Well, I'd sure appreciate it if someone said something. She's basically ghosted me these past weeks. I thought she was supposed to be my girlfriend."

Way to go, spilling his heartache to his youngest sibling. But maybe, because she was female, she might have an ounce more compassion than his brothers would. His brothers, who he was pretty sure were jealous of him, and had always been, simply because he'd been basically headhunted from a young age to join pro hockey and was a million times more successful than them. Apart from in matters of relationships, that was.

"Yeah, that."

Whoa. Judging from Ellie's tone, perhaps compassion had skipped the entire Reilly DNA. Put that down to his loser of a father. He always would.

"Did you ever actually talk to Georgia about her being your girlfriend?"

"Huh?"

"Did you?" she persisted.

Well, "We went out on dates. She said she wanted to see me again." Prior to the kiss at Ellie's wedding, but still, it had been enough to make him think she was serious about him.

"But did you ever have a 'define the relationship' talk?" she asked.

"People do that?"

"Oh my gosh, Mitchell. You're so clueless sometimes. Actually, most times."

"You don't have to be mean," he grumbled.

"No, but you want me to be honest, don't you?"

"Maybe not this honest."

Her chuckle ended abruptly. "Mitch, I think you kissing her at my wedding scared her off a little."

"What? Why?"

"I haven't talked to her, so I don't really know, but I think you'll find she's trying to figure out if a relationship with you is what she really wants or not."

"Wow. And she couldn't tell me this herself?"

"Like I said, this is only what I think. She hasn't said anything to me."

"Can you...?" He swallowed. "Can you ask her?" Man, pride was being flushed down the toilet tonight.

"Aww, poor Mitchy."

"Don't call me that."

"Look, when I next see her, I'll ask her to call you, but there are no guarantees. Mitch," her voice softened. "You need to understand that it's not easy for her with you over there and her over here, four states away."

"I know it's not easy," he gritted out. "I hate being the guy who people think has an imaginary girlfriend because we're never together."

"Then why keep pursuing her?" Ellie said gently. "She's not leaving Seattle any time soon. You know she's committed to her studies here, and her family."

Her family. Georgia's family were very rich, and very small in number. They were the neighbors of the Reilly ranch, and consisted of only Georgia's grandmother and brother, Liam, and now Liam's wife as well. Liam had helped out the Reilly ranch when it had some money troubles a few years ago, so the Reillys owed him. And yes, it was no surprise that Mitch and Georgia pairing up had proved a shock to everyone, himself included. But there'd been something intriguing about her, which he'd pursued, even with all the comments about their different backgrounds, age difference, and living in different states.

But he hadn't got to the NHL by shrinking back at adversity, so he wouldn't let dumb things stop him now. Besides, if God wanted them to be together, then He'd make a way. Wouldn't He?

He wished he had a way of knowing for sure. *Hey God, it'd be good to find some other people who believed like me who I could ask.*

"Mitch? Are you still there?" Ellie asked.

"Yeah."

"Well? What are you going to do?"

"I don't know what to do. She doesn't want to talk to me and I'm trying everything I know."

*Except trust Me,* a little voice in his heart seemed to say.

Whoa.

"You should pray about it, you know," Ellie said.

"I have been."

Ellie laughed. "Wow! I keep forgetting you made a commitment recently."

"Recommitment," he corrected.

"Whatever. It's good you're walking with God now."

Her voice held a softness he wasn't used to hearing from her, forcing him to clear his throat. "Yeah."

"And it means you can trust Him," she said, like she'd peered inside his heart and heard the echo of that tiny whisper too.

"I'm trying to, but I feel like there is still stuff that I can do."

"Like fly over here again?"

"It's too close to preseason. I have too many team things going on."

She sighed. "Come on Mitch. If you want a girl to like you, you need to make an effort."

"I thought I had been. We went on dates. Did she ever say anything about that?"

Judging from Ellie's silence, maybe she had.

"What did she say?" he asked stiffly.

Ellie sighed. "Look, maybe you could afford to be a little bit more, I don't know, romantic?"

"She wants romance?"

"Again, I'm just making a best guess here, but yeah. I think she'd respond well to romance. And I know it's not something any of my brothers have had a lot of practice in, but sometimes a girl likes to feel wooed."

"Wooed? What does that even mean?"

Ellie gave another long exhale. "Mitchell, Mitchell, Mitchell. How did you get to be your age and not know this?"

"I've been busy playing hockey. Hockey players don't woo."

"You need to show her your romantic side."

"Hey, I've sent her flowers. We've gone to nice restaurants and stuff." Nice restaurants suitable for a millionaire's sister that made him grateful he was one of the Wild's highest-paid players.

She laughed. "I think it's the 'and stuff' that proves there's still a long way to go. Come on. You can do better than that."

"But that's the point. Apparently I can't. I thought I was doing okay but it's not working."

"And it will be hard to work when you live so far apart."

"I'm no quitter," he said firmly.

"You know, I really feel like this is a situation where you could afford to quit."

His heart froze. "Are you saying she wants to quit?"

"Aw, Mitch, don't go putting words in my mouth. I'm not saying that. But I feel like you two are probably in a situation where you can pull back and it'd all be fine or you press on and try to figure this out. But long-distance relationships aren't easy, especially if you've already got doubts. Now they're only gonna be squeezed and made harder down the track. So you have to be sure this is what you want."

"It *is* what I want."

"Why?"

He straightened. Since when had his sister gotten so in-your-face?

"Why do you want to go out with Georgia so much?" she persisted.

"Because she's..." Beautiful? Hmm, no, a better word to describe Georgia was striking. She was independent— although a bit too independent, apparently. Why didn't she want him?

"Can you seriously not think of any reason why you want to go out with her? Don't tell me it's because she's rich."

"What? Are you kidding me? I don't need a rich bride."

She choked. "Did you just say *bride?*"

He fought a swear word. "No."

"You did, and you just lied as well. Wow. Hey Mitch, you might want to read the part of the Bible that talks about not lying."

"Shut up."

"Okay."

And she hung up.

What the—? He dialed her back, then instantly stabbed the screen to end the call. No way. His sister might have sass for days but he'd demeaned himself enough already today, and wasn't going to give her any more fuel for pity, especially when she'd likely then snigger about it with Jasper and the rest of the family. Uh-uh.

If she thought he needed to be more romantic, then he'd romance the crap out of Georgia. But how could he do that when she was so far away?

He might be the most lame dude out there, but he flicked open the internet and scoured articles. Ugh, cringe city, but at least it meant there were enough other clueless dudes like him. He opened up a blog post with a list of how to romance your long-distance girlfriend.

1. *Send her flowers.* Check.

2. *Play online games together.* Yeah, she hated that kind of stuff, and he was about to get too busy.

3. *Watch the same sunrise or sunset.* That was hard when they lived two time zones apart.

4. *Start a book club for two.*

He scratched his jaw. What was with all the book stuff today?

But... maybe that last one could work. If he knew what book to suggest. Georgia didn't mind reading, but he couldn't remember the last book she'd mentioned she'd enjoyed. So who could he ask? He wasn't about to ask Ellie anything more—she'd laugh and mock him for sure. And no way could he ask Liam. He likely already thought Georgia was wasting her time with Mitchell.

His phone buzzed with a message from Jack. Then he blinked, and saw a picture of himself standing close to the bee lady from the library. After she'd just kapowed him.

Now maybe she was someone who might know a thing or two about books and romance. She was safe, anyway. Not his type, and in a relationship with her Josh, whoever he was, and her girls.

He studied the picture, then realized what the closeness suggested in that camera angle could imply. Then wondered if someone super helpful out there in internet land had sent it on to Georgia, and what she might assume.

Which meant he had to enact his plan ASAP. Which meant returning to the library tomorrow.

# CHAPTER 4

*B*ritta's ordinariness was on full display today as she entered the library in her plain white shirt, navy pants and black flats. No more busy bee for her. Today was about businesslike professional attire, designed to demand respect.

She smiled at the entry staff and walked up the stairs to the kids' section. Margaret hadn't messaged to say she wouldn't be in, so after this early meeting she expected today would run to schedule. A meeting where they'd debrief yesterday, which just might contain a few fireworks, considering the mess Margaret had made.

She entered the space where they had their desks and smiled at Carol.

"How did yesterday go?" Carol asked.

Be polite or speak the truth? "Let's just say it worked out in the end."

Carol winced, cupping her mug of tea. People weren't allowed to eat or drink in the library but the staff could in this space. "I don't know why she just didn't let you organize it like last year. You did such a good job then."

Britta shrugged. "Maybe that's a question you could ask at the meeting."

"Oh! But I couldn't. That would be very forward."

And herein lay the problem, and one of Astrid's just complaints. If nobody ever said anything, nothing ever changed. But being the one person who always said things meant she was the one who ended up with a target on her back. There was a reason Margaret didn't like Britta much.

Kayla scooted in, and when Carol asked about yesterday, Kayla was unrestrained in her opinions. But just watch her clam up and never say anything outright when Margaret arrived. Britta sighed.

It was five minutes past the scheduled meeting start when Margaret waltzed in, unapologetic for her lateness. "Ah, good, you're all here."

"At nine-thirty, like you requested," Kayla said pointedly.

Nope, not a hint of a blush for being tardy. "Well, I think we'd all consider yesterday a success, wouldn't we?"

Britta blinked. "I'm sorry?"

"You handled things reasonably well, although I wasn't convinced that hockey player was the best choice to have read to the children."

No way was she going to have that pinned on her. "I didn't pick him," Britta said. "You did, remember?"

"Now, now, Britta. I'm sure we all make lapses in judgment from time to time."

"I didn't have a lapse in judgment. I had nothing to do with organizing things this year. That was you, remember?"

"I was simply following your procedures from the previous year, and I know how proud you are of your work, but sometimes we can let our pride get in the way of best practice."

Britta glanced across to where Kayla mouthed *Oh my gosh*. Carol was studying the table. Great. Looked like it was up to Britta to be bold again.

She cleared her throat. "Mrs. Rankin, I think you're being unfair. You decided to run the program this year without consulting anyone else."

Margaret stiffened. "I do not need to consult anyone. This is my department, after all."

Maybe Britta should have asked for HR to come in. This despotic understanding of leading a department was not in any handbook she'd read.

"Anyway, I'm hopeful that with today's debrief we can iron out some of those details and ensure a better result next year."

Hmm, Margaret said that now, but she wouldn't appreciate the points Britta had made. Britta drew out of her pocket the paper with her list of suggestions for improvement, waiting for the opportunity to share her thoughts.

"Now, let's start with the most glaring issue. The selection of the person to read. Can someone please remind me why we must always have an athlete come and read?"

"Because they're the ones who draw the most kids," Britta said.

"But obviously not the ones who can read well."

"I don't think that's true," Britta objected. Oh look, it was turning into the Margaret versus Britta show again. "That's a generalization."

"Is it, though?" Margaret said. "I know we don't like to admit to stereotypes here, but it seems there have been more than a few athletes who do not seem to have a solid grasp of the English language."

"Now Mrs. Rankin, I really must object—"

"I'm afraid that next year we're going to have to find someone who can be guaranteed to pronounce words correctly…"

As her boss droned on and on, Britta glanced across the table. Both Carol and Kayla glanced away. Little help they were.

How could Margaret preach inclusiveness then speak like this behind others' backs?

But each time Britta tried to raise a point, Margaret simply ignored her or spoke over the top of her, until frustration boiled in her veins. This meeting required a report to HR, getting the other two as witnesses, and maybe Margaret's incompetence could be exposed once and for all.

Finally Margaret's spiel reached the end, then without asking for further feedback, she closed the meeting and asked Carol—who was taking minutes—to record there had been no objections.

"But we weren't given the chance to object," Britta protested. She glanced at Carol. "I want it recorded that I object to—"

"Britta, can I see you in my office?"

Britta ignored her and detailed the next of her suggestions, like checking in with the guest reader to ensure they had a copy of the book beforehand.

"That's quite enough, thank you Britta."

Fortunately for Margaret, the phone rang and Margaret hustled away, which left Britta feeling petty as she glanced at the list she'd made. Besides, debrief meetings never accomplished too much. Margaret would do what Margaret had always done and let the chaos continue. And Carol and Kayla would do nothing to help, which left Britta holding both baby and bathwater.

She folded the paper, handed it to Carol, who glanced at it, then offered a wry smile. A wry smile Britta had seen a dozen times before that meant she wouldn't do anything.

"Well, that was a complete waste of time," Kayla murmured as they left.

"You could have spoken up," Britta said. "It'd be helpful to feel like I'm not the only one copping the bullets."

"But you do it so well."

Britta eyed her, lips pressed together as she struggled to find words that would not hurt her friend. "Sometimes I could really use your support and not your silence."

Kayla's mouth dropped open then she huffed and walked away.

Well, this morning was off to a great start. She sighed. *Hey God, I don't know what else You have for me today, but help me face it with grace.*

After checking in with Margaret—who sure enough was still on the phone and waved her away—Britta moved to her usual role, (wo)manning the front desk for the next hour, then shelving and answering questions from the public, before her lunch break at one. Already she could feel the need for a real coffee, the agitation from the meeting roaring through her veins like Red Bull in her system after the lows of hypoglycemia.

Good thing the library had always soothed her, just as it had when she was a small child and her parents' long work hours meant she'd spent many a summer day surrounded by books. She loved books, loved their scent, the weight of them, the anticipation as she opened one of her favorite authors and was ready to delve into a new adventure. Even an old adventure, a well-loved book, still held a ripple of anticipation. For when one already knew how excellent the plotting or the prose or the setting or certain beloved characters, well, it felt like a joy to revisit with old friends. To be blessed with this job and instill that love of books with others was a dream come true.

She was helping a young mother find a picture book for her three-year-old when Carol came to the door of the picture book room.

"I'm sorry, Britta, but there's someone to see you at the desk."

"Oh!" She glanced at the mother. "Please excuse me."

She glanced through the glass, saw a man in a baseball cap peer away. Her heart thudded. Wait. That man looked like someone who'd been here yesterday. What on earth did he

43

want? Another apology? A redo of a reading opportunity? Why did he want to speak to her?

She drew close to the desk, saw the tall, big shouldered man pivot back as if he'd heard her silent approach. It *was* him. "Mr. Reilly."

Too late, she forgot he disliked that name, as he winced. "It's still Mitch."

"Sorry." She subtly wiped damp palms on her trouser legs. "I understand you wanted to speak with me. What can I help you with?"

"I, uh…" He glanced around, and yes, the entire space was watching them. His shoulders slumped. "Can we talk somewhere?"

"Ms. Johnson has her break in twenty minutes," Margaret intoned. "You must leave personal queries until then."

Personal? Margaret made it sound like Mitch wanted Britta in some unprofessional way. "I don't—"

"This isn't personal," he rushed to say.

Margaret arched a brow.

"I mean, I wanted to talk to her, but about books and stuff."

Britta swallowed a smile at the "and stuff".

"Why do you need to speak specifically to Ms. Johnson, then?" Margaret frowned.

"Because she, uh, seemed pretty normal."

Margaret choked, as Britta studied him. "Normal" was just another word for average.

"I mean, not as scary as some."

"Scary?" Britta asked, folding her arms.

He blew out a breath. "I don't know why I'm so nervous."

Poor guy. "Was this about having a redo of your reading?" What else could it be?

"What? No. I don't *ever* want to read again. Not like that, I mean."

"Okay."

He glanced around, but Margaret was still in earshot. "Uh, can I speak to you privately?"

"Why?"

"Not about anything personal. Just about books."

"Ms. Johnson's break begins in nineteen minutes," Margaret called.

"Does she have a stopwatch over there?" he muttered.

"Yes," Britta murmured. "And a whip, so unless you have a children's book-related question, then you might want to come back in nineteen minutes."

He dragged a hand through his beard. "Can I meet you somewhere instead?"

"I beg your pardon?" Didn't the man have a girlfriend?

"Hey, it's nothing weird. I don't want Mr. Johnson to get upset or anything."

He knew her dad? This conversation was getting weirder by the second. "I don't know what it is—"

"Oh, forget it." He turned on his heel and strode away.

"Mr. Reilly!" Regret hit her as his fingers clenched. She glanced at Margaret then hurried after him. "I'm sorry, Mitch." It felt so forward to use his name. "Look, I plan to eat my lunch in the park in case you're wanting to talk to me. But it's nothing untoward, is it?"

"Untoward?" He stared at her blankly. "What does that mean?"

She winced. "Honestly, it's like the books I read sometimes infect my vocabulary. I mean, this is all aboveboard, right?"

"Yeah. Why wouldn't it be?"

"It's just odd that you need to speak to me privately, that's all." And if he hadn't been a well-known celebrity, then she probably would not have said yes. But the park was a public space and he would hardly be the sort of person to attack her, unlike if some random person asked her the same question about a private meeting, which she would firmly deny.

"It's just I need some help. And it's, uh, something I don't want others hearing, that's all."

Something he was embarrassed by, judging from the pink highlighting his cheeks.

"Okay then." She took a step back. "Well, you know where I'll be."

"In eighteen minutes?" he asked, his lips curving upward.

She nodded. "In eighteen minutes."

How bizarre.

IT TURNED out to be longer than eighteen minutes by the time she arrived. Eighteen minutes plus some gave him plenty more time to second-guess himself and question the wisdom of this. Every time he saw someone look at him he wanted to hide. He was too well-known, his face appeared on posters and in magazines, who knew who'd stop to talk to him?

Why was he doing this anyway? He was a big boy. He could look stuff up online. But Georgia's ghosting him made him unsure about a lot of things, and the fact he couldn't always remember stuff made him wonder what he should do.

By the time he spotted her plain attire walking toward him he had nearly chickened out again. Shoot, he was nervous.

"I almost didn't recognize you without the bee costume."

She lifted her eyebrows in a way that made her look not unlike her boss, and doubled his nerves within. Maybe that accounted for the stupid stuff that kept hurtling from his mouth like that previous comment.

"I don't wear bee costumes on Fridays."

Was that a joke?

She placed her lunch bag on the seat, sat down and withdrew a sandwich.

"What are you doing?"

"Eating my lunch."

"I thought I could take you to lunch."

"I thought you had a girlfriend."

"Yeah, I do. That's what this is about." He caught the crease in her brow. "Whoa, don't worry lady, you're not my type."

"Good to know." She bit into her sandwich.

"I'm not that kind of guy..." who hit on other people's girls. And seeing he was a Christian now he didn't cheat on his own. And now without her bee costume he could see this librarian chick really was as unremarkable as she'd seemed remarkable yesterday, almost colorless in her pale shirt and washed-out hair.

She glanced at him, lifted a brow, in another uncanny rendition of her boss. Did they learn that move at library school?

"What?"

"Did you know you and your boss have some of the same mannerisms?"

She sighed. "That is not the way to get a woman to help you. So did you want me to help you or not? I've got twenty minutes."

Best he get on with it. "Okay, fine." Suddenly the words he needed to say weren't there. How could he explain he wanted her help? *Her* help of all people. Yesterday she'd seemed spunky and vibrant and up for all manner of challenge. Today she seemed tired.

"Are you okay?" he asked. "You look tired."

She cut him a narrow-eyed look. "Nineteen minutes." She swallowed more sandwich.

Okay, best to not say that again. "So, uh, you seem to know that I have a girlfriend."

Her head dipped as she eyed him curiously.

Man, he should've practiced this some more aloud, and not just in his head. "So, anyway, this is about her."

"Okay...?"

He clenched his fingers, flexed them. He was going about this all wrong. "I don't know why I felt like I could talk to you about this, but here goes. I need someone to give me some book recommendations."

As if he'd spoken the magic words her eyes lit up, transforming her from plain back into the vibrant creature of yesterday.

"Is 'book' the magic word?" he teased.

"'Book' is *always* the magic word," she said firmly. "Books *are* magic."

Huh?

Maybe he wore his question on his face for she smiled. "Books sweep people up and take us away and help us find hope and joy and answers and escape. How can anyone not love the magical effect a book can have?"

"Okay?" His tone was not unlike what she'd used before. But yeah, okay. Being swept up was exactly what he wanted with Georgia. Swept up into finding romance with him, finding a future, and… "Yeah, that's what I want."

She grinned. "Oh, I *love* how books can do that. So, what is it you specifically want to know?"

"Okay, so this might sound weird, but I'd figured you would know, so I'd love your help with something."

"Yes?" She dipped her head in a way that suggested "get on with it".

So he did, his words pouring out in a rush. "I want to know your tips on the best romance novels."

# CHAPTER 5

Of all the things that Mitchell Reilly might have asked her, that had never been one she could've imagined. "Romance novels?" she repeated.

He jerked his chin. "Look, I know it sounds weird, and I suppose I could've looked it up online, but I don't know, I just felt yesterday that there was some sort of connection, like you understood. It's like I said before in the library, you seem normal and not like your dragon lady boss. And anyway, I was in the neighborhood, so I thought I'd ask."

"In the neighborhood?"

He shrugged. "I had training this morning and that's only a block or so that way. So yeah."

She nodded, as she knew that the Wild players had their training facility nearby. But her mind was still trying to unravel what he had said before. "And sorry, I missed it before, why are you asking me this?"

He shrugged. "I don't know. You just seemed like someone who knows books, and it's worked for you, and yeah."

That was hardly an explanation. What had worked for her?

But before she could ask, he was off and rambling again. "I

just want to know your recommendations for the most romantic novel ever."

"Why?"

"For my girlfriend," he said, as if that was answer enough.

She studied him, chewing her sandwich as he stared at her. His eyes were dark and held something that looked like hope, and maybe a plea. It was funny for all the times she'd thought about hockey players—and for a woman secure in her single-ness, she'd thought about them perhaps a bit too much—she'd never thought she'd see vulnerability. But that expression there, wavering between hope and helplessness, seemed exactly that. Mitchell Reilly might possess a killer check on the ice, but right now it felt like she held him in the palm of her hand.

She shifted her gaze away to study the trees. Things happened when one gazed into another person's eyes for too long, and a wise woman didn't stir things up. Especially when the man was asking for his *girlfriend*.

*Lord, protect me.* She swallowed the last of her sandwich, sipped her drink. "So, just so we're on the same page—"

He clicked his fingers. "I see what you did there."

She shot him a look even as she inwardly applauded his dumb joke. "You want me to find a romantic book for your girlfriend?"

He nodded. "And for me."

"For you? I thought you didn't read."

His shoulders slumped. "Look, I know it comes across that way—"

"I thought I heard you say something like that yesterday," she interrupted.

"Look, here's the deal: my girlfriend lives in Seattle, and I'm trying to find a way to connect with her while we're apart. And I figured reading a book together could be fun."

Her heart melted. Oh, that someone like him had thought to do something like that. She never would've guessed he would do such a thing. Her opinion of the man tumbled. What a wonderful gesture—

"I saw it as a tip for long-distance relationships on the internet."

She blinked. Bit back a smile. Of course he had.

"I'm not that clever," he muttered, as if he was ashamed.

Aww, bless his cotton socks. "I think it's a beautiful gesture. I think any girl should be honored to have someone want to do that with her."

He flushed, and her heart might've melted a little more.

"So, you're saying you want a book that both of you can read and you'll share about this together somehow."

"Yeah."

Okay then. Keep it professional. "So, in that case, tell me about your girlfriend. What does she like to read?"

"Well, uh, that's the thing. Georgia hasn't been super big on romance. Which is why I wanted to do something like this."

"What does she do?"

"She's a student."

"A student?"

"She's twenty-one."

Wow.

"Hey, I don't need you to judge me. Yeah there's an age gap, but she's really mature, and I'm…"

*Not.* She smothered a laugh behind a cough. Peeked at him, caught his frown. Instantly felt bad.

"I don't know why everyone thinks it's funny."

"How old are you?"

"Thirty-three."

She clamped her lips together. She'd had a lifetime of saying what she thought but didn't want to scare off the man. Not when the non-reader was actually wanting to read a book. Although what kind of book would appeal to a couple with such a huge difference in life experience she'd need a miracle to know.

"You think she's too young for me, right?"

She shrugged. "I don't know you or her, so I couldn't comment," she said, as diplomatically as she could.

"That doesn't stop most people."

And why it was stopping her, she didn't want to know. It was not as if she wanted the man around. He clearly had issues, and seemed like a walking red flag. But still, she couldn't be like everyone else; that way hypocrisy lay. Best to keep this focused on the topic. "So, what is she studying?"

"Art and photography."

"So, do you have an interest in either of those?"

"It may surprise you, but no," he said dryly.

Yep, no surprise there. "So what do you have in common?"

"Man, I just need a book recommendation. I don't need you to sound like my sister."

So the sister had reservations, too? Hmm. "I'm simply asking because it's helpful to know what kind of book you both might enjoy."

He blew out a breath and shrugged. "That's why I am asking you. You're the expert, aren't you?"

Some people made their lives more difficult than they needed, simply by opening their mouth. Why she remained here, listening to one of those people, suggested she was a glutton for punishment. Or that God thought she needed to work on her patience today. She inhaled deeply and silently exhaled. "How long a book do you want?"

"As short as possible."

"Are you sure? There is a lot more you can discuss when it's a longer book."

He sighed. "Fine, but don't make it a really long book. I see some of the guys on the planes with those doorstoppers, and I don't want that."

"Why haven't you asked any of your teammates for a book recommendation?"

"Because they'd just laugh at me. I want a romance book, not a thriller."

She nodded, her mental library cataloging then rejecting all kinds of options. Classic? Modern? Straight romance, or suspense? "Do you want contemporary or historical?"

"Contemporary means now, right?"

"Current day, yes."

He shrugged. "I don't care. As long as I can understand it, and sound like I know what I'm talking about when I'm talking with her, that's all that matters."

She glanced at her phone. "I need to return in ten minutes."

"So, what do you recommend?"

"I'm not a computer. I need some time. And to pick one that's appropriate I need to know more about you. So what are you interested in?"

He shrugged. "Sports?"

She winced. "I know that there are a lot of sports romances out there, but I'm not sure that they are going to be your cup of tea."

"I don't drink tea."

No surprises there.

"There are sports romances?" he asked.

"Yes, but most have little to do with the sports, or they're not accurately researched." Her smile twisted. "I read a hockey romance where the author referred to the halves of a game."

"Seriously?" He snorted. "Amateurs."

She shrugged. "I imagine it would be hard to know all the ins and outs of the game when you're an author, not a player, so I can't judge too hard."

"I don't want to read anything dumb like that, though."

"No hockey romance for you, then. Besides…"

"Besides what?"

Now she could feel heat lining her cheeks. "I'm afraid some of those books aren't necessarily romantic. I mean, they might try to sound like they are, but I guess it comes across as more a relationship based on appearance, and, er, lust, rather than real love."

He coughed, and rubbed his forehead. "Well, I don't want that."

The fact he admitted that eased her heart. Not that she wanted to admit to having stereotyped him to be a typical player, but the man had enjoyed a number of relationships in the past, or so Kayla had told her. But then, Mitch Reilly had surprised her in lots of ways today. "So, you want to read something that focuses on real love, right?"

"Uh, yeah. I guess."

"Can I ask then is the ultimate aim to impress her with your novel knowledge? Or are you wanting to read about a guy who performs a romantic gesture?"

"I don't care. Either or all of the above."

"You're not making this easy."

"Hey, you're the one who is supposed to be a professional book lover."

Her eyebrows rose as she studied him.

He flushed. "Sorry. I didn't mean to sound like that."

She rose and gathered her food scraps.

"Where are you going?" Panic laced his voice.

"I need to return to my job."

"But you said you had ten minutes to go."

"And I need to do some things before I return." Like check her blood sugar.

"But what about helping me?"

"What about it?"

"But you said you would."

"I don't recall actually saying that."

"But why wouldn't you? I mean, I know I can be a little too blunt sometimes, but I am a nice guy."

"I'm sure you are."

"Don't you believe me?"

"Like I said, I don't know you."

"But... but could you please help me?"

She hesitated, as his look veered to desperation. And maybe she was a soft touch, maybe she was intrigued, or maybe she was a sucker, but she found herself nodding. "I've got to get to work now, but I'll think about it this weekend."

His face fell. "This weekend? I, uh, I'm not exactly the fastest reader. I kind of hoped to start reading this afternoon."

She eyed him, and felt a moment's shame. She wasn't the sort of person to let a moment's pique trump her good manners. But being taken for granted had never sat well with her, and after her shocker of a morning, she didn't want to be taken advantage of again. "I said I'd think about it, and I will. But I'm sorry, you'll need to excuse me. I need to get back to work."

"Okay." His sneaker toe stubbed the ground. "Uh, how can I get in touch with you?"

She hesitated. Giving out her information didn't seem wise, especially when she was careful with her boundaries.

"Will you be here on Monday?"

Clearly the man didn't know much about the library if he didn't know that "we're closed on Mondays."

"Really?"

She nodded. "We open for half a day Sundays, to allow those who work during the week the chance to come in."

"Are you in on Sunday then?"

"No. I have church, and I like to spend the day with my family."

"Your family, that's right," he mumbled.

"But I will give it some thought, and get back to you as soon as I can."

"But how?"

"You're on social media, right? I'll send you a message via Instagram if I think of something before Tuesday."

"I don't know why this is so hard," he grumbled.

"I don't know why you can't just look it up on the internet," she snarked.

Whoa. That wasn't her. And judging from his widened eyes he hadn't expected that either.

"I'm sorry," she began, before the frustration from before rose up once more, refusing to be leashed. "But do you expect me to drop all other things I'm doing just to help you out?" She glanced at her phone. "And now I'm running late. Excuse me."

"I'm sorry," he called as she hurried back, past Derek who eyed her curiously.


SHE THOUGHT about Mitch Reilly's request and her strange reaction throughout the afternoon.

She thought about it later when eating dinner, and later still when she was supervising the Red Jellybeans that night. Why had she gotten snippy? Why couldn't she find the bravado to actually deal with Margaret instead of wishing she had? And why on earth had she agreed to do this thing for a man who obviously never read books, and didn't seem to value her time either?

But still, she couldn't deny she was intrigued by the concept. It felt like a personal challenge. There were obvious book choices, but would they work for a man who didn't like hard words? And maybe that was just as much of a stereotype as anything Margaret might do, but he hadn't exactly come across as confident with olde worlde language. But perhaps if he could watch a version of the novel she thought the most romantic in the world he could use that as a cheat sheet to understanding the novel.

That night she studied his Instagram, and wondered whether she should message him. It felt icky to do that with someone she didn't know, and even though he'd said he wanted to do this for his girlfriend, that felt a little weird too. Like, why pick her out of everyone in the world he could ask? Did she come across as so vanilla that he didn't think she had a life?

The thought of what her sisters would say if they knew what he'd asked kept her mouth closed. She didn't have the energy for their questions. But as the weekend dragged on, she remembered what he'd said. And while his problems with his girlfriend weren't her concern, she could appreciate a man wanting to impress a girl, and the educator inside of her wholeheartedly approved that it would result in more reading.

So by Saturday night she succumbed and sent a message saying she could meet him at the library at one-thirty PM on Sunday to discuss things.

ANTICIPATION RODE high as he jogged the remaining distance. It wasn't too far from his condo, and after twiddling his thumbs for most of the morning after his online church service, he was glad to get some exercise in.

He met her at the assigned place, a meeting room off the main stairs. Private, but not too private, just like she'd said.

"Hey."

She glanced up. Straightened the piles on the table in front of her. Why did she have DVDs? Did people really still watch them?

"Thanks for meeting me," he said. "Especially on a Sunday."

"It's okay."

"You could've just listed them for me."

Her chin lifted. "I don't like messaging strange men on apps."

"Hey, I'm not that strange."

Her eyebrow lifted.

"Okay, maybe this makes me a little bit strange, but it's part of your job, isn't it? Helping members of the public find good books."

"In all my five years of working here I have never had anyone make the kind of request you have."

"Guess I'm special, huh?"

"You're something, that's for sure."

He chuckled. He kind of liked the fact the prim and prissy woman had some bite and snark. But then, there seemed to be a lot more to her than first met the eye.

"So," he gestured to the books. "What have we got?"

She pulled the first one from the pile and handed it to him. "This is a historical novel called *The Light Between Oceans.*"

He eyed the cover. "It looks a bit, I don't know, lame."

She shrugged. "If you want something that will get you talking, this should do the trick. It's about a woman whose husband tends a lighthouse and she has several miscarriages, and—"

"I don't want sad."

"You want light and fluffy?"

"Yeah, I don't think I want that either."

She tucked the next book with an illustrated cover under the pile. "Okay, next is my personal favorite, and a book that often tops the list of most romantic books ever. Ta-da!" She held up the cover.

"*Pride and Prejudice?*" His nose wrinkled. "Yeah, I don't think so."

"Come on. What have you got against Mr. Darcy?"

"Who?"

She smiled. "Only one of literature's greatest heroes. Millions of women argue over whether he's broody and misjudged—"

He could relate to that last one.

"—or intelligent and devoted. You can't knock it unless you try it."

"Hmm."

"And look, here's a cheat's version." She held up a DVD. "In case reading a book is too much, you could watch this with her, and swap notes."

He huffed. "I can't believe a librarian is trying to get me to watch a movie."

"We're not just about reading books here. We try to encourage all kinds of literacy, and that includes visual representations of the texts."

He didn't want to appear any dumber than he already had by asking what that meant. But he was fairly sure she just meant it was a movie of the book. He nodded to the DVDs. "You've got a couple there. Which one is best?"

"Ah, a question for the ages. The two-hour Keira Knightley version famous for the hand flex or the five hours of perfection that is Colin Firth."

"Did you say five hours?" He sat back in his chair. "That's a solid no from me."

"A shame, because it's far more faithful to the story, and would mean you would barely need to read the book to be able to talk intelligently about what Jane Austen was saying."

He sighed. "You're a Colin Firth movie pusher, aren't you?"

"Look, I just would not want you to get caught out and show that you haven't read the book by saying something dumb, like when they're married at the end and he calls her Mrs. Darcy. It's not in the book, and it doesn't matter how many people wish it was."

"You sound like you have pretty strong opinions about this."

"When it's one of my favorite novels, and people like to pretend that they know Jane Austen novels then prove they don't by giving details that are only in the movies, then yes, I have opinions."

He bit back a smile. Here was more of the feisty Bee Chick he'd first come to know. He glanced at the thicker DVD. Picked it up. Recognized the outfit as something like the meek-looking bonnet-wearing chick had worn the other day. "Your colleague wore something like that the other day."

"Kayla wears something like that most years," she said dryly.

"Whereas you prefer a bee."

"I will confess to having dressed in Regency attire a time or two, but I like to mix it up."

"Nobody wants to be boring."

"The Regency period is not boring," she said firmly. "It was one of the most interesting times on the planet."

"What's Regency?"

She explained about the Prince Regent and how he stood in for his father, the king of England, and shared about how it was a time of explorations and inventions and political unrest. But he didn't really pay that much attention, too intent on the light shining in her eyes. When she did passion, she did passion.

"You really dig this stuff, don't you?"

The light faded. "I'm sure you don't mean to sound patronizing, but it kind of comes across that way."

"Whoa, no need to be defensive. Man, are you like this with your husband?" Pity the poor man.

"My what?"

He shrugged. "The other day. I heard you talking to him. His name is Josh, right?"

"Uh, I'm not married."

"Oh. I thought you said something about your girls, but okay."

Her cheeks pinked. "They're my youth group girls."

"Youth group girls?"

"I help run a youth group at my church."

He stared at her. So she was a Christian. "And Josh?"

"I thought someone was following me, so I made up a name, okay? I didn't want it to seem like I was alone."

Huh. "That's actually kind of smart."

"Please don't patronize me anymore."

"I'm not."

She rolled her eyes.

"Hey, I am one hundred percent *not* patronizing. About that, or before. I just meant that it's just kind of good to see someone who is excited about stuff. Like books, and stuff."

She studied him then nodded. More of a dip of her chin than anything else, but it still counted. "So, which one will it be?"

He fingered the DVD, the one she said she liked, then sighed. "Are you telling me that if I watch this, then I don't have to read the book?"

"I'm saying if you watch it, then it will be like you've read the book. Of course, you can also read the book to *really* connect with your girlfriend."

She said those last three words eyeballing him in a way that shot home the reason he was doing this. For Georgia. To hitch her to the romance train.

He sighed. "And you really think this will work in making her think I'm romantic?"

"I think it would go a long way in any woman's estimation of a man if he was to read that book and talk intelligently about it."

"I can't promise intelligent conversation."

"Oh come on. I'm sure you can find something to talk about. It is quite funny."

Somehow he had a feeling that her version of humor and his weren't exactly the same. But still, she'd done what he'd asked her to, and out of her own time too, so he owed her.

"So, uh, what next?"

"Well, do you have a library card?"

He stared at her.

"I'm going to guess from that expression that the answer is

no." She smiled. "Never mind. We can fix you up with one right now."

She led the way downstairs, and he glanced at her. "Hey, uh, thanks for helping me."

"It's my job." Her gaze slid to him. "As you've pointed out a few times."

Yeah, not his finest hour. "Well, you've gone out of your way to help me and I appreciate it."

"I appreciate you saying that. Thank *you*."

He stifled a chuckle. This chick was a little weird. But he liked that.

Ten minutes later he was standing to one side as she whipped up a library card for him like he was six years old. It meant handing over more personal information than he was truly comfortable giving—she now knew his address and birth date and phone number—but she assured him nobody would look at it, that nobody would even know that the great Mitchell Reilly had been in the library.

When she said stuff like that it kind of zapped his ego a little bit, which was probably good too. He didn't want to be a jerk, with an inflated sense of self-importance like some athletes he'd met.

She handed him the bag that had the book but not the DVD; he'd look it up and stream it. "There you go. A perfect Sunday afternoon viewing awaits. Even if you don't drink tea."

"Guess I know what you'd like to be doing."

Her cheeks pinked but he hadn't meant it to sound like an invitation, so he rushed to say, "Hey, thanks again."

"You're welcome. Happy reading."

She smiled, and he felt an urge to stay, to ask if there was something he could do to repay the favor, but she turned away, and was chatting to someone else who worked here, who then peered at him.

Which meant he had to get out of here pronto. No way did

he need to look like a nerd. Even if holding the cloth bag stamped with Saint Paul Library on it made him feel like a little kid. Too late he remembered he'd jogged here, and would now need to hold the bag all the way to his condo. Which all of a sudden seemed way too far away. Man, he hoped nobody saw him.

# CHAPTER 6

*H*er phone buzzed with a notification partway through watching a repeat of *Once Upon a Time* on TV. She tapped it open, saw the Instagram message app had a message. Her heart tensed as she recognized the name. This. This was exactly what she didn't want to happen. This was exactly why she had met with him at the library. She didn't want to be accused of being the homewrecker who got in the way of a man and his girlfriend, innocent though their messaging might be. It was too easy for things to get misconstrued, misunderstood.

She bit back a sigh and opened the message.

*This movie is dumb.*

Oh, the man was a cretin. She typed back: *Have you watched it all yet?*

*Nope.*

She didn't bother holding back that sigh. A mistake, as her mom asked, "Is everything okay?"

She nodded. "Just a work thing."

That wasn't a lie, was it? She'd met him through work, and he was proving to be a lot of hard work, so that was all true.

64

She typed: *How far through the movie are you?*

*The part where the sister has gone away with her friend the army wife.*

*Ah, you're getting closer to the good bit.*

*Hope so.*

She eyed her phone, but when no message came, she felt herself relax, and get engrossed in the TV show again.

Then her phone buzzed again. *Is the book better?*

Well, that was an easy answer. *Always.*

*Of course you'd say that.*

But her heart felt tense again. She didn't want to message another woman's boyfriend like this. And because she had talked about boundaries with the Red Jellybeans on Friday night, she didn't need to think too hard about what to say right now.

*Don't message me again until you've watched the movie and read the book. You need to discuss this with your girlfriend, remember?*

She eyed her message. Too blunt? Too mean? It would get the message across anyway. Then she pressed send.


MONDAY PASSED as it usually did, with the chance to sleep in and claim the house for herself. Living in the family home with other responsible adults meant there were often days when it felt like they were living on top of each other, so to have the chance to be quiet, to just be, felt really good. It was funny in her world how much time was spent in using her energy on others, and while she wasn't the world's most peopley of people persons, she knew how to put it on when it mattered. Like each Friday night. Or when work needed her to be "on" for the kids' Story Times. So to have a day when she could slop around in her sweats and catch up on her own mail and bills and wash her hair felt really nice.

Even if it allowed a little bit too much quiet time to wonder whether Mitchell had finished watching the movie. She guessed not, by the fact that he hadn't contacted her again. Which was good. The more distance she could put between herself and him the better. In fact, if he dared appear at the library again she should probably sic Margaret on to him. That could be a good experience for all concerned.

She chuckled to herself, then glanced at Bumper, their half-blind terrier who'd been a recent addition to their family from a rescue shelter. Bumper's long shaggy coat seemed to grow at three times the pace of her own hair, which meant it often needed cutting so Bumper could see with what little eyesight he had left. Poor dude.

"Come on, boy. Ready to go for a walk?"

He wuffed softly and his tail wagged fiercely as it always did when he heard that word. She got the blue harness and lead and strapped them around him. Bumper had been pretty hesitant at first, but now recognized the word "walk" as his opportunity to explore new smells and sounds. Five minutes later they were partway down the block, as Bumper paused to sniff a very interesting patch of grass, or so his refusal to move suggested.

"He's still alive?" Mr. Daughtry yelled.

"Yes indeed," she called, to the elderly man who had lived kitty corner across the street for as long as she could recall.

This part of the city saw its residents rarely leave by choice. It was quiet, a good neighborhood, something her parents' long hours had afforded to ensure Britta and her sisters had grown up with extended family nearby.

She took a walk, down to the fire hydrant and back, and by the time she returned it was to see the flag was up on their mailbox. "You've got mail," she singsonged to herself. At least, somebody in her family did. These days most of her mail was online.

But when she opened it, it was to see that she was in fact the lucky recipient of mail. Although... maybe not so lucky, once she saw who it was from.

Her heart tensed. Erica was one of the mean girls from her high school years, and there were no prizes for guessing what this would be. And while a girl had spent a long time working on finding her identity in God, all it took was seeing that name to prick the confidence she'd thought she'd earned.

She took the envelope into the kitchen and studied it. Confident Britta would just open it. The Britta of ten years ago knew exactly what this was. An invitation to revisit the non-glory days when bullying had been exactly like that of *Mean Girls* fame. Honestly, that movie might've been set in Illinois, but it spoke as true here as anywhere.

The longer she eyed it, the more the past reared up to taunt her. And wasn't this exactly what she told her kids not to do? "Don't let fear win."

So she ripped it open, and accidentally ripped a corner of the gold paper as it fell to the table. She swallowed. Yep, just as she'd suspected.

*Dear Brita*

What a surprise. They still spelled her name incorrectly.

*You're invited to celebrate the ten-year school reunion of Palmer Street High.*

The date was four months away but still too close for comfort. And now she'd have several months of wondering whether she'd find the guts to go and pretend the bullying from high school had not existed, or whether she should just pretend this invitation had not existed instead. Because why would she subject herself to more of the same?

Memories flashed. Taunts about her weight, her hair, her glasses.

And it wasn't like any of that had actually changed. Neither had her relationship status. And even though she loved her job it wasn't exactly paying high wages. Really, the best thing would be to avoid all the drama and just pretend to not have seen this. Just like she couldn't let her mom or her sisters see it, as she could one hundred percent guarantee what they would say.

And yet... and yet...

How could she shrink back and let the bullies of ten years ago keep winning? That wasn't right. That wasn't what she taught the Red Jellybeans either. She'd be a hypocrite of the highest degree if she told her kids to brave the jungle that was high school when she couldn't go back and do the same.

"Lord, I don't want to go," she whispered.

*I know*, she thought she heard Him say.

"I don't want to be brave."

*I know.*

She shoved her face in her hands. "I don't want to get bullied like that again."

*God has not given us a spirit of fear, but of love, power and a sound mind.*

She sucked in a deep breath and slowly exhaled. The verse from Philippians was what she'd shared on Friday. How could she ignore its truth now?

She picked up the letter, saw the date to RSVP, and stashed it back in the envelope. She still had time. Time to consider what to do. Time to consider what kind of witness she could be. Or what kind of statement it would make if she didn't show up either.

*Lord, help me.*


Tuesday arrived with no word from Mitchell Reilly, which meant she was able to focus on her job without the weight of having to deal with him, which meant all her energies could be focused on today's program.

The library had thirty-five librarians working across the various sections, not including those staff assigned to administration or security, and it often surprised people to know just how much their job tasks varied each day. Sometimes they were answering messages online, sometimes they were on the reference desk or running Story Time or handling class visits. For Britta and the other librarians committed to the children's area, there was a new teen section as well, which meant activities dedicated to that age group, like last week's visit from the hockey players.

And no, she wouldn't be thinking on them at all, thank you.

"Good weekend?" Kayla asked.

"It was fairly quiet, compared to some, anyway."

Kayla grinned. "We visited Edina and had a picnic in the park. It was so good. I really feel like John is going to pop the question soon."

Britta blinked. "How long have you two been going out?"

"Six months, but when you know, you know, right?"

Not her experience. And Kayla seemed to recognize that too, as she quickly shifted the conversation to something else.

Then paused, mouth agape, as she nudged Britta. "He's here."

"Who? John?" She turned around.

Ah, not John. In fact, a very non-John specimen of male was advancing toward her.

"He looks intense," Kayla whispered.

That he did. She glanced at Kayla, half wanting to push her friend at him and run away, but she was trying to be brave so held her ground instead.

"Mr. Reilly," she said.

He flinched.

"Sorry, I keep doing that." Even though using his last name and not his first was helpful to put more of that necessary distance between them. "Is there something I can help you with? Something *we* can help you with?" she quickly corrected.

"I need to talk to you."

"So talk." She crossed her arms. Anything he had to say could be said in public. It would be better that way.

"In private."

She shook her head. "Sorry, I'm working."

"When's your break?"

"I don't have one today."

"What?"

Okay, that wasn't technically true, even if she'd decided in that exact moment to use her lunch break as an excuse to catch up on computer things. She didn't want to talk to him, and didn't want this day getting any messier than it already felt. "Don't you have work?"

"I've done my training for the day."

"Oh, okay. Then I guess that means you've got plenty of time to have a look through this wonderful facility and find yourself a great book to read. While I have to do some computer things."

She pivoted away and moved her arm out of reach from where he tried to touch her.

"Britta, what is going on?" Kayla murmured.

"Could you please deal with him?" She needed a moment to recalibrate. This was not the way someone who was supposed to be unaffected by him should be behaving.

Besides, she had to visit the bathroom and check her blood sugar again.

"Britta?" he called. "I watched the movie."

"Great! Did you discuss it with your girlfriend?"

"Movie? Girlfriend?" Kayla whispered.

She sighed. Clearly this man had no idea how to make her life easier. She put her hands on her hips. "Well, I'm glad you enjoyed it. Did you read the book too?"

"I read the first page, and that was enough."

"Come on. It's like Shakespeare. It just takes a little while to tune in your ear and then it all starts to flow and makes sense."

"Who's Shakespeare?"

Kayla gasped.

Was he serious?

He laughed. "You two should see your faces. Come on. I might be a hockey player, but I'm not a complete imbecile."

"You've read Shakespeare?"

"I didn't say that. But I've watched a movie or two."

"Let me guess: the Leonardo DiCaprio version of *Romeo and Juliet*."

"How'd you figure that?"

Easy. "It's known as the Shakespeare movie with guns."

"It was way more exciting than *Pride and Prejudice* though."

"Oh my gosh." Kayla fanned herself, then Carol called for her to help Margaret.

It was probably time to get this show on the road, if he didn't want his secret leaking out. "So are you back for another Austen?"

"Nope. But I figured you'd like to know that I did tell Georgia, and yeah, she didn't want to play."

"I'm sorry."

He shrugged, but the flash of hurt in his eyes spoke volumes. "She's busy or something."

Hmm. Something, for sure.

"Anyway, I thought the movie was okay eventually. Like, you were right. It took a while for it to get good, but once that mother stopped all her screaming and Mr. Darcy started to do something instead of just standing around looking depressed all the time—"

"Glowering," she said.

"Glowering? Is that when he's scowling?"

She nodded.

"Yeah, well once he stopped doing that and actually did something for Elizabeth, that was pretty good."

Wow. He actually had watched it, and engaged with it, despite what he'd said before. "See? The grand gesture of a hero. That's the kind of thing that can make women talk about Mr. Darcy until the cows come home."

"Yeah, well, not Georgia. She didn't seem to care."

Strike one. But his love life issues were not her problem. "Well, if she can't appreciate the fact that you made the effort then I guess it says a lot about her."

His face darkened. "I don't need you to disrespect my girlfriend."

"I'm not disrespecting. You need to get over yourself. I'm just being honest." *Like his sister*, a little voice seemed to say.

Except she wasn't his sister. She barely knew the man.

"I'm sorry." She saw that Kayla and Margaret were now both watching with too much interest, Margaret's expression marked with a frown. Uh oh. "You're right. This is not the place to talk about this."

He shook his head. "Forget it. I don't know why I thought this was a good idea anyway."

She folded her arms and watched as he swiveled away, looking for all intents and purposes like he would stride out as he'd done before. Petulant man-child.

Then he swung back. Drew near. "I just wanted to try something new. See if I could do better, and finally connect with her."

Her heart softened. "Mitch—"

"And I don't know why you couldn't answer my messages."

Thank goodness the others couldn't hear this conversation. It'd be hard enough trying to explain his appearance as it was. "I'm not comfortable messaging a man who's involved. I don't think it looks right."

"It doesn't mean anything. Come on. I'm a Christian."

She blinked. "You are?"

He muttered something under his breath. "I don't know why everyone acts surprised all the time. Christians don't all need to look a certain way, do they?"

She pressed her lips together. "I'm sorry for misjudging you. I'll be praying you can connect with her."

He jerked a nod then strode away.

~

*LORD, what do I do? How do I connect with someone who keeps ignoring me?*

He hated feeling insecure, but right now it seemed like a lot of people were closing the door. Women, mostly. Georgia was still on radio silence. Ellie, too, had hung up on him. Even the librarian seemed to want to avoid him. What was wrong with him?

Was it the fact he was still trying to figure out his faith? He'd said no to some teammates who'd wanted to go clubbing. His body wasn't the same as when he'd been in his early twenties and could drink like a fish and still play the next day. Was that why Ellie—and it seemed Britta—had made comments about the age difference between him and Georgia?

No. That was stupid.

But still, loneliness seemed to waft through him, like a cold breeze near his heart. Or maybe that was just the effect of wasting five hours watching a movie, time he'd never get back. Why didn't Georgia want him? He frowned. Georgia wasn't even like the heroine; that was more Britta's domain with her blunt assessments mixed with kindness. Not that he wanted to be thinking of her either.

"Hey God, I really could do with some new friends."

People who were honest, who believed as he did.

He scrolled through Instagram, stopped at a post where one of his teammates had congratulated Luc Blanchard who had gotten married this summer to his dancer girlfriend from that show he'd gone on the previous year. Huh. He'd earned a lot of flak for dancing but Luc didn't seem to care. Now there was a guy who was tough yet unapologetic about his actions.

He tapped into Luc's post, saw he'd captioned it with *He who finds a wife finds a good thing*, and a reference to Proverbs 18:22. He opened his Bible app and sure enough, there it was. A quick scroll back through Luc's posts saw more references to things that made it look like the man believed. A glance at his profile bio confirmed it.

Well, a man could complain about feeling isolated, or he could do something about it. So he added his congratulations to the comment.

The dude was obviously on his phone because a few seconds later he saw Luc had liked it. Here went nothing, then...

He opened the Messenger app and thought about his message. Oh, to heck with it. Just write the words.

*Hey Luc, random question, but as you're a Christian I figured you might know. Any Bible studies for hockey players you know of?*

Nerves bit as he waited for Luc to respond. The man did manage his own social media, didn't he?

*Why?*

Why the heck did he think? Man. How obvious did he need to be?

But a voice that sounded a little like the soft one he'd heard Britta use murmured that he needed to get over himself and just be honest. So he sighed and owned the truth. *Because I'm looking for one.* He winced and pressed send.

Ten seconds later his phone was ringing with the weird sound it always made when someone dialed him via an app. Who? "This is Mitch."

"Since when has Mitch Reilly wanted a Bible study?" Luc Blanchard asked.

He swallowed. Time to get real. "Since I recommitted my life a few months ago."

There were a few seconds of silence, then, "Are you kidding me?"

"No."

"How did that happen?"

"Are you always this blunt?"

"You've known me how long and you ask that question?" Luc razzed.

Fair call. "Fine. I, uh, recently realized I needed to get back to what I believed as a kid." Before life and hockey and girls and pleasure had sucked it away.

"Are you telling me you're a Christian?"

"I'm trying to be."

"You either are or you aren't. Which is it?"

"I am." Regret panged at having hidden his faith, then made him lash out. "Wow. Do you give everyone the third degree? All I want to know is whether there is a Bible study you know of or not."

"I do know of one. Which is why I want to make sure you're legit."

"I am legit," he retorted. "Why? What's so special about it? Do you need a secret code to get in?"

Luc heaved out a sigh. "Man, I didn't mean to sound like that. You caught me off guard, that's all."

Yeah, Luc wasn't the only one who'd been shocked. His own family still couldn't believe it.

"Okay, wow. I'm still wrapping my head around the fact that you're a Christian."

He ground his teeth. Any longer and he'd hang up.

"Yeah, okay, so a bunch of us meet up via video call, and we're always happy to include others."

"Sure didn't sound like it a minute ago," he grumbled.

"Yeah, sorry."

"So, when's the next one?"

"Tonight." Luc filled him in on the rough schedule, which looked like most Tuesdays when guys from NHL teams as far apart as Winnipeg to San Jose gathered for an hour or so to connect, encourage and, when they had time, discuss a few Bible verses that one of them had prepared.

His stomach tensed. "You wouldn't expect a newbie to do that, would you?"

"Lead the study? No. But you are welcome to join us."

"Who's us?"

The list of names held a few people he'd expected, like Calgary's Mike Vaughan, Franklin James and Tom Chavez, but also a few surprises, like Zac Parotti and Drew Stanley from Vancouver.

"And, uh…" Man, he hated feeling insecure, but some of those guys didn't like him. "They wouldn't mind if I came?"

"I think you coming would be proof that God exists."

He chuckled despite himself. "Well, thanks."

"Hey," Luc's voice had softened. "It's awesome you're interested. And you'd be very welcome. I'm sorry if I didn't make that obvious before."

"You didn't."

Luc laughed. "I'll send you a link to our meeting tonight, and add you to the group chat if you like."

"That'd be good," he said gruffly. "Thanks."

Emotion clamped in his throat and he ended the call before awkwardness set in any further.

Today had been awkward on too many levels.

# CHAPTER 7

*"P*lease explain?"

Britta glanced up from where she was writing answers to online inquiries as part of the library's "Ask a Librarian" program. This, their first chance to talk privately since the latest surprise visit from a certain library-card-carrying member of the public, was not unexpected, even though Margaret had done her best to ensure her minions were kept busy. By that look in Kayla's eyes Britta knew what she wanted, but that didn't mean she'd make it easy on her.

"Explain what?"

Kayla rolled her eyes. "Mitchell Reilly. Here. *Again.*"

"A man is entitled to visit a library. We are a public institution, and he's a member of the public."

"No he isn't," Kayla hissed. "He's Mitchell Flippin' Reilly. Who keeps talking to *you.*"

"And why is that a problem?"

"It's not! Except... it's weird. Because... yeah."

For a highly educated woman who dealt with words every day, Kayla could be a little inarticulate at times. But trying to explain what Mitchell wanted with Britta when she could barely understand it herself, felt like opening a door to all kinds of speculation that she'd really rather leave closed. She turned back to the computer.

"What does he want?"

And there it was. She withheld a sigh. "He wanted a book, silly."

Kayla snorted. "But why does he keep seeking you out?"

"I don't know. Apparently I'm 'safe', whatever that means."

"And I'm not?"

"Hey, you're welcome to help him out." Even if she was fairly sure Mitchell Reilly wouldn't want anyone else knowing why he was doing this. Still, keeping the secret of a man who didn't seem to see the potential inappropriateness in asking a woman to help him with his girlfriend issues made her wonder why she should be letting this burn a hole in her heart. It wasn't like she owed the man anything. Well, except as a fellow believer, which was the shock of the century. But still, good for him.

"What kind of book?"

Ah, she'd forgotten how bloodhound-like Kayla could get.

Kayla plonked herself down in the computer and tapped the keys, accessing the database.

"What are you doing?"

A few clicks later, and "Oh my gosh. Are you kidding me?"

Uh-oh.

Kayla's eyes were round. "He really did borrow *Pride and Prejudice?*"

How to answer... "It's a classic."

"Yes, it is, but honestly, not a book I'd *ever* imagine Mitchell Reilly reading, if I could imagine him reading at all."

"Now, now. Let's not engage in stereotypes."

Kayla scoffed. "You heard him trying to read. How the heck is he going to read Austen?"

The best answer at this point was probably none. So Britta shrugged.

"You did this, didn't you?" Kayla asked.

"I don't know what you mean."

"You did. There is no way in a million years that man would ever choose Austen himself. Maybe Dr. Seuss."

"Come on, don't be mean."

"I'm not trying to be mean, just honest."

This conversation felt like it was veering a little too close to honest right now. "We should be glad he's reading, right?" Even if it was only one page. At least he'd tried.

"But why that book?"

"Kayla, a man is entitled to not explain his reasons."

"You know he has a girlfriend, right?"

Britta startled at the abrupt change in conversation. "Yes."

Kayla's glossy pink fingernails danced over the keyboard, then she tapped the screen. "See?"

Britta stared at the image she'd seen on Mitchell Reilly's Instagram a few nights ago. The only picture he had posted of himself with a thin young blonde whose expression and clothes screamed class and money. The complete opposite of her own Target-wearing self. And, it must be said, looking like the complete opposite of Mitchell Reilly himself.

There. That was exactly the kind of hypocrisy she didn't want to engage in. Opposites were supposed to attract, right?

"She's Georgia Darcy," Kayla hissed. "Do you know what that means?"

"I have a feeling you want to tell me."

"She's rich! Like, her brother Liam is a squillionaire."

"And you know this how?"

Kayla's acrylic nail tapped the screen. "Because it says it here. Her brother is involved in all kinds of environmental schemes, and does charity work in places like Africa."

"Good for him."

Kayla studied her, as if unsure whether Britta was serious or not.

"No, I mean it. That's great! Would that more rich people spent their money on trying to help people and save the planet. More power to him." She lifted a fist in solidarity.

Kayla shook her head, and yes, that had probably been weird. Oh well.

"She's a student."

"I know," she said, before she realized.

"You know?" Kayla arched a brow.

"Mitchell's girlfriend is hardly a secret. And he mentioned her when we discussed books." She winced. That was sailing awfully close to the truth. She didn't want to expose his secret, but neither did she want Kayla or anyone else thinking she harbored a secret longing for the man.

"Did he mention she's twenty-one?"

She cleared her throat. "Yes."

"He's a cradle snatcher! Like, he would've been *twelve* when she was born. That's just so weird to me."

"Mmm, no weirder than some of those relationships in your favorite Austen novels. Like George Knightley and Emma, or Colonel Brandon and Marianne," Britta pointed out. Why she was defending the man when she thought exactly the same, she had no clue.

Kayla's nose wrinkled. "I never understood why Jane had to make Colonel Brandon so much older. It's so creepy."

Britta nodded.

"But it *is* fiction. Whereas Mitchell and Georgia are real."

If they were. She blinked at herself. But questioning whether they actually had the relationship that Mitchell seemed to think they did really wasn't any of her business. He was invested enough in it to want to make it work, so that was that. It wasn't like she was his sister and could point out the challenges that distance, age difference and other things could present. Anyway, now he was a Christian—praise the Lord!—she could trust God to work things out for Mitchell's good.

Kayla eyed her with what looked like pity. "So I don't know what he's doing talking to you, but you need to make sure you don't read too much into it. We're not the type of women that guys like that are interested in. They go for models and actresses, like Zac Parotti and Ainsley Beckett—oh my gosh, did you see their engagement pictures? She's *so* beautiful. Anyway, they go for those kinds of women, not ordinary average girls like us."

Ouch. Yet none of this was news to her. Nor needed to be said, especially as her heart was untouched. "I promise you, there is nothing to worry about here," she murmured as Margaret walked into the room.

"Ah, Britta, here you are." Margaret frowned at her.

"Just finishing replying to inquiries, like you asked me to before."

"Hmm. And you, Kayla? Why are you in here and not out there?"

"I was just checking the database."

Britta slid a look at her. Yeah, checking the database to see what Mitchell Reilly had borrowed.

"Well, I need you out on the desk now, okay?"

"Okay." Kayla moved reluctantly, shooting Britta a "don't think this conversation is over" face.

"Britta, I just received a memo from Gwen Lee from the Bookmobile department. Apparently Harold has broken his arm and will be out of action for a while."

"Poor man." Her heart thudded. She had a feeling she knew what was coming next...

"Do you still have your bus license up to date?"

Bingo. "Yes." She needed to for youth activities.

Margaret smiled. "Good. Then I'm releasing you for the next little while to assist the Bookmobile team. I'm sure your presence will be appreciated there."

More than it would be by Margaret here, anyway, it seemed.

But still, her contract meant she was supposed to support the library's ventures wherever she was needed, which meant being at the disposal of their department heads. And as Margaret was her department head, Britta had to go where she was sent. And as she happened to love the Bookmobile, maybe this was a God-given opportunity to insure she was where she was needed. For all sorts of reasons.

What would Jesus do? Walk the extra mile. She found a smile. "As you wish."

Margaret's forehead puckered, like she wasn't sure if Britta was mocking her or not. And truth be told the phrase from *The Princess Bride* had slipped out, no harm intended. That's what being an avid reader did. Certain words or phrases held a sticking power and were woven into one's being, so one couldn't help but accidentally sprout them upon occasion. Such was the power of a good book.

"When do I start?"

"Tomorrow."

"Oh! Uh, okay."

"Is there a problem?"

"No. I just wasn't expecting it so soon."

"Not soon enough." Margaret smiled. "For the Bookmobile patrons, I mean."

Britta didn't like to be cynical, but she guessed Margaret would be happy to see her leave, too. "Sure."

*God, give me strength.*

Mitch tapped the link to the video call that Luc had sent. He'd seen the invitation to join the group chat but hadn't wanted to see the questions and comments sure to be there when he was included. Yeah, he knew how these things went.

He smirked to himself. Far better to shock them all by just appearing in the video call.

His laptop screen square opened and he saw he was admitted to a waiting area. His nerves increased. What would these dudes say? He knew some of them didn't like him. He hadn't exactly held back on hits against guys like Zac Parotti over the years, so he couldn't blame them. But Mike Vaughan was known the league over as a good guy, and Luc seemed legit, if a bit suspicious. Which said it all, really.

He blew out a breath. "God, You better help them see I'm different." Because he knew words were cheap, people believed actions. Still, this was an action that he hoped would help them see he wasn't the same man he'd been before.

The screen suddenly dissolved then split into ten squares, faces he recognized, who all wore their own versions of shock.

"Mitchell Reilly, wow." Mike grinned. "Welcome."

"Uh, thanks."

Various others nodded or lifted a hand in acknowledgment. Just like Luc had said there was Calgary's Mike, along with his teammates Franklin James—whose sports reporter wife Hannah did not like Mitch—and Tom Chavez. Zac and Drew were there, along with Edmonton defenseman and recent newlywed Ryan Guillemette. But he hadn't expected to see Seattle's Kyle Tinker, or veteran Doug Lehtonen, San Jose's blockbuster free agent signing last year.

"We normally have Jai too, but his wife Allie is sick, so no go tonight," Mike explained. "Oh, and Chris Thomas is on vacation with his family, and he says hi. But hey, great to see more new faces. Kyle, good to see you too."

"Thanks." Kyle scrubbed a hand along his jaw like he was nervous.

"I didn't know you were interested in God," Ryan said.

Who was that aimed at? Kyle or Mitch? He didn't want to

assume—because heck, Kyle wasn't exactly the first guy one assumed was a Christian, so he no doubt had a story to tell.

"I saw Jai when we were training at a clinic near the Bay, and he invited me, so I'm just checking it out." Kyle shrugged.

Ah. That didn't sound like the man had made the same kind of Jesus-following commitment that Mitch had.

"And you, Mitch?" Franklin asked.

"I, uh, am trying to get back to it."

"You used to believe?" Luc asked.

Hadn't he told him already? "I grew up going to church, then when I first lived away from home I spent a bit of time with a family who were Christians." He shrugged. "It rubbed off so I made a commitment." In his mid-teens. "Until hockey and stuff took over."

Various nods suggested the others understood. He loved this game, but hockey had a way of demanding full focus. Until he'd figured out how to make the game and its status and money work for him, which soon meant he'd had no desire to fill the hole in his heart with God, a hole that had only widened when his dad left, and one that could be filled with other distractions.

"Well, it's great to have you guys," Ryan said.

He nodded, feeling exposed. He ducked his head, glanced at his phone. He'd never liked feeling like the new kid.

"Well, instead of a study tonight, we figured maybe we'd just catch up a bit, see how everyone's travelling. It's been a while," Mike said. "So, Ryan. Care to share? How's married life going?"

Judging from Ryan's rapidly reddening face, marriage was going fine. "Sylvie's great," Ryan mumbled.

Mitch bit back a smile then clicked his fingers. "She's the one with the tattoos, right?"

"Yep." Ryan eyed him.

"I saw a post on the NHL feed. Looked like you had a great day." A lakeside shot, lots of laughter, big smooches, dancing.

Ryan's expression softened a bit. "It was perfect."

"It was a great day," Mike said, and Franklin nodded.

"Even if some of the guests got a little unruly."

"Sounds like a story."

Ryan shrugged. "Sylvie works at an old folks' home and some of the clients got a little feisty."

"Feisty old people?" Kyle asked.

"Like you wouldn't believe." Ryan told a story about a man called Clifford which soon had everyone in stitches. "I don't think he meant to say it quite like that but it was pretty hilarious at the time."

"And still is two months later."

"And Luc, your wedding day was fun too," Mike said.

"The best. I still can't believe how much Bailey's family has accepted me, especially after—but you guys don't need to hear that. That's a story for another day."

"And now Zac's engaged."

"How long until you get hitched?" someone asked.

Zac shrugged. "I don't want to wait. I've found the right woman so why wait for someone else's timeline on what they think is appropriate?"

"Amen," Ryan said.

Hmm. It didn't seem like these dudes believed in long engagements. But then, that might be something to do with the no sex until marriage thing a lot of Christians seemed to live by. If that was the case, he could understand a man wanting to hurry to get on with doing the deed, so to speak.

The conversation continued, and he started getting peeks at what made these guys tick. God was important, and their families, and community and charitable partnerships. And while not many had a Zac Parotti degree of stardom, most of the guys were involved in causes that proved they cared more about people than money. Such as Mike Vaughan's work with the Mission Possible for Future Generations charity in the Philippines.

He liked that. These guys seemed real deal and genuine, rather than some of the status-climbing fakers he'd come across in his work.

"So, back to the studies," Mike said. "I was discussing with Jai and Chris and Pastor Josiah who originally started this study with Jai years ago. We wondered if instead of an in-depth study we could take turns at sharing what God has been doing in our lives lately."

"Don't we already do that?" Ryan asked.

"Yeah, but maybe share a little more intentionally, like try to think of something specific to encourage each other with."

"Such as?"

"Well, for example, most of you would know my son Ethan is heading into his first year of real school. He's been a bit nervous, but Bree and I have been praying for him and last week Bree had a moment when he was acting out and she prayed, and he instantly settled and calmed down. I guess that shows how God can be quick to answer prayers."

Mitch nodded. "I prayed today that I'd find some people to connect with about God and then spoke to Luc today and voilà. Here I am."

"Love it."

As Zac started sharing, Mitch's mind flicked back to just who had given him that initial challenge to find someone to connect with. Someone who had said she would pray for him. Someone who was not his girlfriend.

Conviction panged. Maybe he was wrong to think about her. But it wasn't like he could completely switch off his brain. A man still had an imagination. Even if the woman he'd prefer to be thinking about seemed determined to not think about him.

Gradually, he became aware that everyone was silent, just looking at him. "Sorry, what was that?"

Mike's mouth twitched. "You looked very lost in thought just then."

"I've just got a bit going on." Like Georgia. And, that's right, he'd forgotten his memory lapses. Which probably meant a visit to the doctor was in order soon. Although as soon as he did that, and the team found out, it would no doubt start the ball rolling toward his retirement. And life felt uncertain enough without stirring up those kinds of questions he might be able to leave for another season. He'd prefer to leave it for another season. He didn't have quite enough banked to leave the sport just yet.

And all this talk about relationships and people settling into their futures only served to remind him that his wasn't secure. And he'd have to be one of the older guys here, but nothing was near certain with Georgia. Was he even right to continue to hope, or was this just a fool's errand like Ellie and others seemed to think?

Others, like the little librarian, whose good manners might have held her back from saying what she really thought, but he didn't need to read between the lines to read her face. It had been obvious that she'd been as shocked to learn of the age difference between himself and Georgia as the guys were tonight to see him attend a Bible study.

Which reminded him further that he probably needed to swallow his pride and see if there was a different book she could recommend.

Which probably meant he should return to the library tomorrow.

# CHAPTER 8

*P*eople who thought librarians led boring lives had obviously never accompanied a librarian on a Bookmobile adventure. Britta enjoyed these opportunities to share the love of books further afield, especially after so many months working in an office. And now, when the leaves were starting to turn, and before it got too cold, was the perfect time to be out delivering the good news that the books were back in town.

The central library had a bunch of suburban libraries it was associated with, and the Bookmobile was considered an essential part of this service, with visits from over fifty thousand community members who might otherwise not have any connection with the library. Last year's library report tabled that over sixty thousand books, magazines and other items had been checked out, and that nearly four thousand books had been given away at community events to build home libraries. Rejoining the Bookmobile team meant she'd probably be expected to be at some of these events, so it was a good thing she didn't have dates to fill her weekends.

Today's schedule would see two hours parked near the mall

in one of the underserved neighborhoods without a library. Then after lunch, she'd head to a nearby retirement community. Last time she'd visited there had been a rush on books of a certain vintage, like the Agatha Christies and Barbara Cartlands from a few retirees with English village reading tendencies.

And while Britta liked a good Agatha Christie as much as the next person, she drew the line at Dame Cartland, some of whose books seemed an imitation of Britta's beloved Georgette Heyer. Not that she would accuse the woman of plagiarism, as she'd read so many books in her life that truly original storylines were becoming rare. But still, one did not need to pollute one's mind with inferior versions. Not when there were so many books being churned out into the world each day. And not when there were so many favorites to reread.

She restocked the shelves from the loading site, and retrieved the requested books, then clambered into the driver's seat and took her turn behind the wheel. Sighed. Harold, the usual driver, was a big burly man, and her height meant she had to move the seat forward and adjust the back so she could see. She pressed the ignition. Crunched the gears a few times. Then, after finally getting the vehicle to move, eased out and flicked the indicator to join the main road.

Nerves skittered through her veins and she exhaled slowly. She shouldn't be nervous. It wasn't like she hadn't done this before. It had just been a little while, and she needed to remember the ins and outs of what was involved. And to remain confident even when she was faced with people who seemed to think that because she was shorter than some that they were entitled to treat her like a child. But maybe those people wouldn't be out today.

She negotiated the traffic, with only one honked horn, then got onto the freeway that led north. Twenty minutes later she was pulling into their designated zone. She needed to yank on the brakes, then leap out to put the chocks under the wheels to ensure it didn't roll away. Harold had learned the hard way that hand brakes couldn't always be trusted.

Five minutes later she had set up the sign and switched on the fairy lights inside that she always liked to use but which she suspected Harold didn't. Twinkling lights made the inside look less like a cave from the entry door.

"Are you open yet?" a little boy asked.

Britta glanced at the female adult with him, who was on the phone. The woman nodded.

"Sure!" Five minutes earlier than their designated start time, but how could she prevent a potential reader? "Come on in."

The inside was lined with over twenty feet of shelves, all set at a slight recline so they wouldn't fall out when they were travelling. For a small space the range was extensive, with everything from travel guides and historicals to a decent young adults' and kids' section with comics, picture books and reference books, and a DVD section with movies and TV shows. There were a couple of little sitting areas where people could read and determine if a book was for them, and the librarian desk where she'd check books in and out. Some Bookmobiles had two staff, but budget cuts meant their Bookmobile was limited to one, unless a volunteer driver who'd completed all of the mandatory checks could be added. It was a big ask for someone to volunteer four or more hours of their day each week to do this.

The boy climbed inside and immediately headed to the kids' section. He must be a regular.

"Yoohoo!"

Britta faced an elderly patron. "Good morning. How are you?"

"Oh, I'm so glad to see the Bookmobile is back. I have a book I requested and I'm hoping you have it in today."

Britta moved to the loan desk and the pile of books requested. "Have you got your library card?"

She scanned it, and moments later had located the book which she checked out then handed to the woman.

The lady beamed, clutching the book to her chest. "Oh, thank you! I have been wanting to read this for forever, and books can be so expensive, can't they?"

"Yes indeed." The average cost of a physical book was fifteen dollars; library patrons could read it for free. Last year's statistics had shown that the libraries of Saint Paul had seen over thirteen million dollars' worth of books loaned. And that didn't include e-books or audiobooks.

"I love the Bookmobile! It's the bright spot in my day."

"I hope you enjoy." After farewelling the lady she checked on the little boy. "How are you doing?"

"I was looking for a book on dinosaurs, but you don't have any on T-Rexes."

"Oh! Are you sure?" She glanced at nearby shelves. Some-times books were incorrectly shelved, and while she'd done a quick scan today, she might've missed one.

"It's okay," the boy said, with a sigh that said it clearly wasn't.

"Tell you what," she crouched to his level. "How about I scan your card, and I'll make sure we put one aside for you for the next time we're here."

"Really? You'd do that?"

"Absolutely!"

"Thank you."

The rest of her morning passed with much of the same. Sometimes the stops they made were longer than others, depending on the clientele of the various locations. Multiple elderly people were a lot slower to navigate than the children at some of the elementary schools they visited.

She was running a little behind schedule by the time she reached the retirement community. But the elderly patrons were so sweet, and some remembered her from when she used to do this a year ago.

"It's Britta! Hello, dear girl."

"Mrs. Ransome. How are you? You're looking well."

"Well, I'm glad I *look* well, for my sciatica is playing up, and has kept me bedbound for quite some time. But nobody wants to hear about that. Nobody around here, anyway, because they just want to concentrate on their own illnesses."

Britta withheld a smile. "Is there anything in particular you're looking for today?"

"Oh, I just want to see what new stock you have in."

"We have some new P. D. James, if that's of interest."

"Oh, you remembered!"

"I could hardly forget now, could I?"

She helped Mrs. Ransome find her book then helped an elderly gentleman find a Jack Reacher. There was no judgment here—well, she might have judgment, but didn't express it. Not in this world where it seemed anything goes. Walking a fine line between supporting patrons with their reading choices and being honest about whether it was a "good" book or not was tricky, and she'd learned that not everyone appreciated her personal morals entering into such conversations about the semantics around "good".

But as she glanced at the cover as she checked it out for Mr. Pimm, she wondered if this book might be more Mitchell Reilly's cup of tea. Then shook that thought away. She had no desire to think on him. Besides, with the monthly Red Jellybeans online training meeting happening tonight, she had best start thinking about that. And just how on earth she was going to have the energy to manage all these responsibilities.

~

"Mitchell, how did the library visit go?" Daisy Pearce, the Wild's community liaison officer asked on a phone call, the next day.

"Uh, good?" How did she know? Oh, she meant the time he was supposed to read for the kids. "Actually, yeah. It probably could've gone better."

"Mmm, that's what I heard."

"You did? From who?"

"Oh, somebody."

He hated when she played games like this. Sometimes he wondered if she said stuff like that to tease in an effort to get him to bite. Jack had mentioned a couple of times that Daisy had a crush on Mitch. Which was stupid, as they had a clause in their contracts forbidding workplace relationships.

The thought she might like him, when the woman he wanted was maintaining radio silence, made him antsy. "Yeah, I could've done with a reminder about which book I was supposed to read."

There was a second of silence. Then, "I'm sorry. I thought you would have taken responsibility as an adult and remembered your obligation yourself."

Now that clearly did *not* sound like the woman had a crush on him. Good. "Well, it's hard to keep track of everything, so maybe keep it in mind for next time."

Her cough held an edge of miff.

"Well, seeing you prefer to be reminded about things, I'll remind you of this. We have a community event coming up that we need some people at, and you agreed to go."

He bit back a sigh. Another thing he'd forgotten. Still, community engagement was where it was at, especially to inspire the next generation of players. "Tell me more."

She mentioned a hockey clinic next week that needed some more leaders. "And we all know that they will respond to you if your name is attached to it."

Provided there was no reading aloud then, "Fine. I'll put that into my calendar."

"Do it now, please. I don't want you to forget."

He stilled. Had word of his memory lapses leaked? He hoped not. But asking was a sure pathway to exposing this weakness, and he wouldn't do that.

"Okay." He tapped it in his phone, set a reminder. "Done."

"Great!" she chirped. "Oh, and one more thing. Actually two. The first is we would like to pencil you in to be a guest at another community event."

"What do I have to do?"

"Just show up, sign a few autographs, take a few photos, just like at the library, but this time without the reading."

"Okay. When is that?"

She told him, and he put it in his phone calendar.

"And the other thing?"

She paused, and his heart knotted. Why couldn't she say it outright?

"Daisy?"

"Look, I'm not sure if your agent has got in contact with you, but there are some photos floating around of you and the woman who was dressed like a bee. I gather that she's one of the librarians and I just thought you need to be careful with how that's perceived, especially considering your relationship with Georgia Darcy."

"What about my relationship with Georgia?"

"Now, now. No need to sound angry."

Hmm. He'd call that defensive, not angry. But apparently building a new reputation would take time.

"Just that you might want to be careful about how things are perceived."

"She's a librarian, we were talking about books. That's all."

"I know that." Daisy laughed. "I've seen pictures of her, and I know she's not your type."

For some reason, even though her words were true, it still felt a little pointed and rude. Britta might be blunt and have her boundaries locked Fort Knox-tight, but she had gone out of her way to help him, and he didn't like the idea that someone might make fun of her. "Then why are you asking me this?"

"I'm just saying you need to tread carefully."

"Are you saying the team doesn't want me to visit the library?" He rolled his eyes.

"Of course not. And hey, if you'd like us to explore a partnership with the library, then say the word. Just don't explore a different kind of partnership if you know what I mean."

"I don't actually think I know what you mean," he said, channeling his inner obtuse. "But I gotta go. I have an appointment."

"Oh, well, don't let me keep you."

"Thanks. See ya." He ended the call and smiled.

Yes, he had an appointment. Not one on his calendar, but one he was now even more determined to make.

To go visit the library and talk to Britta about the next book he should read.

"WHAT DO you mean she's not here?" he asked the meek-looking younger kids' librarian who had dressed like a Jane Austen character on his first visit there. Her name tag said Kayla. "Where is she?"

Kayla glanced over her shoulder, then said in a low voice, "Margaret put her onto community visits."

"I beg your pardon?"

"She's on the Bookmobile run."

"The what?"

"The Bookmobile run. It's where we visit schools and poorer areas and retirement homes and take a selection of books. It helps people who don't have much in the way of transport options, to return books or make their own selections."

He could just imagine how that kind of service would be appreciated. "But why Britta?"

"Because she has her commercial driver's license."

"Wow." Respect. She looked too little to have that kind of license.

"And because I think Margaret would be very happy to not see Britta outshine her here."

"Well, maybe if Margaret was to dress as a bee, she might have a chance."

Kayla chuckled. "You know, for a jock you're not too bad, are you?"

"I like to think so," he said as modestly as he could. He wasn't sure if he pulled it off as she arched her brow and backed away just like her friend would no doubt do too. Yeah, he probably needed to work on sounding modest and not shooting from the hip as he too often did. This following Jesus thing was hard work.

"So, is there something I can help you with?"

Judging from the way she was eyeing him, he suspected that Britta might've told her something. But he didn't want to inquire. If she had spilled the tea it probably wasn't going to reflect well on him anyway. "Yeah, thanks, but I'm good."

Her slightly narrowed gaze suggested she didn't think that at all, but he couldn't afford to get caught in the mental gymnastics of wondering what everybody thought about him. He didn't really care anyway. There were only a few people whose good opinion he craved: his mom, his sister, Georgia, and now Britta. And given one-quarter of those people were not talking to him —or was it half now, with Ellie not talking either?—it meant he probably needed to get some more stuff sorted out. And soon.

"Well, uh, if you're seeing her any time soon, please let her know that I'm ready for the next book."

Why he was saying this to her and not just messaging the woman herself, he didn't know. It wasn't like he wanted this arrangement with Britta advertised to anyone.

"I'll let her know."

She eyed him with an expression that looked kind of too close to a smirk, and made his temper short.

He stalked from the room, then dropped into a normal gait. He wasn't supposed to be projecting angry hockey player, was he? Would Jesus stalk the hallways of a public library? Probably not. He'd be more like Britta, with her smiles and enthusiasm and time for people. Well, except for people like him.

"Mr. Reilly?" He closed his eyes at the woman's voice, fought the temptation to swear. Then opened them. "Yes?"

"Oh, I just wanted to say that my son came to the reading last week and enjoyed it very much."

"He did?"

"Oh, yes. He's not much of a reader, because he loves his sports so much, which is why he came when he saw you and your teammates were here."

"Okay."

"So I just wondered if you were planning to return any time soon. I know Travis would love to hear you read again."

Was this woman pulling his leg? "I didn't think my reading went so well that it warranted a return visit."

"Well, my son would beg to disagree." Her nose wrinkled. "He'll be so disappointed to have missed one of his favorite players."

"I don't come here often."

"But I thought I saw some pictures that you did."

"Yeah, you can't believe everything you see."

She nodded, he excused himself, and skedaddled right on out of there. That was it. He wasn't going to grace this place with his presence again any time soon. If he wanted a new book he'd simply message Britta instead.

# CHAPTER 9

"Hey honey, you're home," her mom said as Britta entered through the kitchen door. "How was your first day back Bookmobiling?"

"Yeah, it was good, but pretty tiring. Sorry, I gotta dash. I've got that meeting that's already started."

"The one for Red Jellybeans?"

"Yeah."

Her mom nodded, then pointed to a covered plate on the counter. "I saved you dinner."

"God bless you. I'm starving." She kissed her mom's cheek, picked up the plate and headed to her bedroom. She was already five minutes late, and Edmond Wallace, the kids' church pastor, was understanding—up to a point. She'd messaged to apologize that she'd be late, and scored Edmond's usual response:

*We only have meetings once a month, so I don't understand why you can't prioritize it. After all, this is the Lord's work we're talking about.*

Ah, there was nothing quite like Christian ministry guilt.

She shoved her plate on her desk and plugged in her laptop,

then raced to the bathroom. Two minutes later she was ready to eat when she realized she needed cutlery. She dashed out, grabbed knife and fork, blew her mom and Milla a kiss, then rushed back to her room. Ate a couple of mouthfuls of lasagna before finally switching into the video app where their meeting was held. Thank goodness online meetings were a thing these days.

She managed another couple of mouthfuls while the host decided to let her in. Oh, so delicious. See, this was what she couldn't count on if she was living in a share house again. Her mom might lead her own hectic life, but she was always ready to mother her with delicious meals. God bless her.

Finally the host allowed her in, and she wiped her mouth and smiled and waved.

"Ah, I see someone else has decided to join us."

Edmond might lead the youth ministries of her church, but she wasn't always sure whether he meant to sound snarky or not. The Christian inside would like to think not, but he said it in such a way that was never completely reassuring.

"Sorry I'm late," she said, before realizing she was muted.

"The mute button is on," Edmond said. "We didn't want to waste time tonight, and already we've had to wait far too long for the stragglers to join us."

She pressed her lips together. Yes, she was late, but only by five minutes, well, ten now. And his little spiel about lateness was only making them later.

She listened as he droned on about a policy and did her best to eat discreetly. Edmond wasn't a fan of those who multi-tasked, which was why he'd objected to these virtual meetings. That was until Calvin Norberg, the lead pastor, had pointed out in an all-staff and volunteers meeting that the church was supposed to be about equipping the saints for the work of the ministry. And if the saints couldn't get there because of family or work circumstances, then perhaps they needed to meet people where they were at, instead of demanding they try harder. God bless Calvin.

But the information Edmond thought was so worth imparting wasn't anything particularly fresh or revelatory. Instead, it was pretty much what she'd heard him say last time. Her eyelids grew heavy, her blinks becoming longer. Oh, she could be spending her evening in so many other better ways. Not least with Georgette Heyer's Sir Waldo Hawkridge.

She peeked at the screen, then propped her chin in her hand, and covered her mouth as she scooped in the last mouthful of lasagna. Yum. Her mom was an excellent cook, even if she rarely cooked the Norwegian meals her own mother had. And while a girl might be supposed to eat more fish, she was very happy for the carbs of meat and pasta and cheese sauce, thank you very much.

She pushed the plate away, then saw her phone had a new message. Kayla. She peered at the screen, her eyes widening at the message. *Guess who came to visit?*

No. She wouldn't instantly go off imagining things. Best to play it dumb. She tapped her screen open, taking care to not be seen, and typed *Who?*

*Him!*

Roughly fifty percent of the world fitted that description. Though probably only one who warranted an exclamation point. Still, she didn't want to fuel Kayla's curiosity any more than it already was. She sent a question mark instead.

*Mitch Reilly. He asked about you.*

She closed her eyes. No, no, no. She was supposed to be keeping him away.

"I'm sorry, but it appears Britta has gone to sleep."

Her eyelids snapped open and she stared at the laptop screen. "Oh, sorry!"

"Still muted, Britta."

She rolled her eyes, then caught the teasing smirks and smiles of others who had been in a similar situation.

"Now that Britta has rejoined us, let's move on to the next policy."

She tried hard to stay focused, truly she did. But Kayla's question had made her itchy to know what he wanted. Probably about another book, but still. This wasn't good.

When Edmond got to another extra dry part aimed at the Tiny Tot leaders, she flicked open her phone again. Saw a message on Instagram. Her chest tensed. There was only one person who had been messaging her on Instagram lately. And sure enough, when she tapped it open, it was the person Kayla had mentioned as *Him!*

*Hey Britta. I tried to find you at the library today, but you weren't in. Hope all is okay with you. Just wondering if you have any other book recommendations for me.*

Oh, she had a world of book recommendations. But should she reply? If she didn't, it could go either one of two ways. He might keep trying to see her, or he might give up once and for all. Yet if she did reply, and somehow found the magical book that helped him connect with his girlfriend, that might keep him off her case. *Lord, what do I do?*

She peered back at the screen. Edmond was busy reading his notes, oblivious to the yawns of the others in the ministry team. She lifted her eyebrows at Ferdy, her fellow Red Jellybean leader, and turned back to her phone and typed, *Do you mean another book for you and Georgia?*

*Yep.*

What to say... Not another historical, that was for sure. But maybe a quasi-historical, another classic that had a movie option. *Still want romance but with some action and fantasy?*

A big thumbs-up came her way.

She nodded. *Then try* The Princess Bride *by William Goldman.*

*The movie?*

*Try the book first. Then if that's too hard, try the movie.*

*I'm not completely dumb.*

She winced. *I didn't mean it to sound like that.*

"Britta? Am I boring you?" Edmond asked.

What? Her attention jerked back to the computer screen. "As if," she muttered, relieved he couldn't hear her.

"I'm glad," Edmond said, his forehead lowered.

Oh no. How could he have heard that?

The smile he gave was not pleasant. "Yes, you've been unmuted."

"Great," she murmured, before realizing she probably needed to stay silent.

"It seems you were more interested in messaging someone than in the subject of tonight's meeting," he continued.

"I'm sorry." She pushed her phone far away, out of easy reach. "I'm one hundred percent focused now."

"I hope you're one hundred percent focused on Friday nights."

"Always," she said firmly, as Ferdy nodded and gave a thumbs-up. Too bad he couldn't be unmuted right now to back her up.

"I hope it was an emergency. You know I don't like people being distracted during these meetings."

"Oh, I know that." She smiled, as others stifled their amusement.

"So, was it?" Edmond pressed.

Was Mitch Reilly finding a book to romance his long-distance girlfriend an emergency? Not to her. Definitely not to Edmond, even though he liked hockey as much as the next Minnesotan-born male. But the fact Mitch kept persisting, suggesting it was an emergency to him, might just make it count. "Let's say it's a situation that needs some prayer to get resolved as quickly as possible."

"Anything you'd like us to pray about?" Edmond asked, as Ferdy's brow puckered in concern.

Hmm, this tiptoeing around the truth was not what she should be doing. "No. It's fine. In Jesus's name."

"Amen," Edmond said automatically.

And it would be fine, she told herself. And especially fine if she didn't see Mitch Reilly again. Not for a very long time.

"So as you can see, you have to learn to master the finite movements," Mitch said, demonstrating proper edge work on the perimeter of the face-off circle. "See what happens when I shift my weight? It's easy to wobble. That takes controlling your hips, your knees, your knee drive, your ankles. Each part contributes to how you hold yourself, your posture, which then affects how you balance, and all affects your ability to hold that edge."

The kids watched him, and he felt a glow inside. Here at today's hockey clinic he felt respected. He mightn't get a lot of things right, but he loved spending time with kids and really enjoyed this aspect of coaching. Which might be something to consider down the track when his body was too worn out to play.

Each man faced retirement sooner or later. And while he didn't like to think of it, he might've contributed to a few men's careers ending sooner than they'd hoped. At least he hadn't been responsible for anything as major as TJ Woletsky's career-ending hit on Nick Grenier. Woletsky had retired now, but he'd been pretty unpopular for a long time because of that hit. He wondered what Grenier was doing now.

"Hey Mitch," one of the gap-toothed kids called. "What about backchecks?"

He explained, then demonstrated, and the kid copied him.

These clinics were all about engaging with the next generation of hockey players, giving back to the community and encouraging those coming after him, just as Len and Linda Gulbrandsen had invested their time and energies into him. Which reminded him, he really should get in touch with them soon, let them know their prayers had finally paid off. Again.

The afternoon finished, and he slung his hockey bag over his shoulder and exited the rink. Like a number in Minnesota this rink was attached to a high school, which allowed for students to practice hockey without fighting for ice time like in lots of other places.

The sky was spitting raindrops now, and he was glad his vehicle wasn't far away as he hustled to place his gear in the back. He closed it, lifted a hand of farewell to his teammates, then got inside where it was warm and dry.

That had been fun. And now he had a frozen meal with his name on it before his second online Bible study with the guys tonight. He was supposed to bring a verse, something that God had impressed on his heart this past week, and while he'd been reading his Bible each day nothing in particular had stood out. He didn't really want to be one of the oldest guys there with nothing to say. That felt lame. And sure, that might be his pride talking, but he still believed God could use a lame brain like him. "Hey God, what is it You want me to say?"

He gripped the steering wheel, but nothing came to mind. Raindrops were splattering on the windshield, and he was extra glad he was inside before that hit.

He started his vehicle then steered from the parking lot. Red taillights suggested he'd be quicker avoiding the highway and going down a side street, so he veered off. As he slowed near an intersection, he saw a big white van with a mural of books painted on it. He blinked. What was happening that he noticed books all the time? For he was pretty sure that van read Bookmobile. And—he squinted—was that someone changing a tire?

The person was small, and looked like a kid. He frowned. Should they even be there? He paused long enough to get honked at by the car behind him, then quickly pulled off first chance he got. He shrugged into his rain jacket, popped the collar and jogged back, just as the person—the woman—crouched beside the tire. And while he believed in equal rights for women and girl power and everything else Ellie had beaten into him over the years, it still felt a little wrong to leave a woman to change a tire in the rain.

"Hey, need a hand?" he called. Man, his voice was raspy from barking instructions all day.

"Thanks, but I'm fine." She glanced across then froze.

He blinked. "Britta." He hadn't dared message her since she'd stopped answering last Wednesday. And now here she was. Again. It was like the woman couldn't leave him alone. Or vice versa. Whatever it was, this was weird. And now he doubly couldn't leave her alone.

"What are you doing here?" they both said at the same time.

He gestured for her to go first, but she shrugged. "Isn't it obvious?"

Obvious she needed a hand. He hunkered beside her. "Here, let me help."

"I don't need your help," she muttered, wrestling with a wrench.

He motioned to it. "May I?"

She huffed out a breath. "I am perfectly capable of changing a tire."

"I don't doubt it for a second." And he didn't. This woman was indomitable. "But I reckon I can get it done faster. Not because I'm more capable, just because I'm bigger and stronger."

She released a frustrated-sounding breath. "Isn't that the same?"

Maybe. "I also don't want to see you get any wetter than you are already."

"Why?"

He shrugged. "Because then you might get sick and won't be able to recommend the next book for me to read."

She rolled her eyes. "Does this mean you actually read *The Princess Bride*?"

"Are you trying to trick me? Where are the sports?"

Her eyes widened behind her fogged-up glasses. "You read it?"

"It was okay." He nudged her shoulder. "Now move over, go get dry or something, and let me do this."

"Oh, but…"

But nothing. He didn't have muscles just for show. Besides, it was just wrong to let an itty-bitty thing like her heft her way through this.

Twenty minutes later he'd changed the tire and was wiping his hands on the wet wipes she provided. "Thanks."

"Thank *you*."

He half-smiled. "You're welcome."

"I hate to admit it, but I probably did need some help. You did that so much faster than I could have. You're like an angel sent by God."

He didn't know about that, but he'd take it. "It's a good thing I was in the neighborhood." He peered at the truck, then at her. "You're here by yourself?"

Her chin tipped. "Yes. So?"

"I would've thought they'd have two people on for safety or moments like this."

She shrugged. "Budget cuts. Anyway, I'm tough."

He nodded, remembering just how tough she was. Still, he didn't want her thinking about how she beat him up, so he turned his attention to the van. "So this is the Bookmobile, huh?"

"Yes."

He winced as another raindrop found its way down his collar.

"Oh, I should let you go."

He shrugged. "Can I look inside?"

"Inside the Bookmobile?"

"Yeah. I've never seen one before."

"Um, okay."

That was hardly the sound of enthusiasm. "It's all right. I suppose you have to get it back."

"I can spare a few minutes for a quick tour if you like."

"Sure."

He'd likely be late for the Bible study tonight but this felt important. So he followed her around the side where she unlocked a door, then dropped down some steps, and flicked on some lights.

"Wow."

The twinkle lights made it seem like a fairyland, where a world of possibilities lay within the pages of the books. And there were probably thousands in here. He whistled. "It's really cool."

"Right? We're due to get the heating fixed, but…"

He shot her a look. "No, it's really cool. Like, awesome. Especially if you're into books and things."

She smiled, like she thought his phrasing was amusing. And he didn't want to appear dumb in front of her, even though he probably was. Maybe that was part of Georgia's problem with him; she thought him dumb too.

"It is awesome, isn't it?" Britta said, glancing around, her hands on her hips. She smiled, even though she worked here and had obviously seen it a hundred times before.

He moved to the kids' picture book section, and pulled out a copy of *Freight Train*. "I remember reading this book as a kid."

"It's a good one."

"Yeah." He traced the spines, recognizing a few other titles.

Somehow in this moment, with rain pattering on the roof, it created a cozy quality, like they were the only two people in the world. And for once Britta did not seem wary of him, as captivated as he was by all the books.

"I love the Bookmobile," she said softly.

"Why's that?" He pulled out a copy of *The Invention of Hugo Cabret* and sat on the wooden seat near a range of DVDs.

She stood opposite, straightening a few books. "I love that it provides opportunities for those who don't normally get the chance to visit the library. So many people don't realize the impact that reading can have on people's lives, so it's awesome to bring it to some of those neighborhoods knowing it can truly make a difference."

"Such as?"

"Studies show that improving access to books results in students from lower socioeconomic areas achieving better educational outcomes."

"I didn't know that."

"And services like this really help bring people together. You saw that recently, when all those people came to hear you read."

"I'd really rather not think about that again."

Was that sympathy on her face? "Hey, we could always arrange a do-over if you want."

"Yeah, that's a solid no."

She chuckled, and the sound was surprisingly throaty. She laughed like a woman, not a little girl. He frowned. When was the last time he'd heard Georgia laugh? "So, what else do you like about this?"

"The Bookmobile?"

"Yeah."

She sighed. "I had an elderly lady thank me today for coming out in this bad weather. She said, and I quote, 'It's the bright spot in my day'. People love to see Bookmobile staff and get a new book to read." She glanced at him. "It's nice to feel like I'm someone people want to see."

"Of course they want to see you. You're nice and bubbly, and —" Man, why was he saying this? "Uh, well, I guess you are to most people, even if you haven't always been that way to me."

She exhaled loudly. "And you were doing so well."

He smirked, and she caught his gaze, her lips flicking up to a smile. And maybe he stared at her a little too long for she blushed, and turned away.

He scrubbed a hand over his face. What was he doing here? Why was he saying these things? They were supposed to be talking about books, he was supposed to be thinking about Georgia, not this little woman with sass and curves and glasses.

He ducked his head, was about to stand and leave, when she said, "So, you never answered me before. What were you doing here?"

"I was at a hockey skills clinic and just so happened to come down this way."

"Hmm, well maybe your 'just so happened' was an answer to prayer, because I might've just prayed earlier that God would send me a rescuer."

"Oh, you did, did you?"

"Don't go getting a swollen head. I prefer to think God was in control and prompted you to come this way."

"Hey, I'm cool with that." He shrugged. "I'm trying to do more of what I think God would want me to."

Her face softened. "So you really are a Christian?"

He nodded. "I attended church when I was a kid, and made a commitment when I came to live with a couple who looked after me a bit when I moved over here as a teen."

"You grew up in Washington state, right?"

"Trinity Lakes. Very small town. No hockey prospects there at all, so it meant I had to move away to get a shot at the big leagues."

"And you made the most of it."

"You could say that." He shrugged. "I made a commitment when I was staying with Len and Linda Gulbrandsen, but as soon as I moved from there life got crazy busy again, and yeah. It's safe to say I wasn't following Jesus for a long time."

"We all have moments when we can stray from doing what Jesus might want us to," she said softly.

"Have you?"

She faced him. "I don't think I really know you well enough to answer that."

"Hey, I've been spilling my guts. You can too."

She shook her head, and he realized for all her directness, she was a pretty private person. Unlike him, with a lot about his life splashed around for everyone to read about. It wasn't a secret. And yet for all their differences, this exchange of information in this cozy setting felt a lot more like tiptoeing toward friendship.

He reared back. He didn't do friendship with girls. He coughed. "I should, uh, probably go."

She eyed him. "Yes."

"Oh, but thanks for recommending *The Princess Bride*."

Her lips tweaked. "So you enjoyed it?"

"It was pretty funny in parts."

"I know! It's one of the wittiest books I've read."

"Even if it's filled with dumb jokes."

"I happen to like dumb jokes."

"I've noticed."

She shook her head. "So did Georgia enjoy it?"

Enjoy what? Oh, the book. His heart sank. "Look, I did my best, but she didn't reply. I haven't heard from her in a while, actually."

Her nose wrinkled, her lips pressing together like she had something to say that she didn't dare.

He sighed. "What?"

She winced. "Are you sure this is what you should be doing?"

"Talking with you?"

"No, I mean finding a book to share with Georgia. I'm sorry, but it doesn't sound like she's interested."

He stiffened.

"And I don't mean she's not interested in you, I just mean perhaps reading a book together is not what you should be doing. It might just be that reading is not her thing."

"Inconceivable," he muttered, quoting one of the most famous lines.

She laughed, and his heart lightened.

"I'll be praying for you both."

His throat tightened. "Thanks," he managed to rasp out. "I really should go."

She nodded. "And thanks again for your help with the tire before, I really appreciate it."

"Any time."

She chuckled. "I hope not."

"Huh?"

"Well, that implies I'll be breaking down more often, and I'd be really happy to never break down again."

He smiled, and drew his jacket tighter as she opened the door and gestured for him to exit while she flicked off the lights.

He waited as she exited and locked the door, then removed the chocks before she hiked herself up into the driver's seat. "That's a bit of a climb."

"Good thing I'm part Norwegian mountain goat."

He stifled a smile and crossed his arms against his amusement. Miss Bee was funny. Funny ha ha, and yeah, a bit of the other kind as well.

She shut the door. Then powered down the window. "You don't need to wait. I do know how to drive this thing."

"Call me old-fashioned, but I'd rather make sure you got off okay."

"You're such a gentleman."

First time in his life he'd ever been called that. But judging from the warmth in his chest, he'd be happy to hear it again. "You know it."

Her gaze met his and held, and for a moment his stomach swooped just like he had the first time he'd ridden a Six Flags rollercoaster.

"Hey Mitch, here's a verse for you: 'You are God's handiwork, created in Christ Jesus for good works, which God prepared beforehand so that you would walk in them.' That's Ephesians chapter two, verse ten, in case you didn't know that."

His mouth dried. But before he could ask why she thought he needed to know that, she started the engine, powered up the window, gave him a wave, and drove away.

He now had a Bible verse for tonight. And now maybe had a bit of a problem.

# CHAPTER 10

"*A*nd look what I have for you, Tyrone." Britta placed the two T-Rex books on the counter, a week later.

The little boy's eyes lit. "Wow! You got these books just for me?"

"Sure did."

She smiled as he clutched them to his chest, and then remembered to thank her.

"You're more than welcome." Her heart glowed. This, this was what the library was all about. Helping people to connect, learn, discover and grow.

The library was trying all kinds of initiatives to help reduce the barriers between people and books. That was part of the reasoning behind going fine-free a few years ago. For too long fines had proved a barrier rather than an incentive to return materials, which meant some people never returned to the library, and the library's precious resources slipped from circulation completely because patrons with overdue items felt too embarrassed to return them. The concept had met with resistance from some, but now people could see how it was increasing patron engagement.

She loved these ideas, whether they be eliminating fines, using the Bookmobile, even employing a social worker so patrons who had experienced trauma or struggled with challenges, like poverty, homelessness or addiction, could find a safe place and be directed to access services that would meet their need. A social worker in a library might be a radical concept for some, but it meant that librarians could focus on their job, and the social worker could help as they were trained to do. She loved to help people, but was glad there was an expert in that field. And while it was a shame people might feel more comfortable to seek help from a library rather than at a church, at least she was still operating in an area where she could help people. And to be out "in the world" yet still be used by God to minister to people's needs felt like a gift.

And if it meant she could engage with kids, and occasionally invite them to pay attention to the noticeboard, where she may just have had a brochure about the Red Jellybeans, well, that was good too.

"So I hope you enjoy." She nodded to the noticeboard where she had some bookmarks and other materials. "Feel free to grab a bookmark."

Now there was a selection of bookmarks the kids could choose from. And if the ones that had red jellybeans on them, and some information about where the younger youth group met, just so happened to be the most visually appealing, well she couldn't be responsible if the children chose those ones over others, now could she?

She smiled at her logic, prayed that God would touch hearts, and draw the people He wanted to Himself. Then her mind flicked back to what had happened last Tuesday. When Mitch "just so happened" to be right where she needed and could help her. And she'd "just so happened" to have that strange moment at the end, when she'd felt her words edged with something that almost felt prophetic as she'd spoken that verse from Ephesians to him.

Maybe that made her weird, but she'd sensed it was the right thing to do. And if he was calling himself a Christian then he probably needed to have reminders that Christians didn't necessarily always do what others considered normal. At least, this one didn't. Anyway, who cared if Mitch Reilly did think she was weird? He obviously did, with that long gaze at the end. She'd wondered why he was staring at her, but obviously it was because he thought her strange.

Mitchell. Nope. She wasn't thinking about him. *Lord, help me not think about him.*

Her phone rang. She glanced at the screen. Edmond. Well, complain as he probably would, she was at her workplace, and was not supposed to take personal calls, so he could leave a message.

And she saw that he soon did, and then when no patrons came, she put her phone on speaker and listened to his message.

"Britta, this is Edmond." She smiled—like she couldn't tell already. "I need to have a word with you about something important so if you could please call me back that would be good."

Her nose wrinkled. Why the man simply couldn't tell her what he wanted always annoyed her. Well, she wasn't going to call him back until her shift was over.

Another patron dropped by, and she was glad for the renewed focus on what she was supposed to be about.

"Oh, I have some books to return and I'm afraid they're a little bit overdue," the upper-middle-aged woman said. "I was almost too embarrassed to return then I remembered that you don't have fines anymore so it should be okay. But I have to admit, I'm glad it's you and not Harold. I'm afraid that man scares me a little bit."

"Harold? Really?" The woman didn't mean that, did she?

"He's just a little bit big and I find that intimidating."

"I'm not sure his height is something he can do anything about."

Just like Mitchell Reilly couldn't help come across as fierce sometimes too. Until that moment last week, when he seemed quite nice and normal. Not that she was thinking about him!

"Harold," she shoved her thoughts firmly where they were meant to be—back to helping this poor lady, "needs some time off, so you'll have me for a while longer I'm afraid."

"Oh, that's good. Now, perhaps you can tell me, do you stock *Fifty Shades of Grey*?"

Britta withheld a sigh. "I'm afraid we don't." Not here in the Bookmobile, anyway. But if the woman chose to believe that was true of all the libraries then that was on her. How that book had achieved such heights of popularity while showcasing depravity she didn't know. Well, actually, she kind of did. There was nothing like the boom in e-readers to make a book previously considered scandalous a popular read. And that, combined with a distinct drop in morals in the world, made life an interesting challenge for a Christian who was "in the world yet not of it".

She cleared her throat. "Seeing as we don't have that one, perhaps I could interest you in a different author who writes passionate romance but in a slightly different style." As in, closed door, no on-the-page sex, even though the couple involved—who just so happened to be married—were quite enamored of each other. And if it just so happened to be by a Christian author, with subtle nods to God, then so be it.

The lady's nose wrinkled. "I'm not sure..."

"Well, that's the beauty of the library, isn't it? You don't have to be sure, you can just borrow the book and then return it if you don't like it. In fact, I could suggest a number of authors for you, and you could consider this a sampler, see if there's one that takes your fancy. You might just discover a fabulous new author and want to read all of their books."

"Oh, I like the sound of that."

Good. Britta spent the next fifteen minutes making suggestions and the woman soon left with a stack of books, including a Georgette Heyer that Britta had convinced her was like an easier version of Jane Austen and twice as funny.

She was nearing the end of her allocated time and was about to move the chocks when a patron hustled in. "Hey, I'm not too late, am I?"

"No. But we're about to depart, so if you know what you'd like then I'd encourage you to make your selection quickly."

The man eyed her, and she instantly dimmed her smile and straightened the pile of heavy books on the counter. Not that she thought he wanted to hurt her, because plain women weren't usually a target, but it didn't hurt to be careful. Especially as a woman on her own. And while there might be cameras inside the Bookmobile, there was no point in having a potential incident filmed if she could prevent it. She picked up her phone and pretended to dial Kayla. Then, as the man advanced, dialed her for real. "Hey, Kayla, it's me. Just letting you know that I'm about to close and we'll be on our way."

"Um, and why are you telling me this?" Kayla asked. "And who is we?"

"We" was because she didn't want the man thinking she was here by herself. "Yes, Harold should be here any second."

"Harold?" Kayla asked. Then gasped. "Are you in trouble? Where are you?"

"Near the corner of Wesson and Smith, and yes, there's one man here but he's about to leave, and—"

"Is he?" Kayla demanded. "Is he really? If you're in trouble, then just say yes."

"Not at the moment," Britta said, eyeing the man who now seemed uncertain.

"Just thought you should know, oh, hold on a minute. I'll be a moment."

She placed the phone down on the counter, pretending to end the call, and prayed that Kayla had enough sense to keep listening and not say anything. "So, was there nothing you wished to borrow at this time?"

"I don't want no books."

"Well, in that case, I'll have to ask you to leave so I can lock up."

"You can lock up, after you give me your money."

Oh, she hoped Kayla could hear this. "I'm not going to give you money because I don't have any. Now please leave. I don't think you want me to call the police," she said in a louder voice. *Lord, please let Kayla have heard that.*

He produced a knife, and her nerves tripled. No way, no way. *Lord?*

"Sir, I really think you should put the knife away," she said as calmly as she could. She had to de-escalate the situation. "We don't keep money on the premises."

He swore.

Irritation flared. "But we do have cameras. Say cheese."

She pointed and he instinctively turned and she picked up her phone. "Call the police," she murmured, praying Kayla could hear.

The man whirled back. "Give me your phone!"

"No."

He lifted the knife at her, and she picked up the nearest large book as a shield.

"Get out of my library."

He slashed the knife at her.

She blocked it with the book. "Get out!" she screamed. If she screamed loud enough, then someone might hear and come to her rescue. "Lord, another angel visit like Mitchell's would be really good!"

He advanced again, slashing the knife and she blocked it again. Poor book. Still, better the book than her. But stepping back like this would mean she'd be blocked in at the desk, so she needed to get proactive. "I don't have any money, so this is about to get worse for you."

"Yeah? How? I'm the one with a knife."

She reached under the desk and drew out the pepper spray kept for emergencies just like this. "And I'm the one with this." She closed her eyes and pulled the trigger.

A stream of obscenities filled the air, and she peeked to see the man stumble back. One of the advantages of wearing glasses was less exposure to onion juice drift and things like pepper spray. She held her breath, picked up her big book and advanced. He'd dropped the knife, was bent at the waist, retching. But not over her nice books. "Get out!"

She used all of her weight and shoved him toward the door, then when he grasped at the doorway, she thrust her booted foot to his back so he tumbled outside. Adrenaline churning, she quickly locked it and then ran to the front, and made sure the driver and passenger doors were locked. She snatched up the phone, spun the driver's seat to drive mode, then tried to start the engine. But her hands were shaky, the man was outside somewhere, and she didn't know where. What if he was lying in front of her and she accidentally drove over him? And then there were those chocks she still hadn't moved! "Lord, help me!"

Blue and red flashing lights suddenly swerved into view, and she slumped into her seat. "Thank You, God."

She picked up her phone. "Kayla? Are you there?"

"Is he gone? I called the police."

"Thank you. They... they've just arrived."

"Thank goodness. Are you okay?"

No. She'd give anything for a big hug right now. "I'll be okay."

"You want me to come down?"

"I'll talk to the police, see what they have to say."

"You'll have to give a statement, and I think I will too."

Someone tapped on the window.

Britta shrieked, then glanced out, relief filling her as she saw the police uniform. "Okay, the police are here. I better go."

"Stay safe, okay?"

She drew in a deep breath and exhaled. "Okay." Then ended the call, unlocked and opened the door.

*So, who's ready for training camp?* Ryan asked in the online Bible study chat.

*Not me.* Chris Thomas. *Still wish I was in Hawaii.*

Eye-roll emojis from Franklin.

*Love Franklin's eye-rolling like he wasn't in Fiji last year.* Ryan.

*Says the man who honeymooned this year in the Bahamas.* Luc.

*Says the man who honeymooned in Paris.* Zac.

Mitch chuckled, stretched and eased into a more comfortable position as the online banter continued. He'd been a part of various NHL player group chats before, but this was the first one where he didn't have to worry about the language or what kinds of images he might see. These guys might tease and razz each other, but they were wholesome, which suited him just fine. Trying to walk a different walk now, to fill his mind with good thoughts and not corrupt or worldly things, meant making active choices about what he watched and listened to and read. And some of the things in the past had eroded the morals Len and Linda had tried to ground him in, making them paper thin. Which meant the chatter here, and that like last week and tonight's earlier study, felt like biting into a fresh new season apple after eating junk food for too long. He hadn't known what he was missing until he tasted the difference.

*I'm counting down the days,* Mitch typed. Training and staying at home was boring. And sure, there might be a few more community events he was supposed to do, but he'd rather get into it and on with it. Still, only two weeks to go...

*Me too*, Kyle Tinker said. *Vancouver's going down.*

*Ha, we've heard that before.* Chris.

*It's kind of cute he says stuff like that here*, Drew said.

*These new boys are feisty, huh?* Ryan wrote.

Mitch gathered from the previous conversations that Ryan was one of the longer-serving members of the group, along with Mike, Jai, Luc and Chris. It made the dynamics fun. But he supposed that's what long-time relationships did. These guys treated each other like brothers, even if Mitch's relationship with his own brothers had never been so easy.

Instead, his memories of growing up had been marked by tension and competition. And while he could blame a useless father who'd walked when Mitch was eight, with three younger siblings, and poor Ellie only a one-year-old baby, he knew enough about himself now to own that he'd let pride trample over developing a close relationship with his brothers. He probably owed them an apology one day.

The banter continued, and he was enjoying it when his phone rang. Jack. "Hey, what's up?"

"Dude, have you seen the news?"

"What about it?" He yawned.

"Tonight. Remember your library chick?"

"I don't have a library chick," he scoffed, even as his soul protested. Okay, he mightn't have a library chick, but he did know a library woman. Which meant—"Wait, what?"

"Put the news on now," Jack commanded.

He pointed the remote at the TV and flicked to the local news station.

Then sat up straight as the Bookmobile he'd visited last week came into view, strobed with blue and red flashing lights. "What the—?"

"Remember the Bee Chick?" Jack said.

He'd never forget. "What about her?"

"Some drugged-up guy held a knife to her—"

"What?" He cranked the volume, watched in horror as the reporter stood in a classic trench coat talking to the camera.

"—and it was only by the bravery of librarian Britta Johnson that a more serious incident did not occur."

"Is she okay?" he barked at Jack.

"Yeah."

Jack's affirmative came as the footage shifted to Britta. Mitch's heart eased. She looked normal, pale, maybe a little shaky, but no obvious signs of injury as she talked to a reporter.

"Yes, it's certainly nothing I've faced before. We have training to de-escalate such situations, but I'm afraid I might've gone with instinct over the rules."

Like she had when she'd kneed him before. "Good on her," Mitch muttered, as the vision shifted to include a police officer.

Mitch studied her, looking for signs of stress as the officer expounded on the need for people to treat others with respect. The perpetrator had been pepper sprayed, and could be seen in previously filmed footage rolling on the ground, crying.

Mitch smiled despite his concerns. Dude got what he deserved.

"Tough chick, huh?" Jack said.

"Yeah." But even tough chicks had their breaking points. Such as what had happened to his sister last year, when she'd been hoodwinked by an international scammer who'd followed her to Trinity Lakes. Poor Ellie had felt so embarrassed, until her best friend Jasper revealed his feelings had deepened into more. Now look at them, happily married.

His heart tipped. For all Britta might feel okay now, that had to have been a super scary situation. He wished he knew for certain that she was okay.

"Hey, gotta go," he said to Jack, as the next news item clicked on.

"Catch ya at training."

"Yeah." He ended the call.

Glanced back at his phone. Saw the group chat was continuing. Wondered... Should he? These guys didn't know about Georgia, or maybe they did. But that didn't change the fact that a woman he knew had been subjected to a violent crime. It was only right to ask for their prayers for her. Right?

He debated for a few more minutes, then saw Luc post: *Did you guys see this?*

Mitch froze. It was new video footage, of what looked like inside the Bookmobile. Yep, he recognized that shelf of books; he'd sat on that seat in front of it a week ago.

*Hey Mitch, this is near you, right?* Luc asked.

He slowly tapped out, *Yes.*

*They breed librarians tough down your way, huh?*

He swallowed. *I know her.*

*What???*

Suddenly his phone was buzzing with requests for a video call. But he couldn't answer. He wanted to talk to her. Make sure she was okay. Even if he had no right, and last week there'd been that long look that passed between them that made things feel weird, he still thought of her as his friend. He hoped she'd feel the same.

*Her name is Britta. She's a Christian. So please pray.*

# CHAPTER 11

"*O*kay, here we are." Her mom steered her to the couch and settled her near the fire, draping a blanket over her shoulders. "Want something to eat?"

Britta shook her head, and drew the blanket up then huddled into it. The adrenaline of before had fast faded leaving her shaky and so, so cold. She'd thought she was tougher than this. But after the attack, and the visit to the police station, and all the interviews, and all the sympathy from her sisters and parents, she was so exhausted. Mentally, physically, emotionally drained.

And even though everyone, from the police to Kayla to the news reporters and her family, had said how brave she was she didn't feel it now. Just felt edgy. A little scared. She couldn't brazen it out. She might have moments of toughness, but she wasn't Mitch Reilly robust. She sank deeper in her seat.

"Here you go." Her mom handed her a cup of tea.

She warmed her hands around it, willing the internal shivers to stop like the external ones had. *Lord, be my strength.*

She didn't want to look at her phone. It had beeped with near nonstop notifications since news of the attack had been broadcast, but part of her still wanted to see what was being said.

"Oh my girl." Her mom sat beside her, and hugged her carefully so she didn't spill her tea. "You must be feeling a million emotions."

"Yep." Understatement of the year.

"I can't believe that man dared try that. Or that you knew what to do."

"We do have training for that kind of thing but it really was mostly instinct."

"Thank goodness you've done those self-defense classes, huh?"

"Yep."

God must have known she'd need those classes for herself as much as for her kids when she'd done them last year. Good thing He knew what was coming her way.

Her mind flicked to that verse from Ephesians she'd shared last week, about being God's workmanship, designed for good works that God had prepared in advance for her to do. Did this count as a good work? Well, the fact she hadn't lost any books or money—or her life!—probably counted. She shuddered, put the tea down. And cradled her mom.

Tears escaped as she let her mom hold her. She closed her eyes.

"Oh, honey. You're safe."

She knew that, but it seemed her body was taking some time to realize it.

Her mom kept her arms around her, long enough for Britta's rapid pulse to ease, long enough for her breathing to slow and her closed eyes to remind her of sleep. And maybe she dozed a little, for when she woke, it was to see she was lying on the couch, blanket covering her, and the room was dim.

She wriggled, her neck stiff and sore, and saw her phone light with a message. She reached across, then hesitated. Opening her phone was an invitation to get sucked into the land of fake news and comparison, and she needed sleep, not to be hounded by questions and concern. Yet another part of her wanted to see if anyone—or a particular someone—had messaged. She could do that, right? It wasn't bad to see if her friends cared. Even if it felt weird to think of *certain* people that way.

Should she? Temptation begged. She glanced at the clock. It was already past midnight. As if anyone would still be up. She should go to bed. Go to sleep. Pretend this day had not happened. That would be the wise and sensible thing to do. Yep, she'd do that. She grasped her phone and stood unsteadily, went to the bathroom, had a quick shower, brushed her teeth, then went to her bedroom. Plugged in her phone.

As she plugged it in to charge overnight, she wondered again about the message. Her pulse picked up. Should she? It wouldn't hurt to look, right?

Before she could think too long she tapped the screen and saw the message.

*Hey, I saw the news. I hope you're okay.*

There. That was innocuous. Nothing to read into that message, was there? She could be friends with a man, even a man who had a girlfriend, right? And the fact he was checking in on her was something a friend might do. *Should* do, actually, if they were indeed friends.

Now, she could either leave it, or reply. Oh, what was the point of replying, and at this late hour? He'd be sure to be asleep. He'd sent this hours ago.

But from what the police had said, and the news reporter had indicated, she suspected tomorrow would be filled with all kinds of inquiries and possibly more interview requests. Her lips lifted without amusement. Apparently people didn't expect mild-looking librarians who wore glasses to have stealth ninja moves. So if that proved true, and there was an onslaught of messages she'd need to deal with tomorrow, she should reply now so she didn't forget later. Not that it would matter if she forgot. He was a big boy. He'd cope.

But still, the fact he'd reached out... Before she could second-guess herself a moment longer she tapped out a reply:

*I'm okay. Thanks for checking.*

There. Done. Now she could put the phone down, and—

Oh. He was still awake, judging from that symbol that suggested he was composing a message. She slid into bed, holding the phone so it could keep charging as she waited for his reply. This was a bad idea. She should just pretend she hadn't seen it, then—

*I'm glad. That must've been pretty scary.*

*Yep*, she tapped back. *I was okay at the time, but now I feel a little spooked.*

*Praying for you.* Praying hands emoji.

Moisture slicked her eyes. When had a guy ever said he'd pray for her? Sure, guys like Ferdy or Edmond did, but they were in ministry, which kind of made them obliged to say such things. To have someone she didn't know that well say he'd pray for her felt different. Felt more genuine, like he wouldn't say that unless he meant it. And from all she'd seen of Mitch Reilly over the years, he didn't seem the sort to say things he didn't mean.

And maybe she was just delirious with exhaustion, but the fact he'd sent that message, was willing to reply to her so late at night, as if he'd stayed up just for her, made her heart soft, like it was surrounded by feather pillows, and meant she could put the phone down and close her eyes and sleep without fear or terrors.

· · ·

"DON'T LOOK AT YOUR PHONE," Milla warned, when Britta finally stumbled from her bedroom the next day, hunger fueling her visit to the kitchen.

"Why?" She yawned. Her phone hadn't charged properly, and was flat. "Is Margaret upset that I'm late for work today?" She had vague memories of being told she didn't have to go to work, but maybe that was a dream.

"The internet is going crazy."

Oh. She didn't dare think what that meant. As long as the video from inside the Bookmobile hadn't leaked—

"The video from inside the Bookmobile leaked," Astrid said. "And now everyone wants to know you. You've gone viral!"

Astrid and Milla's shining eyes suggested they thought that was a good thing. Yeah, it wasn't. Any hope that today might be a normal day felt destined for the scrap heap.

"Stop worrying your sister," her mom reproved, from where she was folding laundry on the dining table.

"You're not at work?" Britta asked her.

"I requested a day off, thanks to our family emergency."

"I'm okay," Britta said. Even if her chest felt lined with tension.

"Are you sure?" Astrid asked. "You look pale still."

"I'm always pale." Those same Nordic genes that had bypassed her DNA while giving her sisters blonde hair had skipped giving Britta the tanned skin too.

"Are you sure you're okay, honey?" her mom asked, a pleat in her brow.

She nodded. "Well, I will be." She readjusted her glasses, sat them more securely on her nose. Then glanced between them. "So, what is going on? What does 'going viral' mean? I mean, I know what it means, but how does that affect me?"

"Everyone wants to talk to you," Astrid said. "Like, there are major TV news networks out there now."

"What?" She moved to the window, to peek out.

"Don't look!"

She pulled back the curtains, was met with the sight of flashing cameras and film crews talking on her front lawn. "What's going on?"

"*You're* going on," Astrid said. "Like I said, everyone wants to know you. They want interviews."

"I don't want to speak to anyone." Last night's interview with the local TV news had been hard enough. She'd only agreed because they'd caught her by surprise. It felt too much to look switched on and engaged when she felt anything but.

"Sergeant Larkin called. The police wanted to clear something up today," her mom said.

Her shoulders slumped. "Do I have to go to the station again?"

"He said it wouldn't take too long."

That was something at least. "What time?"

"I said you could call them once you were up."

So much for not looking at her phone.

As Astrid left for work Britta retrieved her phone from her room, and saw it had charged enough now to let her know it was crammed with notifications about missed calls, messages and emails. Her heart grew tight. Nope. She didn't want to do this.

"Can I use someone else's phone? This is overwhelming."

"Here." Her mom handed Britta her phone, along with a business card that had Sergeant Larkin's number. She dialed it, spoke to him then made the appointment for noon.

She returned to the kitchen table. "Now what? I don't want to go and face the media. I just want my books."

"Then do that," her mom suggested. "Take these next few hours to read a book and just relax until your interview at the station."

Truly, there was nothing nicer than relaxing with a book. And with her mom and sister prepared to pamper her a little, she could do exactly that. So with a Georgette Heyer she'd read many times before, she stretched out on the couch covered with a blanket, and read and snoozed until she was woken to go to the interview, with her mom and Milla as support.

Sergeant Larkin was polite, although built in a similar mold to her own father, with a pretty blunt, bluff personality. He checked a few details from her statement last night, corroborating some things, then asked her to sign the documents, which she did.

It was all coming back to her. "Did you interview Kayla as well?"

"Yes. She was extremely helpful. In fact, she had the presence of mind to record part of your conversation, so we have the offender on tape."

"So that makes it easier to prosecute him?"

"Between that recording and the video of the attempted assault, there is no way that man will walk."

"Is the video that conclusive?"

"You haven't seen it yet?"

She shook her head.

"Do you want to?"

"Should I?"

He shrugged. "Look, let's just say it's probably good for you to see what the fuss is about. You might be shocked to see it in a different context."

"Shocked?" she asked.

He half-smiled. "Look." He pulled out his tablet, tapped the screen a few times, then placed it on the table where she could see.

It was black-and-white vision of the bus, no sound. She was inside, straightening books, then the man walked inside. There was no sign of the knife, but there was the initial verbal exchange. This vision was taken from the camera positioned above the driver's seat, so she could see the way the man advanced.

Her fingers tensed as she remembered, and her mom drew near, placed a hand on her shoulder. Then the muted exchange became more obvious, as he whipped out the knife and she picked up the big book. A copy of *One Duck Stuck* she realized now.

Then the man advanced and she swung the book, blocking the knife.

"Oh, Britta," her mom whispered.

Milla had joined them now too, and she could feel the tension rise as they saw the man step toward her again, and she scrabbled in the desk for the can of pepper spray.

Then Milla chuckled. "This is my favorite part."

Which part? Oh, the part where Britta advanced on him, then barged him out the door, propelling him outside with what looked like a kick, then locking it.

It was like watching a movie Ainsley Beckett might've acted in. As if that woman on the video wasn't her.

She saw herself snatch up her phone then stumble back to the driver's seat, turn it around, then with shaky hands try to start the engine. Her brief phone conversation with Kayla. Then her scream when the first responder had tapped on her window.

She exhaled. "I still can't believe it."

"Look, I know it's a lot, but as far as the police side of things go, I think you can be assured this will be resolved quickly. The man's in custody, he's a known offender, so you don't need to worry about him. He won't be going anywhere."

"Thank you."

Sergeant Larkin eyed her. "The bigger question is whether you want to cash in on your fifteen minutes of fame."

Her nose wrinkled. "I don't think so."

He shrugged. "You know, there are worse things you could

do. It wouldn't hurt for other women to see that self-defense is a good skill to learn. You obviously know a thing or two, so there's that."

"Yeah, aren't you always telling others about the importance of knowing how to stand up for yourself?" Milla asked. "That's what you tell your girls anyway."

"Your girls?" Sergeant Larkin asked.

"My youth group girls. Junior high."

"Well, if I were them, I'd be pretty proud of having a youth leader with that kind of presence of mind. And if I were you, then I'd consider how to make the most of this. Who knows? You might find a local jiu-jitsu group wanting to sponsor you or something."

"You're joking, right?"

"Mmm, I'd be checking into some of those messages and emails your mom mentioned to me earlier."

She didn't know how to answer. So gave a kind of half shrug, half nod thing that might be construed as agreement.

"And I wouldn't be surprised if you find yourself in line for some kind of bravery award."

"What? But I didn't do anything heroic. I was protecting books, that was all."

After thanking him for his help, they soon went home, and Milla left for her shift at work, leaving Britta with her mom. And all those unanswered messages and emails. Including that missed call from Edmond. Ugh. He probably wanted to talk about some policy or something. Still, she knew if she didn't respond, he'd likely keep calling until she did. So she called him back, and sure enough, he didn't mention the bookmobile incident, only wanting to check she'd received the updated safer ministries policy. After assuring him she had, he hung up. Her nose wrinkled. Why couldn't he ask that in an email, like a normal person?

"Everything okay?" Mom asked.

She nodded, but she felt drained. "I know it makes me sound like a wuss but I don't want to look at all these emails," Britta admitted.

"Maybe just check the messages from work."

"Good plan."

As her mom made tea, Britta picked up her phone, swiped through her emails until she recognized the ones from the library. Opened them with bated breath. Read the ones from Margaret and the library general manager both commending her for her work and requesting her to call them when she was able. From what she read it seemed the Bookmobile service would be suspended for a while until safety protocols were reviewed. She winced.

"Bad news?" Her mom placed a cup of tea beside Britta.

"Thanks." She took a sip of comforting English Breakfast. "Not really. It's just a shame for the patrons that they won't have books for a while."

"That wasn't your fault," her mom said. "The man's actions spoiled things for others, not you." Her mom sipped her own tea. "Has Margaret said anything about going back to work?"

"It looks like I'll be back in the main library for a while. They want me to undergo some counseling."

"That's probably wise. Are you feeling okay?"

"I didn't have any nightmares, if that's what you're asking."

Her mom's shoulders dropped. "I'm glad. I know there were lots of people praying for you."

She nodded. "God bless them."

"So many people have reached out to us. Oh, and I should've mentioned it before. You've received some flowers. They were sent to the library, then got sent here."

"Flowers? What for?"

Her mom smiled. "For being a heroine? To wish you well? I don't know. I didn't read the card."

Who would be sending her flowers? That seemed like overkill to her. She didn't deserve them.

But when she went into the dining room and saw the bunch of colorful tulips and roses, she gasped, and read the card.

> To the Toughest Librarian out there,
> You're a ninja.
> Signed: No one of consequence.

She blinked. Did that sign-off mean—? No. That was insane. Why would *he* be sending her flowers? But who else would have a *Princess Bride* quote handy?

She sniffed a pink rose, then shoved it away.

This felt weird, but she wouldn't read too much into it. She had a phone call to make to the library.

NOTHING LIKE A THURSDAY offseason workout in the final prep before training camp. A superset of weights involving dumbbell bench presses, lat pull-downs, pull-ups, then a second set of aerobic exercises like box jumps, med ball slams, and band thrusts, before a third upper set of standing shoulder presses, side raises and hanging knee raises would be followed by several sprints to cool down.

Jack and Matt were here at the training center's high-performance gym. The weight room was over 4,000 feet of weights, bikes, treadmills and more. It even had a forty-foot running track.

And now, with training camp starting in two weeks, he needed to maximize his time and focus on finetuning his body for peak fitness. At thirty-three, he'd be among the oldest of the guys competing for a spot on the starting roster. And while he should be a lock—his contract said he was, anyway—there was never a shortage of younger guys all hungry to bump a veteran and prove themselves worthy of a spot. He wasn't about to sacrifice his spot on the second line for anyone.

Which was why he was here. Pushing weights, doing squats, shoving aside thoughts of a midnight conversation with someone who was intruding into his thoughts a little too often for complete peace of mind.

"Reilly, get your head in the game!"

He refocused, nodded to Jack, who grunted as he lifted his weights. Their trainers wandered through the room, and he was careful to not give them an ounce of concern. He needed to prove he was strong, and deserved to be here on his own merits, not just his history.

He finished the last set of knee raises, then headed to the track. Matt, as always, liked to turn anything into a competition, so what should've been a simple cooldown turned into a race. And because he wanted to prove he still had the fire within, he refused to surrender.

"Call that a cooldown?" His trainer raised a skeptical brow.

Yeah, he might have a way to go to release this pride thing completely.

He was breathing heavily by the time he returned to the locker room and picked up his phone. Saw a message in the online Bible study group chat.

*How is your ninja librarian friend?*

Mitch slumped in his stall and studied the message Kyle had sent. Weird. He didn't know the guy much, and wouldn't have picked him as a Jesus follower, but the fact he was reaching out meant maybe he valued the connection fostered by the group chat too.

He studied his phone, wondering how to answer. After that midnight messaging, he'd started wondering if he should've done that, had felt convicted that maybe Georgia wouldn't have approved. But then, how would he even know when she hadn't responded to any of his calls? Besides, what was wrong with telling someone who'd just undergone a terrifying ordeal that he was praying for her? That was innocent, right? And the fact that he'd arranged for flowers to get delivered to her workplace didn't have to mean anything. She'd probably received lots of flowers, anyway. She seemed that kind of person to have friends everywhere, which meant his flowers wouldn't mean that much. At least, he hoped they wouldn't be misunderstood in any way.

*Last I heard she's doing okay,* he finally typed back.

*Good.*

Mike joined in with a praying hands emoji.

Mitchell smiled. He wondered if she knew some NHL players were praying for her. He bet she didn't. Well, she knew that he was, but he bet she'd be shocked to learn he'd passed this along and asked his friends to pray.

Ha. Look at him, describing these guys as friends. Only a few weeks ago he'd been asking God for friends, and now here he was, exchanging prayer requests with these guys, being more open and honest with them than with his own flesh and blood.

Which probably wasn't quite what God had intended. Which probably needed to be amended at some point. Which probably would have to wait a while until the season was done and the next chapter of his life began.

The next chapter. Whatever that looked like. With Georgia? His heart twisted. Or without?

# CHAPTER 12

"*B*ritta, it's good to see you again."

Britta smiled at Helen Harlow, the library's general manager, and sat at the library's conference room table. "It's good to be back."

"How are you after that horrific ordeal?" Gwen Lee, the head of Bookmobile services, asked.

"I'm okay. Thank you for asking."

"Of course." Helen glanced at where Margaret sat, her hands folded tightly. "I know Margaret is equally glad to see you are safe and unharmed."

Good thing Helen knew that because Margaret was not exactly giving that impression. Still, this special meeting was not a time to nitpick but to consolidate a few things, as Helen had explained in her email.

"Now, I wanted to reiterate the library's offer for you to take advantage of our counseling. It's provided free of charge, naturally, as you're an employee and this happened on government property."

"Thank you. I've had a number of other offers of therapy as well, so I'll talk to HR if I need to access the library's one."

Bev Norberg, her pastor's wife, had reached out, and Ferdy too. She'd been given the night off youth group tomorrow night, which she appreciated, not wanting the focus to be on her exploits, when it should be on the message Ferdy had prepared. Hopefully by the time she returned the following Friday night, people would have had more time to get over things, and she wouldn't be the center of attention.

"Now, we just wanted you to know that the Bookmobile will need to suspend its services for a while, as we want to ensure all staff have completed mandatory safety protocols."

"I'm afraid that some of your actions were not quite from the rule book," Margaret said.

Ah, the rule book. "I'm afraid I was not thinking about the rule book in the heat of the moment."

"Quite understandable," Helen said.

"I don't know why," Margaret complained at the same time.

Helen glanced at Margaret, and pressed her lips together. It looked like there was little love lost between the two women.

"The police have concluded their forensics on the Bookmobile, and it's hoped there are no long-lasting effects on the books," Gwen said.

"I hope not." Although why pepper spray would be offered for such a space if it wasn't safe to use around books boggled the mind. "It was my intention to keep things as safe as possible."

"And we appreciate that. It's just that we need to speak about something we found in the Bookmobile."

"What was that?"

Margaret pushed a certain red bookmark across the table. "Can you explain this?"

The Red Jellybean bookmark. Complete with her church details. There was separation of church and state but this blurred the lines. "I'm sorry."

"Sorry for including it?" Margaret asked. "Or sorry you were caught trying to pass propaganda to impressionable children?"

Now was probably not the time to point out that inviting drag queens to read to small children created its own version of what some might consider propaganda. Funny how "inclusive" seemed to mean everyone except Christians sometimes.

"I am involved in running the Red Jellybeans, and yes, I have had children ask about this in the past, so I have a stock of bookmarks which makes it easier to pass out information about it."

"I see."

Britta didn't think she did. "I acknowledge that this was perhaps the wrong environment for this, so I apologize."

"And it won't happen again?"

"Do you want me to not speak about the Jellybeans, even if someone asks me directly about it?"

Gwen sighed. "I suppose we can't ask you to do that. It's just that we are all trying very hard to be inclusive, and when one community interest group promotes their group above others then it's not very inclusive, is it?"

*Lord, what do I say?*

She sucked in a breath, prayed for clarity, and offered a small smile. "One could say the opposite is true, too. That if you exclude a community interest group, one that has had a long association in the community over many years and been seen as a place that does a lot of good, then that's not very inclusive either."

Gwen studied her for a moment, then nodded. "You have a point."

"You know that I'm passionate about seeing young people connect with literacy and programs that will help them build confidence in life. The programs we have at the Red Jellybeans are about empowering young men and women in life skills." Even if they were rooted in Scripture. "In fact, I had a police officer involved in the case commend me for the self-defense classes we've done, something he mentioned was likely highly valuable in helping protect my life."

Gwen nodded, while Margaret still looked skeptical.

"As I mentioned, I've had numbers of young teens and parents mention they are wanting something like this, so it feels unfair to the community we are trying to serve to not mention something that will benefit them, especially when it's something they have explicitly said they want."

"Well, as long as it's not excluding any interest groups, then I suppose it can stay. But not if it's at the cost of a different group."

"The point of inclusion is not either or, is it? If another group wanted to offer bookmarks, then it would only be fair to have theirs on offer as well." And Britta would do her darndest to make sure the Jellybean bookmarks were the ones demanding attention.

Gwen glanced at Helen who nodded. "Very well, you may keep them."

*Thank You, God.*

"Now, I wanted to talk to you about another event. As you know we had penciled you in for the upcoming community day, but given the recent situation I wanted to make sure you were still willing to do that."

The family day? Britta glanced at Margaret and raised her eyebrows.

Margaret coughed. "I'm afraid that with all the recent excitement Britta may have forgotten our discussion about this."

Yes, Britta was fairly certain she'd remember that. Still, given her win with the bookmarks, she could afford to show grace. "I'm afraid you may have to remind me."

Helen explained about the community family day in a nearby northern suburb, and that the Bookmobile would attend. "But only if you feel up to it."

She checked her phone calendar. "That should be fine."

"And it won't be just you, of course."

Helen winced. "That reminds me of something else we'll need to pass on to the staff. Given the recent incident, we probably need to reconsider whether we can let the Bookmobile service run with only one staff member on board, plus a volunteer driver."

"But I don't know if two people would have been able to deal with that particular situation." Especially considering some of the volunteers they had. They were often retirees, due to age or ill-health, and hardly the kind to take down a strong, armed man.

"Still, this is part of our safety review, so for the moment we will need to reconsider how often the Bookmobile can attend, considering the incident."

Gwen shuffled papers in front of her. "It will mean having to pause the service as we rework the schedule again." Her lips tweaked in resignation.

Britta felt almost like she was supposed to apologize, but kept it in. This wasn't her fault, as her mom had said. It was the man's.

"It is a shame that so many patrons will be inconvenienced by this, but it's the only solution I can see going forward," Gwen said.

Britta nodded. "They will be pleased to see it when it returns to full service."

"Which can only happen if we launch a recruitment drive for more volunteers and drivers," Gwen said.

It was on the tip of her tongue to volunteer to help with the drive, and maybe that's what Gwen had wanted, but when Britta simply nodded, she gave a look of disappointment and said nothing more.

Helen clasped her hands. "So, now we have those matters cleared up, I hope you'll enjoy the rest of your day."

"Back in the children's area?" she asked Margaret.

Margaret nodded.

Helen smiled. "I'm sure there are some people who will be happy to see you."

Britta smiled. "And I'll be very happy to see them."


"You're back!"

"Whoa there, Tiger," she laughed, as Tommy wrapped his arms around her and squeezed. "Have you been eating your vegetables? You seem so much stronger than before."

"I have been, ever since you read that story about the tiger that ate his vegetables." Tommy grinned at her and pointed to his teeth. "See? I lost another one."

"That must make eating carrots tricky."

They discussed vegetables for a while then other children joined them for Story Time. There were more than a few questions about her ordeal two nights ago, and she did her best to skirt questions and offer a bland "I'm fine now, thanks for asking" when the same question was thrown at her twenty times in a row.

By the time Story Time was done, she was ready for a nap. But Kayla wanted to talk, and given her help during the ordeal, she couldn't say no.

"You are okay?"

She nodded. "I'm tired. It's funny, I didn't expect to feel as tired as I am."

"You've had a bit to work through." Kayla smiled. "Any more interviews?"

She shook her head. "I said no. I'm not wanting to relive that event any more than necessary. It's gotten sensationalized, and that's not really me."

"Hmm, well good for you, I suppose."

The rest of the day passed, and she was yawning by the time

the close of her shift came. Then Kayla nudged her. And she turned. And saw a certain person she'd sworn not to think about. The very one she thought might have given her flowers.

She swallowed. "Mr. Reilly."

HE WITHHELD A SIGH, saw her flinch. "Sorry."

He shrugged. Maybe he should just get used to the fact that the woman seemed determined to misremember. Not that he could blame her for forgetting things when he was so good at it himself. Like his resolve to not come here. His resolve to not reach out. But he could resolve until the cows came home, something stubborn inside still wanted to see her.

"What can we do for you, Mitch?" her friend—Kayla—asked.

"I'm here to see if the heroine is okay." His voice softened as he studied her. "You're looking okay."

"It was good to escape the house."

"A few too many reporters, huh?"

She shrugged. "They moved on, which is just as well. I'm not the type of person who wants fame."

No, she seemed the kind to hide her light under a bushel or a basket or whatever weird phrase it was he'd read in one of the Gospels this morning. "You don't seem to care what others think."

Her lips twisted. "It's more I can't afford to get carried away. There are so many people saying do this or do that, each convinced that they are right. I'm not wanting to get led astray."

She eyed him, and he wondered if she meant him. Not that he'd lead her astray. Even if it almost felt like she could lead him on a different path to what he'd imagined.

He blinked. Ducked his head. What was he doing here, anyway?

"So, was there a book we could help you with?"

His lips twisted. "You're always very to the point, aren't you?"

"I try to be."

Kayla was asked to help someone, which left him alone with Britta. "You are okay?" he asked more softly.

She nodded. "Thank you for your flowers."

His cheeks heated. "I wasn't sure you'd know they were from me."

"Right. Because quoting a line from *The Princess Bride* didn't give it away?"

"You recognized that?"

"Of course I did. What do you take me for?"

"Look, I didn't want to be presumptuous, but I felt like it was something a friend would do."

She pressed her lips together, her glasses tilting so he couldn't quite read her eyes. Then she jerked her head. "Well, thank you. And thank you for clarifying. I hope that Georgia was okay with that."

"Georgia?"

She sharply inhaled. "Your girlfriend?"

Pfft, right. "Yeah, I know that. And yeah, she's fine." Well, he hoped she'd be if she ever found out. Although the chances of her ever talking to him seemed to be slimming by the day.

"You've talked to her then?" Britta asked. "Oh, I'm so glad! How is—?"

"Actually, she still hasn't talked to me. It's been weeks now."

"Oh." Her eyes widened, then she ducked her head.

He could tell from the way she bit her lip that there were questions she burned to say. Then she peered at him. "What are you doing here, Mitch? Really?"

He barely knew. Only knew he wanted to check on her, and when he'd seen the library tagged on Instagram along with a picture of Britta reading a book, he'd known he had to be here, come see her for himself. Checking in on her via Instagram or Messenger felt too remote. This, in the flesh, felt far more real.

He cleared his throat. "Like I said. I wanted to check on you, make sure you're doing okay."

"Well, I am." She smiled. "Thank you for asking."

"And I wondered if you wanted to get a meal sometime," he blurted.

Her eyes grew wide. "A meal?"

Heck, why had he said that? Well, friends ate together, didn't they? And the thought of spending another night at home eating a meal for one seemed too lonely. Especially when Georgia was sixteen hundred miles away and didn't seem to care, and here was this woman who threw Bible verses at him and could throw wannabe thieves on their rear, and, yeah. "I figured it would be a good chance to talk about another book."

Her head tilted, her expression skeptical. "Another book? For Georgia?"

He shrugged. "Maybe."

She sighed. "I hate to break it to you, but she doesn't seem that interested."

In reading a book? Or in him? "Or we could discuss finding a book for me."

"For you?" she asked.

"For me."

She studied him a beat then swept her hand behind her. "Well, as you can see, we have a world of books that you can explore. You don't need to discuss that with me."

"But what if I want to discuss it with you?"

She shook her head. "As much as I like talking about books and encouraging people to find their best book match, I don't think this is wise."

He stepped closer. "Why not?"

"Because I have no desire to be eating alone with a man who is dating someone."

Wow. "So is that a no?"

She nodded. "That's a no. But if you want to talk books, I have some time right now and I can show you some of the books you may enjoy. Or introduce you to some of our male librarians who might be able to guide you into finding some good reading materials."

"I don't want them."

"Well, we don't always get what we want, do we?"

He stifled a chuckle. Now there was the feisty woman he'd first come to know. "So you've got some time right now?"

"If you hurry. The adult fiction section is on this floor, and I can think of some action books you may enjoy."

"Action, huh?"

"You don't want more romance, do you?"

He shrugged. "I think I'm about all romanced out."

And not just in books. For she was right. This yearning for Georgia needed to get resolved one way or the other, and the longer he put it off the worse it was starting to get.

So maybe this weekend he should jump on a plane and go visit her, once and for all.

# CHAPTER 13

*N*ot even dressed in her most wacky outfits had she felt so on show.

Whether it was because of her newfound fame as a ninja librarian or the fact she was walking around with Mitchell Flippin' Reilly, as Kayla liked to say, she didn't know. But she did know that eyes on her made her itchy. And made her wonder how a person could ever grow so used to fame that it didn't bother them.

She slid a look at Mitch as he held a copy of a Lee Child bestseller and read the back cover blurb.

Almost had to blink at the sight of the big man holding the book, frowning in concentration. Was that even real? Muscled, strong, mouthy, leading hitmaker of the Wild—reading a book?

She'd misjudged him. She'd thought he was perhaps not as intelligent as she'd hoped, when actually the fact he understood the metafictional aspect of *The Princess Bride* book showed he was smarter than she'd given him credit for. That was if he actually *had* read the book, and not just seen the movie...

He glanced at her, his dark eyes slamming into hers and

forcing breath from her lungs. She flung her gaze away. This wasn't wise. This wasn't good.

"What?"

She shook her head.

"No, don't do that. I hate it when girls don't say what they mean. What's wrong?"

"No, nothing is wrong. I was just wondering..." Hmm, how to ask if he'd actually read the book, and not just cheated by watching the movie.

He lowered the book. "Wondering what?"

"So, um, do you think you might like another book like *The Princess Bride*?"

His nose screwed. "Can I be honest?"

"Have you not been?"

"Hey, I've always tried to tell the truth."

"Except when it came to that book?" She *knew* it. He'd cheated. Watched the movie only. Which was disappointing, but not unexpected, because really, asking a jock to understand that kind of book was like asking a librarian to—

"I didn't read all of it."

She blinked. "I beg your pardon?"

"Well, it took me a little bit to understand that the author was sort of describing himself, and some parts were different to what I remember from the movie. I liked the movie, but when I read some of the book's parts in italics, it said we didn't have to read all of those bits, so I didn't."

Wow. "So you actually did read it."

He nodded. "And yeah, I liked it, but if I'm really honest, I didn't love it, and I don't want another book like it." He held up the copy of a Jack Reacher. "But this looks good."

"You should check the first page. See if you like the writing style of the author."

"Like I did with *Pride and Prejudice*?"

She nodded, her heart full. This was what being a literacy

advocate did. People trying new things. People reading outside of their preferred genre. People *reading*. "So, if you borrow that one, then you could maybe borrow a couple of others as well. That way you can see if you like those. Sometimes the book can take a little while before you get into it so it's worth persisting."

"Are you saying I should've persisted with *Pride and Prejudice*?"

Yes. "Look, I'm just glad you gave that one a go. Not every man would've."

"Well, I'm not every man."

"That's for sure."

His gaze narrowed and her brain glitched.

She hadn't meant to sound flirty. "I meant I'm not acquainted with any man who has read that book before."

"I don't know how many guys would be tough enough to admit it."

"Says the man who read only one page."

"Is that a challenge?"

"Not at all. You said you didn't want to read any more romance, right?"

He studied her, and her cheeks grew hot. So she quickly strode down the aisle and plucked a couple of other books from the shelves. "You might want to check out these ones as well. Jack London is a little old school, but he's so descriptive, and if ever you've had a hankering to know what life is like in the Canadian wilderness, it makes for a riveting read."

"Hankering, huh?"

She nodded.

"A riveting read?" He smiled. "I just love these words you use."

"Well, you too could be using words like these if you read the kinds of books I do."

He chuckled. "I'd like a few that'd help me when I gotta chirp the guys on the ice."

"Oh, in that case you need Shakespeare."

"No way."

"Yes way. Have you ever seen a list of Shakespearean insults?" She wrinkled her brow trying to remember some that might prove appropriate for his situation. Then pulled out her phone. Standing too near Mitch Reilly seemed to be doing away with her brain. "How about 'I'll beat thee, but I would infect my hands'?"

He thought about it a second then grinned. "Nice."

"That's from Timon of Athens."

"Never heard of it."

Not many had. "Here's another, from Henry IV. 'Peace, ye fat guts!'"

He laughed. "I could use that."

She could just imagine him taunting someone trying to check him against the boards. "Or when someone's in your face you could use part of this: 'The rankest compound of villainous smell that ever offended nostril'."

He chuckled. "That's our locker room after each game."

"Or someone who's taunting you, you could say to him he's 'like the toad; ugly and venomous'."

"And here I thought you were trying to get me to treat others as Jesus did."

Wow. Conviction clanged. "Oh, I didn't mean to encourage you to be rude."

He shrugged. "I'm known for my mouth, so it'd be weird if I was all suddenly meek and mild. Not that Jesus was. Like, he called the Pharisees broods of vipers, so I guess I can get away with calling someone—" He leaned closer and read her phone, "'clay-brained' or 'sodden-witted'." He chuckled.

Whether it was the sound of his rumbly laughter, or the fact he knew his Bible well enough to know what Jesus said, or it simply was his nearness where she could catch a trace of something that smelled like Cool Water, like one of Astrid's boyfriends from long ago, her body seemed to heat. A glance up saw other patrons staring, and she quickly shuffled away.

He grinned. "It wouldn't be the first time I had some fun with chirps. Last year when Luc Blanchard was on that dance show it was fun to mock him about his dancing. Telling him to quickstep a time or two."

She smiled. "He did surprisingly well." Another hockey star who had surprised her.

"Which made it more fun to tease him." He glanced at the book again. "But he's a nice guy. I've gotten to know him a little in recent weeks, and yeah."

"He's a Christian too."

He nodded. "I know. After you mentioned you'd pray for me to find some Christian friends, well, I did."

She'd said that? "I'm glad."

"I, uh, joined an online Bible study for Christian hockey players. Luc Blanchard is one of them."

"Really? That's awesome."

He shrugged. "And maybe this will freak you out, but some of them have even been praying for you."

"For me? Why?"

"Because they saw what happened and I mentioned you were my friend and asked them to pray for you."

Emotion clutched her, and she blinked hard behind her glasses, but they fogged up anyway. She pivoted on her heel and gently wiped them. Then wiped her eyes.

"Was that wrong of me?" he asked, his voice tentative.

She shook her head, bracing with a smile. She couldn't explain why this touched her so deeply, whether it was his reference—again—to her being his friend, or the thought that famous people like Luc Blanchard might be praying for a little nobody like her. "Thank you."

"You're welcome."

When she judged herself under control enough, she shifted

back. Not so close as before. She needed distance between them. Physical and emotional space. She dared glance up at him. He was studying her, a wrinkle in his brow like he was worried.

"Hey, is that Mitch Reilly?" A voice called.

They both glanced down the aisle where a couple of people stood pointing.

He sighed. "Looks like I need to go."

"Yep." Her stomach twisted with disappointment. But no, he needed to go. He needed to go far, far away for her peace of mind. "Well, you've got a selection of great books there. If you take them downstairs, they can be scanned out for you and you can enjoy them."

"I think I will." He smirked, as he held up *The Call of the Wild*. "After all, what man hasn't wanted to know about life in the Canadian wilderness?"

"Indeed."

"Indeed." He grinned.

Oh, it was too easy to banter with this man. "You better go." She subtly nodded to the people with their phones.

He quickly sobered. "Speaking of going, I'm going to try to go see Georgia this weekend."

"You are?" She winced at the surprise loading her tone. "That's good. That's *great*."

"Yeah." His face didn't say that. "So, if you get a chance, I'd appreciate it if you pray for me. And her. And... yeah."

She swallowed. See? The man clearly wanted to reconnect with Georgia. He didn't want her. He might smile and send her flowers and pray for her, but he was only being a friend. A *friend*. That was all. An ordinary woman putting God first who possessed a fiction-fueled imagination had no business wanting anything more. So she nodded. Pasted on a smile, and said, "Sure."

TRAVELLING west to Seattle and Trinity Lakes sure felt different this time than all the times before. This time might be a literal flying visit, but he wanted to finally get the answers he was looking for. It felt like *Avengers: Endgame*, like the dice would be rolled and he'd finally have to face the truth, whatever the outcome would be.

And the fact that Georgia didn't seem to want him was a hard truth he didn't want to face. Tough he might be, but he doubted he'd be able to bounce off Georgia's potential rejection with a snide Shakespearean quote or three. He'd invested too much in this to let that slide off his back like water off a duck.

Or maybe this sense of doom had something to do with the weird knot in his stomach ever since that moment in the library when he'd left Britta to face the phone-wielding teens while he'd skeetered off in the opposite direction. He'd felt like he'd disappointed her somehow. Which was weird. He'd hoped to make her proud of him with borrowing the books she'd recommended. The books that he'd then forgotten to take on the plane. What kind of doofus was he to forget that? Three and a half hours was plenty of time to dive into a book, but no. He'd left the little pile next to his bed, hadn't he?

No wonder Britta looked at him oddly sometimes, like she wondered what he was doing hanging around her. And while he might wonder that himself at times, he was also conscious he didn't want to stay away. There was something so... ordinary and yet familiar about her, like they were comfortable with each other and could say what they thought. Which was rare in a woman. Especially rare in the kinds of women he'd come across. Most of them just played the game of appeasing his ego, while Britta didn't seem to care.

Maybe that was part of why he'd first been attracted to Georgia. She didn't seem to care about impressing him either. She certainly hadn't in recent weeks, anyway. Would she even be there when he dropped by to surprise her today?

He slumped in his seat, shifting his legs, mouthing an apology to the old lady parked next to him in the too-small seats, then shutting his eyes again. Eyes closed, headphones on, arms crossed, and scowl face activated usually resulted in a lack of conversation with fellow passengers, which was just the way he liked it. No conversations, no explanations, no dumb small talk with people he'd never see again. There'd be plenty of that once preseason began and he'd be obliged to participate in a million fan events. This, his last chance to be anonymous before the community day next weekend, and training camp the weekend after, felt like his last chance to sort this out with Georgia. This uncertainty had gone on long enough.

He heaved in a breath, then released it, probably scaring the old lady beside him. He clenched then stretched his fingers. *Hey Lord, I'd really appreciate You leading me in this. I don't know what's going on, but You do. So help me to trust You.*

He'd asked the guys in the chat to pray for him about a decision he had to make. Didn't give them any more details than that, and mentioned he was coming this way, which instantly saw Kyle ask if he had time to catch up. He'd had to decline, saying he had family visits to make, which was true, even if he hadn't told them he planned to visit. Having seen the schedule, this would be the last chance to catch up until they had a couple of days free at Christmas. Even Thanksgiving would be too hard, with a game that Wednesday then a road trip starting the next day. And it was only a big brother's duty to check Jasper was treating Ellie as he should, and make sure his mom and younger brothers were doing okay.

But his top priority would be to see Georgia. To figure out if she'd meant to ghost him, or if this was just a season of stupid busyness for a student. Although, a bit of Googling suggested the school year hadn't begun yet. So what *was* she doing?

Thoughts of the Bible study guys praying for him flicked his mind back to when he'd mentioned to Britta they'd prayed for her. She'd seemed so surprised, so humbled, he'd even wondered if she was about to cry.

He flinched. What was he doing thinking about her when he should be thinking about Georgia?

A tap on his bicep drew his attention to the elderly female passenger from before, forcing him to remove his headphones. "Yes?"

She smiled, but wore a furrowed brow. "Excuse me, young man, but are you quite well?"

Honestly, the nerve of some people. He bit back his first response. He was a Christian now, so he should treat her with kindness, even if she seemed nosy. "Yeah."

She seemed to take his non-brush-off as an invitation to continue talking. "Oh, that's good. You seem nervous, that's all."

She paused, as if waiting for him to fill the gap. Which gave him the chance to turn away or find a smidge of grace and answer. "I'm heading to see my girlfriend."

"Oh, that's lovely. Are you living apart?"

He dipped his chin. "Long distance kind of sucks."

"I imagine it makes things very difficult at times."

He peered at her. Something about her phrasing reminded him of Britta. He clenched his fingers. He did not want to be thinking about her. Think about *Georgia*.

The woman's head tilted, reminding him of a bird. "There it is again. You must pardon me for speaking bluntly, but you do seem a little stressed." Her eyes widened. "Are you about to pop the question, is that it?"

Pop the—? "What?"

"I do love a romantic story." She clasped her hands. "I hope it works out for you and she says yes."

How had the conversation escalated into this? "Uh, I don't think you understand."

"Oh, I understand, young man. It's such a big commitment, especially when you want it to last. Good luck to you." She smiled, then tapped the arm of the passing hostess. "This young man is about to pop the question to his girlfriend."

"Hey, no—"

"Oh my goodness! That's *so* romantic."

"Uh, actually—"

"Oh! I recognize you now. You're Mitchell Reilly, aren't you? You play for the Wild."

"Yeah, but—"

"That's so exciting! And you're going to see your girlfriend to propose."

What? By now others were looking, had their phones out, were filming.

"Is she expecting it? Your girlfriend I mean."

He shook his head. "You got this wro—"

"Congratulations," the middle-aged man next to him murmured.

"Uh, there's no need for congratulations," he muttered.

"As if she'd say no to you." The hostess winked. "But if she does, I can give you my number, and a good time."

His jaw dropped. He knew of some guys who had been straight-up propositioned before—Zac Parotti had even had women literally fling themselves at him—but he hadn't experienced anything like that until now. He shook his head. "Uh, no thanks."

"Good luck to you then." She winked again, then continued down the aisle.

"Well done." His elderly companion patted his arm. "Honestly, the nerve of some people these days. A hussy, that's what she is."

He bit back a smile. A hussy sounded like another of those old-fashioned words Britta seemed so fond of saying.

"People seem to forget these days that looks don't last, even money doesn't last, but the character of a person tends to."

Her words carved like a knife, slicing away the weirdness of the moment earlier. Why did he suddenly now feel like this woman might have something of the angel about her?

"So," she peered at him, "I hope it works out for you and your young lady."

Which young lady? His thoughts blurred, tipping, tilting between two. One strikingly attractive, one plain. One skinny, one full of curves. One young, one more his age. No, no, no! He did *not* want to think about her.

"There, there." She patted his arm again. "I'm sure she'll be thrilled to see you."

"I hope so," he rasped, knowing he had to say something.

But the words taunted and teased as much as any Shakespearean insult.

And while the old lady and airline hostess seemed determined to think he meant a proposal, he knew he had a far more simple question to ask. Did Georgia want to continue a relationship with him?

# CHAPTER 14

he beauty of a rare Friday night off meant she had
time to spend with her friends. Kayla had wanted to
visit this cocktail bar downtown, and while it wasn't Britta's
scene, she'd thought it might be a good chance to connect with
Kayla on her own terms. What was the point in Christians
expecting non-Christians to come into church when they never
ventured into their spaces? That seemed pretty arrogant to her.

"Oh, Britta. You really should see this." Kayla leaned close
and showed her phone.

She peered at the screen, adjusting her glasses as she looked
closer. But the bar's darkness made it hard to distinguish. "Who
is it?"

"It's Mitchell Reilly."

Her heart thudded. "And?"

"And apparently he's going to propose!"

She blinked. "What?"

"Not to you, silly. Even though he seems to have spent a lot
of time with you lately."

"Excuse me?" How could Kayla even think she would think
that? But asking that seemed recipe for inviting further specula-

tion that she couldn't afford to stir up—in others or herself. "Oh, never mind. He mentioned he was going to see Georgia."

"Georgia Darcy." Kayla rolled her eyes. "Sister of a millionaire, way too young for him, but he's not letting that stop him apparently."

She knew she was supposed to say something, but what she could say that was actually honest and real she could not find. Except, "How do you know he's going to propose?"

It made no sense. He'd said Georgia hadn't even talked to him for weeks. The man had to be delusional. Georgia clearly had been doing her best to avoid him. But what did she know? She herself was clearly delusional to think that a man who said he'd pray for her might hold an inkling of interest a different way.

Kayla snatched the phone back and tapped the screen. An article appeared. "Apparently there is this airline attendant who often posts to gossip sites, and she heard him say he was going to propose."

"How did she know it was him?"

"She's a big hockey fan, apparently. Recognized him right away."

"He's not the only man in the world with a beard and muscly arms," she muttered.

"Oh, poor Britta. You have it bad, huh?"

"No, I do not." *Lord, please take the tendrils of attraction away.* "And if it makes any difference, the only reason I was helping him was so that he would be able to connect with Georgia."

"By reading books?" Kayla eyed her skeptically.

"Yes. They were romance books, if you must know."

Kayla blinked. "Wow."

"Exactly." Not that it seemed to have done any good. Georgia had never responded, or so he'd said. Which frankly made this whole scenario a little hard to believe. How could he be going there to propose?

She sipped her margarita, wincing at the sour taste. She was more a sweet drinks girl, but the names of the sweeter-flavored drinks on offer here that the bartender had listed to her were ones she didn't want to say aloud. Or even in her brain.

But the thought of Mitchell and Georgia together refused to go away. How would he propose? On the beach? At a restaurant? Would he want somewhere private or take the risk and make his feelings known in a public space? She'd always wondered about the confidence of those men who proposed publicly, their certainty such that they'd risk public humiliation in case the woman said no.

But the fact this airline attendant of all people seemed to know his intentions suggested he'd talked about it, which meant he must have had more conversations with Georgia than he'd told Britta about, and felt a degree of certainty that she'd say yes.

Which was fine. He certainly didn't need to tell Britta everything, just like she hadn't told him all. And while they might've shared a moment or two that had made her think he might care a little bit at least, he obviously didn't.

Her stomach grew queasy, and she pushed away the drink. One sip was more than enough. She attempted more conversation, but every time she tried to lead it toward something God-related, Kayla steered it somewhere else. Kayla seemed more interested in checking out who was coming through the door than in talking with Britta.

Kayla's face lit, and she straightened as John arrived and kissed her cheek. Well, well. Good to know Kayla had arranged this evening out with only Britta in mind. She internally rolled her eyes at herself.

But the way Kayla and John whispered to each other, combined with the thumping music, only increased the thudding in her head. It was obvious these two didn't need her here.

"Thanks, Kayla, but I should probably go home."

"You can't go yet. You haven't finished your drink."

"I have a bit of a headache. It's been a big week," she reminded her. "I didn't get back from the police station until really late the other night, and I'm still catching up." She gave a delicate yawn, fake of course, as John moved to the bar.

"You're not upset about Mitch, are you?"

"Who?"

Kayla's bright pink lipsticked mouth flicked up. Then her expression softened. "He's taken, Britta."

"I know that." She gritted out a smile. "Which is why I was helping him, remember?"

Kayla eyed her for a moment, then nodded. "Well, take a cab or get an Uber. You've been drinking."

"I only had one sip," she protested. Unlike Kayla, who would definitely need an Uber to get home.

"A girl needs to be careful."

"Exactly. So don't stay here too long tonight, okay?"

"Okay." Kayla grinned, as John returned.

She made her farewells then moved outside to where her car was, got inside. But didn't drive home straightaway. Instead, she drove to a nearby park that overlooked the Mississippi and watched the lights of Saint Paul reflect in the river as the sky changed from blue to pink to black. A riverboat was lit up and plying its way along the river, the silhouettes of patrons inside showing they were enjoying their Friday night. On dates, get-togethers. Probably a proposal or two. The things people who weren't stuck leading youth group did.

She pressed her lips together. She wasn't sorry she did that. She *wasn't*. But it would be nice to feel like she could be normal for a change, instead of living this existence that sometimes very much felt like she lived in a parallel universe. Where she had her life mapped out in front of her, Christian service all the way, while others got to taste life a little more. Not that she wanted margaritas. Not that she even wanted a man. But it had been nice to think a man had thought about her. For the first time in her life.

She took off her glasses, and the lights reflecting off the river instantly tripled in blur and size. She wiped her eyes, but everything remained blurry. So she closed them instead.

"Lord, I'm sorry. I don't know what's wrong with me."

Yes, she did. She'd started to have feelings for someone that she shouldn't have. Someone who she couldn't have. The man who had surprised her, who had paid attention to her, who she'd dared to think about. She'd known she shouldn't think about him, or allow those thoughts to stir up her heart. She'd preached about guarding her heart to her girls before. And yet stupid, stupid her had gone and done exactly what so many other girls did half her age, allowing herself to think a guy cared, when really he didn't care at all.

"Lord, forgive me for thinking about him."

Was she really that pathetically desperate and needy that she started imagining things about the first guy who paid attention to her? Apparently.

"Lord, I know that You are enough for me, but right now, I feel lonely. If You have a guy out there for me, can You please bring him across my path soon?" She swiped at a stupid tear running down her cheek. "And if You don't, then take away these feelings, please. I feel so stupid, like such a hypocrite, preaching one thing then acting like this. Lord, forgive me."

She found a tissue, blew her nose. Oh, thank goodness there was nobody here to see her.

She leaned against the headrest. Sighed. "And God, I don't want to be selfish, so please bless Mitchell and Georgia. Help them finally connect. And help me to not let this bother me. I'm sorry, please forgive me."

She shuddered out another breath, then broke down and sobbed.

MITCHELL SHIFTED the bunch of red roses and knocked on the apartment door where Georgia lived. Waited. The doorman had assured him Miss Georgia was home, so he was counting on this to finally work out. The element of surprise, after all.

He knocked again, then the door opened.

Georgia's smile faded, instantly shriveling his heart. "Surprise." He thrust the flowers at her, leaned in for a kiss, but she turned her cheek so his lips found her jaw.

"What are you doing here?"

"Seeing you, of course. Can I come in?"

She glanced behind her, winced.

His heart froze. Is that why she hadn't returned his calls? She had another guy? He peered over her, and saw groups of people talking among themselves. "What's going on?"

She sighed. "We can't talk here."

"Why not?" He pushed the door wider. He'd been here before, but had never seen her place filled with so many people. He noted decorations, balloons, music, food. "Are you having a party?"

"It's the start of our last year, so yeah."

Her last year of studies. Here she was, just wanting to be a normal student, while he'd been hoping she was thinking about him. She clearly hadn't. It seemed she hadn't wanted him at all.

Still, pride demanded he say, "Why haven't you answered my calls?"

She sighed, her shoulders sinking. "Mitchell, look I—"

"Hey Georgia," one of her friends called. "Did you see this article in TMZ? Apparently your hockey dad is coming to propose."

He blinked. "Your hockey *what*?" Had he said dad or dude?

"You're coming to do what?" Georgia demanded.

"Not propose," he growled. Not anything, the way this was going.

"Oh my gosh," she murmured. Then swung the door wide and gestured him inside.

Maybe he was an idiot because he walked inside and all conversation stopped. He caught a round of shell-shocked faces, opened mouths, wide eyes.

"Is that Mitchell Reilly?" someone whispered.

"The hockey dad," someone replied.

"The hockey what?" he said. They hadn't said dad, had they? They'd said dude, right?

"The hockey *dad*," the guy emphasized.

"Justin, don't," Georgia murmured.

"I'm not a dad," he said, turning to Georgia. "Why would they say that?"

The guy called Justin stood. He was about half the width of Mitchell, and had clearly never worked out in his life. But he had a brashness to him as he lifted his chin. "Because you're old enough to be her dad."

"What? No, I'm not." He glanced at Georgia. "You know I'm not."

She ducked her head.

"Did you say that about me?"

"No." She met his gaze. "But it is true that you are a lot older than me. I can't help it if some of my friends started calling you that."

"Excuse me? You can. You can tell them to stop. It's rude. Why would you let them be rude to me?"

She sighed. "Mitchell, I really don't want to talk about this here."

"Then fine. Let's talk about it in the hall. Because I sure as heck haven't come all this way to be blown off by you again." He glared at the kid called Justin. "Or be insulted by a pipsqueak like him."

"Hey!"

Mitch moved toward him and the kid reared back.

Georgia sighed, and Mitch pivoted back, tugging her hand as they went out into the hall.

"What is wrong with you?" she complained.

"What is wrong with me? What's wrong with you? Why haven't you talked to me in weeks?"

She crossed her arms, looked away. "I'm not going to talk to you when you're being this aggressive."

"Aggressive?" Was she kidding? He took a breath, tried to calm down.

She eyed him. "Did you really come to propose?"

"No!" As she reared back, he forced himself to drop his pitch and calm his tone. "Of course not. I've been wondering why you have ignored my calls and messages. And you seemed determined to ghost me, so I thought I'd find out what was wrong once and for all."

"Once and for all, huh?" Her gaze narrowed. "You want to know what's wrong?"

"Yes." How many times did he need to say this?

She drew in a long breath. "Well, I'm sorry but I would've thought that you'd have figured out by now that I'm not interested in a relationship. Yes, we went out a few times and that was nice but that was it."

Each word felt like another axe chop to the tree trunk of his pride.

"You live four states away, I'm over here, it's not going to work. We've got nothing in common apart from where our families live in Trinity Lakes."

"But I thought we had fun. You messaged me, said you wanted to see me again."

"We did have some fun, and it was nice, but I realized I'm not wanting a relationship right now. I'm too young to settle down."

"I'm not asking you to settle down."

"You are. You want me to be the little girlfriend who waits here for your call instead of going out and having fun. I'm sorry, Mitch, but you need to know." She sighed. "I'm not interested."

"You don't like me?"

"Not in that way, no."

He might've suspected that was her answer, but it didn't stop the swirl of pain massing in his chest. "Then why the heck didn't you say that weeks ago?"

She tucked her hands under her armpits. "Because you're not easy to say no to."

Some other women managed okay. He shook that thought away. "What do you mean?"

She gestured to him. "You're pretty intimidating, if I'm honest."

"No, I'm not."

Her chin jerked up. "Yes, you are."

The door opened, and Justin the dweeb poked his head out. "Hey, is everything okay, Georgia?"

"Scram," Mitchell barked.

Georgia raised an eyebrow at him, then turned to her scrawny defender. "It's fine. I'll be inside in a minute."

In a minute? That was it? This would all be over in sixty seconds? His breathing grew ragged. "Did I do something wrong?"

She sighed, glanced at the ground, drew a line on the floorboards with the toe of her shoe. "Remember at Ellie's wedding when you kissed me?"

He nodded dumbly.

"You shouldn't have done that."

"I know," he rasped. "I said I was sorry."

"We weren't at that stage of a relationship, and it freaked me out a bit."

"I was caught up in the moment when the wedding photographer wanted us all to kiss our partners. I told you that."

166

"Well, I don't want someone who gets caught up in their emotions. And you do."

"I'm doing better."

"You're kind of scary, and I don't want that in my life. Not again."

He faintly remembered Ellie once telling him about some guy Gary Wickley who'd tried to get Georgia to run off to Vegas to get married. "I'm not like that."

She studied him, her look unconvinced.

He blew out a breath. "You really think I'm scary?"

She bit her lip.

Wow. He paced back. "So that's it, huh?"

"I'm sorry."

"We're really over?"

She sighed. "Mitchell, we dated a few times, but we weren't ever really together."

"But you'd said you wanted to see me," he reminded her.

She winced. "I know. But that was before you kissed me, which is when I realized we're on different pages about things. Look, I'm sorry. I know I should've told you but I didn't know how and hoped you'd just take the hint."

"I wish you had." He blew out a breath. "I don't give up easily when I think someone is worth it, but if you'd just told me how you felt I could have accepted it and we could have avoided this."

Her gaze lowered, her mouth a flat line.

Humiliation creased his chest, squeezing out the pathetic dregs of his pride. "I liked you."

She threw her hands in the air in exasperation. "I don't even know why."

"Because you're beautiful, and interesting, and different, and, yeah…"

She shook her head. "Maybe you need to find someone who you can actually get to know. You don't really know me. I think you liked the idea of me, but I bet you don't even know what I'm studying."

"Sure I do."

She lifted her eyebrows, waiting.

What a time for his memory lapse to make an appearance. "Uh, it's something to do with art, right?"

She rolled her eyes. "Goodbye, Mitchell."

"But Georgia—"

"No. Don't call me. I'm going to block your number, and talk to Liam about you."

His chest tightened. Liam, the millionaire brother, who had an owner's stake in the NHL's Seattle team. This had the potential to go really bad. "You won't have to."

"I still will." She lifted her chin, eyeballing him in that way that said she meant business.

No. He really didn't need to have people murmuring to his bosses about how he was unfit to play. "I haven't done anything wrong."

"Bye Mitchell."

She turned, opened the door, where he heard Justin's nasally voice ask, "Is he gone? Are you okay? Do you need a restraining order?" before the door was closed firmly.

Leaving him in the hallway, alone, confused, conscious that his career might well rest in the hands of a disgruntled brother of the girl who'd just rejected him. Restraining order? Was the pipsqueak serious?

*Dear God, what am I going to do?*

# CHAPTER 15

*A*fter Friday night's bombshell, never had a Saturday felt so long, dragging on as she filled her day with a million things to distract her from checking social media. Call her a bad Christian, but she didn't want to see he was engaged. Didn't want to know he and Georgia had reconciled. She had to eliminate him from her life, take her thoughts captive, not waste a second on entertaining wrong thoughts.

For they were wrong. She knew that. She'd been selfish. And just like she'd told the Red Jellybeans a million times, one needed to be ruthless to dig out the weeds polluting one's mind. Which meant minute by minute, filling her mind with good things, with godly things, praying for God's blessings to cover her family, her friends, her Jellybeans, her church and work friends. Thanking God for His many blessings, keeping her focus on Him, not herself. That way God could have His way more.

After confessing her frustration with being "stuck" with Christian ministry, she'd contacted Ferdy and asked him for prayer requests for the kids. Using her time like this had to be more valuable than not.

So as she vacuumed and washed clothes and cleaned the kitchen and baked brownies she prayed. And prayed some more. And thanked God. And sang along to worship songs, like those by Sarah Walton from Heartsong Collective. And gradually the frustration and hurt began to ease.

"Britta! You're such a rock star!"

"We're glad you are safe."

"Praise the Lord he didn't have a gun."

"Amen." Britta kept the smile on as Jellybeans and their parents swarmed around her and hugged and welcomed her to the Sunday morning service.

Astrid and Milla rolled their eyes and went to find seats with their friends, leaving Britta in the center of more congratulations, many of whom wanted to know about the Bookmobile incident in excruciating detail.

"Were you scared?"

"Was he high?"

"Is he in jail?"

She was thankful for the service starting, for the music that reminded her to bless the Lord in every circumstance, that they could trust God with it all. The message from Calvin Norberg further reiterated this, the time a chance for her soul to recalibrate and remember that yes, God really was in control.

God had been with her in the Bookmobile. God had been with her on Friday night. God was still with her now.

But after the service, when the hugs eased off and she caught the eye of Bev, the pastor's wife, a wave of latent emotion rose. Bev was one of those people who had always had that effect on her, drawing deep emotion from her like she was a heart magnet.

She smiled, then glanced away, to see Astrid and Milla talking with two guys, and the fact she stood here surrounded by people but feeling alone washed over her again. People talked to her, sure. Yes, they said they cared. But oh, to have someone in particular care…

*You are not alone. You have people who care. Stop feeling sorry for yourself!*

"Britta?"

She turned, and Bev drew close and hugged her. "We're so glad to see you are all right."

It took her a moment. Then, "Oh, you mean the Bookmobile guy. Yes, thanks. I'm fine. It was a shock, but I'm okay."

Her brow furrowed. "Did something else happen?"

"No. Nope, not at all. I'm fine." She smiled.

"Hmm." Her head tilted. "That's a couple more declarations than what I need to be convinced. *Has* something else happened?"

She swallowed. Bev was like her grandmother, and as kind as could be. While Calvin, Bev's husband, was the church's visionary, his wife was the heart. She imagined it was like what it must've been when people spoke with Jesus. People truly felt the love.

"Something has, hasn't it?"

"I can't talk about it here," she whispered.

"Do you want to talk about it?"

"Not really."

Bev nodded, but it felt like one of those moments when she could either open up and be real, or try to hide it to herself. And Bev was in hot demand, so opportunities like this were rare. "I probably would like to, but I'm so ashamed."

Bev eyed her then nodded. "Calvin has a meeting, but I don't need to be there. Want to play hooky and have lunch with me?"

"Of course."

"Good." She hooked her arm through Britta's then called to her husband. "Calvin, I'm afraid I'll be out for a few hours. Britta needs me."

He smiled, nodded. "Well, if Britta needs you, then we can't have you saying no to our favorite kung fu librarian, can we?"

His words, meant in jest, pierced the bubble of self-protection. And while she smiled and thanked him without a wobbly voice, her eyes filled. It took some doing but she managed to hide her emotion from Bev. Until they were seated in Bev's car, and there was no place to hide.

"What do you feel like eating for lunch?"

"I'm happy for whatever. I'm just grateful for you to take time out of your day for me."

"Are you kidding? I hope you know I fully plan to boast about spending time with you on social media." Bev winked. "Not in any bad way. Just making the most of my brush with fame."

Fame. Celebrity. Her thoughts tilted to someone else.

"Britta? I was joking. Well, sort of joking. I'd love the chance to show you off, but I won't if you don't want."

"Show me off? I'm not the kind of person people do that for."

Bev glanced at Britta, her expression softening. "Let's go get something to eat then talk."


THIS PLACE with its ivy-covered walls and river views might look humble from outside, but the food was good, and most importantly, on a cool day like this, they could be inside and have the chance to talk privately. Which they did as soon as the food was served.

"Britta, I want you to tell me why you said that before."

"Said what?"

"About not being the kind of person others want to show off."

She swallowed. Sipped her water. Glanced out the window at the riverboats paddling leisurely by. "I hate feeling this way."

"I could tell something was wrong. What's happened?" Her eyes were wise. "It's not just the Bookmobile thing, is it?"

She shook her head. "I'm so embarrassed to admit this."

"God doesn't want us to live in shame. Jesus died on the cross to set us free from that."

So maybe it was Jesus who wanted Britta to expose this today so she wouldn't live in shame anymore. "So, a few weeks ago I met this guy at the library, and yeah."

Bev forked in her salad. "He's nice? And a Christian?"

She nodded. "I didn't think so at first, but he's surprised me. And I knew all this time he had a girlfriend, and I was trying to help him connect with her, but..."

"But now you have your own feelings to contend with?"

She fingered the edge of the plate. "Which is why I'm so ashamed. What kind of leader am I if I can't even practice what I literally have preached about not stirring up emotions?"

Bev reached across the table and held her hand. "Why did he need your help with his girlfriend? That sounds a bit unfair to me."

"It's my job, like literally my job to help people find the right kinds of books. Which is what he asked, and I obliged, as he wanted to 'romance her.'" She rabbit-eared those words.

"Have you met his girlfriend?"

She shook her head. "She lives a few states away. And now he's gone there to propose."

"Oh, Britta." Bev squeezed her hand.

"See how pathetic I am? It's like I have a hook in my heart that I'm trying to pray away but it won't leave."

"I'll pray with you."

"Thanks," she whispered. "I haven't been able to talk about this to anyone, because I just feel so bad. Like, I'm praying that God will bless them, but part of me still feels sad, like nobody will ever want me." Emotion clamped her throat. But she forced herself to say this next bit. "And he was the first guy I ever met who made me feel like I was actually seen."

Bev nodded. "I understand. Hence the comment before about not being someone who gets shown off."

She snatched up a paper napkin and wiped her eyes. "I'm so pathetic, aren't I?"

"Britta, this is known as being human. You're allowed to want love. You're allowed to want romance for yourself."

She exhaled. "I just feel like admitting that says I'm not happy serving God where I am. Like I'm saying my work with the Red Jellybeans isn't enough."

"Britta, you do so much for them, and you have for many years. When it's time to call that season done, you will know that God has been pleased with your service. You've impacted many lives."

"I know I have. And I know God has used me. I don't know why I'm feeling this way when I've been fine for years. And that scares me."

Bev looked at her with empathy. "Maybe this is a new season you're entering into, and that's why you're finally feeling this way."

"I don't know. I thought I was happy and content but now I'm getting tired of all the clichés. I don't want to be the single who gets told 'it's not your time', or 'God wants you to be content enough in Him then He'll bring the right man along'. I feel like that is a bit of a cop-out. We can't twist God's arm. He's God, and He can do anything at any time."

Bev looked at her seriously. "You raise some good points."

"And I especially don't want to be the single woman who is hankering after another girl's man."

In the echo of the word "hankering" she remembered Mitch's tease and smile.

She clenched her hands. "I want that to stop. I *need* that to stop."

"Do you plan to see this man again?"

"No. But I can't stop him from showing up at work."

Bev winced. "That makes it hard. But you can stop helping him."

"Well, if he's proposed like social media is saying, then he doesn't need my help."

"Social media, huh?"

She shook her head. "I'm going to block him."

"You've been talking on social media?"

She sighed. "He messaged to check I was okay after the attack." She swallowed, then braved up. "And sent me flowers."

"Oh Britta."

"Right? See how bad I am?"

"No. I know your heart is innocent. It sounds like this man doesn't quite know what he wants, and is playing with fire."

No. She refused to let her heart hook onto the "he might want her" train. "He's a new Christian, so maybe he's still figuring out what's not appropriate."

"Hmm. It sounds to me like he's someone you'd be wise to avoid in the future."

She nodded. "That's my plan. As best I can."

Bev nodded. "If you block him on social media, and maybe avoid all social media for a while, and avoid him at work, and get someone else to deal with him, that will help." She smiled softly. "I'm sorry."

She shrugged.

Bev looked thoughtful. "Perhaps we need to find you someone else to take your mind off him."

"Yeah, you've seen the single guys in church. If they're nice or halfway handsome or have a job they get snapped up in a minute." By the pretty girls. Not the plain. Not the ones who were overweight and wore glasses.

"Let me talk about it with some of my pastor wife friends. We don't want to lose you to another church, but by the same token, we know the kingdom of God is big enough for you to find a new spiritual home and be used by God there, if that's what He wills."

"You're going to find me a mystery date?"

Bev smiled. "I'm going to pray that God brings the right man into your life."

"Thank you for letting me share."

"I'm always happy to spend time with you, Britta. You're one of my favorite people on this planet."

Her eyes welled and she had to take off her glasses. "Don't say things like that. You'll make me cry again."

"I can't help but speak the truth."

Speak the truth. That's what Britta needed to do. Be honest. With God and with others about her life, her hopes—and Mitchell Reilly.

SEATTLE MIGHT BE A PRETTY CITY, but it sure felt pretty lonely when he was here by himself. And after Friday night's shocker he'd had zero inclination to see his family and run the risk of bumping into Liam. Who knew what Georgia might've already said to him? And as for having to face the mockery of his siblings—thanks, but no thanks. He felt too raw for anything to be admitted out loud just yet.

So what to do? He didn't want to slink back home, tail between his legs. Especially as some of the guys had come across the stupid proposal thing, and asked questions that he hadn't replied to. Except to say *Nope. Another Fakebook lie.*

He glanced at his phone. Kyle had messaged again and asked if he wanted to catch up. And while he didn't really, he didn't want to be with his own miserable company a second longer than necessary, either. Which was why he sat waiting in this too-buzzy café watching the water like he was cool enough to go eat by himself and didn't care what others thought of him. Even if, right now, he felt extra vulnerable and did.

"Reilly?"

He glanced up, nodded. "Kyle Tinker."

"Kyle is fine."

Mitch half-smiled, then got the attention of the waiter. "We need two coffees."

"I don't drink coffee."

"They're for me." Mitch smirked. "And he's having—"

"A chai latte."

"Seriously?"

"I like them."

"I tried one once and it tasted like dirty water."

"You obviously haven't had one from here then."

No. He eyed Kyle. The dude was someone he'd played against, but they'd never socialized. It was funny how something like renewed faith in God could bring people together. "So, you wanted to meet."

Kyle shrugged. "I might have a degree in finance not psychology, but I'm gonna guess it can't have been easy dating someone in another state, then dealing with media scrutiny."

He exhaled, postponing the inevitable explanation as the waiter returned with his coffee and took their food orders.

Once the waiter had gone he faced Kyle again. "It's kind of sucked."

"You don't have to tell me anything but if it helps..."

He exhaled. Who else was he going to explain any of this to? His family would mock him, and say it was about time he was taken down a peg or three, and he wasn't aware of any other Christians on the team. But he sensed Kyle was genuine, and the fact he'd prayed for others suggested he might pray for him too. So he spilled his guts, trying as best as he could to not make himself look too much of a wuss, doing his best to shrug it off. "So there you have it."

"Still sucks though."

"Yep. And super awesome to have it all splashed about on the internet."

Kyle winced. "Sorry, dude."

"Yeah."

Their food arrived, which was good timing as he needed something to force the lump in his throat back where it belonged. He didn't do emotion. Not like this, anyway. Yes, he got feisty and in people's faces, but not emotion-of-the-weak variety. He'd worked too hard at his reputation to give the impression of being soft.

By the time he'd finished his vegetable stack, Kyle was waiting. "So, what will you do now?"

"Go back home. Chalk it up to experience. Forget her. Move on."

"Yeah."

That wasn't the sound of agreement. "What do you mean by saying it like that?"

"Well, it's one thing to have the intention, but it's not always easy to forget."

He really didn't want to be asking this, but felt compelled to. After all, the guy had given up his Sunday morning to speak with him. "You sound like you had something similar."

Kyle looked away. "Yeah."

"What happened?"

Kyle's lips tightened then he played with his mug. "We were together most of high school, then we were, ahem, 'together', if you know what I mean, just before graduation." He shrugged. "We weren't Christians. We thought we loved each other."

Mitch nodded. Good thing Georgia could only complain to her brother about Mitch's misguided attempt at a kiss. He didn't want to think about the consequences if he'd tried for something more.

"Anyway, as soon as graduation happened, she dumped me

and went away. I got drafted by New Jersey and went east to play on their farm team and we've never seen each other since."

Wow. "What, never?"

"It was a mess, and way too hard, and she'd moved and so had I."

"Your family didn't keep in touch?"

"My family came with me. We were done over here. Then I got traded back here a few years ago."

"And you never looked for her again?"

"What was the point? She's probably married by now. Nope, that part of my life is done, man. It's over."

Clearly it wasn't if the dude looked so miserable and kept going on about it. But why Kyle was stealing the show with his own *poor me* story when he should be comforting Mitch was not cool. Except, maybe it was. Because keeping the focus off himself was what he wanted. He didn't do pity parties.

"So, what are you doing? You still go out to meet girls?"

Kyle shrugged. "I've wondered about dating apps and stuff like that. I don't know. It's hard to meet someone who's genuine. I see these guys like Mike who have known Bree forever and it just makes sense. It's gotta be so much easier when a guy has known a girl for years, like before you were famous, to being someone who is famous and has money and stuff and so you end up wondering about the motives of the people you meet."

"I know what you mean." Which was one of the reasons he'd liked Georgia. She hadn't been impressed by any of that stuff. "You could meet someone famous yourself like Zac did with Ainsley." Ainsley Beckett, the movie star, who seemed the perfect fiancée for the NHL's best player.

"Yeah, I'm not in the same league as him. Which is good. I don't need that kind of pressure in my life. Can you imagine?"

"I don't want to." Living life in a fishbowl? He'd had a brief taste of it with all the speculation over his "proposal". Yeah, no thanks.

"So yeah. I don't know what to do."

Clearly the dude wanted to get back together with the one who got away. Equally clearly, he was scared to do it. Not that Mitch would say anything about that. They might've shared some pretty real stuff, but they didn't know each other enough for him to be pointing out the obvious. But he could say, "Well, you and me seem to be the only ones who are still single in the group, so we have to look out for each other."

"And Doug Lehtonen," Kyle added.

"Oh, yeah. I keep forgetting about him."

"I won't tell him you said that."

"Probably best not to."

They shared a grin. Doug had been trading on his reputation as a badass for years. The fact he was part of this group felt as crazy as Mitch being part of it himself.

"So, if we don't want the others rubbing our faces in us being single I guess we're going to have to keep this on the down-low."

"Keep what on the down-low?"

"The fact you're going to pray for me and I'm going to pray for you."

"About getting a girlfriend?"

"No, about more than that. I don't want a temporary girl."

Because Georgia was right. Mitch did want to settle down, which meant finding someone who had all the qualities of a one-day wife.

And the fact he'd spent thirty-three years on the planet meant he'd had a lot of time to figure out what he didn't want.

He didn't want someone into him for his fame or money.

He didn't want someone obsessed with her looks.

He didn't want someone who was self-obsessed.

As hard as this weekend had been, he at least now had some clarity about what he wanted the future to look like. And he wanted—needed—someone who would spur him on in his walk

PLAYS BY THE BOOK

with God, someone he could laugh with, relax with, grow old with, and be real with.

That person had never really been Georgia. But whoever she was, wherever she was, he was going to trust God to help him find her. Soon.

# CHAPTER 16

There was a lot to be said for going on a social media detox. Again, this was something she'd shared with her kids as being beneficial for mental health, but actually doing it herself was another thing. She felt more free, lighter, without the weight of comparisons landing heavy on her soul. And while a woman might like to think she was strong and secure, recent events had proved just how much she needed a buffer from the toxicity that lay waiting to pounce.

Avoiding social media was proving as helpful to her state of mind and heart as not watching the news, or avoiding spending time with those of narcissistic tendencies. She could get back to being Britta again, and not that strange creature who'd broken down with Bev last weekend. Ugh. So embarrassing, made more so by the fact that Bev had messaged to say she'd contacted her pastor friends and there were plans to pull something together soon. But still, moving forward had to be the way to go. She'd blocked Mitch's number, muting him on social media so he couldn't reach her. She'd spied him in the library yesterday and had begged Kayla to say she was on her break, then gone and hidden in the staff toilets knowing he couldn't find her there. She'd stayed there until Kayla had texted to say he'd gone. She'd do all she could to get him out of her system. She couldn't hanker after someone who hankered after someone else. A woman couldn't force a man to love her.

She drew in a deep breath, shoved the book back into its correct place, and continued with her reshelving endeavors. Just as books had their rightful place, so did people. And while she might like to think she lived in a world where equal opportunity existed, experience made it plain that was more hope than reality. Celebrities dated and married each other—witness Hallmark star Ainsley Beckett and Zac Parotti. See? A perfect match. People like that didn't go for plain women like her. And that was okay. She had to remind her soul that talking with a handsome man didn't automatically mean he was interested. Obviously there had been way too much romantic fiction in her life for her to believe that. No, instead the kind of person that Bev and her friends would find for her would no doubt be committed to serving in the church, and likely wore glasses, was possibly balding, overweight and had a preference for polyester —all of which didn't matter if he loved her and loved the Lord!

But still, the thought that she would never have a shot with anyone else reminded her that while she loved her fiction, she lived firmly in the non-fiction world. That was obviously where God had placed her.

She finished her reshelving and was wheeling the cart back when she heard her name called. She froze. She recognized that voice. She slowly turned, and sure enough her nemesis stood there.

"Britta, it *is* you." Erica Parker grinned. "Wow. You look exactly the same."

Now this was a lie. Britta owned her figure now and didn't wear the dumpy-looking clothes of ten years ago. But while she might've thought she looked better, that was nothing on Erica who had always owned something of that golden touch, from her hair to her skin to her dad's wealth which got displayed in all the high-end clothing and cars that Britta and her family had never been able to afford. "Hi Erica."

Erica looked at the cart then at her. "I didn't realize you worked here."

"Living the dream."

Erica's eyes widened. "Oh, that's right. I remember seeing something on the news. You had some scare with a thief the other week, didn't you?"

With everything that had happened lately that felt so long ago now. "Yes."

"That must've been so scary."

She pressed her lips together, saw that Margaret was glancing her way again. "I have to get back to work."

"Oh, before you do, did you get the invitation to the ten-year reunion? I don't recall seeing your name on the RSVP list."

Because she hadn't thought about it since the invitation appeared. "I've been a little busy lately."

"Right, of course. Well, we'll need an answer soon. I'll send you an email with a link to RSVP, if that's easier."

No *way* did she want to give this woman her personal email. But seeing Erica was standing there, in the library, hassling her about this, maybe she could give her library email. So she did.

Erica noted it down. "So many of the others will be there, Tania and Hailey and Drake will be there."

All people who had bullied her. That sounded like good enough reason not to go.

"Anyway, it'd be great for everyone to see you." Erica's gaze trickled down to eye Britta's finger. She smirked. "And your husband or significant other too."

She knew this was bait, begging her to admit she wasn't married. So she nodded instead.

Erica's eyes opened wide. "You *are* married?"

Oh, she was good. There was no way to get out of it now. "No."

Erica's smile flashed alongside the huge diamond adorning her left hand. "I've been married to Drake for two years now."

"Really? Congratulations." Oh, look at this turning the other cheek she was doing. Jesus was no doubt giving her two thumbs-up right about now.

Then she added, "You two seemed to really suit each other." Both beautiful, both loaded, both mean. She sensed that heavenly thumbs-up turning down. *Sorry, Lord.*

"Thanks." Erica fluffed her hair. "I always thought so."

She fake-smiled. "Well, I gotta go."

"Don't let me keep you."

She nodded and went to move the cart, when her name was called again.

She stiffened. Could this day get any worse?

"Oh my gosh," Erica murmured. "Is that Mitchell Reilly?"

"Excuse me." She abandoned the cart and headed to the librarian's office. If she could make a dash to the toilet then—

"Britta?" Mitchell drew closer.

"He knows you?"

The fact her teenage self's bully seemed shocked was incentive enough for her to pause. But she knew this wouldn't go well. She didn't have words to pretend she was all right with him.

"What?" She internally winced, as Mitchell stood before her. She sounded so rude. But she couldn't do nice. Nice led to stirring her foolish imagination into softer feelings she couldn't indulge. She had to be businesslike. Especially now there was an audience. "Is there something I can help you with?"

His brow creased. "Is something wrong?"

She glanced at Erica, who was unabashedly watching them.

She shrugged and then snatched up a book and held it to her chest as a shield. "Nope."

"You haven't answered my messages."

"Did you enjoy those books you borrowed?" she said, loud enough so Erica could hear.

He seemed to realize that they had an audience, glancing at Erica then back at her. "I, uh, yeah. I wanted to talk to you about those."

"I'm sorry, I have work to do. I can't do that now. Maybe later." Like maybe in a hundred years when she didn't feel so edgy around him.

"But—"

"Britta, you are needed here," Margaret called. "Now."

Never had she ever been so glad to have Margaret interrupt. "Gotta go. Excuse me." And she hurried back to the office and blinked hard against the tears.

THE UNSETTLING ENCOUNTERS kept her company for the rest of the day, and through the online leaders' meeting that night, then Friday's organizing meeting for the community event this weekend.

Gwen glanced around the conference room at the staff and volunteers who had been coerced into the family community event. It was always a huge day, and the predicted fine weather meant they should get good crowds.

Gwen's gaze landed on her. "Now Britta, are you sure you're okay to be in the Bookmobile this Saturday?"

Britta nodded.

"You won't be alone," Gwen assured.

Because the new guidelines emailed to all staff this week had made it clear that people now needed a second person with them, whether they be paid staff or volunteer. Of course, that reduced the amount of hours of availability, which meant people couldn't get the books they wanted as often as they liked. How awful that this had happened on her watch. She knew it wasn't her fault, yet still felt personally responsible for people not getting the books they needed.

"I'll be fine," Britta mumbled.

"Great. We'll have cupcakes, thanks to Carol, and a second-hand book display with those library books removed from circulation. Plus the children's department have their brand new books to distribute."

Britta nodded. One of the best initiatives was how the library gave free books to families to encourage them to build their own libraries at home and promote literacy. God bless those who donated money—and books—and enabled this to happen.

"And don't forget your costumes, people."

Dress-ups again. Anything to get kids to stop and talk, which meant dragging out the princess costume again.

"Okay, well, we look forward to seeing a great response tomorrow."

She nodded.

She had Red Jellybeans tonight then hopefully she'd sleep well and be ready for tomorrow. And if she never saw Mitchell or Erica again, life could be wonderful.

"Okay, everyone knows what to do?" Daisy asked.

He nodded. Honestly, the team's community liaison officer was like a stubborn bull. She'd been on his case all week.

After returning from Seattle he'd wanted to see Britta and tell her what had happened, but it was like she refused to see him. He could've sworn he'd seen her in the library a time or two, but she always seemed to disappear when he was there. Just like his Insta account must've when she didn't answer any of his messages. And while he didn't want to be insecure, he was getting flashbacks of Georgia ghosting him again. But Britta seemed too mature for that. She'd talk about what was bothering her, not hide. And while she'd talked to him two days ago, he'd sensed her tension. But maybe that was because of the other woman standing there, all varnished and glossy, watching them like one of those fancy cats, waiting to pounce.

"So Mitch, we'll have you and Jack standing there, and a selfie center there." Daisy pointed to the other spot. "Okay?"

"Yep."

The community day was their last big event before training camp began next week. There'd be fan ops there, but this was different. They'd joined with a bunch of community organizations, and it was another chance to encourage people to look beyond the Vikings as the Twin Cities' number one sporting team.

Daisy had asked them to arrive ready for a ten o'clock kick-off, which meant he'd had little time to look around, but already he could see this place was popular. They were here for two hours then teammates for another shift would come. Some of these vendors would be here all day.

"Hey, Mitch!"

Good. Little kids he could cope with. They didn't have the kinds of questions some older nosier adults had. Adults, like some of his teammates who had teased about the stupid proposal thing that seemed to have mostly died its death as new vacuous news took its place.

He smiled and signed autographs and handed out player cards and took photos. He could fake it for a while then he'd need to get a coffee or can of pop for another energy hit. The past week of training had taken it out of him. Or maybe that was emotional turmoil.

When he was finally released for a break, he took a walk

around the site with Jack, where they soon found Jack's wife Lena and their kids.

"Hey, Lena." He kissed her cheek, then crouched to high-five the boys. "Dudes."

"Hi Uncle Mitch." They slapped his hands hard and he smiled.

"How are you Mitch?" Lena asked. "I saw the gossip about you last week."

"Yeah, all lies."

"Oh! I thought Jack said you were going to see your girlfriend."

"That's over."

"I'm sorry."

He shrugged. Funny how something that had seemed so huge now seemed so dumb. He hadn't realized just how wrong they were for each other until that moment. And Georgia was right. He wanted what Jack had, to have a wife and a family, and Georgia didn't. They were in different stages of life. So, good for her for recognizing that when he'd been too blind to realize it himself.

"So, who's going on a ride?"

"Me, me!" yelled Toby and Isaac.

Mitch glanced at Jack, who nodded. "Just don't feed them too much sugar."

"I can't promise not too many corn dogs though."

"You wouldn't," Lena said.

Jack sighed. "He would."

Mitch bit back a smile. "You two have fun now, y'hear?"

"Honestly, it's like the man grew up on a ranch or something," Jack teased as he wrapped an arm around his wife and walked away.

"Did you grow up on a ranch?" Toby demanded.

"Yeah, a little one. Out in Washington state."

Isaac tugged on his jersey. "Do you have cows and horses?"

"Yep." Not that Minnesota was lacking in either of those departments.

"Could we come visit one day?"

"Uh… actually, yeah you could. My brother Jackson runs the ranch, and my mom and sister run a ranch stay." And they could always do with more paying guests. "I'll mention it to your mom and dad and see what they say."

"Yeah! That'd be awesome. You're the best, Uncle Mitch."

And right now he felt pretty chuffed. See, he could do this token uncle thing. He took the kids to the rides—pretty tame ones, nothing like what was on offer at the State Fair—and paid for their tickets and took some photos as they went on the merry-go-round.

"Look at me!" Toby called, astride a giant plastic panda.

"I can see you there, buddy."

His heart tugged. Imagine having kids of his own like these two.

The ride ended and Toby and Isaac grinned as they joined Mitch again. "That was fun."

He ruffled Toby's hair. "You looked like it."

"Hey, can we go get some cotton candy?"

"Sure." He paid for two huge puffs of pink sugar. The thought of eating all that sugar made him sick but they seemed to enjoy it, their little faces getting sticky. His heart softened. These two really were "oh fer cute" as the locals around here might say.

"Uncle Mitch, can we get a free book?" Toby asked, pointing to an A-frame sign that advertised that.

"Absolutely, but you probably need to wash your hands first."

"Okay."

A nearby hand-sanitizer pumping station saw several squirts and rubbed hands that he hoped were clean enough for the books.

The books…

His mouth dried as he saw where the kids were leading him. The Bookmobile. The very one featured in a recent news report. Along with the very woman who had been in that news report too.

Britta was here. He pulled his ball cap lower, checked for crumbs in his beard or anything else that might make her turn away. He didn't want her to flee.

She stood with a few other ladies outside the Bookmobile, behind a couple of long tables, one of which held books, the other was like a coloring station. She wore a different outfit today, dressed like a medieval princess in a red dress with wide sleeves and a pointy hat that had a pink veil kind of thing floating from the end.

Britta was smiling at a little girl, and his heart clenched. He could just see her with kids of her own. She'd be a great mom, she was so smart, honest, caring. Soft, yet sassy. Kind, yet knew kung fu. Intelligent, yet inspiring. The perfect mom. The perfect wife. The perfect partner.

*His* perfect partner? He blinked, as something like an internal tornado lifted and shifted, scattering all he'd thought he'd known. No. No way. But... maybe? She was a Christian. She encouraged his faith. Enlarged his world. She was fun. But how could she ever trust him when all she'd seen was him trying to get Georgia to notice him? All his life he'd never really done friendships with women—he certainly hadn't with Georgia—but Britta he considered his friend. Would she ever consider being more? Could she ever care about him?

"Uncle Mitch, we want to color," Isaac whined, tugging at his hand.

He swallowed. "Sure." The kids could color but he wondered what Britta would do if she saw him. Run away? Or be polite and play pretend?

Before he could wonder any longer, Isaac had released his hand and was running to the table. "Hi!"

Britta glanced up from where she was helping the little girl. She smiled. "Hello. Did you want to color too?"

Isaac gave a huge nod.

Britta's smile widened. Gee, she had a pretty smile. It made her face light up. "Okay then. Here you go." Her head tilted. "Is your mom or dad nearby?"

"I'm here with Uncle Mitch." He pointed to Mitch.

Britta's gaze followed and Mitch lifted a hand and waved.

Her mouth fell open. She quickly closed it, nodded, and glanced down.

His heart panged again. Anyone would think from that reaction that she wasn't happy to see him. Did she not like him? Is that why she wasn't replying to his messages? What had he done wrong?

"Uncle Mitch, I want to look inside the book bus," Toby said. "Can we?"

"Sure." He slowly followed as Toby scampered to join the little queue waiting to go inside. He didn't need to go inside. There were too many people bustling about and his big body didn't need to get in their way. But neither did he want to make Britta uncomfortable by hanging around out here.

A woman dressed in a Jane Austen outfit bumped into him. "Ope, sorry 'bout that." She glanced up. "Oh, fer real! It's you again."

Her name tag read, "Kayla."

"You remember my name?"

He pointed to his left pec. She glanced down and giggled. "I forgot I had that on."

"So, do you always dress as Jane Austen?"

"Jane Austen, huh? I see someone enjoyed reading *Pride and Prejudice*."

His stomach twisted. "Britta mentioned that?"

"You both talked about it, remember?"

Clearly not.

She eyed him. "She mentioned a few things."

Like what? He wanted to know but didn't want to ask this woman who seemed too eager to gossip. Yet not knowing where he stood with Britta scared him.

And because he didn't like doing scared, he inched closer to where Britta stood, helping Isaac. See, Isaac. Perfect excuse for him to talk to her.

"So, are you Princess Buttercup?" he asked Britta.

Her glance up was swift and too short. "Obviously not, seeing she was supposed to be the most beautiful woman in the world."

Her words stole his. What was he supposed to say to that? There was an edge to her voice and her look that he'd never witnessed before. "Britta."

"There you go." She moved back to help the little girl. "Well done."

"Thanks Britta. You're the best." The little girl hugged her.

"Uncle Mitch, can you help me?" Isaac whined.

"Ah, sure." He glanced at Britta but she seemed to be avoiding his gaze. "Let me just check on your brother. They're my teammate's kids," he added for her benefit.

A glance at the line showed no Toby. He hurried to peek inside, felt the air whoosh from his lungs when he spotted him on the seat where he'd sat when he'd visited a couple of weeks or so ago.

Two weeks. How had so much happened in such a short space of time? How could he and Britta go from feeling like friends to whatever this cold war between them now was? What had he done wrong? He needed to talk to her and find out. Stat.

"Hey Toby, let me know when you're done, okay?"

"Sure thing."

He exited and returned to Isaac at the coloring station. But there was no Britta.

"Hey, Isaac. What happened to the pretty lady who was helping you?"

Isaac shrugged, intent on his coloring, his tongue poking out his mouth in concentration. "She said she had to go."

He just bet she did.

And his heart grew sore.

# CHAPTER 17

*M*aybe it was a coward's exit, but she was glad to put off interactions with Mitchell Reilly. He was dangerous for her peace of mind. For while he'd been kind and actually really cute with looking after his teammate's kids, she didn't want to get to a place where she was imagining him as a father. That wasn't wise. He was with Georgia now, which was great, which was exactly what she had prayed for. So no, she didn't want to talk to him just yet. It was best to avoid him, just like she was avoiding some of the other questions whirling around her head.

Like the fact she had to make a decision about the reunion. The RSVP was due soon.

That she had to make a decision about her job. After the success of last weekend's community event Gwen had encouraged her to put her hat in the ring for Carol's job. Carol had announced this week that she planned to retire at the end of the year to focus on spending more time with her grandchildren. And while Britta hungered for a promotion, she wasn't sure she wanted to work as closely with Margaret as that promotion would entail. She was fairly sure Margaret wouldn't want that either.

She also had to make a decision about whether she'd attend the Wild fan day tomorrow, like she'd always done with Kayla. Kayla had a ticket with Britta's name on it, but she didn't want to go if it meant seeing Mitch. She wasn't ready to have the conversation she sensed he wanted with her. And the way she kept avoiding him was only making it worse. Ugh, she was so immature sometimes.

And she had to make a decision about what to do about the date Bev had set up for her. She had to say yes, obviously, because Bev had set this up with her in mind, but still, a blind date. Maybe that was good, because if the guy saw her beforehand he'd likely give her a hard pass. This way she might get the chance to have a few words of conversation before he said no.

"OKAY EVERYONE, let's put our hands in the air like we just don't care."

The Red Jellybeans did that, even the cool girls. Oh, if only everything in life could be solved by waving one's hands in the air.

"And I want to see who has the best hula-hoop moves. Let's go!"

She laughed as the junior highs took their hip rotations very seriously. They might have invisible hula-hoops but the way these kids were moving, nothing was going to fall any time soon.

"That's great!" She clapped her hands. "Okay, let's take a seat and get ready for Ferdy to share about our story for today."

Ferdy opened his book and went to stand in the front of the room. "Hey guys, today we're going to talk about a really brave woman in the Bible. Who knows any women in the Bible who might be considered brave?"

"Esther!"

"Mary!"

"Deborah!"

She was glad today's message wasn't about Esther. Who could identify with being so beautiful? She never could. Her heart hurt in memory of what Mitch had said last Saturday. She'd known he was teasing, but still her insecurities had spilled with that comment about Princess Buttercup. She grimaced. How could she expose herself like that?

She motioned to a group of boys to stop whispering, and pointed to the front, then her thoughts continued to wander.

She hoped Mitchell hadn't thought she was hinting at a compliment. She hadn't been. There was no point anyway. If he said she was pretty she'd know it was a lie because she didn't look like Georgia, Erica, Astrid or Milla, or anyone else people considered pretty. She shoved her glasses back up her nose. And she hated how her looks were coming to haunt her again. She'd fought this battle many times, but it still came back to taunt her.

*Lord, help me remember that You love me and that's enough.*

Ferdy continued with the story. "And so when the others were running around panicking, we see Jael found her courage and used what she had to save the day. You don't have to be incredibly strong or popular or smart. God will use you if you're listening to Him and ready to step out. This story reminds us we can be strong in the Lord, and in the power of His name. It's God's strength that makes us strong. So trust Him."

He invited one of the girls out the front to pray, and Britta closed her eyes.

That's right. She blinked back emotion. This story had reminded her that she wasn't weak. With God she was made strong. She joined the echoed "Amen".

She lifted her chin. Which meant she could face the future

with all its uncertainties. Even face Mitch Reilly at tomorrow's fan day.


"Ope! Sorry," Kayla called as they bumped their way through the crowds.

Britta hustled close behind her. There were so many people but then there always were at these things. And she and Kayla had come to every single one in the past five years, so she was glad God had given her that reminder to not let fears intimidate her into saying no.

The fans' open days provided opportunities for fans to meet some of the players. She had no need for this as she'd met enough through her work at the library, so that was better left to those who had never had the chance before. But it was fun to celebrate all things hockey, to get excited for the upcoming season.

They watched kids meet their favorite players, people take turns at shooting pucks to win prizes, and plenty more other fun activities.

They were moving to line up for food when a crowd surge pushed her into the path of a woman dressed to the nines wearing a lanyard with all kinds of stickers to suggest she was someone important. "Ope. Scuse me."

The woman scowled then peered at her more closely. "I recognize you."

"I beg your pardon?"

"You're the Bee Girl, aren't you?"

"I don't understand."

The woman tittered. "You and Mitchell were in some photos or something, weren't you?"

Oh. Back when she had been dressed in her bee costume. "That was a while ago."

"Hmm." The woman flicked her a look. No doubt identifying

Britta's plain jersey as the cheap knockoff it was. Then she laughed. "I don't know why he ever…"

"Ever what?" Kayla asked, her gaze narrow.

"Oh nothing." The woman eyed Britta. "Nothing at all."

"She's so rude," Kayla muttered as the woman left.

"The privilege of the beautiful. They feel entitled to comment on others."

"She's not that beautiful. You wouldn't be able to tell under all those layers of makeup anyway."

"Now, now."

"Come on. You know so many people need their filters on Instagram because they have an image to uphold. It's because they don't look like that in real life."

"Well, no image to uphold here," Britta said. "What you see is what you get."

Kayla hugged her. "That's one of the things I like about you. You keep it real."

Wow. Kayla had never said that before. "Thanks."

"I mean it. Like, I bet if you got all dolled up like that chick you could look just as good."

"I doubt it."

"No, seriously. I recently saw a picture of Meghan Markle without her makeup on, and I swear she looks just like my niece."

"You must have a pretty niece."

"She's okay, but not beautiful."

Britta mock-gasped. "You can't say that. That's not very Minnesota-nice of you."

"Maybe I'm just being Minnesota-real."

Britta laughed.

"See." Kayla nudged her. "When you do that, you have this light to you. You kind of glow."

"Please."

"No, I mean it. It's the same as when you smile."

"Did they put drugs in your hotdog?"

Kayla shoved her gently. "Fine. I'll stop, but you need to stop thinking you're not worth it."

She swallowed. Maybe God was talking to Britta through Kayla today.

Makeup was one of those things she'd never felt too sure of. That, and doing anything fancy with her hair. She'd always preferred reading her books than plaiting Barbie's hair. And while she didn't want a Cinderella-like makeover, it probably wouldn't hurt to swallow her pride and ask Astrid and Milla for some tips, especially before the blind date. There was no reason to scare off any dude because of her frizzy hair. Although if a guy was going to be scared off by that, then he wasn't the kind of guy she wanted.

Kayla led the way to their seats and they watched the entertainment prior to the scrimmages.

The team would play in reds versus greens, the practice jerseys different to the usual colors.

The team were introduced and her heart tensed as Mitchell's number 54 appeared. But no, she'd clap for him like she would for every other person out there. A camera gave a close-up of him, and he lifted a hand and smiled. But she could tell his smile was forced. She'd seen a real smile from him and it didn't look like that.

She watched him play, noting his dexterity, the way he and Jack worked together seamlessly. He had skills, this man.

He shot toward the goal and scored and she joined the others in standing as they cheered. He glanced up in the stands and for a second she was sure his gaze locked with hers.

Then a teammate pounded him on the back and she breathed again.

Kayla nudged her. "Did you see that? He looked right at you."

She shook her head. "There's too many people." Besides, why would he? He had Georgia now, didn't he?

"Not too many if you know what you're looking for."

She exhaled. But that was the thing. He wasn't looking for her. And he never had been.

~

"DUDE!" Ryan Guillemette's jaw dropped. "What happened?"

"Did you get into a fight with some scissors?" Luc teased.

Mitchell rubbed his naked chin. "It was time."

"Been a while since you felt some fresh air down there, huh?" Chris winked.

"His version of the revenge haircut," Zac said, smiling.

"How's it going?" Kyle asked.

"Whoa, give a man a chance to answer."

"Are you doing okay?" Mike asked.

Man, there was nothing like a group of guys for prodding him with questions like an eager Grandma. Not that he could remember his grandmother ever getting into his business like this. His grandparents had died when he was little.

"Mitch?" Kyle asked.

Oh, right. "I figured I'd mess with the team's PR girl. We had our team photos yesterday and I shaved it off this morning."

Doug chuckled. "Now that is a Dougie-approved move."

Yeah, he didn't know if the others would approve if he shared the real reason. But he was straining his brain to figure out why Britta still was ignoring him. He was sure he'd seen her at one of the scrimmages. Positive. When he next looked up, it was like she disappeared again. Why did she keep doing that? It was just like at the community day when she'd been there one minute, gone the next. But then she'd said she was a fan of hockey, not of him. So probably that was good for his pride, even though his ego felt plenty fragile right now. And she still refused to answer him. Insecure him was sure she was ghosting him. Was she more like Georgia than he wanted to believe?

His appearance had caused more than a few dropped jaws this morning at practice. Daisy's among them. "What is the point of you having a team photo with your beard on then shaving it off?"

The point? He was trying everything to figure out what it was that might make Britta dislike him. Maybe she didn't like the beard. So he'd change it. He'd change everything for her if he thought it would give him a chance to explain.

"Well, how is it going with you and Georgia?" someone asked in the video call.

He shrugged. "It's not going. We broke up. How do you not know this?"

"Because unlike a proposal that was spread everywhere, there's been nothing said since."

Oh. He'd kind of assumed Kyle would spill the beans, but apparently not. Huh. He supposed there had to be a first time for everything.

The conversation shifted to the others' first games and road trips. Preseason games were an opportunity for teams to figure out their lines and pairings. Mitch's many years on the team meant he was a lock in his position, but others weren't so sure, like the newbies desperate to prove themselves.

"We're playing you next," Luc said.

"Great."

The call soon finished, but Kyle asked for Mitch to stay on. One guess why that might be.

"Dude, you don't seem happy," Kyle said, after the others had gone.

He shrugged. "I'm fine."

"Are you? Are you okay with the whole Georgia thing?"

"I've moved on. I want to find someone who wants a family. I'm not getting any younger."

Kyle nodded. "Yeah, I think it'll be cool to be a dad."

"One day, huh?"

"One day." Kyle pointed at him. "But only if you find the right woman first, huh?"

"You betcha."

ELLIE CALLED him not so long after, demanding to know what was going on. "Because I finally got the truth out of Georgia. You two have broken up and you didn't tell me?"

Another mistake. "I should've done that, huh?"

"You think?"

He sighed.

"Okay, so what's that sigh for?"

"Man, you're pesty."

"You should know."

Yeah, he'd been called that a time or two. He didn't quite have agitator levels though, so he preferred to think of that quality as persistence.

"Do you miss her?"

"Who? Georgia?" he added quickly, realizing how that sounded.

"Whoa, whoa, whoa. Is there something I'm missing? Have you got another lady friend?"

At the moment it didn't feel like it. "No."

"I'm not buying. What's going on, Mitchell John Reilly?"

"Don't you Mitchell John Reilly me."

"I'll Mitchell John Reilly you anytime I like, thank you." She gasped. "There *is* another girl. You're deflecting."

Sometimes he hated that his sister knew him so well. "Look, I wondered if there was, but now she's avoiding me."

"Poor Mitchy."

"Don't."

"Oh, but it's kind of funny, but also kind of sad to think the womanizer has no women interested in him."

Ellie's last comment might not be true, judging from the way

Daisy looked at him sometimes. Still, "I really hate that you say that about me. I'm not a womanizer." Sure, a few years ago he'd had a healthy interest in women. Now he had a healthy respect for women. And he knew what he wanted, and what he didn't. Even if the one he did want didn't want him. Apparently.

"So what are you gonna do?"

"I don't know. I've tried to talk to her but she ignores me."

"I'm getting a sense of déjà vu."

He rolled his eyes. "I really appreciate your support here, sis. Thanks."

"Well, get over yourself. Get back on the horse and try again."

"Yeah? Like how?"

"I don't know. If these two women aren't the right ones for you then find the one that is. Unless you want to stay Uncle Mitchell forever."

He didn't. He'd had a tiny taste of that and now knew he wanted a family for himself. "I just don't know how to find a genuine woman who wants me."

"Are you praying about it?" she demanded.

"What do you take me for?"

"You really don't want me to answer that."

He chuckled, despite himself. "No, I don't think I do."

"Look, there are Christian dating websites and apps."

"I don't want to go on a dating app."

"Don't knock it. It worked for Cooper."

He huffed. "He knew Jess for years."

"Doesn't mean it doesn't work for others. It might work for you. Seriously, you gotta be out there, not hiding at home feeling sorry for yourself."

"Wow. Are all of us Reillys so brutally honest?"

"I think it's part of our DNA."

Huh. Maybe it was. But her words reminded him of another woman who was direct and unflinching in her conversation.

Until she proved to be as misleading as the rest. But then, she'd always said she liked fiction.

"Hey, have fun this week."

"Thanks." A road trip to Dallas to start the preseason, then he'd play back-to-backs at home before a Saturday off, then another road trip to Winnipeg and Chicago, then another game at home. They'd get a few days off before the regular season began, and he'd be playing every two to three days either at home or away. How was he supposed to build any real relationship with a woman with that kind of crazy schedule? God would need to do a miracle to pull that off.

"I'll be praying for you, bro," Ellie said. "That the woman of your dreams will sweep you off your feet."

"And I'll be praying for you and Jasper. That he'll be able to put up with you."

She laughed. "Love you."

"Love you too," he said gruffly. Had he ever said that to her before? Recent events had made him soft.

But the thought she'd pray for him reminded him of another woman who'd said she'd pray for him. The one who was now avoiding him. The other one he was going to have to get over.

# CHAPTER 18

"$\mathcal{A}$re you sure about this?" Britta asked Astrid. "It just looks like a lot."

Astrid wiped on more eyeshadow. "I thought the day would never come when you would ask me and Milla for a makeover. So this is years' worth of makeup today."

"Spackle," she muttered.

"Don't be like that. And spackle is really for those who don't have great skin. And your skin is not bad. Not anymore."

"Gee thanks."

"No, I mean it. You can barely see the acne scars these days."

Acne that had pitted her soul, marring her in ways she preferred to deny.

"And you're a bit pale, but you'll do. Especially with all the color we're adding tonight."

"I just don't want to look like a clown."

"She's so rude," Astrid muttered to Milla.

"I just think that everyone is used to seeing me look pale so I don't want to look like someone I'm not."

"But that's the point of a blind date, isn't it? You don't know these people so you don't have to look like you usually do."

"But what if someone there actually does like me and wants to see me again? Are you offering to do my makeup for the rest of my life?"

"You don't think you're going to be marrying someone you meet tonight, do you?"

But wasn't that the point? The Christian mingle might as well have been named the Last Chance Saloon of the Desperate and Dateless. Her heart clenched. Unless Astrid meant she didn't think any of the guys there would like Britta. She eyed her sister.

"Wait, I didn't mean it to sound like that. Maybe you will meet Mr. Right."

She tried to shrug off the hurt. "You're right though. I probably won't. So it doesn't matter. Do what you want with me. I'm your doll to dress up."

"Finally."

She let her sisters play with her hair and finish her face and nails before they tackled her ensemble. "You can't wear that," Astrid said about the white blouse she'd planned to wear. "It'll make you look washed out."

She couldn't believe anything could make her look washed out with all the color on her face. "Are you sure this makeup isn't too heavy?"

"Trust us."

Well, they were the experts and she was the guinea pig. She pulled out another top. A perfectly serviceable beige blouse over jeans.

"Nope, you can't wear that. It makes you look like a potato."

Milla laughed as Britta protested. "I don't look like a potato."

"You kind of do."

"Talk about rude," she muttered, as Astrid hurried out then back in. "Look what I found."

"Is that my dress?" Milla asked.

"Your too-big dress, remember?" Astrid winked.

Britta withheld a sigh. Always great to be reminded that she was larger than her sisters.

"Now this." Astrid held up Milla's red wrap dress. "This has potential."

"It's too cold for that. And it's probably too small. Plus it's red." Red meant she'd stand out. And wasn't that color traditionally associated with streetwalkers?

"It's got enough stretch that you'll be fine. And you're not going to this event wearing what you wear to work. I'm not letting you wear jeans. And that's final."

"Fine. But how am I going to stay warm?"

"By talking to all those handsome young men."

She rolled her eyes.

But yes, men. Plural. When Bev had contacted her, she'd found out that what she'd thought was a blind date had actually escalated into a combined churches speed date setup.

"For once we started talking, we realized there are a number of singles in our churches, and we thought this would be a great opportunity for you all to mingle and, you know, get to know each other," Bev had said. "You might make some new friends."

Milla studied her, head tilted as Astrid held the red dress up against Britta. "I think the color works."

"Great." Her fake smile slipped into natural. "No, really, I do appreciate your help."

"It'll be fun. And if nothing else, it'll be a good chance to practice talking to guys."

Even that felt fake. The whole evening felt fake. She felt fake. And after years of preaching how important it was to be yourself and to be real, she was starting to have a problem with this.

But after Astrid and Milla worked their magic, and the wrap dress went over black leggings and boots with the belt, cinching her waist, she could see what the fuss was about.

"Wow."

The dress made the most of her curves. Her hair was styled,

looking smooth for once, and the makeup job made her eyes look bigger.

"Are you sure you want to be wearing glasses and don't want to wear contacts?" Milla asked.

"Contacts always hurt my eyes."

Astrid looked at her critically. "Maybe one day you should invest in some new frames, you know, that don't make you look like an old lady."

"Wow. Why don't you tell me what you really think?"

"You're not ready for that."

Britta laughed, and then instantly relaxed. Okay, so tonight would be hard in some ways, but in others, it could be good. Like Bev had said, she'd get the chance to practice talking to guys. Still, it would be good to have a wingman with her. "Are you sure neither of you want to come?"

"I have a date," Milla said.

"And I'm out with the girls from school, but I'll see if I can swing by later," Astrid said. "But to be honest, I don't really want to hang out with all the Christian losers who can't find their own date."

"Wow. Thanks."

"Oh, you're not a loser. There just literally has been no suitable guy come into our church."

"What do you mean by suitable?"

"You know, someone who is smart, and funny, and who likes books as much as you."

"Do you really think he needs to be the same as me? You don't think opposites can attract?"

"Sure they can. But a couple have gotta have enough to hold them together after the attraction fizzles."

"Wow. You're so romantic."

"I'm what's known as a realist, Britta. I don't always have my head in a book or in the clouds."

That was for sure. "Well, thank you for making me look

pretty."

"You *are* pretty." Milla hugged her. "And you need to walk in there and feel confident. You've got a lot to offer."

"Like lots of good book recommendations?"

Astrid laughed. "And a sense of humor."

"Fine. I'll go slay."

"You do that."

ALL THOUGHTS of slaying disappeared as she entered the church hall's front door. Other nervous-looking people glanced at her. And while she had felt cool at home, right now she felt over-dressed. Why were others wearing jeans when her sisters had insisted she wear this dress? And she looked *so* made-up in comparison to the others. And yes, she could see why people might think Christians were boring because it looked like some of these women were just like her and didn't know a mascara wand from a hair tong.

*Lord, I don't want to do this. I want to go home. I want You to magically make my Mr. Right fall from the sky and land in front of me.*

But running away wasn't going to help her be brave. And it wasn't going to help her show the Red Jellybeans what courage looked like. And while she might be overdressed in comparison with some, at least she wouldn't be overlooked.

She moved to where a woman sat behind a table wearing a cardigan and a smile and a name tag that read *Deirdre*.

"Welcome, welcome," Deirdre said. "It's good to have you here."

Her heart was racing, as every fiber within longed to back right on out. "Thanks."

"Now, you are…?"

"Britta."

"Wonderful. Please, put on your name tag," she did so, "take your card and pen and go inside to meet the others. Help your-self to a glass of pop and mingle."

She nodded. Pop. No champagne or cocktails here. They might've helped. She stifled a laugh, and quickly downed a glass of lemonade then took a glass of water.

She entered, and sure enough, the room was filled with people who looked a lot like she did normally. Ordinary. Plain. Glasses. The Marys of the Bennet family, not the Elizabeths, Lydias or Janes. Still, the fact they were all here meant they attended church, so that was something they had in common at least. And if they attended church, there was a high chance they were Christians. She didn't think that Bev would put her into this mix if there weren't a couple of suitable contenders. And for someone who had preached her whole life about not judging a book by its cover, she shouldn't be making assumptions. Especially when she knew just how painful it felt to be on the other side of such judgment.

She headed to a couple of other women who looked equally nervous. Still, the fact they were here and they had likely come with an equally genuine goal to meet a partner meant they weren't so dissimilar to her. So she acted as she usually did whenever new people attended the Red Jellybeans, and smiled.

"Hi, I'm Britta. I'm so glad I'm not the only one here tonight."

They introduced themselves, then the chestnut-haired one—Leanne—murmured, "I didn't know what to expect, but I kind of hoped there would be at least one handsome guy here."

Britta winced, remembering her own similar thoughts. *Sorry, Lord.* "I'm sure they all have good hearts. I know I'm no beauty, so I hope others can see past that and give me a chance."

"Oh, I didn't mean to sound like that. It's just that single Christian guys can seem a bit boring sometimes. Like all they want to do is get married and have five children."

"Well, I haven't met many single Christian guys, so I guess we'll see if that proves true tonight."

Leanne frowned, like she didn't get Britta's joke. Which was fair enough because it was only really half a joke. Would the guys who came tonight fit that stereotype or not?

Others entered, and their host asked them to take a seat. Britta joined the others in taking a little plate and filling it with a selection of cheese cubes, crackers and grapes, not that nerves let her eat any. She took another sip of water. Wearing this dress had reminded her that she should probably be a little more careful about her diet. She'd felt a hum since the Bookmobile attack that suggested her body was still recovering and didn't need extra stress from sugar highs and crashes.

"Now this is how tonight will work," Deirdre said. "You'll each have five minutes with a member of the opposite sex before a bell will ring and you will move on to the next person. I will give a verbal warning at four and a half minutes so you know to wrap up the conversation. Please check the name of anyone you would like to meet again and then at the end you'll hand your card in and we'll see which of those match up. Of course, if you are confident enough, you are welcome to make the most of those connections yourself. Unlike some speed dating scenarios, everyone here is part of a church and has been vouched for by someone who is in Christian leadership, so we're not expecting any abductions or assaults."

A titter of amusement rippled across the room, but Britta couldn't laugh. Sweat was slicking down her back, pooling under her arms. Oh, she hoped this dress wouldn't show wet patches.

"I'll give you a moment to finish your snacks and for the ladies to take their seats then we'll get started."

She glanced at where her name sat on a card waiting for her. Lamb, meet slaughterhouse. She glanced at the place card next to hers: Leanne. Well, at least she'd have a friendly fellow victim to commiserate with.

"Okay, ladies, you'll stay seated and the gentlemen will move clockwise. And remember to take turns in asking questions and in giving your answers." Deirdre tinkled the bell. "You may now begin."

Britta took her seat and smiled as the first man took his place. He held out his hand and she shook it. "Hi, I'm Britta."

"Jon." He smiled.

He had a nice smile, although he owned a few extra pounds too. She could imagine if they were to get married they'd be the tubsy twins before too long.

"Britta sounds like you're Norwegian."

"My mother's side."

"Do you know how to make Tater Tot hotdish?"

Did she—? "Is this one of your questions?" she teased.

He eyed her seriously. Oh, okay. He didn't share her sense of humor, apparently. So perhaps it was.

Food seemed to be a favorite topic of his, as his next questions were in a similar vein. Then he asked, "Do you have any family diseases I should be aware of?"

Wow. "Like diabetes?"

His face closed, his nose wrinkling in dismay.

She wouldn't take it personally, and persisted. "What's your favorite book?"

"Do you mean of the Bible?"

Oh. "I guess we can mean that."

He shook his head. "I don't read anything but the Bible. The rest is sin."

Okay, well that was an easy cross against his name.

The bell rang and she thanked him for his time and the next man took his place.

Dwight wore a *Star Trek* T-shirt and had long dark hair that fell into his eyes. And while she didn't want to judge people, she couldn't help but think he looked a bit like a serial killer.

"Red pill or blue pill?" he asked without preamble.

"Excuse me?" Did she look like she did drugs?

"It's a *Matrix* reference."

"Oh, okay. Well, in that case, neither."

He looked disappointed. "You have to give an answer."

"In that case the red pill."

"Like your dress." His gaze dipped to her neckline.

Ugh. "I guess."

He nodded, like that was the correct answer.

"You?"

"I'm the blue pill."

He was definitely something, that was certain. She asked about his favorite book and he said *The Hitchhiker's Guide to the Galaxy*. Well, at least this man read fiction. She shared about *Pride and Prejudice* then it was his turn again.

"Do you identify more with Shrek or Donkey?"

"Uh, Shrek?"

"I think you're more of a donkey."

"Scuse me? And you know this how?"

He shrugged. "Just a feeling I got."

Good to know. "Okay, well how about you? Shrek or Donkey?"

"Definitely Donkey."

That was true. The man was definitely a donkey. "Okay, my turn to ask a question. Are you a hockey or football fan?"

"Neither."

"Seriously?"

He shrugged. "I like sci-fi and video games."

Of course he did. Strike two.

The bell rang and after Britta thanked Dwight for his time, the third guy came along. He was dressed a lot more formally than the others. She held out her hand. "Hi, I'm Britta."

He shook her hand, reluctantly it seemed, and nodded. "I can tell from your name tag. I'm Mark."

Like she couldn't do the same. "Hi Mark."

She glanced at her list of questions, but before she could ask he said, "What church do you go to?"

She told him, and his face fell. "Oh."

"How about you?"

He told her, then proceeded to give a list of the ways their churches differed in theology, most of which seemed to suggest her church was in the wrong.

She glanced at her notes again, but before she could ask her question, he said, "How many kids do you want?"

"I think it was my turn to ask," she said.

"You are the woman, I am the man, so I don't have to submit to you."

She crossed her arms and arched her brow. Yep, that was another solid no.

The silence pulsated between them, and her left leg started to twitch. She was glad when an interruption drew attention to the door.

Deirdre stood there. "Oh, I'm so sorry to interrupt."

"Don't be," Britta whispered.

Leanne glanced at her and murmured, "Right? Mark is so rude."

"It appears we have a last-minute addition," Deirdre called. "Another man."

Britta smiled at her new friend and raised her brows.

"Hallelujah," Leanne murmured. "I hope he's handsome."

Or at least not a chauvinist, Britta thought. She was getting a headache. This room was too warm.

She peered behind her to see who stood beyond their host. Gasped. Then turned around, sinking in her chair.

In the course of his career, Mitch had had many moments that could be counted as humiliating. But few were as all-encompassing as this. Why had he allowed himself to get talked into this? That's right. Nobody had talked him into it. It had just randomly popped up on his social media feed. How the mighty had fallen to be reduced to trying to pick up a chick in a Christian mingle speed dating event.

He glanced over the contenders. Yep, sure enough the guys looked exactly like he expected. Like the nerds from school had mated with the holy geeks and spawned, leaving their children to die here in a vat of awkwardness. The women didn't look much better, all variations of the same. And while he knew he wasn't supposed to be filled with pride or be prejudiced—that book had a lot to answer for—he still hoped to find someone who might connect with him beyond believing in Jesus. But it didn't look like any of the women here knew what hockey was, let alone could appreciate a game.

Except... why was that woman in red at the back not looking at him? Everyone else was. She stood out, not just because of the bright color of her dress but because she remained seated with her back to him. He frowned. It was kinda hard to tell, but there was something familiar about her...

"Okay, well, I'm afraid it means we have one more young man than we have ladies. Oh, wait, we have another late arrival. Can I help you?"

Mitch pivoted to face the woman. She smiled at him, then her eyes widened. "Wait, I know you. What are *you* doing here?"

"Uh..." How to answer that without sounding lame. "The same thing as you, I guess."

She frowned. "I'm here as my sister's wing woman."

Man, that would've been a good idea. "Who's your sister?"

She scoffed. "Come on. You know her."

"I do?" He didn't recognize any of the women here.

"Yeah." She pointed at the other end.

Where the woman in the red dress had finally turned around

and was looking at him. His heart skipped a beat. Then another two.

"Britta."

But unlike any Britta he'd ever seen before. He swallowed. She might be sitting down but she could've been dancing a solo on the dance floor like Luc's dancer wife for all he noticed anyone else. That red dress was hot, her hair and makeup... "Wow."

The woman next to him chuckled. "She looks good, huh?"

"She looks so different."

"And the best looker here tonight, right?"

He couldn't drag his eyes away, even though Britta had turned away and wasn't facing him anymore. He'd never forget seeing her eyes widen in surprise, her lips in a perfect pout.

"So, I guess if you're here then you haven't proposed like they said."

"Proposed?"

"To Georgia. Your girlfriend, right?"

"She's not my girlfriend." He winced. "Wait. She thought that?"

"That's something you should ask her."

He glanced at her. "Who are you, by the way?"

"Astrid. Britta's older younger sister."

"There's another?"

"Milla. But she's out on a date." She smiled up at him. "So what else do you want to know?"

# CHAPTER 19

*I*t was quite possible that the lightheaded feeling she was experiencing was not due to low blood sugar. That instead, it was the sight of her sister talking to Mitchell Reilly that was enough to make the blood rush tsunami-like through her system. She had to get out of here. But then the thought of why on earth he was here when he had a girlfriend— or was it now fiancée?—made her pause.

Deirdre-of-the-Cardigan clapped her hands. "Right, well, I guess we'll start this round again, and perhaps you two could take this seat here and begin."

What? No. She had no desire to talk to Mark a second longer. And no desire to see her sister talking to Mitch. Did he know Britta was Astrid's sister? The night that had already felt challenging enough was getting worse by the second.

"Well?" Mark coughed, reclaiming her attention. "I don't know what people see in people like that."

"Excuse me?"

He jerked his chin at where Mitchell and Astrid were now talking.

She peeked across. Were they talking about her? Or was that just her insecurity talking? Why did he have to be so far away? She still had another five guys to get through before he'd be able to talk to her. And she desperately wanted to know why he was here. What had happened to Georgia?

"I see you're just like the rest of them."

She dragged her attention back to Mark. "I beg your pardon?"

"You. You're like every other woman I've ever met. You want to talk to the handsome dudes, not the ordinary ones like us."

"I don't think that's fair."

He pshawed. "Please. I know your type."

"My type?"

He gestured to her outfit. "You'd do anything for a man's attention, with all your makeup and clothing that says 'look at me, look at me'."

"Yeah, you sure know me so well." She narrowed her gaze at him, her irritation bubbling over. "I think you'll find the lack of women interested in you has got more to do with your attitude and the way that you speak to women, not how you look."

He coughed. "I can't believe you said that to me."

"Well, if this is you putting your best foot forward, then you might want to reconsider how you come across, and not go putting it in your mouth."

"I don't need to listen to this."

"You probably do if you actually want to get married. And I —"

"You're wrong."

"No, please talk over the top of me because I *love* it. In fact, every woman on the planet likes to be ignored, and told that they're wrong. So you have fun trying to find a woman who will deal with that."

"She's not you, that's for sure."

"One hundred percent."

"I wouldn't want a painted trollop as my wife."

She blinked as a rush of blood went to her head. "How dare you?"

The other conversations ceased as their hostess came closer. "I'm sorry, what seems to be the trouble here?"

Britta pointed a finger at Mark. "He called me a painted trollop."

There was a collective gasp.

"Oh dear me, no. You must've misunderstood."

Leanne put up her hand. "I heard him."

"She made me say that." Mark glared. "She was being disrespectful, and I don't tolerate disrespect."

"Disrespect?" Britta pushed her chair back, snatched her bag and stood. "You're the one who is disrespectful, and doesn't know how to speak to a woman."

She turned and hit a large chest. "You!"

Mitch steadied her, then scowled down at Mark. "Did he really insult you?"

"He called her a painted trollop," Leanne murmured helpfully.

"No way," Astrid muttered, eyes slitted.

Britta's cheeks heated to firestorm levels, and would probably soon cause the "paint" Mark found so objectionable to slide off.

"A what?" Mitch asked.

She didn't want to hear it again. She'd known dressing like this was a mistake. This wasn't her. She couldn't bombshell her way into a relationship even if she had dynamite. Dizziness caused her to stumble. She had to get out of here. She inched to the side.

"Stay," Mitch whispered.

"But—"

"He owes you an apology."

He sure did. But she wasn't feeling good, was feeling light-headed, shaky.

"Look, I don't know who you think you are," Mark said to Mitch, "but you can't come in here and tell me how to speak."

"No, but I can tell you that this woman here doesn't deserve your disrespect. She's an amazing, kindhearted Christian woman, and you need to treat her and speak to her as you should a sister in Christ."

"But—"

"But *nothing*. Britta deserves an apology."

"How do you know her name?"

"She's wearing a name tag," Mitch said, like Mark was an idiot.

She bit her lip, trying to hold back a hysterical laugh as Mark muttered something that might've been an apology.

She was all set to accept it when Mitch said, "What was that? I didn't hear you."

Mark heaved out a loud breath. "I'm sorry. And I'm sorry that I ever came here. I just want a wife who can help my ministry. I don't have to like her, or find her attractive. Why is that so hard?"

"Mark, I think it would be best for all concerned if you were to leave," Deirdre said finally. "I don't feel like you are a fit for what we're trying to do tonight."

Mark stood, and he scowled at Britta but she crossed her arms. "You're welcome to her," he spat at Mitch.

"I'm not yours to give," she shot back, as Mark exited.

She felt a shift in the air and glanced at Mitch to see he was holding back laughter. Was he laughing at her? Did he think her makeup was too much? Oh, she wished she knew what he was thinking. And what on earth was he doing here anyway?

She moved, bumped into a chair, and staggered. Mitch swooped to catch her, and held her shoulders. "Hey."

"What are you doing here?" she whispered.

"What are *you* doing here?" he murmured back.

"Making a fool of myself?"

"You? Never."

"You'd be surprised."

He smiled, and her heart jogged a little. Oh, she definitely wasn't feeling well.

The hostess clapped her hands. "Right, well, we should probably get back into it. But now we are one man down I'm afraid we'll have to have one of the ladies sit out for a turn."

"I'm not staying," Astrid called.

"You're not?"

Astrid shook her head, and winked at Britta, then moved to the door.

Her heart sank. Was that because she and Mitch had made plans?

"How about you?" Mitch asked. "Are you wanting to stay, Britta?"

And feel the sting of being called painted trollop for the rest of the night? But better that than being forced to wonder about what Astrid and Mitch had talked about. Nausea rippled within. Maybe there was someone nice here whom she hadn't met yet. She planted her feet more firmly to stop the shakes.

"If you're staying, can I be your next date?" he asked.

She blinked. "You?"

He nodded, his lips tweaking. "It's felt like forever since we talked. And you and I both know there are things we need to say."

HE WATCHED AS SHE HESITATED. The makeup, which did so much to carve contours on her face, could not hide her embarrassment. Indignation heated his chest. How dare that guy before be so rude? He'd like to do women the world over a favor and slapshot him. Poor Britta. Was that why she didn't want to talk to him now?

She wet her bottom lip. "Mitch, I…"

"It doesn't have to be here," he said quickly. "Anywhere."

"And Georgia?"

"That's what I want to talk about."

She studied him a moment, then slipped back into her seat. "Okay." She closed her eyes, wincing like she might be in pain.

"Are you okay?" he whispered.

"I have a headache." She sipped her water.

"You're staying?" the hostess asked. "Oh wonderful. Now, Mitchell, perhaps you can take this seat opposite Britta. Actually, no, the other couples have already spent far too long with each other. I'm sorry but I'm going to have to ask you to move to the next one."

"But I want to talk to Britta."

"And you can when it's your turn. I don't want to have to remind you that you came late."

He cut a look at Britta, saw her lips twist into a wry smile, and yeah, okay, the idea of this old lady in a cardigan ordering him around must look a little amusing. "Are you sure you want to stay?"

She bit her lip, then gripped the edge of the table as she stood. "Actually, I've changed my mind." She glanced at the hostess lady. "I'm really sorry but I don't feel well. I think I need to go."

"I understand. That young man before was certainly *not* what we imagined when we set this up."

"Thank you for your hard work." She nodded to the others. "Good luck to you all."

"You too," they chorused back. Apart from the brunette who had been sitting beside Britta. Her gaze kept swinging between Britta and himself, and the twist to her mouth suggested she didn't like what she saw.

Well, too bad. He turned to Britta. "Let me walk you out."

"I don't need you to."

She kind of looked like she did. She was trembling. "I want to." He saluted the hostess. "Thank you, and good night."

"You said that like a TV host," Britta murmured as they left the room.

She reached the coat rack, pointed to a gray coat. He handed it to her, but she couldn't do the buttons, her fingers were shaking so much.

Aww. Poor thing. That guy had really done a number on her. "Here, let me help."

She jerked away. "I'm fine."

She clearly wasn't, but he didn't want to add to her stress. "Look, I don't want to be presumptuous, but—"

"Are you two leaving?" Astrid, the sister, stood from the chair where apparently she'd been waiting in the foyer. She narrowed her eyes, and he could see the family resemblance. "You better not mess with her."

"Astrid," Britta protested, blushing.

"I'm not messing with anyone," he said.

"Right, you better not be. I have a tracker on her phone and if she's not back at a reasonable hour then I'm going to hunt you down."

His lips curved. "I see feisty runs in the family."

"Only us two. Milla is far more mild."

He glanced at Britta. "Does that mean I can take you?"

"Take me where?"

"Anywhere you want."

"But I drove here."

She didn't look like driving was a good idea now. Britta seemed really out of it. Her face held a sheen of sweat.

"Oh my gosh, Britta. He's asking you out on a date."

"Well, actually, I just wanted a chance to talk."

Britta's cheeks flushed to a new red. She ducked her head. Shivered. "I think I should go home."

"But you promised."

"I'm really tired now."

"Is that girl-speak for you're embarrassed?" he teased.

She shook her head. "I'm sorry. I really need to go to the bathroom."

Huh? "Britta, wait."

But she was stumbling away, and he didn't want to chase her. That wasn't a good look. Given all that had happened before, he didn't want to look like a stalker.

"Is she okay?" he asked Astrid.

"I'll go check."

He didn't know how long he waited in the foyer. Long enough to hear a couple of bells ring from the function room. Maybe Britta was sick. Maybe she was sick of him. No, it wasn't that. Was it?

He blew out a breath, clasped the back of his head as he read the noticeboard. He probably needed to find a church he could visit, maybe one day join, even though his playing schedule wouldn't allow for too many Sunday services. From what he gathered from the other guys in the online Bible study group, church attendance was a bit hit-and-miss, hence the need for gathering together online. He wondered which church Britta attended.

By the time Astrid and Britta appeared, it was obvious that Britta wasn't well. Obvious, too, that she'd been crying. There were smears under her eyes where her makeup had been.

His stomach dropped. "Britta."

Astrid shook her head at him. "She needs to go home."

"I can take her."

"Yeah, no. I think she needs family right now."

"Is there anything I can do?"

"You could pray."

He watched as the strong woman he'd once called a ninja was led by her sister to the parking lot. He followed, not knowing what to do but hating feeling so helpless.

Astrid led her to a car then opened the passenger door and encouraged Britta to get in. Then closed the door. Britta put her seatbelt on, then slumped against the window.

"There must be something I can do," he said.

"Look, there really is nothing except pray."

"What happened?"

Astrid glanced at him. "She had a hypo."

"A what?"

"She sometimes gets low blood sugar and has these attacks. She used to have a lot when she was in high school, which is why she was bullied so much."

"What?"

Astrid's hands clenched. "Some days I would like to throttle some of those people who did things like that. She's struggled with her self-esteem ever since. Even though she tries to hide it."

"But she's amazing."

"I know. But hide it as she does, she still struggles with thinking she's worthy."

"Of course she is."

"I don't just mean that 'God loves her and Jesus died on a cross for her' kind of worthy. I mean the fact that tonight was the first date she's ever had."

"What, ever?"

She jerked her chin, her eyes glistening. "And that fool before has made her second-guess everything again."

No. Poor Britta. He glanced at her, still slumped against the window.

"Which is why she got so stressed, and then you showed up and started acting like you were gonna take her out on the date, and then you said you wouldn't." She snarled at him. "Is it any wonder she had another attack?"

"I…" Had he acted like that? "I didn't realize. I'm sorry."

"Uff da. Yeah, well Britta doesn't like to mention it, but if you're gonna act like you care, then you probably need to know."

"Know what?"

She eyed him. "Britta has diabetes."

# CHAPTER 20

*S*he hadn't had an episode like this in years. Not since her senior year when stress had made her miss a bunch of days at school after one bullying attack too many. Stress did that to her. Had always done that. And since the attempted Bookmobile robbery and then Mitchell's proposal had made her realize she'd fallen for someone she shouldn't, she'd felt a low hum of stress rippling through her body that had peaked when Mark the Neanderthal had said what he had in front of Mitch.

Then, when she'd heard Astrid say what she had, her humiliation, which she thought was complete, had discovered new depths of utter misery.

She hadn't gone to church yesterday. Had missed today at work. She knew Mitch had a road trip and had gone away but she wouldn't blame him if he never came back to see her again. Why would he? She had a vague memory that he might've said a few nice things on Saturday night but she couldn't recall the details. How could she, when all she was conscious of was the fact that he'd pitied her. *Pitied* her. Rightly so, but still. He now knew the reason she loved fiction so much was because she got to live her happily-ever-afters vicariously through books, not in real life.

A tap came at the door, then the door opened and her mom came in. "Hey honey, how are you feeling?"

"I'm still tired."

"Hmm. What's your latest blood sugar reading?"

"70."

"That's still too low for my liking. We may need to take you to the doctor if you still feel like this tomorrow."

Hypos meant she needed to regulate her carbohydrate intake, to make sure the sugar releasing into her system was of the slow-release kind, not the quick churn-and-burn of sweet things like lemonade or chocolate that contributed to fast highs but even faster drops. When her body experienced too many fast falls like that, it struggled to keep up, which then affected other internal organs and compounded her health issues. She was usually careful with her fuel intake. Obviously stress had made her careless.

Her mom was usually pretty patient, but her nursing background meant she took things like this seriously. "I want you to be careful."

"I'll be better tomorrow." She had to be. Today's Bookmobile visit had been canceled because she couldn't be the second person they needed. She couldn't be responsible for more cancellations.

She dozed a little more, too tired to even read a book, and woke when Astrid returned from work and tapped on the door, then walked in without waiting for a reply, just as she usually did. Her sister, the traitor. Even though she masqueraded as an angel of good.

"Hey, how is the patient?" Astrid pulled out Britta's desk chair.

"A little better, but I'm still exhausted."

"You poor thing."

*You poor thing.* The words that had reverberated through the years. Pity for being the ugly sister, the dateless sister, the one overlooked because personality and character and grades didn't matter as much as looks. Oh, she hated pity.

She peered at Astrid. Yesterday she'd been too tired, but right now she had to push through the mental fog and be honest. The longer she left it, the more this played on her mind, and the harder this conversation would be.

"What is it?" Astrid asked.

"How could you say that about me?"

"What are you talking about?"

"I heard you on Saturday night." Her eyes filled with tears. "How could you humiliate me like that?"

"What do you mean?"

"You told him."

"Are we talking about Mitchell?"

She nodded. "You told him about me. I heard you. If I wanted him to know, then I might as well get a loudspeaker and yell into it and tell him myself."

"Britta, you're not making sense."

She tried really hard to focus, to make her thoughts and words coherent. "You told him I was sick."

"Come on. It was obvious you'd just puked."

She cringed. How bad had she looked? "But you didn't need to tell him I've got diabetes."

"Britta, he was concerned."

"I don't know why."

"Don't you?"

Oh, this was too hard to understand. Maybe she shouldn't attempt to go back to work tomorrow seeing she couldn't make sense of anything right now. But there was something else she wished Astrid hadn't said. "But you said…" What was it? It had been there a second ago. Oh, that's right. "You said… you told him that I've never had a date."

Astrid bit her lip. "You heard that?"

"Yes! How do you think that made me feel?"

Astrid came to sit on the edge of her bed. Britta lacked the energy to push her off.

"I'm sorry."

"Now he just thinks I'm pathetic."

"I'm sure he doesn't think that."

How could Astrid know? What had he and Astrid talked about? "What was he doing there anyway?" What had happened to Georgia? Oh, she was too tired for any of this to make sense.

Astrid sighed. "Look, I really think you should talk to him."

But talking to him meant having to cope with his pity, meant being vulnerable, and it felt like she'd already exposed—or been exposed by her sister—enough already. If he cared then why hadn't he contacted her somehow? He might be away on a road trip, but he'd sent flowers before. Why couldn't he again? Wasn't that just proof he didn't care? Or was that just sickness-induced unreasonableness? She still felt dizzy most of the time so that she didn't know what was going on.

"I can't talk to him," she said petulantly. "I'm off social media, and I've blocked him."

"Then unblock him."

Her eyes filled. Oh, she *hated* being so weak.

"Hey." Astrid held her hand. "Hey, it's okay."

"I don't know what's wrong with me." She wiped at a stupid tear. "I'm such a mess."

"You're sick. You're allowed to not have it all together."

"I don't have anything together." She sniffled. "I can't believe he saw me dressed like that." *Look at me, look at me…* Ugh! *Lord, take Mark's words away.*

"You looked amazing. He even said that."

"He did?"

"Yes."

But why would he say that when he was going out with Georgia? Or was that simply her being overly sensitive about what guys in relationships should say to other girls? What did she know anyway? Were they even together? How could they be? "I don't know what to do."

"Let the man talk to you."

"But I don't want to get hurt." And she'd already proved she didn't have the strength to take the thoughts captive that longed to whirl into romantic fantasy.

"Britta, give him a chance to explain. I get the feeling he wants to be your friend."

Her *friend*. See, that was all. She didn't need to get carried away. He probably wanted to make sure she wasn't making much ado about nothing, or mountains out of molehills, and every other worn-out cliché. Another memory trickled back, something about how Astrid had mentioned Mitch could take Britta on a date, and he'd corrected her, saying he only wanted to talk. Had he seen how she'd leaped to hope then been crushed by his correction? Oh, how *humiliating* that he'd witnessed that! Did he think she wanted to go out with him? How could she even be thinking like this—what had happened to Georgia?

She pressed her lips together. So many questions. So many unknowns. And she felt too weak to deal with any of it. *Lord? I need Your strength, because I've got none.*

〜

*LORD, I need Your wisdom. I've got little.*

Mitch taped his stick, round and round and round. He'd done this for years so it was like being on autopilot, he could do this with his hands while his mind and heart focused on other things.

Like the person who had scarcely left his thoughts since the incident two nights ago. *Lord, bless her.*

He didn't know what to do. Not since her sister's words had made him face himself, face his actions. Things had gotten complicated. And extra tricky since she'd gotten sick. And while part of him wanted to send flowers, another part realized now just what that meant.

Because Britta had never dated, she might read into his gift more than he wanted at this time. He wanted her to trust him, to see him as a friend, a friend who could one day be more.

Besides, she had her own stuff she was working through, health challenges and esteem issues, just like him. Her sister was right; she'd hidden them well.

Everything with her felt so tentative, like one wrong word and she could run away. And after weeks of the cold shoulder, it felt so good to have her talk to him again; he couldn't let that go.

But what exactly should he say?

He had to tread carefully, to be gentle. Man, he still hadn't even explained to her about Georgia. And while she had to know that wasn't a thing anymore, he still probably owed an explanation to the woman who had done so much to help him try to woo another woman. He winced. He was such an idiot sometimes.

"Dude, you okay?" Jack asked.

He nodded, forced his thoughts back to tonight's game against Winnipeg. He really needed to snap out of this funk.

YEAH, he *really* needed to snap out of this funk. His captain didn't hold back as he verbally sprayed the team after their loss to Luc's team. And yeah, it was preseason, and they were still finding their feet and tweaking their lines, but Mitch knew he'd had a brain fart or two and done some dumb things. Things he couldn't even really explain to anyone else about, let alone himself. Except it was hard to care about a dumb play when it felt like he was at a crossroads in his life, something that would affect the rest of his life, unlike the outcome of this game which literally meant nothing.

"And Reilly? What the"—expletive—"was that performance?"

"Jiminy Crickets, keep your shirt on."

He spoke too soon as he scored a personal invective that would've left a lesser man crying. He folded his arms instead.

In moments like these he sometimes wondered what was the point of all this. Giving his all, night after night, putting his body and literal head on the line—for what? Money? What price a brain injury? Fame? Nope, not interested. What he wanted was to start his new life, find a wife, build a family. He glanced at Jack. He wanted what Jack had, to have someone to come home to, someone trustworthy, someone who believed like him, someone who believed *in* him, someone who liked kids, who was sweet and funny and…

He groaned.

"Bro, are you all right?" Jack asked. "You need to see the medic? That was a heavy hit you took before."

He shook his head. The room suddenly tilted. Then he blinked and it cleared again. "I'm fine."

He would be fine. Once these moments of blurriness passed. And especially once he figured out what he'd do with the rest of his life. And how he could convince a certain woman to take a chance on a broken man, and prove he was trustworthy after he'd shown himself anything but.

*Lord, I need Your wisdom.* He rubbed his hands over his face.

He slowly stripped as the others threw their gear into the basket. He'd have a shower soon, but he really needed an ice bath.

The medic paused, glancing at his chest. "Hey, that's a bruise."

He peered down at his ribs. "I've had worse."

"Ice it." He handed him an ice pack. "Better than nothing."

"Thanks."

But he was slow to move.

"You feeling okay, Mitch?" the medic asked.

"I've just got some things I'm figuring out."

Like, how long was too long in this game? Retirement was one of those things he really should consider. He wasn't as fast as the young guns, his body hurt too much to hit like he had in the past without him feeling it for days after. The pace he'd played at in the past wasn't sustainable anymore. So what was next?

*Lord, I could really do with some wisdom.*


"HEY MIKE, thanks for staying a little longer."

The online Bible study group chat had just ended, and he felt the prompting to talk with Mike. He had to talk to someone. And while it had been good to talk with Kyle, he needed someone a little older, someone who had gone through the ups and downs of a relationship, someone who was married. And when Mitch had been praying for wisdom, Mike Vaughan had been the name that had come to mind.

Mike nodded. "So, what's up?"

He exhaled. "I wanted to talk to someone in the group who's a little older like me about…" He swallowed. *Come on, just say it.* "About retirement."

"Wow."

"Yeah."

"Does anyone else know?"

"Nup."

"I won't say anything."

"Appreciate it."

Mike exhaled. "Okay, so you're thinking about that too, huh?"

"You are?" he asked quickly.

"Bree and I have talked about it, about what comes next. I figure I've got another year or so in me but then who knows, right? Our times are in God's hands."

"Yeah."

"And I haven't made a career of the kinds of hits you have, either." Mike's brow knit. "Are you healthy?"

Play pretend or admit the truth? Oh, what was the point of this video call if he wasn't being honest? It wasn't like there was anybody else he could be really real with. "I've had some issues with my memory and eyesight since I took a hit last season."

Mike winced. "I'm sorry. Have you spoken to the staff about it?"

"Not yet."

Mike looked at him.

"I will. I've just had a lot of other things on my plate this summer."

"Like your non-proposal."

He groaned. "That's such a mess."

"What do you mean? I thought it got sorted."

"Yeah, I did too, and I'm all cool about ending it with Georgia."

"But…?"

"But someone else I think has got the wrong impression."

Mike whistled. "You're a fast worker."

"No. I've known her a while now."

"Let me guess: the ninja librarian."

"What? How'd you know?"

"This group has a reputation. When a guy asks for us to pray for a girl, then we know it's serious."

"It's not serious."

Mike eyed him.

"Okay, look, this is the other part I need some wisdom with. I don't want to mess with her or mess this up. And she's seen all this stuff with Georgia, and now she'll just think I'm some loser who's rebounding fast who she shouldn't waste her time with."

"You said she's a Christian, right?"

"Yeah. It's just I feel like things have been really awkward between us, and I don't wanna make things worse."

Mike nodded. "I understand awkwardness." His mouth tweaked wryly. "Back when I was playing for Boston and before Bree and I were dating, I once flew to Toronto to help Bree for something I thought was a Valentine's Day date. I didn't realize she had organized it for someone else."

"She arranged for you to go on a date with someone else?"

"The things we do for love." He shrugged. "Anyway, that's another story."

Sounded like a good one.

"Let's just say it put some strain on our friendship and I had to take some time out from her, to kind of detox. It was hard. I've known Bree most of my life and known that she was the girl for me for most of my life, but she took some convincing. But I kept trusting God and I kept doing my best to be her friend. And like I say, it wasn't easy, but was worthwhile."

"And look at you now. Married, four kids, doing well."

"We were friends first—she's Brent Karlsson's twin—so the three of us spent a lot of time together growing up. She knew she could trust me."

"That's what I have to do." Get Britta to trust him.

"You want to marry her?"

"What? No. It's *way* too soon to talk about stuff like that."

"Is it? How old are you?"

"Thirty-three."

"And you're talking about retirement and what's next, so surely a family is part of that."

Who was he kidding? "Yeah, it is."

"Then if you think she might be a suitable candidate, then pray for her, be her friend, give her time, give God time to work in her heart, and trust Him. He's got good plans for you."

"Even if I've got concussion issues?"

Mike winced. "It's that bad?"

"It's not good."

"Then you need to see a doctor. See a private specialist if necessary, but get it checked out. Concussion issues aren't to be messed with. I remember when Holly, Brent's wife now but she was his girlfriend then, had a concussion before the Olympic Games. It was scary stuff, and she needed time to heal which meant time off short-track skating until she was completely better. So talk to the doctors soon, don't put it off. If you do, there's a chance you're only one bad hit away from a major brain injury. And you only get one brain."

He sucked in a breath. True.

"Then once you've talked with them that'll help you know what to do next. And that will help you know what to do about this girl. What's her name again?"

"Britta."

"Well, Bree and I will be praying for Britta, and praying for you. I think you know what to do."

"Yeah."

"So go do it. But let me pray for you now." Before Mitch had a chance to close his eyes, Mike was off. "Hey Lord, thank You that You see Mitch and know his questions. I pray that You will help him to trust You, to thank You, to fill his mind with good things. And if there is stuff in his brain that You need to heal, then God we ask for healing. And we pray for Your healing in this relationship with Britta as well. Thank You for the peace that surpasses all understanding guarding Mitch's heart and mind in the knowledge of You. Amen."

"Amen." Mitch cleared his throat. "Thanks."

"Any time. And I mean that. If you need to talk, I'm a brother in Christ and I'm happy to talk and pray for you."

"Appreciate it."

Mitch ended the call, his spirits lifted at last. He still might not have all the answers, but he knew the next step to take. And that meant talking to the doctors.

# CHAPTER 21

"Oh, Britta, it's so good to have you back."

It had taken a few more days than she wanted, but she was finally back in the children's section of the central library. She literally did not have the energy to drive the Bookmobile. She barely had enough strength to drive her own car. She'd explained that to Gwen and Margaret and they'd understood, so she was back here for Story Time.

She adjusted her hennin, the pink princess pointy hat she'd worn before, that she liked to wear when she dressed up for Story Time.

"Now, what are we going to read today?"

She held up a selection of books and let today's group of children pick their favorites. Thank goodness Margaret had been understanding. Britta might be sitting down, but already she felt exhausted. Managing her energy levels was hard, especially when the spirit was willing but her body was weak. Maybe she should've taken the whole week off.

But if she'd done that, she would've been even longer in bed, thinking about Mitch and wondering what next to do. She'd watched a few of his games, and knew he'd have his first real game next Saturday. It would be good to see him and finally have that conversation, but she wouldn't want to interrupt his preparation. But still, she'd sensed the need to pray for him, to ask God to keep him safe. *Lord, be with him today.*

"Right." She smiled, and slid her glasses up her nose. Oh, she must be tired if even that action hurt. "So, what will it be?" she asked the group of children sitting on the reading mat. *"The Very Hungry Caterpillar?"*

"No-o-o."

*"Clifford the Big Red Dog?"*

"No-o-o."

That was a shame. "How about *Oh, the Places You'll Go!* by Doctor Seuss?"

There came a chorus of "Yes!"

"Excellent choice, may I say. Okay, shall we begin?"

She glanced at the little kids as they nodded, their parents and carers perched in the little chairs nearby. She smiled, slowly opened the first page, then began. "Congratulations, today is your day…"

This story held extra poignancy today. It might've been written for children, but there was a reason it was given to graduates of all ages. People often lived in the "waiting place" of life, waiting for something to happen. And while the children were excited by the various opportunities and options that might lie in their future, as a Christian she knew she had to trust God for the right opportunities at the right time. After all, God was writing the story of her life. But just like in this book, she still had a choice. She could sit still and never take a risk, or take a chance and step out into the future.

God didn't promise to make life happen when she was sitting still doing nothing. Sitting still because she was paralyzed by her fears or by what she could see wasn't faith. And God was calling her to walk by faith. Walking by faith meant moving, shifting, placing one step in front of the other, step by step, day by day, trusting. She didn't know what the end of her story would look like, but God did. And He was good, and He loved her, and the Bible said He had good plans for her so she could trust Him.

She reached the last page, and read aloud, "'Today is your day. Your mountain is waiting. So… *get on your way!*'" She closed the book. "Who enjoyed that?"

Nearly all of the children put their hands up, along with most of the adults.

She smiled at them. "I remember receiving a copy of that when I graduated from high school." Some other adults nodded. "Still holds true, doesn't it? We don't know what the future holds, but we can look forward to unexpected opportunities, or we can shrink back. Hands up those who want adventures!"

She joined the kids—and some of the adults—in putting up her hand.

"Excellent. I hope you'll see some new adventures and opportunities soon. Okay, we're now going to have some coloring time, so if you would like to join Kayla over at the table, we can get you set up and started."

When Story Time was finished, she was really ready for a nap. But considering a nap wasn't one of the services offered at the central library, she had to make do with taking her break while answering some of the library inquiries.

So, after changing her outfit, she ate her sandwich and checked the inbox.

*How many librarians do you have employed at the central library?*

She typed her answer: *35*

*Do you have a map of the central library?*

*Sorry, we don't have one of the library itself, but we have one that shows our branch locations. I'm attaching a link to it here.*

There was nothing else, so seeing it was her break, she took a moment to check her own personal library email inbox. Saw a message from Helen Harlow. Clicked it open.

*Dear Britta,*

*Your name has been recommended to the city's committee for citizen of the year for your brave endeavors last month concerning the Bookmobile incident. You have been invited to a special brunch in December.*

She rubbed her eyes. Checked it again. Was Helen for real?

She sat back. Oh, she remembered why that date felt familiar. It was the day before the school reunion. Her nose wrinkled. The school reunion she still had to RSVP for. And while the thought of attending did not fill her with anticipation, she still sensed she should go. Maybe someone would be there that God wanted her to speak to, to encourage. Just because people hadn't seemed eager to hear the gospel at high school didn't mean that life hadn't knocked them around enough to want to hear now. And even though she physically felt kind of crappy now, it was still another couple of months away, which also meant she had more time to regain her strength.

So, before she could hesitate any longer, she found Erica's email, opened the link, complete with her misspelled name, and bought the ticket. There. Done.

Her phone buzzed in her bag, and she checked it. Mom. Checking she was okay.

*I'm fine,* she messaged.

She hesitated, looking at her phone's Instagram app she hadn't touched in weeks. And while she still didn't want to get sucked into the death spiral of social media comparison land, the story she'd read earlier reminded her that nothing came of sitting still. Yes, she could be still and know that God was working things out. But sometimes God needed her to face her fears and take a step of faith. And she felt the strangest impulse to be bold in this instance. She tapped open the app, ignored the bunch of notifications demanding her attention, and scrolled to the messages, found a name, tapped it open.

Mitch. *I hope you're feeling better.* Followed by a praying hands emoji.

She took a breath, and slowly typed back, *Yes.*

～

"MITCHELL." Dr. Larrimer, the neuro specialist, shook his head. "I really wish you had come to see us earlier than this."

He wasn't the only one wishing that right now. The barrage of tests had left him lightheaded and headachy, and even though he didn't want to admit how much the tests had affected him, he was trying to be honest.

"So, what's the verdict?" He couldn't pull off casual. Too much was on the line.

The doctor glanced at the papers, the printouts from the tests today. Thank goodness the team had a day off so he didn't have to give explanations about where he was. As it was, he was fairly sure the doc would be urgently advising he contact the team's medical personnel ASAP.

"Look, I don't think it will come as any surprise when I say that repeated hits to the head are a known cause of chronic traumatic encephalopathy. The symptoms you've described, and from the initial results we've seen today, suggest that you are at high risk of this progressing."

Mitch pressed his lips together. No. *Lord, no.* Weren't things supposed to work out for his good? How was this good?

The doctor eyed him. "And I feel it is only my duty to say that the nature of your work suggests you are likely to experience similar trauma again. So it's my advice—"

*No, don't say it.*

"—that you retire, effective immediately."

*No, no, no!* "And if I don't?"

"That is on your head. Literally. I'm not joking. I mean that quite literally."

He swallowed. "You're saying I should quit."

"Yes."

"Is there no chance of improvement?"

The doctor sighed. "Look, I'm not going to say never, because I've seen some wild things in this field that can't be explained."

Like Holly Karlsson's miraculous recovery from a concussion three months before the Olympics. Mitch had read the articles. He'd seen experts describe her recovery as inexplicable. *Inconceivable.* His lips twitched, despite himself.

"This is no laughing matter."

"I'm not laughing. Not at all. I'm trying to wrap my head around this and I don't mind admitting that it's overwhelming."

"Have you got a support network around you?"

His chest tensed. No. Not like he wanted.

"My advice is for you to talk to the team doctors. I can send this information to them today."

"No, not yet."

"Look, if you don't tell them and something happens, then I will not be held responsible for what happens."

"Nobody is blaming you, doc. I just need a little bit more time to process this."

"You don't have a lot of time. You need to make a decision, and the longer you delay, the more likelihood you have of reinjuring what is the most sensitive and fundamental organ in your body."

"I thought that was the heart."

"That's the most fundamental for the circulatory system, but it's the brain that tells the heart what to do. And I've seen cases, many cases, of older people who suffer dementia brought on by CTE."

His skin prickled. *No, no, no.* "Are you saying I'm going to have dementia?"

"I'm saying that CTE dementia is caused by repeated or

severe blows to your head and it's often seen in those people who play contact sports or sports with a history of knocks like football, boxing and hockey."

"I didn't realize that."

"Not many people do. They love the game, but they don't realize that the game does not always love them."

He gritted his teeth as his heart shrieked in protest. *Lord, help me!*

"So, shall I email these results to your team doctors?"

As soon as they got these results, he'd be pulled from the team and he'd likely have to stand down. He'd only just made the grade. They hadn't even started the regular season.

So much felt out of his control, but at least he could determine what happened now. "I need a few days to decide."

"What is there to decide? If you keep playing hockey, your brain will get worse. And you only get one brain."

"Well, like I said before, I need a few more days to think about it. So I think I'll be fine to take a few more days before I tell them, okay?"

"It's your brain," the doctor said, in the way that someone might say *it's your funeral.*

"Exactly."

His fingers were shaking by the time he returned to his car.

He slumped in the driver's seat, the car a bubble from life's reality. How could this have happened? He knew exactly how this could happen, but still, why him? Why now? Wasn't God supposed to protect him from this? Wasn't the fact that he was trying to follow Jesus supposed to keep him safe from harm?

Except he knew bad things happened even to good people. And while he knew he wasn't that good, he knew goodness didn't matter, as anyone could suffer an accident or chronic illness...

His mind flicked to someone who suffered with a chronic illness, yet did so without complaint.

*Lord, bless Britta.*

Britta knew how to keep following Jesus, despite life throwing her some vicious curveballs. He wished he hadn't been one of the curveballs in her life. Or maybe she didn't consider him a curveball at all.

*Stop.* What was he doing thinking about her when he had just received this heart-numbing information? He needed to focus. Which was exactly the point, the doctor had said. Mitchell couldn't focus, not so easily anymore. And with his family four states away, who exactly was there around here as his support system?

Panic rose. *Lord? What do I do?*

He drew in a deep breath, slowly exhaled. God was in control. Mike said that. Could he call Mike? But a quick check of Calgary's schedule suggested Mike was likely on a plane. He couldn't call him. Not yet. He needed someone here. Not in the team. He couldn't run the risk of anyone there knowing just yet. He needed God to send an angel his way to remind him that God was in control. *Lord, help me.*

He glanced at his phone. Saw a notification. His heart pounded. He opened it. And suddenly knew where he could go.

# CHAPTER 22

She was so ready to end today. She needed whatever time she could get before she had Red Jellybeans tonight. And after having time off lately, she couldn't leave it to Ferdy to do it himself, not again. It wasn't fair for Bev to have to step in once again.

She tidied the kids' area, closed her computer, said goodbye to Margaret and Carol, and walked with Kayla out the front doors.

"Bye Derek," she called. "Stay warm."

"You got a pastry for me?"

"Sorry, not today. I've got my kids to get to."

"It's Friday. I forgot." Derek grinned. "It's easy to forget when one is just living the dream."

"Uh, Britta," Kayla nudged her.

*God bless him.* "See you, Derek."

"Britta," Kayla whispered urgently.

Britta turned, then nearly stumbled over the gutter at the sight of the man.

Mitch Reilly. But unlike any Mitch Reilly she had seen before. The man might be known for his intimidating presence, but right now he seemed wounded, hunched in his jacket, like he was trying to hide from a nonexistent gale.

"Hi Mitch," Kayla said.

"Hey, it's Mitchell Reilly," Derek called.

He nodded, but his eyes remained on Britta.

Her heart shivered. Something was wrong. What did he want with her? "Uh, Kayla, I think I need to talk with Mitch. See you tomorrow."

"You're working tomorrow?" Mitch asked, his voice gravelly, like it had lacked use.

"I'm supposed to."

He dipped his chin. Scuffed his shoe.

This wasn't the man she'd seen six days ago, when she'd been at her weakest. It was like the tables had turned. *Lord, what has happened?* Is this why she had felt that prompting to pray for him today? To send that message today?

"Okay, well, bye you two." Kayla grinned, then made a *Call me* gesture to Britta as she left.

Britta half-shrugged. She would only call her if there was something she could say. And judging from the man's face, she wasn't sure that was possible.

"Did you, um, want to talk?" she asked.

He nodded, glanced away. Shoved his hands in his pockets.

Okay, then. She gestured to a nearby park bench, but he shook his head. "I don't really want to be with other people right now. Is it okay if we go somewhere else?"

She glanced at her watch. "I actually have to help run my youth group tonight. That starts in just over an hour."

His shoulders slumped. "Oh. I didn't realize."

"But we're usually done by eight thirty. We could meet then, if that's not too late for you."

He nodded, but his expression shadowed. "It's okay. I don't want to waste your time."

"No." She moved forward, grasped his arm.

He glanced at her hand.

She dropped it. "Mitch? What's wrong?"

He shook his head, his lips tight, and she suddenly felt an overwhelming urge to hug him. Like she would her sisters. Or her friends. Or even when the Red Jellybeans were upset, even though she knew that would be frowned upon by people like Edmond who feared accusations of impropriety.

And even though she suspected Mitch might object, she also sensed he needed a hug. So she stepped into his personal space and wrapped her arms around him.

He slowly wrapped his arms around her, and held her. Leaned his face upon her hair. She closed her eyes. Felt a drop of wetness in her hair. Was it raining?

No, a peek at the sky showed it was cloudy but no rain. Then... she tensed. Was he crying?

She pulled back slightly, but he held her tight still. "Mitch? What's wrong?"

"I can't talk about it here." His voice was raspy still.

"Where is your car? Do you want to talk there?"

"You have your kids to get to."

"But you're important too."

He released her, rubbed his face, glanced away, his hands clasped behind his head. "Look, you're gonna be late if we keep standing here."

But she couldn't leave him like this. "Do... do you want to come with me? I've got to go home and get changed and have dinner, then go to youth group, but you could come with me. We could, uh, talk in the car. You could have dinner. It's usually only something basic, but you'd be welcome. I'm sure there's enough. Mom always cooks a ton, and..."

And look, she was babbling. Because she'd never invited a guy to her house before, let alone to have a meal. And yeah, this was *this* man, and he'd now say no, and an awkward situation would be made ten times worse, and—

"Your mom?"

It took her a moment to realize what he meant. Cue more embarrassment. "Uh," her nose wrinkled, "I live at home with my parents."

He nodded, then shook his head. "I couldn't."

What—couldn't live with his parents? Or couldn't visit her house and meet hers? Well, the man probably didn't do parents of the women in his life. Not that she was exactly "a woman in his life", but still. She was a woman, and he was standing in front of her, so perhaps that counted. She wondered if he'd ever met Georgia's parents. Well, he *must've* if he'd gone to propose.

She cringed. That's right. How could she have forgotten that? She might be a painted trollop, but she felt like a hussy right now. A flaming-cheeked one at that. How to extract herself from another embarrassing situation... "Never mind."

"I, uh, didn't mean to sound like I don't want to meet them. I just don't want to impose."

"Oh!" Phew. "You're not imposing."

"Really?"

"They'd be *thrilled* to meet you. My dad especially. He's a huge hockey fan, and..." Her voice trailed off. His face had shuttered. "But we don't have to talk about hockey or anything at all. I can plonk you in front of the TV and you can wait there till I return."

"Did you say plonk?" His lips shifted in a half-smile.

"I said plonk."

"Could... could I maybe come with you to youth group instead?" He shrugged, shoved his hands in his pockets again. "I don't have to come inside. I can sit in the car. I just don't really want to be talking to people."

"Well, sure, but I'm afraid the kids would combust if they saw you." As would Ferdy. "Do you have a police clearance to work with kids?"

"Yeah. We need one to do the community stuff with kids, but

hey, I don't want to be in the way." He took a step back. "I should just go—"

"Stop. You're coming with me. And it's up to you what you do when I have youth group. But I think we both know that you need a friend right now, right?"

He nodded.

She sucked in a breath and gestured to where she had parked her car. "Okay then. This way."

HER SURPRISE at Mitch's appearance, and her dismay at the state of her car—she'd needed to collect a dozen wrappers before he'd shifted the passenger seat back far enough to get in—was nothing compared to the shock her family met her with as she walked through the door.

"We have a visitor," she announced, as Bumper made Mitch welcome with slobbery kisses hello.

"Who—? Oh my golly, it's you!" That was Astrid.

Her dad put down his newspaper. "Mitchell Reilly?"

He held out a hand. "Sir."

"Uh, it's Pete. I'm a big fan." Dad shook his hand, glanced at Britta then back at their guest. "To what do we owe this pleasure?"

Mitch glanced at Britta.

She smiled. "We bumped into each other down at the library and he needed a place to hide out."

"What?" her family said.

"Huh?" Mitch tilted his head.

"Okay, fine. He's coming to youth group with me and I need to eat, and if there's enough, Mom, he might like some, too."

"We're having Tater Tot hotdish." Her mom glanced at him anxiously. "Is that allowed for you?"

"Sounds amazing." He shrugged. "I don't eat a lot of home-cooked meals. I usually cook what my trainer has prepared for me."

"Sounds healthy." Britta wrinkled her nose.

He shot her a glance. "A little too healthy sometimes."

"Well, you don't need to worry about that around here."

"Britta," Mom protested, as Mitch smiled.

There. That was what she wanted to see. He needed to relax. Which probably meant she needed to say something like, "Now, nobody is allowed to ask Mitchell about anything except the weather."

"Britta." He rolled his eyes. "It's fine."

"No, it's not. I'm not letting them ask you what I want to know. Okay?"

"She's always been a little bossy," Astrid murmured.

"Says you," Britta muttered.

"It's okay," he murmured. "Britta reminds me of my sister."

His sister. See? Not the first time he had said that either. Anything else had to be firmly stuffed back in its box. She concentrated on eating her meal fast. On not looking at the others. She didn't want them seeing the heat on her cheeks and seeing she'd misunderstood things again. Why was he here? What did he want to talk to her about? It was amazing how such a mystery had chased away the exhaustion before.

She finished quickly, glanced at the kitchen clock. "Okay, I'm just going to get changed then we're going to go, okay?"

He nodded, and she rushed to get changed in what was probably her shortest time ever. She couldn't leave him out there, talking to her family and spilling secrets she really wanted to know.

By the time she returned he was rinsing his plate and hers at the sink. Oh. That was nice. She caught Astrid's raised hands and mouthed *what is he doing here?* She shrugged. She didn't know either. "Okay Mitch, are you good to go?"

He turned. "That was fast."

"That's me. I'm a speedy ninja librarian, remember? So, are you ready?"

He nodded. "Yeah. Let's go."

HE'D LIED. He wasn't ready. But all the way to her house, and through the meal, and on the drive to youth group, he'd felt a yearning for something he hadn't known since the Gulbrandsens had virtually adopted him when he'd been living away as a teen. He hadn't grown up in a family like Britta's. His family had been dysfunctional and broken even before his dad disappeared. It hadn't been long before he'd been playing in the east, visiting Trinity Lakes less and less, his family more of a concept than his reality.

But oh, he wanted it now. Wanted a family now. *Needed* a family, especially now. Today's news had shattered him, so Britta could lead him into youth group like a trick pony on a lead and he'd do whatever she asked. God bless her for not asking questions yet. God bless her for not asking if he'd cried earlier. No way could he live it down if she knew that. He blew out a breath.

"You okay?"

"Just dandy."

"Mm-hmm." She peeked at him again as they stopped at a red light. "So, are you wanting to stay in the car or do you want to come in?"

"Is it okay if I stay here?"

She nodded. "It might get a little chilly, and if someone sees you, there might be questions."

"Will that make it awkward for you?"

"I'm tough. I can cope." Her lips tweaked. "Even if I haven't appeared like that too much lately."

"I think you're amazing." Who else would have known exactly what to do? Her hug had been just what he needed. Her offer of food and shelter, perfect too.

"Right." She rolled her eyes and pulled into a church building parking lot. "Well, I have to now go and be amazing with the Red Jellybeans, so I'll leave you here. Yes?"

He nodded. "Wait, did you say the Red Jellybeans?"

"Mmm. Because they're hyperactive for Jesus."

He laughed. "That's funny."

"Or in the words of my pastor, 'Oh, fer cute'."

He smiled. Living here the past few years he'd heard that expression a lot. "I'll catch some z's."

"Okay. Well, if you get bored we will be in the function room which is off the main auditorium. We won't be hard to find. Just follow the noise."

He reclined his seat. "Thanks Britta."

"You're welcome, Mitch." Her smile was soft. "Then as soon as I'm done, we'll talk."

His heart thudded. "Okay."


HE WAS glad she'd parked near the edge of the parking lot. It meant he got to watch as various kids were dropped off by parents and siblings, a few by white-haired peeps he guessed were grandparents. It gave another glimpse of another world, one he'd never really known. But being here, in Britta's tiny, messy car, made him feel like he could reach out his hand and touch it. This world could be his if he dared.

And sure, there had been some challenges along the way, but he recognized the warmth Britta possessed, like a fire drawing him in from the cold. And while she would never be conventionally pretty, there was something far more magnetic about her looks. She possessed a vivacity that lit up her face. It had been fun to watch her at dinner, to read the emotions and guess what had caused her to blush. He liked that he could read her face. That she didn't mask it like she had at the speed dating thing.

He groaned. Oh, there was so much that needed explanations. Not least of which was his appearance today, but also to finally explain about Georgia.

He closed his eyes, prayed for the Red Jellybeans, smiling at the name. He probably would've been considered hyperactive back in the day, though not necessarily for Jesus. Just hyperactive for himself. Which had pretty much carried on in his life, living for himself, and living for hockey.

Which made him wonder who he'd be without hockey. If his brain was glitching, what could he do? He'd need to do something. But what? See if the Wild would pity him enough to work in the front office? Be a scout? Coach, maybe? Or should he move back to Trinity Lakes? Buy his own ranch? Well, that last he could cancel out. He didn't love cows and horses, no matter how much his younger siblings did. Well, not Cooper—he loved numbers as much as their oldest brother, Dermott, loved plants. Dermott ran a gardening company on the Independence Islands just off South Carolina. Maybe he could beg Dermott for a job and work there for a time. He still had some muscle, even if he didn't have all his brain.

His fingers clenched; he actively relaxed them. No, he wouldn't think like that. His brain worked perfectly fine. Maybe God would even heal him.

But he also sensed some of what Mike had said was true, too. Which reminded him that he should message him, let him know, get him to pray. Because Mike was right. There were seasons for everything and maybe Mitch's season of hockey had finished a little sooner than he expected. Which meant the upcoming conversation was all the more important.

"Lord, I don't know the future, but You do. Help me to trust

You. And be with Britta. Give her energy and strength to deal with the kids tonight. God bless them. Touch their hearts. And give her the energy and strength to deal with me. And give me the wisdom to know what to say. Amen."

# CHAPTER 23

*B*ritta glanced at the clock. Today, which had already felt so long, held the promise of taking a lot longer still. And she was so tired now she needed this evening to be done. She needed that conversation with the man who was still sitting in her car. She shivered. Oh my goodness. Mitchell Reilly was sitting in *her car*, maybe even *sleeping* in her car.

"You okay, Britta?" Ferdy murmured.

She nodded. "I've got a meeting after this, so I'm a little antsy to finish."

"Hey, me too. Happy to finish soon, even though I don't have a meeting." He peered at her. "Who's it with?"

He'd yelp like a banshee if she told him. "Oh, just someone from work." That's how she had first met Mitchell, so that was the simplest explanation. Few people ever inquired too closely when she told them where she worked.

But even though both of them might wish to finish soon, there was no point when the kids weren't due to be collected until 8:15, and that left plenty of time for people to still be late to pick up their children. God bless them. At least they came.

Time to wrap this session up, then the kids could eat supper while the leaders cleaned up.

She clapped her hands. "Okay guys and gals, let's pray. I'm going to check what's in the prayer tub and hand it over to Ronaldo who is this week's pray-er extraordinaire. Let's give it up for Ronaldo."

The Jellybeans clapped, and she invited him to come up on the stage to take the microphone. Giving the kids opportunities to minister like this, complete with microphone, built up their confidence to one day do that in church or other events too. She pulled the list of prayer requests from the cardboard box that comprised their prayer tub, quickly checked through them, then handed the appropriate ones to Ronaldo. Some were too personal to be read aloud; others were too silly. Nobody needed to hear about requests for five million dollars.

The kids bowed their heads, she did too, and Ronaldo prayed,. "In Jesus's name, Amen."

"Amen," she echoed.

Then Ronaldo swore.

Her head jerked up. And when she saw how he was staring at the function room's doors, she joined the others in staring at the man at the back of the room.

"Is that Mitch Reilly?" someone murmured.

"The Wild's 54?"

Uh-oh. The buzz of excitement rippling across the room was about to explode in three, two, one...

It was like watching a tidal surge seeing the kids race up the back, crowding Mitchell as he looked on, bemused. Well, she'd warned him, and he'd made his choice. This was one hundred percent on him.

"What is he doing here?" Ferdy asked.

Ah, this was going to be tricky. "That meeting I mentioned?"

"*He's* your meeting? I thought you met at the library."

"We did. He was doing a thing there. I was dressed as a bee."

He rolled his eyes. "Of course you were."

"Look, I don't know what your problem with dressing up in costumes is, but I guess mine was a bit hard to forget."

He smiled at her. Hugged her in a brotherly side hug. "You sell yourself short."

She peeked across, saw that Mitch was staring at her. She lifted a hand and smiled. He nodded. She raised her brows. "So, we better go rescue him."

Ferdy whistled to get everyone's attention. "Okay everybody. Yes, Mitchell Reilly is in the house. Let's give it up for him."

Cheers filled the room.

Britta beckoned him forward. His appearance meant he'd asked for this. "Mitch, perhaps you'd like to come down the front. And maybe we can have a super quick question and answer time while we wait for everyone's parents to arrive. Is that okay?"

Mitch nodded, making his way down the aisle.

"Hey kids, while he's coming, if you want to grab a quick snack from the table, do so." The supper snacks were provided by a couple of local businesses; one was a bakery that gave the Red Jellybeans their unsold baked goods for the day. They went a long way in dealing with hungry junior high appetites.

"Welcome Mitch," she said into the microphone as he climbed the three steps to the stage area. "Hey guys, let's give him a really big Red Jellybean welcome."

Sure enough, the traditional welcoming call involved gorilla grunts from some of the vocal boys. Mitch chuckled, waved a hand, and she handed him the microphone.

"Hey," he said in his deep voice. "Thanks for letting me interrupt."

"You asked for it," she murmured, away from the mic. "I thought you were gonna stay in the car."

He held the mic at arms' length. "I wanted to see what all the fuss was about."

"Well, you're about to." She grabbed the mic. "Now, some of you may be wondering why Mr. Reilly is here. Sorry, why Mitch is here." She pulled the mic away. "You up to telling them that you're a Christian?"

Ferdy gasped. "You are?"

"Yeah." He grabbed the mic. "So, as Britta said," he pulled the mic away and glanced at her, "you are Britta here, not Ms. Johnson?"

"Yep."

He faced the kids. "Okay, so as Britta said, I'm here because I wanted to see what all the fuss was about. She's mentioned how much fun you guys always have."

A kid waved his hand. "How do you know Britta?"

Mitch glanced at her. "We met at the library where she works. She's my friend."

Her heart glowed. She smiled. "Tell them about becoming a Christian."

"And yeah," he faced the kids again. "I'm a Christian."

A ripple of "whoa"s flowed across the room.

"And I'll admit I haven't always been, but lately I've come to realize just how important it is to have faith in something bigger than yourself."

She prayed as he shared his testimony. God bless this man.

"We can't predict the future, but we know Someone who can." He pointed upward. "God is always there for us in times of trouble, and I don't know about you, but sometimes I feel like I'm in trouble."

"With Britta?" someone asked.

He laughed. "Yeah. No, not really. My conscience does a pretty good job of telling me when I've done things wrong. Anyway, I just wanted to encourage you all and say that being a Christian is nothing to be ashamed of. God is good, He loves you, and we can trust Him with every aspect of our life."

She studied him, sensing his words held a weight beyond the obvious. What had happened?

He cleared his throat. "And like I said earlier, we don't know what our future holds, and we can't trust that what has been will always be. But God is Someone who is always trustworthy. That's actually why I'm here tonight. I prayed today and God gave me an answer, and it just reminded me that He's faithful. So if God is faithful with me, I know He'll be faithful with you. You can trust Him too."

Britta stared at him. He'd prayed and God gave an answer? Was she part of that? The only reason he was here in this exact space at this exact moment was because of her.

Her throat filled, and she gestured for Ferdy to close the meeting. By now, several of the parents were standing at the back of the room, and they joined the applause as Mitch waved, and then good-naturedly agreed to pose for some selfies.

"I can't believe what I'm seeing," Ferdy said.

"He was really good, right?" She had seen him at presentations before, but there was a world of difference between how he'd read at the library and how he'd spoken now, with the kids eating out of his hand. If the man wasn't a hockey player, he should be a youth leader.

It was much later than 8:30 by the time they could finally lock up. So much for getting out of here fast.

"You looked like you were having fun," she said as they finally walked to her car.

"Don't tell anyone, but that actually kind of was."

"I thought so! I actually thought you'd make a great youth leader if you weren't doing hockey."

A strange expression creased his face. "Yeah. Maybe."

"Mitch?"

He exhaled. "Hey, I know it's getting late but is there somewhere around here where we can eat without being bombarded with lots of people?"

"Oh! Uh, sure." It couldn't hurt to eat with him now, could it? He was in trouble, in need of a friend. And obviously something was up with Georgia seeing he'd showed up at a singles event. "There's a hotel not too far from here that has a dining room and a lounge that's open to the public. It's not usually too busy, especially this time of year."

"Okay. Let's try that."

She drove, and fifteen minutes later they were walking through the door. One of the servers asked if they were staying at the hotel, and she blushed. "Um, we're just having some food."

"Dessert? Cocktails? Coffee?"

He glanced at her. "If you've got some menus, we'll let you know."

"Okay, well the kitchen closes in twenty minutes, so if it's food you want you need to order soon."

Britta led them to a quiet area, near where a fire would blaze in winter, but right now was filled with decorative pine cones.

This felt so weird, sitting on a plush couch at right angles to Mitch, his knee bumping hers. She studied the menu, decided an apple pie was fit reward for her past week, and when the server approached, gave her order.

"I'll have the same," Mitch said, then eyed her. "Nothing to drink?"

"Water is fine." If she was going with the sugar rush of an apple pie, then she probably needed to offset that with her drink consumption. She usually could tell when a hyper attack was coming, and so far felt fine, but it was best to not push things.

"So." He shifted to study her.

"So."

His lips tweaked.

Her heart pounded. "So what's this all about?"

~

IT WAS funny how all the explanations that had rushed through his head seemed too hard to grasp right now. He'd spent an age in the car trying to figure out what to say before the questions in his head made it impossible to stay inside. He needed to explain three things. Georgia. Last Saturday. And today's shocking health news.

But first he wanted to know something else. "Why did you finally respond to my message on Instagram today?"

She studied him, her eyes wide, the lights flickering off her glasses. This space was quiet, perfect for this kind of conversation. It felt too important for prying ears and eyes.

"Um, I don't know. That sounds lame, I know, but I just felt this sense that you might need me to reply today. That sounds weird, but—"

"I did need you."

"Oh." She sat up, her glasses a little skewed. Kind of adorable. "Um, you weren't exactly radiating joy when we met at the library earlier."

Looked like they'd be starting with point three, and not point one. "Yeah. I kinda got some bad news today."

Her face softened. "I wondered. Is it your family? Is everyone okay?"

He nodded. "Yeah, they're all fine." *But I'm not.* The words stayed stuck in his mouth.

Her head tilted, and the glasses slanted a little more. "But you're not okay?"

He shook his head, the action releasing a few more of the stars that blurred his vision. He groaned.

"Mitch? What is it?"

He closed his eyes for a long moment, until he could judge that the motion sickness had departed. "You know what you said before about me being a youth leader if I wasn't doing hockey?"

She nodded, biting her lip.

"Well, turns out I might not be doing hockey for much longer."

She gasped. "Mitch."

He shrugged. "I saw a neurologist today because I've been having bad headaches for a while now. Since I got a bad concussion earlier this year."

She covered her mouth. "I'm so sorry."

"He advised me to quit, and I'd just come out of his office when I saw that you'd replied to me." He shrugged again. "Call me crazy, but I took it as a sign that you were willing to be my friend." He swallowed. "And I really kind of needed a friend today."

Her eyes glimmered, which sparked his own emotion. But no way was he about to cry in some hotel restaurant, where anyone could see him. Thank God there was no one here with their phones out today.

She grasped his hand. "I don't know what to say."

His fingers tangled with hers. "Just telling someone makes a world of difference."

"Nobody else knows?"

"No."

"Not even the club?"

"I haven't told my family or my agent. Admitting it aloud makes it feel too real. I don't want anyone else to know. Not yet, anyway."

"Of course. I won't tell anyone."

"Thanks."

She squeezed his hand, and he could almost feel her tangible sympathy. He was grateful for the arrival of their desserts. Eating gave him something to do other than notice how soft and small her hand was.

"It must've been God that prompted me to message you today," she finally said.

"Yeah." He glanced at her. "Thank you."

She smiled softly. "You're welcome."

"And thank you for inviting me to go to your parents', and youth group. And this now. I would've been a basket case if I was trying to figure this out alone at home."

"God is still with you even when you are alone at home."

"I know. But sometimes you need God with skin on, don't you?"

She nodded. "It's good to have friends who are believers who understand." She carved off another piece of pie. "So, who would you count as your Christian friends?"

"Apart from you?"

"You know, I really feel kind of special that you would think of me as your friend."

He loved when she said stuff like that, showing her innocence and humility. "You are special."

She rolled her eyes.

"But to answer your question, I can't remember if I told you before that I'm part of an online Christian hockey players' Bible study group. People like Mike Vaughan, Luc Blanchard, Kyle Tinker, Zac Parotti, Doug Lehtonen."

"Wow. All of them?"

"Right?"

She smiled. "Did you see all of those kids tonight? They were saying exactly the same thing about you. 'Wow! He's a Christian.' Like a cool one."

"You think I'm cool?"

"I think if I was to answer that the way you want me to, that'd give you a big head."

He laughed. "You're still sassy, huh?"

"I have my moments."

She sure did. He swallowed another piece of pie. "It was cool to talk about God stuff tonight. I've never really done that before."

"You should do that more often. You're a natural."

"Well, maybe if I can't do hockey I'll be a youth leader with you."

She coughed. "You could be a youth leader anywhere."

But it'd be more fun with her. She was fun. Georgia had never been fun. He winced.

"What's wrong?" she asked quickly.

"I just remembered."

"That you've got a game tomorrow?"

"You do keep tabs on our schedule, don't you?"

"I'm Minnesotan. I love hockey."

Her glasses were skewed again. How could she see? He leaned close and adjusted them.

She reared back. "What are you doing?"

"Your glasses were crooked."

The light had faded from her face. "I don't need you doing that."

Oh. He studied his pie.

Then he remembered that he was trying to go slow, trying to prove to her that he could be trusted. It was weird how today's interactions had shoved that from his brain. Maybe that was just more of the forgetting thing.

"Sorry," she said. "I didn't mean to snap. I just got a flashback to last week's horror when Neanderthal Mark was trying to fix me." Her smile flashed. "Good luck with that."

He half-smiled. "I couldn't fix you. Not just because I wouldn't dare—"

She gave that throaty chuckle again. He really liked her laugh.

"—but I think you're pretty amazing the way you are."

There. That still counted in the friend territory, didn't it? A friend could say that without it being weird.

But from the way she was looking at him, maybe it was unusual. Or at least unusual for her. "Mitch."

"Britta."

She shook her head. "Why are you saying things like that? What happened to Georgia? I thought—I heard—you were going to propose to her."

"You mean you haven't heard what happened?"

She shook her head. "I've been on a social media detox, and it's been great. It's really helped my mental health. But it does mean I'm out of the loop with some things."

What a thing for her to be out of the loop on. "So, yeah, about Georgia. I was never going to propose."

Her eyes were wide behind her glasses. "You weren't?"

"Nope."

"Then...?"

"I finally went to talk to her to figure out if this was a relationship anymore. She basically told me it wasn't and sent me packing."

"Oh, Mitch. I'm so sorry."

"It was good to get an answer at long last." His lips pulled wryly. "Even if it meant that you and Ellie were right, and I finally realized that Georgia and I are in different seasons."

She bit her lip. "It must've hurt though."

He shrugged. "It stung at the time, not gonna lie. But I guess now, looking back, I can see there was never any real relating in our relationship. If I'm completely honest, I don't think I ever really loved Georgia. I don't think we were even really friends."

He winced. What was it about Britta that made him expose all the dark recesses of his heart? Maybe it had something to do with the chocolaty softness of her eyes, the fact he could feel her tangible care. "Anyway, that was a while ago now."

"It was?"

"Well, yeah. But I wasn't exactly in the position to make public announcements about any of it." Like, how was he supposed to announce something like that to the world? Even though he had tried to tell Britta in person, and via messages, but she'd ignored him. He studied her. "So that's why you looked so surprised when I was there at the mingle last week."

She nodded slowly. "Last I heard you were still trying to woo Georgia, then you showed up at a Christian singles event. I didn't know what to think."

"That was a hot mess, wasn't it?"

"Oh my gosh. Christian singles. Who'd be one?" She rolled her eyes, her self-mockery evident. "I felt so embarrassed. Then to see you there." She laughed.

"What?"

"You should've seen the way the other women perked up as soon as a handsome Christian guy walked in the room."

"You think I'm handsome?" he asked.

Her gaze lifted to his, connecting. And suddenly, he wanted her to say he was. He knew he didn't own Zac Parotti levels of Tom Cruise handsomeness, but the insecure boy in him wanted her to admit she found him attractive, even if it meant he sounded like a tool.

"That's kind of an unfair question."

"How?"

"I mean, it's obvious you are. Which is why the other women all perked up when you came last week."

The other women? Not her? He remembered that she'd been the one woman who hadn't turned around. "You didn't turn around."

"Because I thought you were with Georgia," she murmured.

"Is that why you said that's an unfair question?"

She shook her head. "Forget it. I shouldn't have said that."

He grasped her hand. "No, I want to know what you mean."

"Mitch."

"Come on, Britta. You're not the kind of woman who plays games. And you don't hold back on telling the truth. So what is it?"

"Fine." She sighed. "You're the kind of person who can enter a room and everyone looks at you. I'm the kind of person who walks into a room and nobody notices. If I'd come here tonight, just by myself, I bet you that I'd still be sitting here and not be served."

"Britta."

"No, it's true. And you can't say it's not true because you haven't lived my life, so you wouldn't know."

True. But if that was her experience, then, "That is unfair."

"Right? But it's something I've known all my life. And I guess that's why I'm pretty passionate about trying to give those people who might feel overlooked an equal chance."

He'd seen that. The way she'd given the kids with glasses the chance to ask the first questions at the library day. The way she'd encouraged the kid to pray tonight. He loved that about her. "I think that's an awesome quality about you."

She peeked at him. He nodded, willing her to believe it. Then she relaxed. "Thank you."

He sipped his water. Remembered last week. Hoped she was taking her meds or whatever it was so she wouldn't have another hypo. "Uh, are you feeling okay? Astrid mentioned that you had a hypo."

She sighed. "God bless her. I don't advertise my diabetes. It's just always been part of my life."

"I looked it up a bit this week. Are you type one?"

She nodded. "I got diagnosed when I was young. I've learned to be careful with my blood sugars. And it's usually not a problem unless I'm stressed."

"You've had a bit going on lately."

She ducked her head, as if remembering the stressors of last week.

He winced. He didn't want to be causing her more pain. But by the same token, it was necessary to clear the air. "Are you okay now?"

"Yes. I had some time off work because I got kinda sick."

Regret knotted his heart. He should've sent her flowers, sent a card, proved he was her friend. Her *friend.* He'd had plenty of relationships, but he couldn't count many—any—of those women as being friends. Until now.

She'd been right before. This relationship they shared was special. Something they could build on, if she ever learned to trust him. "I'm glad you're better now."

A yawn escaped her. "Oops, sorry." She chuckled. "This is the latest I've stayed up all week so it's past my bedtime."

"You need your beauty sleep, huh?"

She eyed him uncertainly, then he remembered what her sister had said. That she'd doubted her looks. Is that what she'd meant before, about his unfair question?

"I didn't mean to suggest you needed beauty sleep, Britta."

"It's okay. I've learned that no matter how much sleep you get, you can't improve this."

Her words might be edged with bitterness, but he didn't have the chance to explore more as she excused herself and headed to the bathroom.

Man. He'd failed that one. *Lord, it was going so well.*

# CHAPTER 24

*B*ritta studied herself in the hotel bathroom mirror. It had been going so well. *Had* been. Then her old insecurities pricked at his words and had spoiled things again. Well, not spoiled things. She could still redeem things if she went out there and pretended all was well. But a lifetime of snubs and jokes had made her soul feel like paper that was spotted by tears. It didn't matter how gentle the cleaning, it was marked for eternity. Just like she was.

And while tonight had been confusing, with some questions answered while so many still remained, she couldn't let her own insecurities spoil tonight. If nothing else, they were friends. And that was good. That was *great*. God obviously knew that Mitchell needed her and had prompted her to send that message right when Mitch needed it. And she was glad to have been the person he could turn to, someone he could trust. She wouldn't let the old demons steal that joy.

She wiped under her eyes, pulled her hair back. The tiredness from before had returned, and she didn't want her blood sugars affected by staying up much later. So, she would once again have to practice what she preached to the Red Jellybeans and put her own self-interest to one side, and focus on what would bless him. Which reminded her—how was he going to get home?

She hurried back, smile on dial. "Sorry. I just remembered. I need to take you back home."

"Oh, shoot. I kind of forgot."

"Because you're having such a good time, huh?" she teased.

His eyes were intent on hers. "Yeah."

She swallowed. Well, friends had good times together. That was normal. She had fun with Kayla. Although she'd never looked into Kayla's eyes this long...

She blinked. "I need to go. And so do you. You don't want to be too tired for your game tomorrow. That is, if you're playing."

"I'm still playing. I need a bit of time to figure some things out before I quit."

"Is that safe though?"

"It's all a big unknown, isn't it? It's not exactly like I can guarantee if I'll have a hit to the head or not. But look, I don't want you to worry about me."

She studied him, bit her lip, nodded. *Too bad, buster.* She'd try not to worry, but she'd be praying her guts out for him.

He motioned for the bill. "Are you coming to watch it?"

"No. Have you seen the prices for the tickets to those things? Oh wait. You don't need to. You *are* that thing."

"I can get you some tickets if you want."

"I wasn't begging."

"I didn't think you were." He shrugged. "We get tickets that we can give to family and friends. As I don't have family around here, I'd like to give them to my friends."

And that's what she was, wasn't it? A friend. Well, at least he'd settled the question of Georgia, so she didn't have to feel like she was poaching on anybody's territory. Not that she was poaching. Mitchell Reilly did not seem the sort of man who allowed himself to be poached.

Fortunately, the waiter returned and Mitch paid, and she had no compunction about letting him. After all, she had driven him around, fed him dinner, and provided a solid night's entertainment with the Red Jellybeans. And it looked like she'd be driving him home.

The waiter left and she stood, collected her jacket. "So, where am I taking you to now?"

"Your house?"

"Excuse me?"

He flushed. "I don't mean it to sound like that. I just mean you've been driving me around a lot and I don't want you to have to drive me back downtown when you come back this way again."

"I don't mind." It'd be fun to see where he lived. Then she yawned.

"Yeah, that's the sound of someone who needs her sleep."

That comment walked a little too close to what he said before. But she was being a big girl and not taking offense. For the moment, at least. "So you'll catch an Uber?"

"Yeah."

"You don't need to do that. I'm happy to take you."

"I know. But you've been sick, and I don't want to be responsible for you having a relapse by staying up too late. Especially if you have work tomorrow. I mean it." He pulled out his phone. Tapped the screen. "Actually, it looks like it would take just as much time for me to catch a ride from here as it would from your place. Are you okay if I did that? Or do you want me to come in the car until your place?"

"I've driven myself home alone many times before. But thank you for the offer." That was sweet.

He nodded. "I'll order one now then."

"Okay."

He tapped the screen a few more times, then glanced at her.

"It's probably better this way. That way people aren't wondering why I'm at your house."

"They might think you met someone at the hotel instead."

He winced. "That doesn't sound great when you say it like that either."

It was true, though.

Another yawn erupted from her, which seemed signal enough for him to insist on walking her outside to her car, where he paused. "Now are you sure you're okay to drive? I don't want you falling asleep at the wheel."

"I'll be fine."

"Are you positive?"

Oh, it was sweet how he worried. "One hundred percent."

He nodded, one hand on the roof of her car. "And do you want tickets for tomorrow's game?"

"The season opener? Are there any tickets left?"

"There will be for you if you want them."

Her heart thudded at the intense look in his eyes. But he was only being a friend. She wouldn't read anything more into it. "Then yes. That would be amazing. Thank you. But are you sure you should be playing?"

He rubbed his jaw. "I keep forgetting."

"Mmm. They say that that's a sign of too many concussions."

He glanced at her.

She smirked. "Too soon?"

"You're funny."

"My mom works as a memory care nurse." She shrugged.

"Really?"

Her chin dipped. "You'd be amazed at the stories we've heard."

He studied her another moment. "Come here."

What? Oh. He pulled her to his chest and wrapped his arms around her. And while she knew this was a friend hug, she couldn't help but close her eyes and notice the way his heart beat against her ear, the way his scent of Cool Water tickled her nose. The way his arms felt so secure and protective. A girl could die happy in this hug.

A car's headlights strobed the parking lot, and he released her. "That might be my ride. So, you're sure you're okay?"

"Yes."

He waved to the Uber driver, and glanced at her. "Thanks for today. You'll never know how much it means to me."

And he'd never know just how much his hug had meant to her. She might never marry, but she'd always have the memory of his hug to fuel her dreams.

He waited until she got in the car, then waved as she drove off.

All the way home she replayed the events of the evening. All the way home she remembered how his big body had filled the space of the car, and noticed how his scent still lingered. Tonight felt part miracle, part movie, part dream. And if she could keep squashing any romantic fantasies down to where they belonged then this could be good.

By the time she pulled into the driveway, she was almost fully reconciled at tapping out at friendship. But then she opened the door and was met by her parents and Astrid and Milla.

"Um, I wasn't expecting a welcoming party."

"We weren't expecting you to be as late as you are."

"Come on." She hung up her coat, and tugged off her boots, then collapsed on the sofa. "I'm twenty-eight. I don't have a curfew."

"And you haven't been out on a date with a hockey player before." Milla joined her parents as they claimed the armchairs and lounge.

"It wasn't a date," she scoffed. "He came to youth group, that's all."

"You should see what they're saying on the church Facebook

page." Astrid perched on the coffee table and took out her phone.

"You should know that I'm not looking at social media." Although now she *really* wanted to know. "So what are they saying?"

Astrid laughed. "They think that you and him are a thing."

"Well, we're not. He made that very plain. We're friends, that's all."

"Oh." The disappointment washing over her mom and sisters' faces was so sharp it could shovel snow.

"Is he doing okay?" her dad asked. "He didn't look super well, but I didn't want to say that before."

"He's playing tomorrow, so he can't be too bad." She hoped. *Please God.* "Speaking of, he said something about getting me some tickets for tomorrow night's game. Now I don't know if there's anyone here who might be free to join me, in case there's a spare ticket, but I'm open to bribery."

Milla smiled. "He likes you."

"Yes, as a *friend*, okay? And I'm gonna say this once: I'd really appreciate it if people did not tease me about him or say anything about him, because I don't want to think about him in that way, okay?" Darn these stupid tears. She blinked them back.

"The fact you're getting emotional says—"

"Don't." She pointed at Astrid. "That's not helpful. And if you love me, I *need* you to not tease me or make a fuss. My heart feels fragile enough so I don't want to be trying to protect it from my family, as well as everyone and everything else."

Astrid looked at her then murmured, "I'm sorry."

She nodded, pressed her lips together, and hugged her family members good night, then headed to the shower and then bed. Oh, she had so much to think about, she didn't think she'd ever get to sleep.

∽

HE'D BARELY SLEPT last night. Wondering about his actions yesterday, whether he'd been wise. But surely it had to have been a sign from God that Britta had messaged him, just when he needed her. Their time together had been easy, relaxed, and he'd been open and honest. Well, honest about most things, except insisting on calling her a friend when she felt like so much more. Then he'd wondered if his stupid, off-the-cuff comment about beauty sleep had made her cry. Then chewed over whether she was right and if he should even play today given his news yesterday. Then there was all the wondering about whether he should tell the team this morning. He knew as soon as he opened that can of worms there was no putting them back.

He blinked, refocused, but the blurry vision of yesterday wasn't here right now. *Thanks God*. He'd take that as a sign that he was good to go.

"Okay, let's gather round."

He listened to the coach's instructions. He knew the drill. They were playing Chicago today, who weren't the Stanley Cup-winning team of several seasons ago, when Jai Mullins had lifted the Cup. And it was a season opener at home, so it was important to get a win tonight to prove to the fans that their support was worth it. And the fact that Britta would be out there somewhere made it feel especially important to prove to her and himself that he was okay to play.

He'd messaged her that the tickets could be picked up from the box office, and hoped she'd found some people to bring along. He'd suggested her family, as a bit of a thank-you for crashing their meal last night. Whatever happened tonight, he hoped she had fun.

He finished taping his stick, then found a permanent marker and drew a cross. He needed the reminder that Jesus was with him, especially tonight.

He joined the lineup and headed out for the warm-ups,

soaking in the roar of the crowd. This, he'd miss this when he retired. And while he loved skating, and loved the game, part of him also did love the energy of people invested in him, cheering him on. Although, come to think of it, he'd got a much milder version of that last night when he'd spoken to the Red Jellybeans.

"Yo, Reilly," his captain barked. "It's time to *focus*, not stand around looking happy."

"But what if I am happy?"

"I don't—" expletive "—care."

Yeah, the captain wasn't a local. That Minnesota-nice thing hadn't rubbed off on him.

He joined the others in shooting pucks and did his best to stay focused, even as part of him wanted to see if Britta was here. Daisy had said she'd arrange for the tickets, so he hoped she'd gotten good ones. He hoped Britta could see well and that she'd be proud of him.

He took a shot, then Jack did, and he worked on his angles. He tended to take wrist shots, and often aimed for the upper left over the goalie's shoulder. Wrist shots were quick, requiring less time to set up than a slap shot, and Mitch liked to think of himself as spontaneous, looking to take advantage of other's weaknesses. Of course, if word of his own issues got out there'd be plenty of people wanting to take advantage of his own issues. Mike Vaughan was right: Mitch had made a career of ticking off other people with the kinds of solid hits that still got him booed like whenever he played in Vancouver. He'd apologized to Zac— it was nothing personal—but the fans weren't buying. And hey, it was good for the game and the crowd to have someone to root for, someone to consider a villain. It was just with Britta in the crowd he'd rather be the hero.

He skated around the back of the goal and glanced up, and saw her. She was sitting with her dad and Astrid and the youth leader dude from last night. He skated over, waved, and she smiled and waved back. Yeah, that was what he wanted. Someone there, just for him.

She pressed her hands together in a praying gesture then pointed at him, and he tapped his heart.

"Who you getting gooey with?" Jack asked.

"Nobody."

Jack glanced up. Britta waved to him, too. Man, these nice Minnesotans were everywhere.

"Ah, I see." Jack smirked. "So that explains all the books."

"It never hurts to expand your brain."

The words echoed in his ears, and his stomach twisted. *Lord, protect my brain and every other part of me tonight.*


"THAT WAS SUCH A GOOD GAME!" Britta's grin could power the entire state, her face lighting up the Wild's family room. "Congratulations on your goal."

"Thanks." He hoped he looked modest, even though his heart was fit to burst. "It was a nice way to start the season."

"Four zip is a nice result any day of the week," Britta's dad said.

Mitch nodded. He was glad Pete had come. From his brief visit last night, he'd gotten the impression they were a hard-working family who might enjoy hockey but tended to watch it at home more than live.

"I hope you'll be able to come to some more games," he said. His gaze fell on Britta.

"It was so much fun, it'd be nice to come again." She pushed up her glasses.

He wondered what her eyes would be like without them. He'd gotten a glimpse the other day but she'd been hesitant. He didn't want to push into her personal space. "I have tickets, and I'm real happy if they go to people who care about the game."

"I can't thank you enough, man," Britta's youth group co-leader dude said. Mitch had already forgotten his name.

"You're welcome. Glad you enjoyed." Thank goodness so many conversations didn't require the use of first names, not these days anyway. Was forgetting people's names a sign of this stupid CTE? Or was it just the symptom of someone who didn't care? He probably should investigate if it was the former.

"Tonight was really fun." Astrid smiled as Matt walked past and winked at her. "I'd be happy to come again."

And even though Matt had a girlfriend, he'd bet Matt would be happy to add another notch to his bedpost. Although Astrid seemed to share her sister's values, and seemed pretty capable of looking after herself. "So, are you all heading home, or got time to grab a quick meal?"

"You're going to eat at this late hour?" Britta asked.

Oh, that's right. He'd hoped she'd be up for another meal like last night—well, he'd need something more substantial—but maybe her blood sugar meant she had to be careful what time she ate. "I have to eat soon, otherwise my blood sugar crashes."

"You don't have diabetes too, do you?" Astrid asked.

"No. It's just the natural crash that happens after a big game. I gotta refuel and soon."

"Ah, well, we hadn't exactly planned for that," Pete Johnson said. "I'm on early service welcome duties at church tomorrow, and I don't want a late night."

"I'll come," Britta's co-leader said.

Oh. He wasn't the person his invitation was aimed at.

"Yeah, Ferdy, I don't want a late night either," Astrid said, elbowing him. "And I think I saw your name on the roster too."

"What? I don't remember that." He pulled out his phone, then Astrid pulled him aside.

Okay, his estimation of the woman had gone up a hundred points.

Britta glanced at the others then gave an apologetic-looking smile. "I suppose if they are going home, then I should too, because I'll need a ride."

"No, no, you should stay. I'm sure Mitch would be very happy to give you a ride home. Right, Mitch?" Astrid glared at him.

*Hold your horses, honey.* "Of course," he said, as casually as he could. "I owe you a ride after yesterday, anyway."

"Oh, but…" Britta bit her lip, her eyes wide and anxious.

"I'd really like it if you could stay, for a little while at least."

"Really?"

He nodded, then, when she nodded, gave an internal fist pump.

Mitch turned to her father. "Mr. Johnson, I promise to take good care of your daughter and get her home before midnight."

Pete glanced at his daughter, then back at Mitch, speculation in his eyes. "She's twenty-eight years old, Mitch. And as I heard not so long ago, she doesn't have no curfew."

"Twenty-eight, huh?"

Her chin lifted. "What's wrong with that?"

"Nothing. It's a good age. A great age."

"A great age for what, Mitch?" Astrid asked.

*Scram*, he mouthed at her.

She laughed, and hooked her arm through her father's. "Come on, Dad. I think they're still selling last year's scarves. We should see if we can get a discounted one for our girl here."

"Hey, if you need scarves or jerseys or anything, you only need to ask. Just tell me your sizes and I'll get some."

Pete shook his head. "Now that's real nice of you, but we don't accept no charity."

"I'm happy to accept charity," Astrid said. "I'm a medium jersey." She winked. "You can put that hot guy's name on it if you like."

Yeah, he didn't.

"Astrid," Britta murmured.

"Hey, if the offer's open to everyone then I'm an extra-large," Ferdy said. "Reilly's fine on mine."

"Oh my gosh," Britta moaned. "Look what you started."

He smiled at Britta. "It's no biggie. And it'd be nice to have a few more jerseys out there with my name on it."

"Insecure, are we?"

"So insecure." Especially around her. She was so smart and seventy million kinds of amazing that she made him nervous. "So, anyone want anything else?"

"Look, I really think we should go. It's already going to be a killer with the traffic," Mr. Johnson complained.

"Thank you for coming, sir." Mitch held out his hand. "And as I said, I promise to have her home soon."

"Take care of her."

"Yes, sir."

He shook Ferdy's hand too, and gave Astrid an awkward hug, which then left him and Britta.

She seemed shy, glancing around the team's family room.

"Want me to introduce you to anyone?" he offered.

"Oh no. They're all family and WAGs and I'm just me."

He drew near, picked up her hand. "You're not 'just' anything. You're Britta. Hey, that reminds me. What does Britta mean?"

She glanced at their hands. "It's Scandinavian and means strength or exalted one."

"It suits you."

"What does Mitchell mean?" she asked.

"You know, I've never thought to ask. Maybe we could look it up on the way to getting food. I'm sorry but I'm starving."

"Where do you want to eat?"

He smiled. "I know the perfect place."

# CHAPTER 25

*M*aybe some people would be freaked out by the fact Mitchell took her to his apartment, but she wasn't too concerned. Despite the weird disappearance of Astrid, who she was *sure* would've liked to have come, she felt safe. She was only his friend, after all.

And when he took her there, it certainly made sense why he could be at the library as often as he was. His apartment was just two blocks away, right near where they trained. It was the perfect downtown location. Especially as it had a restaurant down on the bottom floor, that already knew his order, which he collected before taking her to the elevator that took them to the ninth floor.

"This is okay, isn't it?" he asked her, as they ate the meal at his small dining table.

She nodded. "Better than okay. This feels luxurious to me." He'd ordered a couple of different pastas, salads, and a dessert that looked chocolate-based, so unfortunately wouldn't fit in her blood sugar diary. She scooped up another tiny taste of ravioli. "Yum."

"I'm glad you like it. I just thought this was nice and quiet and we can talk. I promise not to take advantage of you."

"Take advantage of—? Oh." She blushed. "Well, as if you would do that to a friend."

"Exactly."

Her head tilted. "Unless that's a line. That's what a line is, right? I've never had anyone use a line on me so I don't even know that I would recognize it if someone used one."

"It's not a line, Britta. And I hope that you know I would never try and use some cheesy line to persuade you to do something you don't want to do."

"What if it is something I want to do?" Heat rushed to her cheeks. Oh, why did she have to have a mouth with an unfortunate tendency to run away on her? "Not that I mean *that*. But— oh, never mind." Although every single pore in her body minded. What was wrong with her? Maybe this was why Bev thought Britta needed practice speaking with men, seeing as her mouth couldn't be trusted to not embarrass her.

He eyed her, and she wondered what he was thinking. Then he exhaled heavily. "I think we're better off leaving the flirty talk aside."

Flirty talk?

"I just want you to trust me," he said.

"I do trust you."

"You do?"

She nodded, glad to put aside that earlier embarrassing moment and focus on something else. "Call me naive, but I've seen the way you are with others. And I think you're a pretty solid guy."

His lips curved. "You do, do you?"

"You live up to your name."

"You looked it up?"

"While you were getting the food. Mitchell has Hebrew origins, and is related to Michael, which means 'who is like God'. It has links to the archangel Michael who fought and defeated and hurled the devil from heaven. So the name conveys a sense of power, bravery and strength." She smiled at him. "That's a pretty good meaning."

He swallowed like he was moved. "I…" He glanced away.

His hand lay on the table near her own, tempting her. They were friends, but this eating alone together—gosh, that phrase sounded weird—and then some of their conversation felt like it was starting to blur the lines. She slid her hand back.

Then he reached across and grabbed it.

She peeked up at him, he was still staring at the table, his mouth pulled down in a frown. "What's wrong?"

"You know, I don't think I ever told you why I don't like the name Mr. Reilly."

"Why is that?" she asked softly.

"Because it makes me think of my father, and I hate my father. Well, I hated him. We found out earlier this year that he died."

Her chest cramped. "I'm so sorry."

He shrugged. "He left us when I was eight. Left my mom to take care of five kids twelve and under. My sister, Ellie, she was only one."

"Oh, that's awful." She squeezed his hand.

"My mom did the best she could, but it was hard, y'know? We have a ranch in Trinity Lakes."

"How big a ranch?"

He described it, then shared about his siblings: Dermott, Jackson, Cooper and Ellie, each of whom had found love in recent years. "Even my mom, after being on her own for so many years, seems to have a man friend."

"Good for her."

"Yeah. Good for her."

He glanced at her. His look held weight, and she wondered what he was thinking. She licked her lip, nervously. "What is it?"

He heaved a sigh, sat back in his chair, but his thumb played across the back of her hand sending shivery thrills in her insides. This wasn't what friends did, was it? Or was she so completely clueless she had no idea? Probably should lock in Option B, Peter.

"Mitch?"

He glanced at her. "My family don't come east too often, but when they do, would you be willing to meet them?"

"Your family?"

He nodded. "I don't think Jackson would leave the ranch. His wife is pregnant, so I don't expect to see them over here. I try to get tickets when we play in Seattle because sometimes he can make it then."

"And who else is there?"

He ticked off his fingers. "Dermott and Mindy live in the Independence Islands off South Carolina, then the others, by age, Jackson, Cooper and Ellie. She's the baby. But she got married this year." His lips curved. "She married her best friend, Jasper. He was pining for her for years."

"Aww, that's so sweet."

"He's a good guy."

"That seems to run in the family."

He glanced at her.

"Well he is, and you are..."

His face grew soft. "I have never met anyone like you before."

Her heart kicked, like she'd just sucked down a Red Bull. But she couldn't get carried away. "Someone ordinary and plain?" As soon as she got home, she was telling Astrid to dye her eyelashes. And maybe see if they could find some contacts that didn't hurt her eyes.

"Britta, why do you keep saying things like that? I don't see someone ordinary. I see someone extraordinary."

Her usual retort would be a joke, something along the lines

of "someone needs to get his eyesight checked". But the way he kept staring at her locked those words in her mouth.

He shifted to the seat next to hers, then moved closer still, until he placed her hand in his upon his heart. "I don't see someone plain. I see someone whose eyes are filled with light, just like her heart, and when she's happy, her whole face lights up, and makes everyone around her happy."

Emotion bit at the back of her eyes, then fogged up her glasses. She had to remove them, one handed, because he still hadn't released her hand.

His breath caught, and he leaned near some more, then pushed a lock of hair behind her ear. "Britta." His voice held a rasp, and he brushed his knuckles down her cheek.

Her heart started pounding, and his nearness meant she closed her eyes. Friends didn't do this. He was going to kiss her. To *kiss* her. Oh, she hoped she'd know what to do. She might've watched a million movies and read a billion books but there was a world of difference between reality and make-believe. She leaned closer, felt his breath on her skin, then...

He sighed. The air cooled between them. She opened her eyes.

What had happened? Had she done something wrong? She could've sworn he was about to kiss her. So why hadn't he?

"I'm sorry," he murmured, not looking at her.

*He* was sorry? She was the one who had just been denied her first kiss.

Did he not want her? Did she not meet a certain special standard? Did her breath smell?

She pretended to rub her nose, but took a quick sniff. No, it smelled normal. So what had happened?

"Britta, I..."

She suddenly didn't want to hear his explanations. Didn't want to hear where she had failed. Didn't want to hear how she didn't fit in with the rest of the beautiful wives and girlfriends she'd seen in the family room tonight. A memory sparked. Hadn't he once said she wasn't his type? Oh, how well she knew it. And why she was disappointed, why she was even thinking about this, only proved that she'd wanted more than he was willing to give, and proved her imagination would be the death of her.

"I...I think I need to go home if that's okay."

"Home?"

"Yes. My home. But hey, it's okay, you don't need to take me. You used Uber the other day. I guess it works the other direction too."

"No, I'll take you."

"You really don't have to."

"I do. I promised your dad and I'm not gonna break my word to him."

But what about his word to her? How could he lean in for that magical moment then leave her shortchanged? That was a promise as much as anything. "I want to go now please."

"Is this because of..." He swallowed, then gestured between the two of them. "This?"

A classic line from *Jane Eyre* begged to be uttered. "Do you think because I am poor, obscure, plain, and little, I am soulless and heartless? You think wrong! - I have as much soul as you, - and full as much heart!"

Instead, she shrugged. "I don't know what you mean."

"Britta, I didn't mean to upset you."

"I'm not upset." She feigned a yawn. "Like I said yesterday, I turn into a pumpkin if I stay up too late."

She held his gaze, willing him to believe her, then he nodded. "Fine. Let's go."

❧

HE WAS SUCH AN IDIOT. The night had been going so well, and then he realized how much he wanted to kiss her and had been about to, then realized if he kissed her he'd be breaking the personal code he'd set himself. He wouldn't take advantage of her. And it was late, they were in his home, and she was innocent, and he wasn't, and he knew where kissing alone could lead to. So he pulled back. Then so had she. And now it seemed, from the way she was walking fast to his car, she couldn't get far enough away from him.

The first half of the drive was silent. And maybe she actually was tired because she had her eyes closed for part of it. Maybe that was simply her praying, asking God to get her back safely in one piece.

His heart hurt. He couldn't finish tonight on this sour note. "Britta, I'm sorry about before."

"It's okay. You're tired, and so am I, and there's been a lot going on so it's really easy to misread things."

Misread things? Is that what he'd done? He'd thought her closing her eyes was an invitation for him to kiss her. Had she just been tired, after all?

"You know I like you," he began.

"I know we're *friends*." She emphasized that last word. "And that's okay. That's great! Because apart from Ferdy, I don't have that many guy friends, so this is good, figuring out how this can be."

No, no. She didn't mean that surely. "Britta, I—"

"So, have you thought anything more about what you're gonna tell the team?"

"Tell the team?" he repeated.

"About what the specialist said."

Oh, that was a low blow, changing the subject like that, putting the focus back on him. Still, her question demanded an answer. "I want to take a little bit longer. It went okay tonight. Not a single blow to the head."

"Wow."

She didn't sound impressed. "What's that supposed to mean?"

"Well, you know that the neurologist is really concerned. You can't afford to pretend it's not going to be an issue."

"Thank you, Dr. Britta."

"Don't be petty. I told you that my mom deals with patients who have suffered brain injuries, and are now living with the consequences. Some of those are people who made choices to continue to do activities that put their lives at risk."

"I'm not putting my life at risk," he scoffed. "Come on. You saw me tonight. I was fine."

"So you're fine tonight. What about tomorrow? What about the next day? When was the last time you had symptoms?"

Yesterday. But he couldn't say that out loud.

"I'm guessing that it was recently if you don't want to tell me."

He dug deep for patience. "Britta, I appreciate that you are concerned. This is my business."

"And as your *friend*," she kept saying that in a weird way, "then I consider it my business to point out when my friends are doing dumb things. And you, my friend, are doing a dumb thing by continuing to play and pretending that you're okay and not telling the team."

He clamped his lips together, drummed his fingers on the steering wheel. "Are we almost at your home?"

"Really? You're going to ignore me now, huh?"

"I think you said everything you need to say. It's nothing new."

"Wow. Okay, then."

"Okay."

They were not okay. He hated this tension between them, especially as he knew it was his fault. He wished he could go back thirty minutes to the almost kissing moment before. He should've just dived in there. He pulled up outside her house. "Britta, I'm sorry."

She was quiet for a long moment, then nodded. "I'm sorry too." She glanced across at him. "But I'll be even more sorry if you have an injury and you're in a wheelchair at the age of fifty."

He sucked in a deep breath. Exhaled. He guessed from the way she was picking up her purse that he had ten seconds to put this right. *Lord, help me.* "Britta, I'm sorry I disappoint you."

Some of the tension left her face as her shoulders dropped. "I'm sorry too. You're right. It's your life, and I should trust you to make the best decision."

*Best decision.* Like pulling back from kissing her so he could focus on building a friendship with her rather than jump straight into the physical like he'd always done. Well, not that he'd done that with Georgia, but then he hadn't exactly focused on building a friendship with her either.

"I want to be your friend," he said.

Her lips pressed together and she nodded.

"And I gotta admit I'm rusty at that. Worse than rusty. I don't think I've been a friend to a woman before."

"Not even Georgia?"

"No." He glanced at her. "You and Ellie were right, you know. Georgia was too young for me, and in a different stage of life. It would never have worked out."

She nodded, but didn't say anything. Bless her for not saying *I told you so.*

"So, uh, how do we be friends?"

She peeked across at him. "That sounds like such a kindergarten thing to say, doesn't it?"

"It sounds lame, but it's still true. I want to be your friend. I want to know you. And your family. And your church, and yeah, everything."

"Well, if you're serious, you could come with my family and me to church tomorrow."

"Didn't your dad say he was going to early church?"

"Yeah, but he stays for the second service." She shrugged. "Then you could come back and have lunch with us if you want to know my family more."

"Really?" His heart hungered for that.

"But you probably have training or something like that to do, so—"

"Actually, no. We have a trip on Monday, which means we have tomorrow free. Tomorrow or today? I don't know what time it is."

"It's late o'clock, that's what time it is." She emphasized that comment with a yawn. "Um, thanks for the meal, and the tickets, and driving me home."

"Thanks for coming. Oh, and do you want me to send the jerseys here or to the library?"

"Oh, you really don't have to do that."

"I want to. And I said I would, and I'm trying to be a man of my word."

"Well, I wouldn't want to get in the way of that then. Here is fine."

He nodded, making a mental note. He hoped that mental note stayed in place. Then he remembered what she'd said before. "Did you mean it? About me coming to church tomorrow?"

"Of course. I don't say things I don't mean, either."

"Apart from that comment before about everything being okay," he teased.

"Well, apart from that. Obviously." She rolled her eyes, but a small smile peeked out anyway. "But I think things are more okay now."

"Way more okay now," he agreed. Apologies tended to do that. As did admitting his insecurities, like needing her help in order to be her friend. Of course, he couldn't admit to too many insecurities or expose his heart too much. That way she'd be sure to be running for the hills.

But right now, it felt like they had a shot. A shot at friend-ship. And if that could be solid enough, maybe even a shot at love.

His stomach fluttered. "Come on. Let me walk you inside."

# CHAPTER 26

$\mathcal{C}$ould there possibly be anything more weird than sitting in her family's living room, watching a *Pride and Prejudice* adaptation, next to Mitchell Flippin' Reilly?

She peeked across, caught his smile, then shifted her attention back to the screen, but not before seeing Astrid and Milla smooth away smiles. Honestly, for all that she was watching a Regency-era movie she might as well be living in one, given that everyone had decided to be her chaperone this afternoon.

She knew Astrid did not like this version, but did that stop her sitting down? No.

And Milla, too, had apparently blown off a date to join in. Even her mom was watching, although Britta suspected she was watching the Britta-and-Mitch sideshow as much as Keira and Matthew on the screen. And it must look pretty funny seeing a big hockey player crashed out on their lounge, arms folded as he nitpicked his way through the movie.

"Why is Keira the only one not wearing gloves at the ball?"

"An excellent question, my friend," Astrid said.

*Her* friend? No, he was Britta's friend.

"Why do they have animals running through the house?" he

continued. "I thought Mr. Bennet was supposed to be a gentleman."

"You thought that, huh?" she asked.

He shrugged. "I might've read a little bit more."

"You've read *Pride and Prejudice*?" Milla asked, her incredulity obvious.

"Your sister set me a challenge." He glanced at Britta.

"One you still have to meet."

"I plan to meet it one day."

The intense look in his eyes sent her stomach into somersaults. He couldn't *not* mean anything by that, right? Judging from the smirk-swapping between her sisters, they seemed to think so too.

The whole morning had been weird, a complete contrast to the emotional highs and lows of last night. Today's appearance at church, when he joined their pew, had caused not a small amount of kerfuffle. She'd heard the whispers of "Look, it's Mitch Reilly!" and known people must be wondering what he was doing sitting next to her.

*He's only my friend*, she wanted to scream, but one didn't do that in church. But surely he must know what it looked like to single her out like this? When the service had finished, he'd shaken a few hands then exited out the back, where she found him later, surrounded by some of the Red Jellybeans from Friday night.

The sight of him talking with them, laughing with them, caused a twinge of tightness in her chest. He looked at home there, like he was in his element. Finding her footing in this friendship with him was tricky. She didn't want to read too much into things, and she didn't want anyone else to read too much into things, either. She had to hold this loosely. If she invested too much of her heart, she was bound for disappointment.

"I heard he was a smash with the Jellybeans on Friday night," Bev had said at the service.

"He was a natural. Like he'd been doing it all his life."

"I'm sorry I didn't get a chance to talk to you before, but Deirdre Messinger told me you had an unpleasant encounter at the speed dating mingle."

Wow. She'd almost forgotten that. "Yes, one of the gentlemen proved to be a little too old-fashioned for me. Or any woman born in this century or the last."

Bev laughed. "But it seems you don't need to worry about Mr. Wrong, not with Mr. Reilly proving to be a hit, or so I heard."

"We're just friends."

"Mmm. Well, some of the best relationships I know have stemmed from friends who became more."

"I can't afford to think like that."

"Well, I'll be praying. And I'm glad he's here, even if the mingle did not turn out the way you'd hoped."

"I'm so grateful that you and the ladies put that on, so thank you. I hope some of the others made some connections."

"I think we'll see some good results." Bev had winked and moved away.

She hoped Leanne and the others had made connections. It would be good if some of them could find new friends at least.

She glanced back at her own new friend, still watching the movie on the screen, and studied his profile. She hadn't had much of an opportunity to really look at him since he'd shaved his beard. Now she could see the scars on his chin, the square jaw and bump on his nose. His hair was thick and dark, the strong eyebrows communicating so much in a single lift or lower. Right now that was lower.

"What's wrong now?" she asked.

"I don't like her voice," he grumbled.

"Whose voice?"

"Keira's." He'd refused to call her Elizabeth. "I can't even hear what she's saying half the time. And everyone just talks too fast."

She bit her lip, glanced at her mom. Was that one of the symptoms of CTE?

Her mom met her gaze then smiled. Okay, that didn't look like an expression of concern.

"I've always thought her voice sounds too wispy and thin." Astrid said. "And his sounds too deep."

"She sounds like a girl, not a woman," Mitch complained. "A man needs a woman, not a girl."

Her heart grew tight. Was he referencing more than just the movie? Judging from the way Astrid and Milla were smiling at her, maybe he was. But she couldn't get carried away. They were friends, that was all. She pulled a cushion to hide her stomach. A woman's stomach, a little soft and squishy, like she'd had a baby, when she hadn't experienced the act that led to that. How could she, when she hadn't even had a kiss?

The movie ended, and she caught his huff and roll of eyes at the "Mrs. Darcy" moment at the end.

"Not your cup of tea?"

"Look, I'll admit the music was nice, and it was good to not have Mrs. Bennet acting so hysterically all the time, that got really annoying in the first one. But you can understand more in the Colin Firth version."

"That's the difference between a five-hour adaptation and a two," Milla said.

Astrid folded her arms. "I've never really liked this version."

"I think a lot depends on which version you watch first as to which one you prefer," Britta said.

"You prefer the other one, right?" Mitch said.

"I think it's a more accurate representation of the book."

"The book, the book. You like things played by the book, right?"

"Always."

"So, was that scene when Mr. Darcy dives into the lake in the book?"

"Well, no."

He smiled. "What about the bathtub scene? Is that why you like that version?"

"No!"

"You keep telling yourself that."

Her jaw dropped, as her sisters sniggered, and even her mother smiled.

He laughed. "She's fun to tease, huh?"

She flung her cushion at him. "You can leave now."

His laughing eyes softened. "Do I have to? This has been fun."

It had been. After the service he'd joined them at home where he'd given them their new jerseys, then they had lunch, then watched the movie. All the time her sisters had eyed him, then eyed her, and she'd had to keep silently mouthing "We're only friends" to them, just as she had when she'd finally got in the door last night.

"He didn't try anything?" Astrid had asked last night.

"No." Well, he'd tried, then changed his mind, so that didn't count. "He said he wants to be my friend."

"Oh." The obvious disappointment washing over their faces had matched that in Britta's heart.

But today had been good. Relaxed, easy. And while she hadn't had a male friend like him before, he seemed to fit in even more easily than Ferdy had done. He was comfortable in his skin, owned a confidence she wished she could portray, and seemed to understand that in their family, tease was as natural as hugs and eating multekrem at Christmas.

Christmas. She shivered. Would he still be around by then? Would things have changed? But before then there was Thanksgiving, and... Oh! Should she mention her school reunion to him? No. He wouldn't want to go. He probably had a game on, anyway. But she had a funny feeling that the Wild's playing schedule that was burned in her brain said he'd be free...

He got a phone call, and excused himself to take it.

As soon as he was gone from the room, her sisters rushed to her. "I can't *believe* that man just watched a movie with us." The size of Astrid's eyes could rival helipads.

"He likes you," Milla whispered.

"No, he said we're just friends, so I'm trying my hardest not to read anything more into it than that."

"But—"

"But nothing. Please don't make this any harder than it is."

"Aww, poor Britta." Milla hugged her. "He seems nice."

"He does," her mom added. "Very polite and respectful."

"He wants to make a good impression on us," Astrid said.

"Please stop."

"Fine." Astrid rolled her eyes, but her smile said she likely wouldn't. "Hey, are we going to decorate this afternoon or what?"

"Decorate?" Mitch asked, returning to the room.

"Our street has one of those competitions between neighbors about who decorates their house best for Halloween," Britta explained. "We don't love Halloween, but we like decorating and dressing up."

"I've noticed that about you," he said.

His smile caused another glitch in her heart.

"Oh, Britta gets into it so much." Astrid wrapped her arm around Britta's shoulders. "She's so good with kids, she'll make a great mom one—"

"So, did you need to go now, Mitch?" Britta's voice was far too high just now to sound convincing. Any moment now and her voice could be accused of being Keira-worthy wispy and thin.

He shook his head. "Can I help decorate?"

"You betcha," Dad said, from his chair in the dining room

where he'd been reading *Popular Mechanics*. "I don't mind having somebody else get up on a ladder instead of me."

"Sure. I'd love to help."

"You would?"

Mitch shrugged. "I've never really decorated for any holiday. I did a bit when I sometimes stayed with the Gulbrandsens when I first left home. That was them on the phone before. They want me to visit, they live in a small town not too far from here, so I'll try to see them soon, maybe next weekend. But while they were nice as all get-out, they didn't do Halloween." He shrugged. "So I didn't really decorate ever."

"Not even a Christmas tree?"

"There's not much point when I live by myself and travel so much."

"Do you see your family for Christmas or Thanksgiving?"

"Not Thanksgiving," he admitted. "Our schedule is usually too tight then. I try to make Christmas, but it depends on our games."

"Do you ever see your family?" Milla asked.

"Yeah. But they live a long way away, so it's not easy. I usually try to get there each summer, but even so we're not close. I mean, I love them, don't get me wrong, but it's not like this." He gestured to the kitchen, with her mom's heritage on display in the carved spoons and special glassware in the illuminated cupboards. There was history here, a family's love.

She remembered what he had told her about his family, and her heart grew sore. She glanced at him, and his lips pressed together and he shook his head at her a little, like he was saying "don't pity me now".

"Well, if you need a place to come for Thanksgiving, you're welcome here," her mom said.

"Really?"

"If that's okay with Britta, of course."

Way to go with giving her an easy out. Not that she wanted one. "Of course that's okay."

"Yeah, if you come, you can watch the Mormon *Pride and Prejudice* version," Milla said.

"The what?"

"It's a contemporary version, set in Utah, so it's kind of fun."

"And the heroine works in a bookshop, so she's a little bit like Britta."

Britta rolled her eyes at Astrid. "I don't think we need to be watching any more *Pride and Prejudice*. Not until somebody finishes reading the book, at least."

"Whoa, shots are fired," Astrid murmured with a grin.

"Are you saying I need to read the rest of the book before you'll watch it with me?" Mitch said, lips twitching.

"I can't believe you would even want to watch another one."

"I would if it means spending time with you," he said in a low voice.

Her heart squeezed. But friends weren't meant to say stuff like that, were they?

"Ooh! Let's go grab the popcorn," Astrid said. "Who needs a movie when we can watch this?"

Mitch arched a thumb at her sisters. "Are they always like this?"

"You've got no idea."

"I like it." His expression softened. "I like this."

Her dad walked into the room and dropped a dusty box of decorations onto the counter with a thud. "So, are you gonna stand around all day chatting up my daughters or you gonna help me with some of this?"

"I'm helping, sir."

"We're all helping," Astrid said. Then pushed Britta toward him. "Here, Britta wants to help you too."

He steadied her, grasping her upper arms. "Thanks for today, it's been fun. I've never really spent much time with a family like this."

"I'm glad you could come." And she meant it.

MITCH GLANCED across at where Britta sat, watching the red and gold trees flash by. October was one of the prettiest months in upstate Minnesota, and a time when leaf peepers made the most of fine Sunday afternoons like this.

And while he hadn't been leaf-peeping, he'd been glad for the chance to spend a rare Sunday off to go to church this morning then visit the Gulbrandsens this afternoon. Church had gone well. People hadn't seemed so surprised to see him this second time around, and he and Britta had been able to escape quicker than expected to travel an hour up north to where he'd spent two formative years of his life. The late lunch with Len and Linda had been another reminder of what he wanted one day. A house, a family, filled with love.

"So you had fun?" he asked her now as they returned.

She peeked across. "It was really good to meet Len and Linda. Although I still don't know why you wanted me to come."

Because he was trying to slowly introduce her to his world. To help her know and make her comfortable with those he loved. He'd explained a little of that to Linda, but he couldn't admit that to Britta, so he went with the other true thing. "I thought you'd enjoy meeting a fellow bookworm."

She eyed him, like she wasn't sure whether to believe him, then nodded.

When Len had been showing off his roses to Britta, Linda had murmured, "She's sweet, but not quite the kind of woman I imagined you introducing us to one day."

"How so?" Indignation rose up. Linda was kindhearted, surely she didn't mean—?

"She's a woman, not a girl, for starters. And she's smart and likes books, so that's an instant plus for me." The ex-English teacher had laughed. "And she's got depth and such a passion for the lost. I don't mind admitting that Len and I have been a little concerned for you over the years, and praying so hard for you to come back to the Lord. I'm so pleased you have, and that you brought her here."

"She's good for me," he'd admitted.

"I can see that."

"But we're taking it slow," he warned, seeing the wedding bells in Linda's eyes.

"Are you? From what I gathered, you were proposing to one girl one minute, then with Britta the next."

"Britta and I aren't together, and there was no proposal. That was officially ending something that I'm now realizing existed mostly in my imagination."

She patted his arm, her sympathy plain. "And this one?"

"I want her to trust me, so we're building a friendship."

"Wise man."

Wise in one way, maybe. He still hadn't owned up to the team about his concussion results. Britta had mentioned it again this week but had backed off when he asked her to, which he appreciated. He needed more time to figure out what to say. Mike had messaged, asked how he was doing, and he'd fobbed him off with *It's fine.* And it *had* been fine. The past games on their road trip to Toronto, Montreal and Ottawa had seen a return of his usual grit and fire. No hits to the head. *Thank You, Jesus.* So he'd been fine, and would remain so. *In Jesus's name.* But he remained grateful that she hadn't raised the topic today.

His conversation with Britta on the way up had centered mostly around the sermon and how the Gulbrandsens had featured in his life. He'd told her about spending time with them when he had a scholarship to one of Minnesota's high schools that had produced more NHL players than almost any other. Told her about finding faith with them, which had been eroded when the perks and grind of the NHL had set in.

Now, however, on their return journey as the sunset gilded the trees, they could talk about the past week. And the upcoming one.

"I'm really glad you could meet them, not just for their sake, but for mine. Because it's nice to see you rather than message or speak on the phone." He glanced at her again. Saw her blush.

He liked that about her. She was so honest and direct it felt like even her skin couldn't hold a lie.

"So, last we messaged, you mentioned the past week has gone well at the library."

"Yes. It was good to finally get back into the Bookmobile again. I forgot how much I missed it."

He listened to her chatter, loving the way the soft late afternoon light lit her face as she mentioned various people and their books and their funny experiences.

"I just love how we can provide a service that really blesses people, you know? So many people have said the Bookmobile is the highlight of their day, especially in winter when snow and ice-laden sidewalks keep people indoors, it's so good to be someone that brightens their day."

"You do that all the time. Brighten people's days, I mean."

"Mmm, that's not exactly true. Margaret, where I work, I think she's convinced I'm coming for her job. She doesn't see sunshine but a threat."

"Why? What's happened?"

"Oh, it was just a silly thing. Gwen and Helen, the library head, were having a meeting the other day and I was walking past, and they called me in to check on me, which was sweet. But then Margaret saw, and as soon as I returned to the kids' section she was pumping me for details and hinting that I should take a position in Saint Anthony Park."

"That's miles away."

"Exactly."

"She's jealous of you."

"I don't know why."

"Because you have a passion for what you do, and everyone can see it. I mean it. It's like what the pastor was preaching about this morning. You have a gift of encouragement, and it brightens people's lives."

"Wow, Mitch. That's… thank you."

"It's true. I see it in how you treat your Jellybean kids, and treat total strangers. You have a warmth with people that brings out their best."

She chuckled.

"What?"

"Well, that's obviously not true. I don't think Mark at the Christian mingle event thought I had any warmth at all."

"I don't want you *ever* thinking about him again," he said firmly. "He's got an iceberg for a heart, which means you made him sweat."

"Pretty sure I was the one sweating that night," she murmured. "Among other things."

"I didn't notice. I only noticed how good you looked."

"You liked it when I dressed up?" she asked tentatively, fingering her jeans.

"You looked great then, and you look great now, and you even looked great dressed as a bumblebee."

She snorted. "How much of Linda's bundt cake did you eat? I didn't think it had hallucinogenic properties."

"Why do you do that? You put yourself down, and you shouldn't. You're special, Britta."

Her breath caught, and she glanced out the window again, biting her lip.

He was about to ask her what was wrong when his phone rang. He glanced at the vehicle's dash screen which indicated it was Ellie.

"Hey, want to meet my sister?"

"What, now?"

"She's calling. You could answer if you like. Mess with her a bit."

She smiled. "Okay." She pressed answer on his phone. "Hello?"

"Oh! Is this Mitchell's phone?"

"Yes."

"Who is this?" Ellie demanded.

"Britta."

"Britta? Uh, why are you answering? Is Mitch there?"

"Who is this?" Britta said.

He stifled a chuckle.

"This is Ellie, his sister. Would you put him on please?"

"Sure." She pressed speaker, and the car audio switched on.

"Mitchell? What floozy have you got answering your phone now?"

"Ellie, you're on speaker." He winked at Britta, who looked to be holding in her own laughter.

"Oh my gosh. Uh, Britta, are you there?"

"Why yes I am, Ellie."

He chuckled.

"Mitchell, this isn't funny, and you're making me think I won't come and see you now."

"Whoa, are you heading over this way?"

"Jasper has a hardware store convention—"

"That's a thing?"

"It's in Minneapolis next week," she said, ignoring him, "and I thought I could go with him, and come see you for part of that, and maybe watch a game."

"That'd be awesome." He could count on one hand the

number of times his family had come to see his home games. And if it meant she and Jasper could meet Britta too…

"But now I'm not so sure."

"Aww, come on Ellie, don't be sore. You and Britta should definitely meet."

"Why?"

"Because you're both interested in similar things."

"We are?" Britta said. "I thought you said she ran a ranch."

"Has he been talking about me?" Ellie asked.

"He mentioned that he loves you, and you're his favorite sister, and—"

"Yeah, I'm not sure about the first, but that second thing is definitely something he would say. Mostly because I'm his only sister."

"Well, from what I've gathered the first is true, too," Britta said.

"Who are you and what have you done with my brother? Mitchell, have you been abducted by aliens? Use the code word if that's true."

Mitchell laughed. So much for messing with his sister. Between Ellie and Britta, they were doing a pretty good job of messing with him. "I think you two will get on fine. When do you get in?"

Ellie shared some details and he glanced at Britta who seemed to be enjoying the show. He soon ended the call. "Sorry about that."

"You're not sorry. And I'm not either. She sounds like fun."

"She's like another Astrid."

Her eyes gleamed. "Then this will be fun."

# CHAPTER 27

The following Wednesday, Britta swallowed as she swiped her hands down her jeans. Nothing like meeting Mitch's family for dinner. At his apartment, no less. She gripped more tightly the straps of the cool-bag that held her dessert.

"Ellie and Jasper, this is Britta. Britta, meet my sister and favorite brother-in-law."

"His only brother-in-law, but whatever." Jasper rolled his eyes. Held out his hand. "Nice to meet you."

"You too."

Ellie seemed to take her measure, then held out her hand, too. "Finally."

"I'm sorry?"

"Don't be. If you're the woman he's been waiting for, then it's been worth the wait."

Heat flushed Britta's cheeks. "We're not—"

"Ellie," Mitchell growled.

Ellie laughed, and in that mischievous grin she shot her brother, Britta could see why Mitch thought Ellie shared qualities with Astrid. Those two would get on like a house on fire.

But as the evening progressed, with perfectly cooked steaks and healthy vegetables like Mitch knew exactly what she should eat, it seemed he was right, and she and Ellie did share a number of things in common. They both enjoyed studies—Ellie with her history, Britta with her English Lit. They both shared a fondness for historical dramas and rom-com movies of the 90s and 2000s. But Mitch was a little off the mark in one area.

"Mitch, you know that me running a history museum in Trinity Lakes is not the same thing as Britta working at a public library in Saint Paul, right?" Ellie rolled her eyes.

"I just kind of thought they were. You both deal with people."

"Who doesn't deal with people?" Ellie said. "Even Jasper works with people, and he works in a hardware store."

"Until recently Cooper didn't deal with people," Mitch grumbled, then glanced at Britta. "He's my youngest brother."

She nodded.

"Second youngest in the clan," Ellie volunteered. "He's a tech geek and super smart. I think he and Jessica are ready to set a date."

"Really?" Mitch asked, a pleat in his brow.

She studied him. Why would this concern him?

Ellie snickered. "Come on, bro. You don't need to look worried. Jess is perfect for him, and just think of all the bills that Jackson can save if a vet marries into the family."

Britta chuckled.

"That's not it," Mitch mumbled.

"Then what is?"

He glanced briefly at Britta then shrugged. "Nothing. Hey, who wants dessert?"

"What is it?" Jasper asked.

"How do you say it, Britta?" Mitch asked.

"Tilslørte bondepiker. It's a Norwegian dessert," Britta said. "Like a cross between a parfait and apple crumble."

"Now you're talking."

She produced it from Mitch's fridge and served it, and it quickly disappeared to murmurs of approval.

"That was delicious," Ellie said. "It's a little tart and a little sweet."

"Just like Ellie." Mitch smirked.

"Hey, my wife is not a tart," Jasper protested, winking at Britta.

"I meant—"

The others laughed. Aww, poor Mitch. She placed a hand on his back, which Ellie instantly seemed to notice as her eyes brightened. Britta dropped her hand. Hurried from the dining area to the kitchen. Wished she could shrink so she could slip down the sink.

What was she doing here? Why did Mitch keep inviting her to meet important people in his life then kept insisting they were only friends? The longer he kept this up, the harder it was getting to be.

"Hey."

She jumped. "I didn't hear you come in."

"You were lost in your own world there." He leaned against a kitchen cabinet. "Is everything okay?"

"Yes." It would be. When she left, maybe. It was much easier to do the friend thing when they were apart. But here, in his presence, catching the occasional drift of his scent, seeing his eyes darken when she held his gaze, it was enough to befuddle a girl. Or a woman. Especially one who was old enough to know better.

She lifted her gaze, saw his attention firmly on her, and there it was again. That intensity that made her heart flutter and made her wonder just what he was looking at.

"Are you sure?" His brow lowered. "Is your blood sugar okay?"

"Yes." It was time to get this conversation off herself. "How about you? Have you had any more concussion symptoms lately?"

"Britta." He pressed his lips together as his sister wandered in.

"Did I hear you say concussion symptoms?" Ellie asked, glancing between the two of them. "What do you mean?"

Mitch heaved out a breath. "It's nothing."

Britta crossed her arms and raised a brow.

Ellie pointed at her. "That is not the look of nothing. What's going on, Mitchell?"

He shook his head.

Oh, she'd ticked him off now. But Britta wasn't sorry. His family needed to know. This was a secret she was getting tired of keeping.

"If you don't tell me, I'm gonna ask your girlfriend."

"I'm not his girlfriend," she mumbled.

Mitch shot her a look that suggested that right now he might not even consider her his friend. She turned to the sink, filled it with hot water, and began cleaning the gold-rimmed glasses as the siblings squabbled behind her.

"Look, it's nothing for you to worry about," Mitch insisted. "I get headaches occasionally, that's all."

"*Is* that all?" Ellie demanded.

When Mitch said nothing, she said, "Britta?"

She sighed, and turned to face her. She couldn't look at Mitch right now. "I don't know the details, but from what he said, a neurologist has advised him to quit hockey."

"What?" Ellie shrieked.

She risked a glance at Mitch. He was glaring at her, arms crossed. She shrugged. "Your family needs to know."

"I can't *believe* you never told us this." Ellie thumped her brother's arm. "Why are you still playing?" She gasped. "Have you not told the team?"

A muscle throbbed in his jaw.

Ellie glanced at Britta.

Britta shook her head.

"Oh my gosh. What is wrong with you, Mitch?" She hit his shoulder then glanced at Britta again. "I knew my brother was stubborn, but I didn't realize he was stupid, too."

"He's not stupid. There's just a lot to process."

"And I bet it's really hard to process if he doesn't have all of his brain working. Gosh, Mitchell. Do I need to contact the team? Obviously your girlfriend isn't game."

Indignation flared. "I'm not his girlfriend, nor his keeper. He's a grown man, and if he wants to make a decision that could permanently affect his life, then that's on him. It's his life." From her peripheral vision she caught Mitchell's nod.

"But it's not just his life he's affecting," Ellie retorted. "It's the life of whoever he ends up marrying. She's the person that's going to have to look after him if his brain is so compromised that he can't function properly."

Britta froze. How many times had she heard her mother share stories of exactly that scenario? Mom had never shared names, of course, but the situations she'd described felt eerily similar. Brain injuries could happen for all kinds of reasons— accident, assault, all manner of awful things. But the ones her mom could never understand were those people who played sports or continued risk-taking activities when advised not to, who got one knock too many. Their personalities changed, they isolated themselves, and their families were left to pick up the pieces when dementia or other diseases ravaged their minds or bodies.

And she, she'd started to care for this man who was stubborn, just like his sister said. This man who refused to listen to a doctor's wise counsel. Who would likely blame her for saying something about his own failings, when all she'd done was try to help. But was Ellie right? Was staying silent simply enabling his condition to worsen? Nausea rippled through her stomach. She was so ashamed of herself.

How could she let him walk into a future that felt fraught with failure? How could she let another woman bear that burden? It wouldn't be her—he'd made that clear.

Her heart buckled. The whole evening now felt like a farce. "I think I should go."

"Oh, Britta, I didn't mean to upset you," Ellie said. "I'm just upset that my idiot brother—"

"He's not an idiot. Please don't say that."

"But he's taking such a risk with his health. Aren't you worried about him?"

"Of *course* I'm worried about him. Of course I think he should quit. But what do you want me to do? I'm not his girl-friend. Right now I don't even think he thinks I'm his friend."

"Britta," he murmured.

She pressed on. "But I *am* concerned, which is why I told you. You're his family and I'm not, okay? So I'm going to leave you three to have some fun family discussions while I go home. I've got a big day tomorrow."

He reached out a hand but she shrugged it off and got her bag. He could keep the glass bowls she'd made dessert in; she wouldn't be back. And forget his promise to drop her home tonight. She'd get a taxi.

"I'll drive you," he muttered.

"No thanks."

"Britta." He stretched for her again.

She jerked her arm away. "Just like I can't tell you what to do, you can't tell me either."

"I don't want you mad at me."

Emotion roared. She blinked it back. Then bit her lip to stop the tremble. With what felt like extraordinary effort, she managed to calm enough to say, "I'm not mad at you. I'm mad at this situation. And I'm mad at myself for wanting things to be different." For him to have never been injured. And for him to love her. She pulled away as he tried to touch her again. "I can't do this anymore."

"Britta, no."

"No. That's exactly the right word. No."

"Why are you doing this?" he muttered. "I thought you were my friend."

"Faithful are the wounds from a friend, Mitchell. It's better than the deceitful kisses of an enemy." She headed to the door. Then paused, glancing at a shell-shocked Ellie and Jasper. "It was good to meet you."

"Britta, don't go," Ellie pleaded. "I didn't mean for you two to break up."

She scoffed. "We're not breaking up."

"You're not?" Ellie asked, hope in her eyes. Behind her, Mitch took a step toward her.

"How can two people break up when they're not even together?" She glanced at Mitch. "Just friends, remember?"

His body sagged, but she couldn't stay a second longer.

He'd made his choice. And now they both had to live with the consequences.

≈

"Oh my gosh, Mitchell, I didn't mean—"

"Ellie, shut up."

"Did you see the look in her eyes? Oh my gosh. I feel so bad."

So did he. If his sister and bro-in-law weren't here he'd probably cry.

"You should go after her," Ellie said. "Your apartment is nice, but this area is no place for a woman to walk alone. There were some weird-looking dudes out there."

"I'll go," Jasper said, moving to get his keys.

"No, I'll go." Even though she was probably calling an Uber as they spoke.

Mitch snatched his keys and jacket and pounded down the stairs. The elevator wasn't the fastest, and after the emotions of the past half hour he needed to burn off some energy.

Why hadn't he seen it from that perspective before? His refusal to quit—or at least his delay—meant he was risking the future of not just himself, but whoever else shared his future. And he knew beyond a shadow of a doubt who it was he wanted to share that future with. The person who'd been honest with him, had tried her best to support him, who'd been far more than just a friend, who was everything he wanted. His lungs were burning as he rounded the last set of stairs on the ground floor and exited the stairwell into his apartment building's foyer. The person who he wanted was walking out the glass doors.

She was on her phone, wiping her face. He'd made her cry. He'd made her *cry*. Well, it had probably been the combined effort of himself and Ellie, but still. He didn't want her to cry.

"Britta, wait."

She turned suddenly, then tilted, like she stumbled.

"Whoa." He rushed to catch her.

She shrugged free. "Get your hands off me."

"Britta, please don't go."

She backed away. One unsteady foot behind the other.

"Please, hear me out."

"I have an Uber arriving in three minutes."

"Then let me say this fast." His mind suddenly blanked. There was so much to say, he didn't know where to begin.

Her gaze narrowed. "Say what?"

Oh, he *hated* that she was mad at him. His heart shriveled. But still, he had to say the most important thing. "I'm sorry."

"Yeah, right. Okay."

She didn't believe him? "Please forgive me."

"Forgive you for what, Mitch?" She sounded so weary. "It's your life. Your brain. Tell the team or not. You do you."

*You do you?* What kind of dismissive statement was that? But... was it dismissive? Or had she just given up? His heart panged. Was that really what she thought of him? That he'd ignore everyone else and live his life his way, selfishly? He wasn't trying to be selfish; he just naturally was.

No! He was still figuring out what this would mean for his future. He wasn't *selfish*. Was he? No, He'd been set free from that. Hadn't he? Oh, it was so hard to think!

"I..." Suddenly the three most important words were so hard to say. His throat seemed to have clamped up.

Her eyebrows rose. "You?"

He might be feared on the ice, but this short woman in glasses had the power to weaken his knees and steal all his words and sense. He didn't need a long history of concussions. She was enough to have messed with his brain.

She heaved out a sigh and pivoted, moving to the curbside.

*I love you. I need you. I want you.*

Three phrases, three words long, that he'd never said to any woman before.

She shrieked and he sprinted after her. She was shaking. "What happened?"

Her breath shuddered. "Nothing. It was just a turkey."

"They're everywhere these days, always getting in the way," he mumbled. He could slap himself. Why was he talking about the city's pesky turkeys when he should be talking about what really mattered? He was the real turkey here.

A car pulled alongside, a sticker pronouncing its Uber status.

"Britta, please don't go."

She shook her head. "I can't do this anymore. I don't think it's healthy for me." She signaled the driver and moved to the door.

"I don't want you to go."

She hesitated, her fingers on the door handle.

His heart took flight. Maybe there was a chance, after all.

Then her shoulders slumped, as she peered up at him. "Well, it looks like none of us are getting what we want tonight."

And her look of sadness clamped his throat as she got inside, closed the door, and the vehicle drove away.

# CHAPTER 28

*N*ever had she been so thankful for the distraction of Red Jellybeans. And work. And family. And church. Maybe it was immature but she'd had to block Mitch again. She couldn't pretend she was okay. She wasn't.

She didn't watch his games. She didn't wear his jersey. She didn't think about him. Well, tried not to anyway. But it seemed like his fingerprints were everywhere. In the string of pumpkin lights hung up across the front porch. In the jersey Astrid had left hanging on the back of the door. In the game her dad was watching that filled her ears as she returned from the Jellybeans on the Friday after Halloween. The way she kept expecting him to appear at the library. But no. He hadn't appeared.

And the fact he hadn't appeared—yes, she knew he had road trips, but he hadn't contacted her at all—only reinforced that she'd been the foolish one thinking there was more to this relationship than there was. He obviously didn't. It didn't matter what her family or Kayla or Ellie or anyone else might say. Her stupid romance-hungry imagination had leaped to impossibilities that had proved to be exactly that—impossible.

She knew she couldn't be friends with him. Knew he obviously didn't consider her much of a friend, seeing he hadn't bothered to get in touch. And while part of her knew it was unreasonable to say he wasn't being her friend when she wasn't exactly being friendly in return, she also knew she had been wise to call a time-out. Because Mitchell Reilly was dangerous for her heart.

She couldn't be friends with him, because she wanted more. And the fact he didn't seem to want the same hurt. So, call her a hypocrite, but while she knew she had to protect herself and not have anything to do with him, she still hungered for him. Did that make her crazy? Maybe. But her heart was such a mess it felt impossible to think straight.

THE NIGHTS WERE COLDER NOW, getting darker earlier, too. A recent snowfall had scared most of the red leaves from the trees, leaving the branches twisting up to the heavens like pointy witch fingers to the sky.

She was glad when the Halloween decorations came down. Glad to see Thanksgiving would be celebrated soon. Not that she could find much to be thankful over.

Actually, that was a lie. She had plenty to be thankful for. She *knew* that. It would just be easier to be happily thankful rather than gritted-teeth thankful. But still, she thanked God for His blessings, day by day.

As for Mitchell Reilly, she prayed that he'd diminish from importance in her heart. He'd made his choice; it hadn't included her. And that was that. If he really wanted to connect with her he could; he knew where she worked and lived. But the fact he hadn't showed he'd chosen not to. Proving this friendship was built on sand, not rock. And any thinking he might like her was foolish fancies, no doubt fueled by too much fiction that she'd imagined could somehow be proved real.

· · ·

"Have you lost weight?" Kayla asked.

She shrugged. "Maybe a little." That's what not eating her feelings did. It was hard to eat her feelings when she felt numb.

"You look great, by the way."

Given the choice of dressing for today's Thanksgiving-themed Story Time and activities as a turkey, a Native American or a pilgrim, she'd chosen Option D, thanks Peter. A funky—in a good way—dress patterned with turkeys, with her black corset, black tights and black boots. Coupled with her new black-rimmed glasses, she could almost believe Astrid this morning when she said Britta looked sexy.

"You're the one who needs glasses, Astrid."

"You're the one who should take a good hard look at yourself and stop pining over a certain somebody."

"I'm not pining."

"You are."

"I'm trying to be brave."

"Have you even watched a game since you broke up?"

"We were never together," she said wearily. How many times did she have to repeat this?

"Then if you weren't, why are you still acting like you were?"

"I'm not."

"Prove it, and watch a game."

Maybe it was childish to take the dare. But she shrugged, and said, "Okay."

So that night after work she sat and watched the game with her mom.

Flinched when she saw his jersey on the ice. "Whatever happened to him?" her mom asked.

"He got busy. Lots of road trips, you know that." She'd made sure to mention that whenever his name came up with Ferdy or the Red Jellybeans or even Derek, when they'd chatted a few times after work. Derek had asked questions about Mitch, after seeing them hug, and she'd deflected as best she could.

Mitch was busy with his games, training, community responsibilities, pretending he was okay. She was busy with her work, the Beans, and pretending she was okay. Win, win.

She got up to make a cup of tea. Then her mom cried, "Oh no!"

"Oh no what?" She hurried back and saw a man on the screen, lying flat on the ice. Her empty cup fell to the carpet. "Oh *no!*"

The Wild player lay on the ice, surrounded by medics. Her mom grasped her hand, then prayed aloud, "Lord, be with him, heal him right now."

Britta's breath was shaky. She couldn't do this. Couldn't watch. Some might have the strength to do so, but right now, she felt fragile. *Oh God, please heal him.* She covered her eyes.

"What is it, honey?" her mom asked.

"Mitch," she whispered. "I told him he should quit."

Her mother rubbed her back. "He'll be okay."

"No. He got told by specialists weeks ago to quit because of the number of concussions he's faced, and he refused to tell the team."

"Oh no."

She blinked back the blur in her eyes. "That day his sister was in town I asked how he was doing and she overheard, then she blamed me for not saying something, because of the risk of something just like this happening to Mitch."

"You can't blame yourself, honey. He's a grown man."

"I know."

She peeked through her splayed fingers and stared at the screen. A gurney was slowly moving to the sidelines as players from both teams tapped their sticks on the ice.

Her mom sighed. "It's awful, but it's part of life. People make their choices."

Her heart hurt. Mitch certainly had. Rejecting her. Rejecting sound advice. And look what had happened. *Lord, be with him. Heal him, please.*

THANKSGIVING LUNCH WAS USUALLY a loud and raucous affair but this year felt a little more subdued. Maybe that was due to the awful event in last night's game that the media had barely stopped talking about. The possibility of spinal damage to one of the Wild's star players? She couldn't talk about it. Could only pray for all those involved, pray for him, pray for God's healing power to work in the midst of this terrible situation.

She helped her mom with the preparations, helped Astrid and Milla set the table. In addition to family members, there were a few people from church and a couple of neighbors, including Mr. Daughtry, Bumper's new best friend. Most people brought a hotdish or something to share, which made catering easier, but the day was bound to get hectic, bound to be noisy. Which was probably perfect for distracting her from regrets and sorrow.

The first guests arrived at eleven, then the men settled in the living room to watch football, while the women nattered in the kitchen. She checked her blood sugar—all good, but she didn't want to waste her carbs on unnecessary snacks. There'd been enough emotional turmoil yesterday, and grief at what could've been still clung heavy to her heart.

She welcomed people and chatted and kept busy. Fended off questions about a certain person she'd known who had carved a hole in her heart. How ridiculous that it had been weeks since she'd seen him yet she still felt this way.

"I haven't seen you post anything on Facebook or Instagram in ages," her aunt said.

"I've canned my social media."

"What, forever?"

"For the last little while, and the foreseeable future. I don't like how it messes with my head, so I've been having a social media detox for the past few months."

"Well, good for you. I much prefer real relating like this," her aunt said.

"Yeah, we don't do it as much as we used to, do we?"

"I think we get so busy that we think connecting with someone via a little screen is better than taking the time to really speak to someone and really hear them."

She nodded. She knew that. She'd spoken about that to the Red Jellybeans.

"Now, whatever happened to that friend of yours?"

"Which friend?"

Her aunt's eyes gleamed. "I believe he played hockey."

"We haven't seen each other for a month. He's busy, and to be honest, I don't really want to talk about him, either."

Her aunt looked at her, then nodded. "Okay. I'm praying for you, honey."

"Thanks." Her voice was small—wispy and thin, some might say.

"Britta, could you take this platter out to the men?"

"Sure." If it got her away from the interrogation in the kitchen.

She grasped the platter and took it out to where the pregame football show was muted, and the men were swapping comments about the recent weather.

"How about that snow, eh?"

Her uncle sighed. "Nine months of winter every year."

"Gonna head up soon to the cabin up on the north shore and do some fishin'. Wanna come?"

"You betcha."

She deposited the platter on the coffee table, deflected their comments on her single status, and was heading back to the kitchen when the doorbell rang.

"Britta, can you get the door?" her mom called.

"Sure." She took off her ruffled apron, smoothed her hair, pasted on a smile, and opened the door. Then nearly had a non-blood sugar-related hypo.

It was him.

~

HE DIDN'T KNOW why he was here. Just knew this place felt like coming home. Seeing her was like coming home. It had been far too long. His senses were drinking her in.

"Mitchell." Her voice was so soft, like she thought him an illusion. "What are you doing here?"

"I..." Needed her. After the past twenty-four hours, everything had become crystal clear.

And the events of the past twenty-four hours slammed into his chest, felling his composure as his eyes filled. Man, he wasn't supposed to be so weak.

"Hey." She drew him inside, closed the door.

The sympathy on her face undid him, and he didn't care if it seemed inappropriate, he needed her, her hug, her warmth. He needed *her*.

So he bent his face to her shoulder and drew her to himself, as her arms tentatively enfolded him. And in the safety of her arms he let the emotion of the past day spill over.

He didn't know how long he stood there, his humiliation on show for anyone to see, but she must've gotten concerned for she hushed him and rubbed his back. "Hey, it's okay."

"It's not," he rasped.

"Hey, come with me, this place is crammed full of guests and you don't want to see them."

No. He wanted nobody but her.

He palmed his eyes, snatched a tissue from a nearby box, and followed her quickly through various people, some of whom called after her, after him, but she ignored them, leading him down a hall to where he guessed the bedrooms were.

She opened a door and led him inside what must be her room. It was pretty, pink, soft and dainty, filled with books, just like her. She gestured for him to sit on her bed while she moved to the desk chair, but he needed someplace firm, that wouldn't make him think things he shouldn't, so he took the chair instead.

Her expression was half wince, half shyness. "I wouldn't normally ever bring a man to my room, but considering the place is crammed with others, I think this is the most amount of privacy we can get."

He drew in a breath. Tried to calm. *Lord, I'm a mess, I need You.*

"Can I get you anything to eat or drink?"

"No. I…" He scrubbed his hands down his face. "Look, I'm sorry for barging in like this. I didn't know where else to come."

"Hey, it's okay," she soothed. "I know that must've been a huge shock."

And a huge wake-up call. "I felt so bad when they wheeled Matt away. He's just a kid. I can't believe they're talking about him needing spinal surgery."

"We've been praying for him."

"I have been too." He leaned forward, elbows on knees, head in his hands. "I visited the hospital this morning and prayed for him while he was lying in the bed. His girlfriend looked at me weird but his folks appreciated it."

"I'm sure they did."

He shuddered out a breath. "It made me realize how lucky— how *blessed* I've been to not have had a worse injury."

She pressed her lips together, and her eyes behind her glasses seemed to shimmer with tears. Tears that spoke of her compassion for Matt. And, he hoped, her compassion for him.

The thought she might have tears for him propelled words to his mouth. "I'm going to quit."

"You are?" She blinked, her eyes growing wide.

He nodded. "I actually spoke to one of the medics on the team last night, just sounding things out. Obviously with Matt's injury there will be a gap on the team, so I don't feel right stepping down immediately, but I can't do this anymore. I want to step down as soon as I can."

"So you'll speak to the coach?"

"I need to speak to my agent, so many people." He groaned. "But I know it's the right thing to do."

"It *is* the right thing, but I'm still sorry."

"No, I'm the one who is sorry. I shouldn't have made you keep this secret. That wasn't fair to you."

"It's okay."

"Is it? I hope you'll forgive me. I've been such a fool. I should've stopped you from leaving that day, then come to visit you, but I didn't know what to say." There were so many things he shouldn't have said. So many words left unspoken. "Then we had those long road trips, and the longer it went on, the more I started thinking that you wouldn't want to see me. I've messed up so many times. And I know it's a lot for me to be here today but I didn't know where else to come." He offered an awkward smile. "Well, I did, because I missed you so much, but I wasn't sure you'd ever want to see me again."

She bit her lip, like she wasn't sure whether to believe him. Which was fair. He'd flip-flopped back and forth so many times, he was amazed she hadn't kicked him to the curb as soon as she'd opened the door. The fact she hadn't, spoke of her generous heart. A heart he still foolishly hoped she'd let him come inside.

"Britta, I… I haven't stopped thinking about you since that day with Ellie. And ever since then it's been like there's this dagger in my heart that digs deeper every day. Please, would you consider being friends again?"

She nodded.

"Really? You'd be my friend? Even after all my mistakes?"

"Of course."

"I can't believe it," he whispered.

"You should try." Her smile was an invitation.

So he had to hug her again, then as he held her, was conscious of a shift. When the hug became... different. When awareness flowed, and his nerve endings tingled, and every pore seemed hyper-conscious of just how perfect Britta Johnson was. In his arms. In his life. Like God had made her for him.

He pulled back, smiling, as her glasses were angled haphazardly. "I missed you so much."

"I missed you too. I...I've been praying for you every day."

"I've been praying for you too." He exhaled, knowing he had to get this off his chest. "I'm sorry I've been so stubborn."

"I can be stubborn too."

"I'm sorry I didn't come sooner."

"I'm sorry I didn't make the effort either."

"We make a good pair."

His words drifted around the room, echoing in his heart. They would make a good pair. The best pair. They might be opposites in many ways, but in the fundamental ways—faith, values, desire for family, even a sense of humor—they were a perfect match.

She studied him, as fresh awareness vibrated between them. Her eyes, intent on him. His, intent on her. Only her. Now and forever after only her. And even though he didn't want to push things, on this day that already felt miraculous, he dared once again, drawing closer then tracing a finger down the soft skin of her cheek.

"Mitchell," she whispered. "What are you doing?"

He drew back. "Sorry."

"It's okay."

"Really?" Hope flared again. "See, I don't want to presume, even though I wanted to be more than friends. I *want* to be more than friends." He groaned. "Man, that sounds like something a little kid would say. But it's true. Even though it doesn't seem right or fair to say that."

"Why?" she murmured.

"Because I feel bad when I know that if we were to be more than friends you'd be stuck with a broken man with my kind of problems in the future. I didn't think it was fair to be this wreck of a man with nothing to offer."

She shook her head. Was that a no? Did she not want him? Oh, what right did he have to beg her to consider him?

"That's not true," she whispered. "You've got so much to offer."

Oh, how he wanted to believe her. But she'd always been an encourager, someone whom light shone through.

"None of us are perfect," she said softly. "My health challenges mean I'm not supposed to live a super long life either."

His heart reared back at that. "You can't say that."

"Why not? It's true."

Her eyes held his, daring him to say this next thing. "Are... are you saying we'd make a good match?"

"That's up to you."

Was she saying that he might still have a chance?

"None of us know how long we have," she murmured. "Our futures are in God's hands."

He knew that. Nothing was guaranteed. Which meant they could live in fear about the unknowns or step out in faith and trust God that He'd be with them, anyway. "You really want a future with me, even though it might not be easy?"

"Easy things are never valued as much as those things you've had to fight for. And besides, God will be with us, in the big moments and the small. We can trust Him."

He swallowed. "In that case, Britta, would you be willing to consider being more than friends? One day, when you're ready."

"Oh Mitchell."

Her face fell, as did his heart.

Then she peeked up. "I've been ready for months."

Hope flared again. "You have?"

She nodded. "But you said I wasn't your type."

He'd said that? He didn't trust his memories, so he'd trust hers. "I'm sorry for ever saying that. Because you are exactly my type. You're fun and funny and smart and so pretty it's like you light up the room when you smile. You make me a better person."

Her expression said she didn't believe it.

"It's true." He eyed her hand, lying loose in her lap, then suddenly knew he needed to grasp it, needing her to ground him, even as his stupid hopes threatened to carry him away. He'd built a career on taking risks, and this felt like the most important one to date. "Britta." He swallowed and scooted from the chair to kneel before her.

Her breath caught as he gripped her hands, their faces at eye level. "What… what are you doing?"

He had to say this right. This moment felt as weighty as when he'd sat waiting to hear his name called at the NHL Draft. "Britta, ever since we met at the library it's like you have been tapping at my heart, waiting for me to open up. I realize now I got it all so wrong with Georgia, I wasn't even friends with her. She never knew me, not like you do. And I sure never knew her, not like I know you. We never wanted the same things."

"What do you want?" she asked softly.

He swallowed. Crunch time. "I want a family. I want a wife. The other way around, but you know what I mean."

Her lips curved. "I know what you mean."

"Georgia is not a woman. Not like you. Nobody is like you."

He dared to lift his hand to her hair, tangling his fingers through her soft hair as her breath suspended again.

Her eyes filled with something that looked like a cross between uncertainty, hope and fear. Oh, how he wanted to wipe that uncertainty from her dear face, a face that had become more dear and more lovely the longer he'd known her. How could he have ever thought her plain? Her face held light and life and mysteries and dreams and he wanted to spend forever getting to know her. If she'd agree to give him one last try.

She wet her bottom lip, and his gaze instantly fell there. He yearned to know the taste of her lips, had dreamed of it a thousand times since their near miss weeks ago.

"Britta, it's been hard to take things slow and try to be your friend when I've really struggled with wanting more. I didn't want to freak you out by appearing to be some tool flip-flopping from one woman to the next. I didn't want you to ever think you were a rebound when really, you are the first woman I think I've ever really gotten to know. So that makes you the first, the only, woman I can say I've truly loved."

"Loved?" she whispered.

"Loved."

"Truly?" Her face glowed.

"Truly. One hundred percent. Absolutely. I even read the rest of *Pride and Prejudice* to prove it."

"You did?"

He nodded, then tried to concentrate. "I have to admit, my memory is not too great but let me see if I can remember this right. Britta Johnson, you must allow me to admit how ardently I admire and adore you."

Her eyes sparkled, and a tear trickled down her cheek. "Does… does this mean you were going to kiss me that time at your apartment before?"

He nodded. "I wanted to, but I wanted us to be friends first. And that was going so well. Until it wasn't."

"And now?" she asked.

"Now do I want to kiss you?"

"No!" Her cheeks pinked.

"Because I do."

Her breath hitched.

He touched her glasses. "May I?"

When she nodded, he lifted them off. "Now I can really see your beautiful eyes." Dark, with the sweetness and warmth of chocolate. "Your eyes are so beautiful. They're like windows to your soul, looking straight into your sweet heart."

"Mitchell."

He bent to her face, closed his eyes, inhaled her skin, nuzzled her cheek. "So soft."

Her hands slipped up his arms, along his neck, to his jaw, her touch like fire on his skin.

His lips grazed her cheek, bumped into her nose. He could feel she was very still, barely breathing. He peeked to see she'd closed her eyes. Why hadn't he noticed how long her eyelashes were before? "May I kiss you?"

"Yes, please."

He smiled and angled his face and gently skimmed his lips over hers.

She sighed, and her hand slid to the back of his head and pressed him closer.

He'd take that as permission to continue, so he did, kissing her again and then again in soft feather-like brushes, a tentative exploration. Then her lips firmed as she pressed back, and he fought the temptation to take it deeper. Not yet. This was perfection enough.

A tap came at the door then it opened, and they sprang apart.

Astrid stood in the doorway, smirking. "Well, it looks like a couple of people are feeling pretty thankful today."

"What do you want?" Britta said, her lips swollen, her cheeks bright pink.

Astrid held up her hands. "Don't shoot the messenger. I've been sent to tell you that dinner is being served."

"Okay."

"I'll go," he murmured.

"Actually, that was the other part of the message. Mom wanted me to tell you that she's set a place for you, and for me to—what was it she said again? Oh yeah. 'Don't let the poor boy go home without staying. It's Thanksgiving.'"

Britta squeezed his hand. "Please stay."

"Are you sure?"

"I want you to."

"I know my place, then. I'd better submit."

She laughed. "I like how you think."

"I thought you might." He kissed her cheek.

"All right!" Astrid did a *woot woot* movement. "Thanksgiving is in the house!"

# EPILOGUE

"*D*o I look okay?"

"Britta, relax. You look beautiful."

Words she'd never heard a handsome man say to her before. But she meant more whether her dress label was in and everything appropriately covered. Mom, Astrid and Milla had assured her it was but the way Mitchell's eyes had widened suggested she hadn't covered quite enough. "You look fantastic," he'd whispered, before kissing her so thoroughly she'd needed to redo her lipstick.

She smiled as she watched the lit up buildings flash past as Mitch drove. So no, she didn't exactly mean did she look beautiful or not. She might be needy, but wasn't needing to hear compliments so much. Especially now she'd discovered what all those books meant when it came to how great kissing was, and was starting to realize just how hard it was to stop. So while she might want his kisses, she now understood how desirability could be a two-edged sword.

Knowing Mitch desired her had helped her grow more secure in her looks, even if others—like the team's PR lady—couldn't understand why Mitch and Britta were together, judging from the raised brow looks Britta earned each time she showed up at games. Britta had asked him about her, and he'd laughed, saying some of the guys thought Daisy had a crush on him. Whatever. The fact his eyes remained only on Britta chased insecurity away.

Besides, she was learning—again—to be content to be herself. She didn't need to look like Daisy, or Georgia, or Astrid or Milla. She was comfortable being Britta. Sometimes that meant she didn't wear makeup. And sometimes, like tonight, she let Astrid and Milla work their magic. Sometimes she wore glasses, sometimes she did not. Tonight she'd chosen to wear them, partly because she didn't want to give in to some Cinderella stereotype that said a woman wearing glasses needed to lose them to look good. And partly because Mitch had admitted recently that he thought she was sexy in her glasses.

"Call me lame, but it's like when I see you, nose in a book, I just think you're so beautiful. Like, I don't want to interrupt you, but then I also do, because I want to be the hero you're thinking of, not another Mr. Darcy."

"You really think I'm beautiful?"

"I really"—he'd kissed her right cheek—"think you're"—he kissed the left—"beautiful."

And his passionate kiss on the lips suggested that.

He parked, then, as if sensing her tension, grasped her hand, squeezing gently.

Peace stole through her soul. "Did you just pray for me?"

"Yes."

She smiled, caressed his chin. "Thank you. I love you." Then, as his eyes widened, realized she'd never said that to him before.

"Really?"

"Really." Her hand cupped his smooth cheek. "You are a good man, Mitchell Reilly. You're strong, protective, kind, and caring." Her heart softened as he drank in her words. "You might look tough, but I know your heart is soft and sweet."

"Don't go telling anyone now."

"It's too late. The Red Jellybeans already know, and I'm announcing it on the library's social media."

He laughed. "I can't believe you wait until now to tell me this," he grumbled, laughter in his eyes as he drew near.

But she got the feeling from the way he kissed her thoroughly that he didn't really mind.

The flash of another car's headlights made her aware that they could be seen, so she pulled back, adjusted her hair, checked her lipstick in the passenger visor mirror. "Am I still okay?"

"You're perfect."

That was overstating things, but she'd take it. "Well, here goes nothing then." She exited the car and he held her hand as they entered the function center where tonight's school reunion was being held.

"Oh wow." The blonde woman behind the table looked her up and down. "I love your dress."

Britta smiled, not recognizing her. "Thanks."

"Name?"

She cleared her throat. "Britta. Britta Johnson."

The woman blinked. "Are you kidding me?"

Mitchell squeezed her hand. She'd told him about some of the bullying, and he'd insisted on coming tonight. "And I know I didn't RSVP my date, but I have a plus one."

"Oh." The woman—oh, that was *Tania*? She'd put on weight —glanced at Mitch. "I, um, need to see what Erica says."

Erica. Her heart tensed. Then she actively relaxed. God was here, in this moment just like all the others, and she didn't need to stress over what misguided people might be thinking.

"Whoa. Are you... are you Mitchell Reilly?" a man asked. His name tag said Drake.

Well, it looked like the years hadn't been so kind to him either. One of the good things about being an ordinary person meant she had no pedestal to fall from, unlike some people here. In fact, the opposite was true. Instead of falling, she could only go up in other people's estimations, which, judging from the growing crowd's murmurs about her dress and guest, seemed to be the case so far.

Drake tried talking to Mitch, but Mitch didn't leave her side, the perfect attentive boyfriend. The people here didn't know he was retiring soon, so she was glad to make the most of it. And he was too.

He wrapped his arm around her waist, their height difference a little easier to negotiate given her heels. "I'm sorry but I'm here with Britta. She's my sole focus tonight." He smiled. "And every waking moment."

Hmm. He was putting that on a little strong. Nobody here needed to get ideas that she wasn't still as much a Christian as she was back then.

Erica arrived, glanced between them, and frowned. "Are you two together?"

"Yep." Mitch kissed Britta's knuckles. "Britta is so amazing. I can't believe I'm so lucky to go out with her. Did you see her get that award from the mayor yesterday?"

"Award?" Erica asked.

"For bravery." He chuckled. "I don't know how many times I've watched that video of my ninja girlfriend kicking butt. I love it. I love you," he said to Britta.

"Aww," Tania cooed.

"I remember hearing something about it," Drake mumbled.

"She's a rock star, even if she's a librarian." Mitch winked at her. "And making the world a better place."

"Mitch," she whispered, her cheeks hot.

"What? I can't help it if I think you're awesome. I'm just agreeing with the rest of the world, anyway. And hey, doesn't she look beautiful?" he demanded of Erica.

Erica nodded stiffly. "That's a very nice dress."

"No," Mitch said. "Well, yes, the dress is nice. But *Britta* is the one who is so beautiful. Like, a star. The most beautiful woman here tonight, right?"

Erica glanced up at her, and her expression changed, softened. "You look really good, Britta."

Tears beckoned but she blinked them away. "Thank you."

"I'm glad you came."

She nodded. "I figured it was time to deal with the past."

"What do you mean?"

She drew in a deep breath. Felt Mitchell's reassuring touch on her lower back. Then said the words she'd practiced for years. "I forgive you for bullying me through high school."

Erica gasped, but Britta wasn't finished.

"I was never sure if you knew I had a medical condition, and I'd hate to think your heart was so mean that you made fun of me when I was suffering. I prefer to think you were just oblivious."

"But we knew…" Tania's voice trailed away.

Britta lifted her chin. "Then I hope you have changed. And I'm praying that God will touch your hearts and reveal His love to you so you can be set free from the need to make yourself feel better at the expense of others. I know that God can do miracles and change your hearts too."

She smiled at their gobsmacked expressions, picked up the skirt of her dress and walked inside.

"Proud of you," Mitch murmured, his hand finding hers and squeezing gently.

She exhaled. "That felt good to say. Releasing, you know?"

He nodded. "Have I mentioned that I think you're awesome?"

"Not in the last two minutes."

He chuckled, instantly drawing people's attention. Then the whispers began of "It's Mitch Reilly!" "Plays for the Wild!" "He's here with Britta?" "No way! That's Britta?"

She recognized a few people, but paid attention to those she remembered as being like her. A little—or a lot—on the outer, those who hadn't aged as well, those whose faces wore the strain she recognized as dread. She swapped details with a few, promising to catch up, not by Facebook, but in person, setting dates, arranging times. "Because if we don't do that now, we both know we won't do it at all, right?"

Trays of canapés waited on the tables, but suddenly she didn't want to be here. She'd come, she'd made an entrance, she'd reconnected with the few she needed, said what she needed to say. She glanced at Mitch. "Do you mind if we leave?"

"You don't want to stay?"

"No. This is the past. I've seen who I want and have the details of those I want to stay in touch with. I want to go somewhere else where I can relax and not worry about being gossiped about."

"I'm not sure if that's going to happen if we're together."

"*If?*" She arched a brow.

"Okay. Wrong choice of word. Like I could ever let go of my ninja librarian."

She laughed. "Just as well."

"Well, your wish is my command. Where to?"

"Anywhere that would make all the effort I went to with this dress worthwhile."

"Hmm." He eyed her, then picked up her hand and spun her around so her dress flared out. Oh, Marilyn had nothing on this. She felt like a va-va-voom-alicious bombshell. "I think I know just the place."

Twenty minutes later they were inside an ivy-covered restaurant where her outfit fitted in with those of other patrons. They were being escorted to a table when her name was called.

She paused. It was Helen Harlow, who was seated with the mayor.

"I thought I recognized you." The mayor looked her up and

down. "Wow. What's the occasion?" He glanced at Mitch, then his eyes rounded. "Say no more. I think I understand."

What? He wasn't implying what she thought he was, was he?

Mitch wrapped an arm around her shoulders. "One day, sir. If she keeps me around that long."

Oh my goodness. She smiled at Helen who wore her own *Aww* expression.

"Congratulations again on that award, Britta," the mayor said. "It's so good to know we have people like you serving our community."

"Thank you, sir."

"Now, before you two go, can I get a photo with you both?" The mayor grinned. "I like to post these on social media."

They agreed, then he asked the waiter to take their photo.

She smiled and posed like she was used to doing this all the time.

The waiter led them to a cute corner table near the window. Mitch seated her, and then took her hand. "That was okay, wasn't it?"

"Meeting the mayor again?"

He nodded. "I figured it's always worthwhile to build connections. And hey, let's hope Erica sees." He laughed. "This would so mess with her."

No doubt. Not that she cared. That part of her life was done. Oh, it felt so good to have those shackles finally released.

They were handed menus, then their drinks and meals were ordered, and she relaxed and laughed and enjoyed herself.

There might be uncertainty in the future, nothing in life was guaranteed, but in this moment, she could unwind and enjoy and trust that God had the future in His hands.

Mitch smiled at her, with that smile she might once have thought was arrogant but she now recognized actually held a soft strain just for her. "So, do you think you could come with me to Trinity Lakes after Christmas?"

Her heart stuttered. "You want me to meet your family?"

He nodded. "It's only fair. I've met yours. I'm telling the coaching staff the week before Christmas, so they've got time to find a replacement during the break. I know as soon as they do they'll put me on medical leave, so I figured it's a good chance to go see the fam. And I happen to know that Ellie has a lot of groveling she wants to do."

"She doesn't need to grovel."

"Yes, she does. She's my sister, so it's only right I make her pay. So, will you?"

"I... I would need to check my work schedule. But," she added in a rush of courage, "I'd like to meet them."

He grinned. "Awesome! I think you'll enjoy it there. And I know Ellie wants you to feel welcome."

"God bless sisters."

"Amen. But I don't want to think about them. I want to focus on you."

She shivered at the intensity in his eyes. "What do you want to focus on?"

His gaze slipped to her lips, and she knew exactly what he wanted to be doing.

She mock-sighed. "Fine."

He grinned, and took his time kissing her, and she was quickly lost in the romance of the moment. Then a cleared throat drew them apart. Oh! Helen.

Her cheeks were hot. "Um, hi."

"I'm sorry for interrupting, but Britta, I thought you might like to know that there is a vacancy in the role of head of the children's department at the library, effective immediately."

"Why? What's happened to Margaret?"

"I got a call this afternoon from Margaret's husband. She had a fall and has broken her hip quite badly. It seems she's had a form of osteoporosis she's hidden for a long while."

Her heart softened. Poor thing. "I didn't know."

CAROLYN MILLER

"None of us did. Anyway, her husband said the doctors are convinced that she'll need months of rehabilitation, at least half a year, if not longer."

"That long?"

Helen nodded. "And while Carol would normally be the natural choice, she's already submitted her resignation because she wants to spend time with her grandchildren. "

"That's right."

"I was originally hoping you'd apply for Carol's job, but understood that there might've been, ah, some challenges given the personnel, shall we say." Helen's wry look said she knew more about the internal politics of the children's department than she was prepared to speak aloud. "Anyway, in thinking about a suitable replacement, I really don't want to have to go through the ins and outs of training a suitable out-of-towner, so I was discussing with the mayor just now about the possibility of filling Margaret's role in-house. And he saw you and suggested your name and I agree, you'd be the perfect fit."

Mitchell gripped Britta's hand. "Amen to that. Britta would be awesome."

"I don't know what to say."

"You don't need to say anything yet," Helen said. "Carol remains in her role until the new year, so we can iron out some details then. But just give it some thought, okay?"

"Thank you. I will definitely give it some thought and lots of prayer."

"Please do. Now, I don't want to interrupt a special evening. You two enjoy your night."

"Oh my gosh," Britta murmured, as soon as Helen left. "Can you believe that?"

"Actually, I can. God is good, right?"

She nodded. "All the time."

"And this shows that we can trust Him with the future, whatever comes, wherever we may be."

"Are you thinking you'd stay? Even if you can't play for the team?"

"Of course I'm staying. I love you."

"I love you too."

His eyes lit like he'd never get tired hearing her say that. "See? How could I ever want to move when you say such sweet things? If you're here, then I am too. I might study to do youth work, or help the homeless like Derek, somehow. But I'm not leaving you." He kissed her hand. "Wherever you are is home to me."

MITCH TAPPED on the laptop and the screen opened into a bunch of squares.

The Bible study guys waved and welcomed and he smiled. "Hey all. Happy new year."

"Happy new year to you too!"

Mitch smiled. It had been a very happy new year. To know he was loved by the sweetest woman in the world—what could top that? After speaking with the team, he'd scored medical leave which meant he'd had plenty of time to take Britta west to see his family in Trinity Lakes. They'd all—especially his mom— been huge fans of the petite librarian with stealth moves. Like the way she'd stolen his heart.

His brothers had also been huge fans of his apology for his arrogance over the years, and praised Britta for helping soften his heart. And yeah, he'd had to swallow what felt like more than his fair share of humble pie, but for the first time in a long time it felt like the bonds connecting them held simple love, rather than the edge of pride and competition. God—and Britta —had helped to change him for the better.

"Good to see you, Mitch," Ryan said.

"Yeah, it's gonna be my last one, I'm afraid."

343

"No way." That was Luc. "I feel like you've only just joined us."

He'd explained before to the guys about his concussions, and the team's medical advice to sit out the rest of the season while monitoring his symptoms, and they understood. There was nothing like Matt's devastating accident to make people realize the challenges of this sport.

"How is Matt?" Franklin asked.

*Lord, heal him.* "They say he's out for the season, and they'll need to assess for next year."

"Poor dude."

"Life can change like that." Kyle snapped his fingers.

"We'll be praying for him," Jai said, which met with a chorus of Amens.

He'd really miss these guys.

"You can still join us," Mike said.

"Thanks. I'll see how I go." He'd talked with Mike who'd connected him with Holly Karlsson, who had shared a bit about her experience post significant concussion. And while he had no plans to become a doctor like Holly, she was proof that just because one career ended didn't mean that God didn't have something exciting around the corner.

"What will you do now?" Zac asked.

"I'm going to take some time off." A good few months. "I was wondering about maybe getting involved in youth work, youth pastoring maybe or helping the homeless. There's this guy at the library who I've had a few good talks with, and yeah." He shrugged. "I don't know. I'm praying about it."

"A new year means a new start, right?" Kyle said.

"For sure."

"How's your ninja?" Doug asked.

He joined the others as they laughed. "She's good. Got a promotion at work she's excited about."

"Looks like Mitch is the latest to fall," Ryan said.

Oh yeah. He'd fallen, all right.

"Hey Kyle, it must be your turn next," Luc said.

"She'll have to be a pretty amazing woman to match the one I let get away."

"Deets?" Luc pressed.

Kyle shook his head, glanced away.

"Clearly there's a story waiting to be told there," Doug teased.

Mitch's heart softened. He wondered how long it'd be until Kyle felt ready to share his story. Still, the dude obviously felt embarrassed, so he had to take the heat off him. "So, what's everyone else's news?"

Zac shared about his fiancée Ainsley's new role in a people smuggling movie with Lincoln Cash. "Her fans are so excited to see those two reunited."

"That doesn't bother you that she'll be kissing another guy?"

"Yeah, from what we've seen of the script there's no kissing involved, so we're good."

"But if there was?" Mitch asked. He couldn't stand thinking of another man kissing Britta's lips. He felt so humbled that she'd kept hers for him.

"If Ainsley has another romantic role then I've volunteered to be her kissing coach," Zac said. "Or even stand in if need be."

"The man knows all the moves," Doug said.

"How about you, Dougie?" Luc asked. "What's happening in San Jose?"

He shrugged, but remained tight-lipped. Hmm, looked like something was brewing in that neck of the woods also.

"So, anyone else?" Jai asked. "Ryan, you're looking a little excited over there."

"Well, I think it's only fair to let you all know that there will be a little Guillemette this summer."

"What? No way."

"Yes way." Ryan laughed, as the others plied him with congratulations and tease.

Mitch smiled. It might still feel like early days, but he couldn't wait to share similar news one day. Once he'd convinced a certain ninja librarian that she didn't need a fictional hero. Not when she had him in her life.

After all, a person might plan their life, but God would direct their steps. And for however long that life was, trusting God meant they could always be sure that the Lord who held their days in His hand could be trusted with them. The Lord who had written their lives, not with ink, but by the Spirit of the Living God, not on tablets of stone but on tablets of human hearts. The God who would continue to write His story in Mitch and Britta's hearts.

The End

Want to meet the woman Kyle let get away? Then get ready for *Second Shot at Love.*

# A NOTE FROM THE AUTHOR

Thank you for reading *Plays by the Book,* the fifth book in the Northwest Ice romance series. It's always fun to catch up with the guys and see what's happening in their lives! And it was super fun to see Mitchell Reilly finally get his story after his siblings in the Greener Gardens and Trinity Lakes series romance series. If you want to know more about the Reilly family, make sure you read *Regaining Mercy* (Dermott's story), and *Love Somebody Like You, Tangled up in Love,* and *Only You Can Love Me,* which feature Jackson, Ellie and Cooper's stories.

Don't forget to check out Kyle Tinker's story in *Second Shot at Love,* releasing in 2026, and the other books in the <u>Northwest Ice hockey series:</u>

Fire and Ice
The Love Penalty
Pointe, Shoots, and Scores
Faking the Shot
Plays By the Book
Second Shot at Love

~

Big thanks to Megan Hamilton, Rebekah Deedrick and Nicole House for their Minnesota insights, and the other ladies in my ARC and review team.

Reviews help other readers find new-to-them authors, so if you can spare a moment to write a quick review at Amazon / Goodreads / your place of purchase, I'd be very grateful.

~

If you enjoy hockey romance you may also want to check out the Original Six series, a sweet & swoony, slightly sporty Christian contemporary romance series.

The Breakup Project
Love on Ice
Checked Impressions
Hearts and Goals
Big Apple Atonement
Muskoka Blue

Romance fans who enjoy small town life may also enjoy reading the Muskoka Romance series, that starts with *Muskoka Shores*.

I'd love for you to check out my other books and to sign up for my newsletter at www.carolynmillerauthor.com where you can be the first to learn all my book and contest news, and discover more behind-the-book details and photos. Newsletter subscribers can also get an exclusive bonus book free, so grab your copy of *Originally Yours* here.

May God bless you - and happy reading!
Carolyn

# ABOUT THE AUTHOR

*Carolyn Miller lives in the beautiful Southern Highlands of New South Wales, Australia, with her husband and four children. A long-time lover of romance, especially that of Jane Austen, Georgette Heyer and LM Montgomery, Carolyn loves to write contemporary and historical romance that draws readers into fictional worlds that show the truth of God's grace in our lives.*

*To find out more about Carolyn's books, and to subscribe to her newsletter, please visit www.carolynmillerauthor.com. By subscribing, you can also get a free novella, Originally Yours.*

*You can also connect with her at*

# ALSO BY CAROLYN MILLER

Contemporary:

The Original Six hockey series

The Breakup Project

Love on Ice

Checked Impressions

Hearts and Goals

Big Apple Atonement

Muskoka Blue


Northwest Ice hockey series

Fire and Ice

The Love Penalty

Pointe, Shoots, and Scores

Faking the Shot

Plays By the Book

Second Shot at Love


Three Creeks Ranch Romance series

A Cameo for a Cowgirl

A Valentine for a Vet

A Second Chance for the Dancer


Muskoka Romance series

Muskoka Shores

Muskoka Christmas

Muskoka Hearts

Muskoka Spotlight

Muskoka Holiday Morsels

Muskoka Promise

Muskoka Miracle

Trinity Lakes collection

Love Somebody Like You

Tangled Up in Love

Only You Can Love Me

Our House on Sycamore Street

The Lost Daughter's Irishman

The Fairall Romance Legacy

An Irish Kiss

The Greener Gardens Romance series

Restoring Fairhaven

Regaining Mercy

Reclaiming Hope

Rebuilding Hearts

Refining Josie

The Silver Teapot Series

Not Exactly Mr Darcy

Not Precisely Mr Knightley

Historical:

Regency Wallflowers

Dusk's Darkest Shores

Midnight's Budding Morrow

Dawn's Untrodden Green

Regency Brides: Legacy of Grace

The Elusive Miss Ellison

The Captivating Lady Charlotte

The Dishonorable Miss DeLancey

Regency Brides: Promise of Hope

Winning Miss Winthrop

Miss Serena's Secret

The Making of Mrs Hale

Regency Brides: Daughters of Aynsley

A Hero for Miss Hatherleigh

Underestimating Miss Cecilia

Misleading Miss Verity

'Heaven and Nature Sing' from the Joy to the World Christmas
novella collection

'More than Gold' from
the Across the Shores novella collection

'Convincing the Circuit Preacher' from
The Courting the Country Preacher novella collection

www.ingramcontent.com/pod-product-compliance
Lightning Source LLC
Chambersburg PA
CBHW030526190726
48283CB00006B/1788